HONORED VOW
Mary Calmes

Published by
DREAMSPINNER PRESS

5032 Capital Circle SW, Suite 2, PMB# 279, Tallahassee, FL 32305-7886 USA
http://www.dreamspinnerpress.com/

This is a work of fiction. Names, characters, places, and incidents either are the product of author imagination or are used fictitiously, and any resemblance to actual persons, living or dead, business establishments, events, or locales is entirely coincidental.

Honored Vow
© 2011 Mary Calmes.

Cover Art
© 2011 Anne Cain.
annecain.art@gmail.com
Cover Design
© 2011 Mara McKennen.
Cover content is for illustrative purposes only and any person depicted on the cover is a model.

ISBN: 978-1-61372-217-6
Digital ISBN: 978-1-61372-218-3
First Edition November 2011

Printed in the United States of America
10 9 8 7 6 5 4 3 2
∞
This paper meets the requirements of
ANSI/NISO Z39.48-1992 (Permanence of Paper).

For all those who have come along with me
on Jin and Logan's journey, thank you.
It's been a privilege.

Glossary

aker	A leadership position in a large tribe that is fought for. The position reports to the maahes. Akers are always appointed in sets of twos, as manu and bakhu.
amenta	A panther who lives in the territory of a tribe not their own without permission.
apophi	A panther who is a disgrace and burden to the tribe.
aset	(Throne) The appointed mate of a semel in the event of the death of their reah. An aset can only be chosen, made, by a reah.
beset	Companion of a reah.
duat	A panther who has promised, on pain of death, to live only as human and never shift.
epeboi	An initiate.
heru-ur	A bacchanal orgy that takes place during the Feast of the Valley.
khatyu	The soldiers of a semel.
khet	A term literally meaning "separated by fire," each dead to the other.
khonsu	A man standing second.
maahes	Prince of a tribe, the emissary of the semel.
maat	Balance, harmony, correct action.
mastaba	Mistress of a semel's home, normally the widow of the previous semel.

menat	Tribute.
menthuel	Honor challenge.
phocal	Leader of the Shu cats, an elite group of werepanthers that serve the priest of Chae Rophon.
reah	True-mate of a semel.
semel	Tribe leader.
semel-aten	Tribe leader of the werepanther capital city of Sobek, considered the leading semel of the world who makes werepanther law.
semel-netjer	Tribe leader blessed with a true-mate who is a nekhene cat.
semel-re	Tribe leader blessed with a true-mate, a leader who has found his reah.
sepat	Honor challenge.
sheseran	Mate of a sheseru.
sheseru	(Flail) Enforcer of the tribe, guardian of the mate of the semel.
sylvan	(Crook) Teacher of the tribe, counselor to the semel.
taurth	A yareah who has been cast aside because a semel found his true-mate.
wosret	An unmated reah claimed by the semel-aten as a concubine.
yareah	A mate of a semel who is chosen, not the semel's true-mate.

HONORED VOW

Chapter One

As I walked down the long, cold gray corridor behind the medical examiner, I realized my heart had stopped beating. I had no idea when the organ that pumped blood through my body had given up, but I suspected it had been the day before, when I had received the phone call that my best friend, Crane Adams, was dead. Everything inside me had ceased working. I had stopped breathing at that moment… I just hadn't noticed.

I had not been able to drag air into my lungs, form words, or, for one terrifying moment, see. Not that I had been able to convey the terror, as I was mute. Funny how quickly your life gained perspective when something real happened, something that changed everything.

"Jin?"

Never could I be expected to be the same from that moment on.

"Love?"

I turned my head to look up into the honey-colored eyes of my mate, the semel, leader of our werepanther tribe, the tribe of Mafdet, Logan Church.

"I can go in alone."

It was what he wanted, but there was no way. I had to know; I had to see for myself. I shook my head—it was not even a possibility.

"Mr. Rayne?"

I looked back at the man we had followed from the front desk. We had all stopped at a door. It was steel, and there was a small window cut at eye level for someone at least my size of five eleven.

He cleared his throat. "Just you, Mr. Rayne, and Mr. Church," the examiner told us, glancing at Domin and Yuri. "You both will need to stay out here."

"Sure," Yuri agreed fast, his eyes flicking to mine.

He was worried, had been since the day before, when I had stopped talking.

"We'll be right here," Domin assured me gently.

And when my eyes met his, I found that between his steady gaze, the cadence of his voice, and his musky, sweet scent, I could momentarily stave off a breakdown. His presence was soothing, girding.

That revelation was disconcerting, because we weren't friends and I knew he was only there out of duty. But… after we picked him up, just the calm that washed over me when he sat down in the back of the limo, the way his hand slid over my knee as he moved by, had helped. And we weren't friends, we weren't close—the maahes, or prince, of my tribe and I were more like roommates than anything else, or had been, before he moved out. Now when he came to see Logan on tribe business, we barely had two words for each other, so it was weird that his being there meant anything at all. Yuri made more sense; he was my sheseru, there, as always, to protect me, keep me safe, and so his solid presence comforted me. But Domin, that he mattered at all, especially since his duty was to Logan and not to me, was confusing. Why being swallowed in the deep dark brown gaze shored me up I had no clue.

Logan put his hand gently but firmly on the back of my neck before he told the man we were ready. As I walked into the antiseptic-smelling room, I realized his touch was the only thing keeping me vertical. If Logan were not standing beside me, I would have been on the floor. I had no strength of my own, only his. As werepanthers, touch was always comforting—animals craved contact—but at that moment it was all there was.

Inside the room we were introduced to Althea Nelson. She was the assistant medical examiner for Clark County, and she began with an explanation.

"There was a fire, his townhouse burned, so I want you both to be prepared for what you're going to see." She was a small woman, thin, compact, with clear, piercing brown eyes. Her look managed to be sympathetic and matter-of-fact all at the same time. "Are you ready?"

The body of my best friend was lying under a black plastic sheet on a cold metal table in a brightly lit room. I had never been less ready for anything in my entire life. My heart hurt.

Two hands came down on my shoulders as I felt my mate's chest press against my back. There was more of his strength coming my way, transferred by heat and touch through my clothes, through my skin, deep into me. It was all I had.

The sheet was folded back.

It took a second because my brain questioned, but my stomach rolled, and so I was briefly overwhelmed, drowned under a landslide of emotion before the scream tore through my brain. Because I was the reah of my tribe, one of my gifts was that during the change from human to animal, I normally retained my logic. Being a reah was the only reason I was able to take a breath and finally speak. In that moment, the cat in me, and not the man, was more useful.

"That's not Crane Adams."

Seconds of time clicked by before the assistant medical examiner figured out what she wanted to say to me. I watched her, saw the concern flit across her sharply cut features. She probably heard disbelief a lot. "Mr. Rayne, you—"

"This man looks like him." I coughed because my throat was dry from not being used. "But that is not his face."

She cleared her throat. "Mr. Rayne, how can you tell what—"

"No," I cut her off. "I know what you're thinking, but I'm positive. I've been looking at him since I was six years old. It's not him."

"Mr. Ray—"

"And if you check for an appendix and find one, then you'll know you're looking at the wrong man too."

There was thundering silence.

I heard the clock on the wall. It was one of those white faces with black numbers, nothing artsy about it, function being its only offering.

"Mr. Adams had his appendix out?" She looked startled. "That wasn't in his health records that we received from Chicago."

"Because it happened in Arizona when he was twenty-one," I informed her, and even though it was horrible and some poor man was dead, my relief was overwhelming. A whimper passed my lips as I recalled Crane insisting he was not hungover, he was really sick this time, goddamn it! The whining had gone on for hours before I finally broke down and took him to the emergency room. He had been way up on his high horse as they wheeled him into surgery, all that righteous indignation because for once, I was wrong. The last thing I'd heard as the doors swung closed was that I was a self-righteous prick.

"Do you remember the hospital, Mr. Rayne?"

"Good Samaritan," I told her.

"Let me see if I can get those records to confirm, but if you're certain…." She trailed off, leaving the question for me to confirm.

"I'm very certain." I sighed, and it was a long drawn-out one, because from the look on her face, I was guessing the man lying there in front of me still had his appendix. "I was there."

"Mr. Rayne—"

"Does this man have an appendix?"

Her eyes met mine. "Yes, he does."

"Yes, he does," I echoed her before I turned around, lifting up to wrap my arms around Logan's neck, pull him down to me.

My mate buried one hand in my hair; the other pressed to the middle of my back as he held me tight.

"I'm so sorry for putting you through—"

"No," Logan said as his arms tightened around me. "You were doing your job."

"I'm just so sorry."

So was I, since my brain was starting to wrap around a new truth. Leaning my head back, I looked up into his face.

"I know, love," he said, nodding. "We'll find him."

Slowly, insidiously, I started hyperventilating.

"I swear, Jin. We'll find him. Please breathe."

And I had to believe him, since he'd never let me down before.

I HAD known Logan Church for a year and a half, but in that time my entire life had gone through a drastic metamorphosis. I had changed from being a loner, traveling from place to place, town to town, with my best friend, Crane, to finding my mate and having a home. I was the reah of my tribe of werepanthers, the mate of the semel, and my voice was second only to his. I went from having nothing to having it all.

Normally reahs were women. Since I wasn't, when my father and my old tribe discovered what I was, I had been beaten and exiled from the home and family I had grown up in. The only person who remained loyal, who loved me and stayed with me, was Crane. And first he'd been dead, and now he was missing. I was barely holding it together.

When the door opened, I rose from where I had been sitting on the couch in the luxury suite at the Venetian in Las Vegas, flipping channels on the TV. Domin came in first, holding open the door for those who followed him, a stream of people, some I didn't know, before finally Logan was there. I would have crossed the floor to my mate, but Yuri Kosa, the sheseru, enforcer of my tribe and my guardian, put a hand on my shoulder, holding me where I was.

"They all come to you here, even your semel."

I knew that. The hotel room was like a home away from home, and as such, Yuri was there with me, as was Artem Varda, his second. Because we were in the territory of a semel who shared a bond with Logan, Yuri did not bring any more men with him to guard me. But still, when strangers were entering the room, Yuri kept himself at my side, and everyone moved forward to me. I wasn't allowed to defer to anyone, being seen instead as the power player. It was stupid werepanther posturing, but there were rules that had to be observed, so I minded my sheseru without question.

When Logan was close enough, I reached for him, and he took my hand in his. He did not look pleased.

"What happened?" I asked quietly.

Quick shake of his head before he turned to look at Domin. I saw the maahes of my tribe holding court, facing the men who had followed him into the room.

"I present my reah," Domin said, acknowledging me with his hand.

I watched as they all knelt in front of him. I recognized Calvin Reynolds, the semel of the tribe of Opet, the tribe that called Las Vegas home; his sheseru, Roger Tsang; and his sylvan, Amanda Dove. I assumed the other ten or so men were his khatyu, fighters. As my eyes traveled over those on one knee in front of Domin, I found my gaze drawn to Amanda. She had a good face and gave me a trembling smile when she noticed my regard.

I had been surprised that in the two tribes I had regular contact with—my own and the tribe of Pakhet, that of Christophe Danvers, who lived in Reno—there were not more women in one of the two roles that served as counsel for the leader. In my travels across the country with Crane, I had seen many tribes that had a woman as either the sheseru, tribe enforcer, or sylvan, tribe teacher. In Logan's tribe, both places were held by men, as they were in Christophe's. It had struck me as odd.

Certainly Logan would have chosen the person most qualified, but I didn't know about Christophe. I wasn't sure how antiquated his ideas about women were. And he had a scary, jealous mate who probably wouldn't have liked another woman living under her roof. Normally the sheseru and sylvan lived with their semel until they found mates of their own.

"Jin."

I looked up at my mate. Usually I could find myself in his amber eyes, find any needed salvation right there in his loving gaze. "Tell me what happened."

"Calvin will tell you," he said, gesturing back to the semel of Opet, who, having shown me the proper respect as befitted my station as the reah of my tribe, was now standing. All the others were still kneeling, as Domin had not given them permission to stand. Only Calvin didn't have to wait.

I lifted my eyes to his.

"My reah," he said, clearing his throat. "I'm so sorry that I let you walk into the morgue thinking that your friend was dead, but the men from the tribe of Anuket had my daughter up until an hour ago, when they released her for my compliance in this charade."

If Logan hadn't grabbed me and tucked me under his arm, against his side, I would have dropped to the ground.

"Anuket, that's your old tribe, right?" Calvin asked.

"You know it is," Logan told him. "Finish so we can go."

He let out a deep breath, took a step closer to me. "Jin, they kidnapped my baby and held her and threatened to rape and kill her if I didn't let the whole thing play out. I'm so sorry, but we're talking about my child."

I nodded fast, hating him and being completely sympathetic at the same time. I thought about his daughter, Jacqueline: Jackie, Jack, J…. She was cute and adorable. She got straight As and was captain of her swim team. Since I had been the captain of mine back in the day, back in high school, we always had lots to talk about. I loved her sweet face, her huge chocolate brown eyes, and her bubbly personality. With Crane living and working in her father's territory, I had been seeing a lot of him, and her. She had confessed to me that she had it bad for a guy at school.

"He's a white boy, Jin; can you see me with a white boy?"

I told her I could. White, black, any color, any flavor she wanted. "Your dad won't care," I told her, certain I was right. Calvin had every color of the rainbow in his tribe, just like Logan did, just like most did. What you were on the outside didn't mean anything to him, to Logan, just as long as you were—

"But he's not a panther."

—a panther on the inside. "Oh crap," I had breathed.

"Oh God," she'd moaned, hurling herself back on her bed. At sixteen, it was the end of her world.

"Jin?"

I shook my head, clearing it. "I get it, Cal," I assured him. "I do. Just tell me what they said."

He coughed softly. "You need to call, or I should say that Logan was directed to call Archer Pike as soon as you realized you weren't looking at Crane Adams."

"Who—" I coughed. "Who was that at the morgue?"

"I have no idea."

"Not one of your cats?"

"No, I was told he was not a panther."

"He was a panther," Logan told him. "I suspect you're missing someone."

The look on his face was like Logan had hit him. I didn't understand that. Whether the man was a panther or not, I didn't care. Human life or panther life, both were precious and sacred to me. In my mind, and I knew in Logan's, as well, there was no difference.

"Jin." Logan said my name, drawing my attention. "We have to call Archer Pike."

I nodded.

Logan had to get on the Internet, which he did from his phone, access the secure database, and look for the number he needed. It took only moments.

"Are you ready?" he asked me softly.

My nod let him know I was.

Minutes later, we all sat around the phone in the living room listening to it ring. Logan had put it on speaker.

"Hello?"

"May I speak with Archer Pike?"

"This is he."

"This is Logan Church," my mate growled, his voice low, hard. "You have the beset of my reah; I want him returned now."

Heavy sigh. "I apologize for the ruse, semel-netjer, and I apologize to the semel of the tribe of Opet for borrowing his daughter, but I needed to get your attention."

It felt like ice water had been injected into my veins.

"You have it."

"I tried to speak to you in Sobek, but you wouldn't listen, and then you announced to the priest that we were *khet*, dead to each other, and so I had no recourse but this. The tribe of Mnevis is trying to take over my territory. I need you and your sheseru and your khatyu to come and align with us and help us drive them out."

"Why would I do that?"

"Your reah is the son of my sylvan, this was his first tribe, and we have a covenant bond."

"You're insane," Logan said flatly. "We have nothing, and your sylvan is dead to me, as are you and the rest of your tribe."

"If this is your final word, then I will have no choice but to put to death the beset of your reah, who I have in my possession."

I didn't make a sound, and when Logan's gaze caught mine, I saw his eyes glow with pride. That I trusted him, that I had remained silent, I could tell, touched him deeply.

"If you do not return the beset of my reah, Crane Adams," Logan began, turning back to look at the phone, "I will come and take him, along with your head. I have, as you know, a member of the Shu living in my home, and once he speaks to the priest on my behalf, I will have a mandate for your life, semel of the tribe of Anuket."

There was a long silence.

"You thought I would just say yes because you know that Jin loves Crane. Your sylvan, Jin's father, and your sheseru, Crane's father, were probably in agreement with this plan, but I will not grant you aid for one man, especially as I have a true covenant bond with the man seeking to take your territory from you, Derek Jackson."

"He's filth! He's—"

"He's passionate," Logan said, cutting him off, "and younger than you and stronger than you. He wants a tribe that is racially mixed, not racially pure. He wants diversity because he wants the strongest tribe, the best, and accepts all based on nothing but their desire to stand with him. It makes sense to me."

"You cannot—"

"I have, I did. It cannot be undone; it's sealed in blood, mine and his. So you will return Crane Adams and all will be well, or I will come with my sheseru and my khatyu and however many members of the Shu the priest decides to send with me, and I will kill you, your sheseru, and your sylvan, destroy the tribe of Anuket, end its lineage, and leave it to Derek Jackson. Choose your course."

Archer was breathing hard over the line.

"Now!"

Every eye in the room was on Logan. He was absolutely still, absolutely certain of his decision. And I held my breath because I wanted Crane more than anything, but I knew, in my heart I knew, that if they didn't choose to give him back to Logan, I wasn't getting him back at all.

"You must come for him and speak your words to my tribe, in front of my tribe, and tell them all that you refuse to aid us," Archer told him.

"I will aid *them*, semel," Logan assured him. "They are all welcome to come and take refuge on my land and with my tribe if they do not want to become part of the tribe of Mnevis. I would welcome them all."

"You said my tribe was dead to—"

"*Your* tribe, semel," he clarified. "If any panthers come to me seeking sanctuary, seeking shelter, I will take them in, and so they are then members of *my* tribe. Do you understand?"

Archer had no idea the kind of man that Logan was, and that had been his biggest mistake. Logan would never, ever turn his back on fathers and mothers and children. He'd pay to relocate them all, speak to Derek Jackson on their behalf, and do whatever was necessary to create a smooth transition if and when he had to.

"Your answer, semel," Logan demanded.

There was a deep exhale of breath. "Come, then, and claim the beset of your reah."

"I will leave tonight," Logan told him. "I will call you after I meet with the semel of the tribe of Mnevis, and you will grant he and I, our sylvans, and our retinue safe passage."

"You will not bring your sheseru?"

"I will not."

"Then who will—"

"As I stated before, I have a member of the Shu here on my land, Taj Chalthoum; he will act as my sheseru and come in Yuri Kosa's place."

"I do not understand you leaving your sheseru behind if your reah is—"

"Never, ever concern yourself with my reah," Logan said, his voice going from cold to warning in seconds.

"But we request the presence of your reah."

"Your request is denied."

I would have said something, because I wanted, needed, to go, but if Logan forbade it, I could never protest… at least in public. He was going to get an earful when we were alone.

"My sylvan wants to see his son, as does his mate, your reah's mother."

My mother no more wanted to see me than my father did. It was crap.

"My reah will not step foot into your territory, and that is my final word. Now I will speak to Crane Adams, or you will prepare yourself for a challenge in the pit."

I heard Archer suck in his breath. Everyone had seen Logan fight in the pit the previous summer. All the leaders of the werepanther tribes traveled to Sobek, between Giza and Cairo, in Egypt, once a year for the Feast of the Valley. At the last feast, Logan had killed the semel of the tribe of Dendera because he had kidnapped and tortured me. In the pit, everyone had seen his size and how very lethal he was. The idea of a one-on-one challenge could not have been appealing to Archer in any way.

"I cannot grant your request, Logan Church, for Crane Adams is not conscious at this moment. Before I was present at his inquisition, he was scourged by my sheseru."

I had to grab for the back of the couch as the room tilted sharply to the left. A wave of nausea hit me, and I started to shake.

Crane.

They had tortured my best friend, and I hadn't been there to stop it.

"He was scourged," Logan said like he was confused.

"Yes."

There was no air in the room; my chest was in a vise as my eyes filled with tears. I bit the inside of my left cheek so I would not make a sound.

He had been tortured and then disfigured. To be scourged meant you were cut into with a blade, your blood was spilled, and in some way, your body was mutilated. It was different from being marked as apophi, a disgrace to your tribe. When a semel marked one of his cats, scarring them or taking an eye, it was done fast, never meant as a killing stroke but as a testament, carved in flesh, of a failing. It was done at a tribe gathering or during a challenge in the pit with everyone there as witness.

Scourging a cat was what a group of panthers of one tribe did to another that trespassed on their land without permission. Scourging was normally done at the end of a hunt and was led by the sheseru. The first night I had met Delphine, the sister of my mate, she had been alone on another panther's land. She could have been scourged had Crane and I not interfered and if Markel, Domin's sheseru at the time, had wanted to do anything more than scare her. A cat who was scourged could, or could not, be expected to live, based on the level of punishment the enforcer of the tribe chose to inflict. Pain was a precursor to being maimed and, in some tribes, defiled as well. There was no way to know what my best friend had been forced to endure without asking. The fact that his own father had disfigured him, allowed others to hold him down and torture him, hurt him, make him bleed, was beyond my understanding. There was no way I could not go now. None.

I turned and walked to the window, looking out at the Las Vegas strip.

"Semel," Logan said, his voice low and edged in ice, "I have changed my mind."

"About bringing your reah?"

"About bringing my sheseru," he told him. "I will bring Yuri Kosa with me, and when I arrive, your sheseru will meet mine in the pit, and it will be a fight to the death."

"You cannot demand—"

"I do demand!" Logan roared. "And I will contact the priest tonight and have Shu warriors there to witness it!"

"I—"

"He's dead! By my sheseru's hand or by that of the priest, he is dead!"

"Yes," Archer said breathlessly.

"What made you think that you could touch the beset of my reah? Mine! I am not a friend, semel; we have no covenant bond between us!"

"I—"

"I am semel-netjer!"

Even over the phone, not even standing face to face, Logan's fury terrified Archer. His whimper came over the line.

"You will give me the names of any man who helped the sheseru maim the beset of my reah."

Maim.

The word conjured too many horrors to think about.

"Did you hear me?"

"Yes."

"If Crane is not in a bed, bandaged and cared for by a physician when I reach you…." He took a breath. "I will end your house, Archer Pike. Do… you… hear… me?"

"I do."

"We will be there tomorrow with Derek Jackson and his men. Do not make the mistake of having me look for Crane or you. Understood?"

"Yes."

"Yes?" he hissed, his fury and hatred boiling over.

"Yes, semel-netjer."

I heard Logan hang up, and then I heard something shatter. I didn't turn around. My guess was that he had wrenched the phone out of the wall and hurled it across the room. I saw his reflection behind me in the glass seconds later, saw him heaving for breath, saw the pain in his eyes, and felt the heat rolling off him.

"Jin…."

I shook my head. If I spoke I would break down, and I was not ready to do that.

"Go," I heard Domin say behind us to the men still kneeling on the floor.

"Semel-netjer," Calvin Reynolds began. "I am so—"

"Leave us," Yuri said, cutting him off. "We thank you for our accommodations here, and we will leave shortly."

There were no more words. I heard them go, and when the door was closed, a silence fell that sucked all the air out of the room.

"I'll call Taj from the car," Domin said, his voice dark and low. "Let's get home and get you all packed."

I turned, walked around Logan, and headed for the door. Yuri was right behind me.

"I'll kill them all, Jin."

And even though as a reah my first instinct was usually forgiveness, in this instance his words wrapped around my heart and gave me comfort.

"I promise."

It was all I could ask.

Chapter Two

I WAS sitting on the chaise in my bedroom. Logan had knocked out a wall and put in heavy glass doors that slid open sideways onto the covered patio. There was a fireplace outside as well as in, and the floor that had once been tile was now black-veined marble. It was beautiful. He had completed it over the summer so it would be ready for winter.

"You're going to freeze," Logan said, walking around me, wrapping me in a heavy down comforter, rubbing my arms to warm me faster. He bent and inhaled my scent, pressing his nose to the side of my neck, and I turned and kissed him.

I made slow love to his mouth, licking, sucking, biting, my tongue sliding over his, rubbing hard. I loved the taste and feel of my mate, but this, of course, had a purpose.

He leaned back, gasping for breath, sounding drugged when he spoke. "I forbid it."

I shoved him away from me.

"And that's my final word."

I couldn't breathe. Didn't he understand? How could he not understand?

"I will never allow you back in that city. I will never let you step foot back in the territory where they hurt you. Once upon a time, I thought it would be fine. I thought your father would come around, I thought your old tribe would see the error of their ways. But your father and Crane's father, they spoke to the priest of Chae Rophon and told him that you were an aberration. They said that my mate should have been killed. Does it make sense to you why, knowing all the facts that I know now, I will never let you go back there?"

I looked out at the snow.

"You need to trust me to bring Crane home. You need to let me punish them."

Tears welled up in my eyes.

"Crane's father will fall to Yuri and yours to me, and that's the only way it can be. There can be no mercy, the wound is too deep. I thought once that there would be nothing between our two tribes, but now I know I was wrong. There will be blood, Jin, there has to be. I see no other recourse."

I shivered hard as tears rolled down my cheeks.

"I will call you when I get there and tell you what was done," he said, moving forward again, trailing his fingers through my long hair, which ran through his hand like water. "You will wait for me and not leave. Do you hear me?"

I nodded.

"I know you're furious, I can feel it rolling off of you, but I can't do what I need to do, be what I need to be, if you're with me and I have to protect you."

Anger wrapped around me and squeezed my heart in a vise.

He was silent, his fingertips tracing over the line of my jaw, brushing away hot tears.

I shivered hard as I tried to get my body under control.

"Listen," he said, steadying his voice, "I know you're scary and strong, but faced with Crane being hurt, you won't be yourself, and I can't be the catalyst for your transformation if I'm in my shifted form as well. We don't know yet the true power of a nekhene cat, Jin, we don't know what you can do, but this… with Crane… this is not the time to find out."

I couldn't see anything through my tears.

"Please have faith in me."

But I had faith; I just needed to see my best friend. I needed to be the first face he saw.

"You think he won't understand if it's me and not you, but, Jin, love, he will. And he needs his semel to claim him, not his reah. Crane must be shown his value, and his value must be understood by others. The mate does not claim cats from the territories of others, only the semel does. That is maat. This is not a negotiation, this is war. Do you realize what could happen because of this? What I will be forced to do? Jin? Do you?"

I needed to go to Crane; that was all I knew.

"You will not be allowed from the grounds for any reason."

But I had to work. He knew I had to work.

"I called Ray, told him we had a family emergency and that you would be out for a week. Don't test me. Stay here."

I would get off the grounds somehow.

"If you show up in Chicago, it will show everyone that you violated my order, that I'm weak. Is that what you want?"

I wiped at my eyes.

"We are one, you and I; you can't go against my mandate. I need to know that you're here and safe so I can concentrate on only one thing. Do you understand?"

Again, not a question of understanding, instead a question of desire—mine for Crane.

"I'll be right back," he told me, hand under my chin as he tipped my head so he could see my eyes. "You do realize that every drop of pain that I'm looking at now I will visit on Archer Pike. He brought my mate to tears; this cannot end well."

I took a breath as he bent and kissed me.

When he was gone, I went back to staring at the gray sky of winter. Incline Village, Nevada, a quick trip up Mount Rose overlooking Lake Tahoe, lay under a blanket of white. It was icy cold, the grounds were covered under several feet of snow, and flakes fell from the sky morning, noon, and night. I had so been looking forward to spring.

Logan returned a while later, took my hand, lifted me up off the chaise, and led me downstairs. He deposited me in the living room beside the huge fireplace there. I stared into it but didn't move. I felt like the eye of a tornado as the house spun around me, everyone in motion, moving.

Delphine, Logan's sister, packed for her brother; Domin was on the phone, making arrangements; and Taj Chalthoum, the member of the Shu who had come home with us from Egypt six months ago, spoke to his phocal, Jamal Hassan. He asked permission to speak to Hamid Shamon, the priest of Chae Rophon, who made the laws for every werepanther in the world. He was asked to send an emissary on Logan's behalf to inform Archer Pike that the semel-netjer of the tribe of Mafdet had the priest's blessing and support. Once Taj was off the phone, he reported to Logan that Hamid had members of the Shu dispatched to Chicago. It would take them an entire day to make the long trip from Cairo, but they would be there to be witnesses for Logan.

Six months ago, at the Feast of the Valley, it was discovered that I was not only a reah, which was an extremely rare kind of werepanther, but also a nekhene cat. Being the mate of a nekhene cat changed Logan from being a semel-re, a semel who had found his reah, to semel-netjer, a semel mated with a nekhene. As Logan was the only one in the world with that honor, as far as we knew, when one of the Shu called on his behalf, it was more than likely Hamid would send whatever aid was needed.

"Jin." I heard Taj say my name from a distance. "The priest is sending Shahid and four other of my brothers to Chicago as we speak."

I nodded.

"Jamal says that he will come himself if you wish."

The leader of the Shu, the phocal, would come to help me retrieve Crane and watch over him. It was very kind.

"Do you wish it?"

I shook my head.

"All right, then." He reached a hand toward me but thought better of it. "I'll call him and give him your thanks."

Final nod, and he walked away a moment later.

"Jin," I heard Delphine say beside me. "Crane still has some things here for when he visits, so I'll pack that up for him too, alright?"

Another nod.

"Okay," she said softly before she walked away.

My chest hurt because my heart ached, and holding in the sobs when I wanted to break down and bawl was making breathing difficult.

Yuri was the only one besides Logan brave enough to get close to me and stay, and though the man could never be called perceptive, because he was a sheseru and I was a reah, our bond, hardwired into both of us, sometimes inexplicably verged on psychic.

"So you don't have to leave the house, Koren, as Logan's heir, will attend any events in your stead, standing at Domin's side as he heads the tribe in our semel's absence."

I knew who did what; I didn't have to be told.

"Although with Domin and Koren not speaking, it will be uncomfortable, I'm sure."

I was quiet even though I knew, like we all did, where precisely the blame fell for the fallout.

We had all anticipated a mating ceremony. I thought when we returned from the Feast of the Valley in Sobek in late June that sometime in July, August at the latest, Domin and Koren would exchange vows. But something had changed when we got back, and Peter, Logan's father, who had arrived a week before us, could shed no light on the mystery. All I could see, all that either man would say, was that due to the fact Koren was heir to the tribe of Mafdet, they needed time to reevaluate the true nature of their relationship.

"What?" Delphine had been as confused as I was.

When Koren brought the first of many women home, bringing them for the evening to meet his parents and his brother, the semel-netjer, I started to understand.

In October, right before Halloween, Delphine mated with Markel Kovac, who had at one time been the sheseru of the now-defunct tribe of Menhit. He had once been to Domin what Yuri was to Logan. The ceremony was beautiful, the banquet lasted three days, and as a gift, Logan knocked out two walls on the second floor toward the back to give the newlyweds what amounted to an enormous studio apartment within the house. They loved it, the privacy of being alone with the closeness of family. Panthers needed the community of others like them. Solitary was not the way for us to live.

When Crane and I had been traveling for years, just the two of us, from place to place, the reason had been me. As a reah, I had been much sought after, but once I turned a semel down, when they realized they were not my mate, things normally turned ugly. They wanted to keep me. I wanted to leave. More than once I had been in a fight for my life with someone who felt, in the frenzy of the moment, that they loved me. The process was too hard to keep repeating, so Crane and I had steered clear of all werepanthers, and normally, as soon as we became aware of any, we were gone. Everything had changed, though, the night I met Logan Church. His need had never been his alone. As soon as I saw him, it had been mine as well.

After we rang in the New Year earlier in the month, I had finally cornered Koren about what had happened. He didn't look happy to me, and Domin didn't appear any better. Why the forced separation?

I was stunned as I stood there and finally heard Koren's confession. He loved Domin; he just wasn't sure he was ready to give up the idea of a female mate and children born without a surrogate in the mix somewhere, and while the idea of having a mate at all was appealing, so was not having one and being free, especially as the growth of his real estate business took him to different cities and time zones.

He wasn't ready to settle down. Or more importantly, he was too scared to make a commitment and have it be the wrong one. He was not prepared to say, in front of everyone, that this one person was his life and that it was forever. Logan had been ready from the moment he laid eyes on me; Delphine had decided Markel was the one; but not Koren. There could be someone better out there, and the promise called to him, the lure of what could be just around the corner. And, as I suspected, the turning point had been when Peter returned from Sobek. He had come into the house and admitted to Koren that when he found out that his second-born son was gay, he had been devastated. It had been hard for him to have his first-born take a male mate, and when he found out that Koren would as well, or was thinking about it, he was overwhelmed. He wanted grandchildren, wanted to ensure his lineage, and even though he had claimed to be keeping an open mind, the reality had been painful for him.

In Sobek he had gone to the priest to make sure that Logan was forced to take a yareah and procreate. But before Logan could even inform me of his father's ultimatum and adamantly assure me he would never, ever have children with anyone but a surrogate, I had given him the news that I had asked his sister for the gift of life. Together, Delphine and I would make the next semel of the tribe of Mafdet. As patriarch of the Church clan, Peter was guardian of the line until he died and so had been well within his rights to talk to the priest. But the news that I had asked Delphine to be my yareah, to help me, as a barren reah, to reproduce, had basically just made the man's year. The second he got home, he shared his overwhelming happiness with his second-born.

What Koren heard was: *you can be whatever you want to be now…. I don't care. Logan will carry on the Church bloodline with his reah; I don't care what you do or with whom.* At which point Koren realized that what he wanted was his father's blessing and understanding, wanted his life to be as he had thought it would be growing up. He wanted exactly what his parents had, and that picture did not include another man. It especially did not include Domin Thorne.

Maybe.

Or maybe it did.

Koren was, again, for the millionth time, on the fence.

He couldn't say he wanted Domin, but he didn't want anyone else to have him, either. He loved him, and dear God in heaven, he wanted to sleep with him, but the rest… the rest was tricky.

I had not even been able to look at him. After our talk, I put distance and, normally, Yuri between us. No one talked to me without Yuri allowing them to, so since I didn't want to see Koren, I simply didn't.

"He's an idiot," Logan had told me as we stood together on the balcony watching Domin move out. Even though Koren was not around much, it was still his home first, and so our maahes had chosen to buy a loft in King's Beach, just down the hill from us. He was only a twenty-minute drive away, but still, it was distance Logan didn't care for.

"Who's an idiot? Domin for leaving, or Koren for not asking him to stay?"

"Domin for leaving," my mate had rumbled. "If you want something, you fight for it."

"Yeah, but Domin waited for Koren to grow some balls the first time, and now he's right back to where he was. How many times does your brother get to use Domin's heart for a doormat?"

"Koren will figure out what he wants."

"And by then it will be too late," I had said, my eyes never leaving the scene below me, watching Domin direct the movers.

"That's awfully pessimistic of you," he had teased, leaning sideways to kiss my temple.

"Someone else will discover Domin Thorne," I had told my mate very seriously. "He's a pain in the ass, but the man is beautiful to look at and very passionate, and now, since he's been your maahes, loyal and fair. You've changed him, your faith in him, your kindness, your acceptance, all of it—he's different."

"He's always been that way," Logan had told me. "He just forgot for a while."

Domin had been a good guy? "Are we talking about the same man?"

"Yes."

I hadn't wanted to argue; I knew Logan had made all the difference in the growth of his maahes, even if he didn't. "Koren's a fool."

"Why don't you tell him that?"

I had sighed deeply before I had turned and looked at my mate. "Because no one listens to me. They're supposed to, but they don't. Crane left, too, and Russ.... Everybody's leaving our home, and I hate it."

"I'll never leave you."

Which was more comforting than he could have known.

"Your teeth are chattering," Yuri told me, bringing me back to the present.

The reason being that I was cold inside and out.

"I know you. I know you're terrified about Crane and scared that I'll get hurt exacting the revenge you yourself want, but, Jin,"—his voice cracked, lowered—"I am the sheseru of my tribe. It is no one's place but mine."

I leaned forward, elbows on my knees, face in my hands.

"Right?"

I nodded and stayed like that with him sitting silently beside me.

It was dark by the time they were ready to leave, and I was still, wondering about Crane. Was he scared? Conscious? Had he called for me when they brutalized him? Did he, at that very second, want me with him? Had he felt powerless or abandoned? Had he been raped? Everything was swirling through my head.

I was going right out of my mind, which was no good for anyone, not just me. My power, it seemed, was no longer contained in my skin or with the shift. Some of it, as I'd learned in Sobek before I was reunited with Logan, was the power of a reah, the ability to broadcast what we were feeling. Before I knew why or what, I had been able to suddenly flood a room with my pheromones and emotions. The jump in power had been a surprise, and the priest of Chae Rophon had provided the answer in a name: nekhene.

I was a nekhene cat, hawk-cat, the only one of my kind, and powerful in ways that were unknown because, as far as Hamid knew, the last one before me had lived and died a thousand years ago. The power of the nekhene to transform at will, to shift from man to beast in the blink of an eye, was one thing, but the rest of it was a learning process.

The problem was that because we didn't know, we didn't know what to expect. So far, the only thing Logan and I and everyone else knew for certain was that the reah in me trumped the nekhene, so my love for my mate grounded me, gave him dominion over me. But how long that would last—if it would—that, too, was unknown. As it was, unfortunately, because I was a reah but also a nekhene, when I was in pain, if you were a panther, you knew it because you felt it as sharply as if it were your own. The normal control my family and friends and other panthers had over their own emotions and desires was stripped away, and there was only the continual assault, the constant barrage and battering, until the only refuge for the mind was the shift to animal.

Once people were panthers, there was only that consciousness. They could shift back and forth if commanded or reminded because it was simply an innate ability. A semel could order his khatyu to shift, and they would change only because they were told to. Only reahs retained the knowledge that they were humans even when they were in cat form. Semels, the strongest of all, only preserved the knowledge of their mate and nothing more once they shifted. It was frightening to think that with my pain alone, I could transform an entire room of people into panthers.

But pain was not the only reason people shifted. There was passion as well, lust and desire. Apparently my scent, when I was throbbing with my nekhene power, was intoxicating, and there was no way to tell what the trigger would be or to gauge my response. It terrified Logan. Hamid, who was continuing to dig but finding scarce little in the way of information on nekhene cats, said the most important thing we could do now, from what he had read, was to show the nekhene the bond between myself and my semel.

The only reason I had been able to contain myself at the morgue and not let my power run out of me was Logan. If he was there, right there with me, hands on my skin, the nekhene was contained. The reah that I was first was Logan's mate, so the nekhene responded to the familiarity of the bond. But if he was not close enough to touch me, kiss me, maul me, the wild creature that my body housed got restless when it was hurt or frightened or threatened.

The priest had told me before I left Sobek that some of the ancient texts spoke of the nekhene as not a kind of cat at all but instead as an inherited power. But I knew the truth; it was simply a mutation of speed and size. And yet, in all shifts I had ever seen before mine, basic composition did not change, only musculature shifted. But now, for me, I morphed into something else altogether. It made sense, then, that the nekhene was power and not simply biology. And yet how could that be? Shifting wasn't magic, so nekhene power had to be the same, something that could be explained logically.

I told myself about logic and reason and science every single day, and every single day it made less sense. My skin, sometimes, was all that kept me from flying into a million pieces.

"Jin."

And when I didn't feel like me, I lost myself just a little.

"Please, Jin," I heard Yuri whisper from where he sat beside me. "Please try and breathe. Please calm down."

I had trouble focusing past whatever it was that had coaxed the nekhene power from me.

"Jin!"

My name, yelled, finally brought me from my thoughts at the same time I realized my heart was pounding in my ears and I was breathless.

"You're making me sick," Mikhail growled from across the room. "Please, Jin, please breathe."

I got up and walked to the picture window and stood there, my forehead pressed to the cold glass.

"What's going—oh," Delphine gasped behind me. "I think I'm gonna shift."

There was shuffling in the room. I heard the front door lock open, the door hitting the wall with a bang, and then Yuri's roar for his semel.

There were others close by; I was aware of them, but my eyes were closed as the ache swelled inside, got bigger and suffocating, and the pain overtook me.

"What's—Jin." I heard Logan say my name, felt him closing on me.

"Logan," Taj said from somewhere close. "Do something. I feel like I'm going to claw my way out of my own skin."

"I—" Mikhail gagged. "I'm going to shift right here. I can feel it."

"Logan," Yuri panted, and I could hear his fist slowly pounding on the wall. "Please, I can't… I'm gonna shift too."

"Jin!"

When I felt Logan's hand in my hair, I tried to lean away, but he was stronger and so grabbed me and held tight, not allowing any movement.

"Stop," he ordered sharply. "You think if I touch you, you're gonna break. You won't."

I didn't turn to look at him.

He yanked hard, cocking my head back at the same time his other hand wrapped around my throat. His mouth was at my ear. "You will submit to me because I'm stronger than you."

I took a deep, shuddering breath and felt something deep inside deciding. I could even imagine the gentle swish of a cat's tail like a pendulum, thinking… thinking….

"You're mine, and all your pain is mine too. Trust me with it, my reah."

But how could I? He was leaving me, and I needed to reach Crane.

"Stop," he ordered.

I tried to pull free of his hold.

There was a growl from his throat before he bent my head forward, moving my hair, baring my shoulder, and he buried his fangs in the curve of my neck.

I jolted under him, and a sob rose from my chest.

He was stronger, I was weaker, and I calmed because he had reaffirmed my place at his side, in my tribe, so that my world settled and I could breathe.

We stayed frozen there together, and after long minutes, he gently withdrew his teeth. He licked at the spilled blood, at the wound he had made, and kissed and suckled at my skin.

"Mine," he told me as he rubbed his chin over me, his cheek, marking me with his scent, putting it all over me. "You're mine."

I twisted around and buried my face in his chest. His arms wrapped me up, and he tucked my head under his chin. I was shaking hard, clutching at him, holding on for dear life.

"Baby, you haven't slept in days. Let me put you in bed, you need to sleep. You need to close your eyes. I have you, I'll always have you. You'll always belong to me."

"Oh my God, thank you," Delphine gasped, and I heard her drop to the floor.

"Christ," Mikhail moaned, and I opened my eyes in time to see him slide down the wall so he was sitting with his knees up, looking completely wrung out.

"Thank you, Logan," Markel muttered.

Yuri took a deep breath.

"Rest, Jin," I heard Mikhail murmur, his voice edged with pain. "Please."

"Yes," Taj muttered. "Please."

I inhaled Logan's scent and concentrated on the sound of his heartbeat. I wished I could lie down with him, curl around him.

"When I get back with your beset, my reah, I'm all yours."

I had only his promise to comfort me.

Chapter Three

DELPHINE WOKE me the following morning and brought me the cordless phone.

"Who is it?" I asked, because Logan and anyone else close to me would have called my cell; it had to be someone else.

"I'm not sure," she said, squinting at me, her hand on my face. "But I think maybe it's somebody who knows Russ."

Someone who knew Logan's youngest brother? "Russ?" I said, putting the phone to my ear. "Hello?"

"Hi, uhm, is this Jin?"

"Yes, who's this?"

"Really?"

"Yes," I said irritably.

"Sorry," the woman said quickly. "I just, I think I thought with a name like Jin that it was short for Ginger or something."

"I'm sorry, who is this?"

"No, I'm sorry, I'm Samantha Ritter, uhm, you know, Russ's Samantha."

Russ's Samantha… Russ's Samantha….

"He said he told you about me?"

He had told me… crap! "Oh." I sat up in bed. For the first time in days, some part of the world did not center on Crane. "Yeah, he told me. How are you, Samantha?"

"I'm not that good, actually. A couple nights ago Russ didn't come home, and the police found his car this morning, and from the looks of things, he was attacked by an animal."

Fuck.

"I've been really trying not to freak out, and people have been saying that he probably just went out with the guys and lost track of time, but I checked with everyone, and nobody's seen him, and, God, I just don't know."

She was rambling because she was terrified, and I understood that.

"And I called the police, and now they're not sure, because I think they thought he was just out doing whatever, too, but that's not like Russ, he's such a grownup, you know, but now, with his car and everything, I just…. And he said that if anything strange ever happened to him, which makes no sense but it's what he said—he told me to call you."

"Okay. Uhm, Samantha, did Russ happen to tell you where he was going the night he didn't come home?"

"Yeah, he was supposed to go see a man named Blake… Blake Dempsey."

I moved the phone away from my mouth and covered the receiver with my hand. "Delph!"

She didn't turn around.

"Delph!"

Nothing.

I pulled my sock off, balled it up, and beaned her in the back of the head with it.

She turned from where she was looking outside and faced me. "What the hell are you—"

"I need you," I whispered, hissing at the end, pointing at my laptop on my desk.

"What?" She was chuckling now because I was probably the least scary thing she'd ever seen in her life. In bed, disheveled, barely awake—baby bunnies were more frightening.

"Check the list on my desktop; see who the semel in LA is?"

"Semel in LA?" she asked, moving to the chair, pulling it out and sitting down. "Why?"

"Just do it," I whispered.

"Jin?"

"No, no, I'm here," I said softly. "So, Samantha, do you have any idea what Russ was supposed to be meeting Mr. Dempsey about?"

"No, he said he wouldn't be long, had to clear up some misunderstanding with a friend of ours, Jimmy Tamaki."

I cleared my throat. "What did Jimmy do?"

"I don't even know, it's all sort of fuzzy, but as far as I can tell, Jimmy and Russ went running together, and something changed, and they wound up in some weird part of town and got into a fight. Which is so weird because neither of them are, like, big he-man types, you know? I mean Russ and Jimmy work at the same animation studio, for goodness' sake!"

I understood exactly what had happened. Russ, who had never wanted anything to do with the werepanther world, had, without meaning to, found another werepanther, and the two of them had shifted and gone for a run. Unfortunately, they had run in someone's territory without permission and were probably in very deep trouble as we spoke.

Before the Feast of the Valley in the summer, Russ had gone to Los Angeles for a recruiting convention and finally landed a job at Ironwood Studios, which was supposed to be the next Pixar. He was scared and excited and most of all happy to be far away from his family. The thing about Ruslan Church, the youngest of Logan's brothers, was that he absolutely hated being a werepanther. He felt the culture was barbaric and that everyone should just do their very best never to shift and live their lives as humans and nothing more.

And so he had moved to LA, against Logan's express orders, and had told him he did not want Logan to speak to or in any way alert the semel of Los Angeles to his presence there. He was not a semel, he was a normal cat; no one would know unless he shifted, and he never, ever would. When he had left, he had a shouting match with his father, and Peter struck him with the blow that this was the reason he had never even thought to ask Russ to carry on the Church line—he was weak because he hated his heritage. They had yelled some more, and finally Russ had told his father to go to hell, and Peter had stormed from the house. It had been quite a day.

I had followed Russ out the door, grabbed him, and turned him around to face me. After a heartbeat of time, he had dropped his bags and lunged at me, hugging me tight.

"Promise to call me," I told him. "E-mail me and let me know what's going on."

"I will, Jin, but you can't ever visit. I mean, I'm nothing, but you're a reah, for crissakes, or a nekhene, or whatever the hell you are... but other werepanthers will know if you visit. I don't want anyone to ever find out that my brother is semel-netjer. I'll get sucked into all the bullshit all over again. I mean, I don't think you even get how much I just want to be a regular guy, just some guy doing his thing in LA."

"No, I know."

"I hate the pit, I hate Mikhail. I—"

"You hate Mikhail?" I teased.

"Yes! I hate them all! I hate Yuri! I hate Markel and Ivan, and I hate Logan, and I know you love him, but fuck! I hate gatherings, I hate the hunts, and I hate my father preaching the fucking law. Most of all, the fact that we can never have someone in our lives who is not a werepanther is fucked up. I want to meet a nice girl, marry her, and have very normal, very boring, very healthy, and very without-teeth-and-claws babies. I just want to be human."

"I know." I smiled at him.

"You get it 'cause you used to want that too."

"Yes, I did."

"So I'm gonna find a girl and never see my stupid family until they can accept me for who I am, and that's it."

"Are you done?"

He smiled at me. "I'll really miss you."

I hugged him again, and he put his head down on my shoulder when he embraced me.

"You always smell so good," he growled, and I shoved him off me.

"I'm not saying I wanna sleep with you or anything."

I nodded.

"But see, I could get hurt for wising off to the mate of my brother."

"No, you couldn't."

He grunted, threw the last of his bags in the front of his Audi, and drove away, the U-Haul trailer he was pulling following behind him. I had sent Crane to his new place a month later and got video of a very nice loft that he shared with the lovely Samantha, who was a computer programmer. They kissed for the camera, Crane had given me an eyebrow waggle, and that had been it. When Crane got home from his secret mission, we did not mention it to Logan; he reported that Russ looked happy, was happy, and that everything was going well. Russ didn't come home for Christmas; they went to see Samantha's family instead, but Eva and Delphine and Markel went to California for New Year's and took enough food and goodies to feed an army. Samantha had apparently loved her gifts and loved Russ's mother, sister, and brother-in-law. They stayed only three days. It was as long as Markel felt was safe. Russ had told them not to mention one word about werepanthers. And now, less than three weeks later, he was missing.

"So, Jin, do you think you could come and help me find Russ? The police have no idea what to even do."

"Of course I will."

"Oh God, thank you so much. I mean, you and his mother and his sister, you guys are the only ones he talks about when he talks about home, you know? I would love to visit, but he won't… and I am in this with him, he's so beautiful and smart and funny and ohmygod, if I lose him, I—"

"I'll fix it, don't worry."

"Oh, thank you."

"I'll call you when I get there."

"Thank you, Jin," she said and hung up.

"I'm sorry, where exactly are you going?" Delphine scrutinized me.

"Your brother's in trouble."

"Which one?"

"Ruslan." I smirked at her.

"Oh shit."

"Oh yes," I groaned, getting out of bed, striding across the room to stand over her.

She pointed at the screen. "It looks like you've got a Miguel Garza there in LA."

"Garza? Not Dempsey?"

"There's a number here. I can call his sylvan."

"Forget it, just pack."

"Pack? Me?"

"Yeah. You and I are going to LA."

"How?"

"What do you mean how?"

"I mean how do you plan to get off the grounds?"

"You—"

"Not me," she said with a grin. "I can leave whenever I want. You're the one who's under house arrest, dear."

"But us getting out of here starts with you," I assured her.

"How?"

"Just put on your gym clothes and drive out the front gate."

She stared at me.

"I'll pack a bag and drop it off the balcony, and then I'll go down for a run. When everyone's trying to figure out who's gonna go with me, you get the bag and throw it in the back of your car. Once we're off the grounds, we're out of here."

"Jin, they'll never let you off the grounds, honey. They'll follow you and—"

I arched an eyebrow for her.

"Oh," she said, nodding, "right. They won't even be able to keep up."

"Taj is the only one who can keep pace with me, and he's gone."

"Logan can too."

"For a short time." I swallowed down my heart.

She nodded. "Okay. How far down do I meet you?"

"A mile."

"How fast can you do that?"

I waggled my brows for her, and she giggled.

"He'll skin us both, you know."

A shudder tore through me, and her eyes filled that fast as I allowed her, for a second, to feel the breadth of my pain.

"Oh, Jin," she whimpered.

I took a deep breath to calm my racing heart. "He left me here, and all I wanted was to go to Crane. He forbade me from going with him. And I understand why, I do, but staying here... I—I will go right out of my mind. And Russ needs us. If Logan's gonna save Crane, then you and I, we're saving Russ."

She nodded, taking a breath. "Okay."

"Aren't you worried about him? Don't you think we should go?"

"I do."

"So let's go."

She turned for the door.

"Shit."

"What?" She looked back at me.

"Markel."

"Oh, no, it's okay; he's working on a new piece for his gallery opening next week, so he's at his studio morning, noon, and night."

"So he won't even notice you're gone."

"Probably not."

"Good. We'll be gone; he'll have more time without you bugging him to have sex."

"Exactly."

We had a pact.

And two hours later, our escape was seamless. I met her, alone, in her Lexus, a mile away from the front gate of our home. She had clothes and shoes for me and a big smile. Ivan, who was at the front gate, had let Delphine leave to go to the gym without question. He didn't even check to see how many bags there were in the trunk of the car. But why would he have?

I had shifted, ostensibly to exercise, and Artem, Yuri's second, and three others had started the run with me. I left them after five minutes, and they never caught up.

At the airport, I paid for the one-way tickets to Los Angeles in cash, having taken a wad from the safe in my bedroom and given it to Delphine. Once we were taxiing down the runway, I felt like I could breathe.

THE COLD January air smelled good, faintly of the sea, which soothed me, and it was not nearly as freezing in Santa Monica as it was in Nevada. Delphine had used her phone and booked a room at the Surfrider Motel, which was on Ocean Avenue, and I drove us there after we used her card at the rental-car counter. Once we had checked in, each of us claiming one of the twin beds, we left our bags and Delphine navigated to Russ's loft.

He lived off Fourth Street, and Delphine told me that once we found him, we should all go for crêpes at this place he had taken her the last time she visited. There was no question in her mind that everything would turn out fine. At six that evening, we knocked on Russ's door.

The woman who answered was breathless. "Hello?"

"Hi again." Delphine smiled, pushing around me. "Remember me?"

"Ohmygod," Samantha sighed, lunging at Delphine. "I wanted to call you so bad, but Russ was very specific and told me that if anything ever happened that I should call Jin, not you, and I don't know why, but he was so—*so* adamant, and now… ohmygod, thank you so much for coming!"

The two women hugged tight, and slowly, Samantha calmed enough to meet me. Her eyes took me in. "It's so good to talk to you in person. Russ always goes on and on about you."

"Well, I kind of like him a little bit too."

She nodded fast, eyes filling. "I don't know what to do."

But I did. "Samantha, could you tell me and Delphine where Russ went to meet Mr. Dempsey?"

"Of course."

After we left the apartment, promising Samantha to call and give her an update in a couple of hours, I told Delphine that now was the time to scrutinize the list for Los Angeles again.

"It's a huge city," I told Delphine when we were back in the Dodge Neon with me driving this time. "I bet the semel here has a maahes and several akers below him, it's the only way."

"Oh, Jin," she said, grimacing. "I have no idea what you just said."

"About what?"

"What's an aker?"

I shot her a look.

"What?" she snapped at me. "We just—our tribe wasn't like that, Jin, you know that. And especially me and Koren and Russ, we didn't receive any formal training in werepanther law at all. Only Logan got that, and even he didn't get enough. Until Logan made Domin his maahes, I had no idea what that even was."

Domin.

"He's gonna kill you when he finds out you left."

"So guess it's lucky for me that he's not living at the house anymore."

She made a face. "I miss him."

"Me too."

"I hate this."

"What?"

"Never mind."

"Just say it."

"No, I—it just sucks."

"What does? Domin and Koren?"

"Yeah," she sighed, finally turning to look at me from staring out the window. Her eyes were red-rimmed.

"Awww, sweetie, don't cry; they'll figure it out."

"Oh, Jin, I don't give a shit. If we're being honest, I hope Koren gets home from one of his many business trips and finds out that Domin's mated and adopting babies. It would serve him right to lose the love of his life because he's too big of a coward to claim him."

I snorted out a laugh. "Really? This is your brother you're bashing."

"I know, but look at my brothers: I have Logan, who knows exactly who he is and what he's about, and Russ, who's the same kind of guy, if you think about it, and then we have… Koren," she finished, disgust dripping from her voice.

I started laughing.

"Who is a wishy-washy pansy piece of crap!"

"He does love Domin."

"I don't think so."

"Delph, you know he does."

"If he did, he would be able to make a commitment."

"He's bisexual and he's not sure what he wants."

"The bisexual has nothing to do with anything and by the way—bisexual, my ass! I have never seen the man light up like he does when Domin walks into a room. He melts like butter. I don't even make cow eyes like that and I'm a girl!"

"Are you sure?"

She smacked my leg really hard, which just made me laugh harder.

"Ohmygod, Jin, how stupid is Koren? He knows who he wants to screw him and that's about it," she said irritably, obviously disgusted. "He's so fuckin' scared of taking a chance, he's terrified of what my father will really think, and he's worried about missing out on some perfect picture of the perfect family that he's got stuck in his head. He's absolutely terrified of making a choice one way or another just in case it's wrong, so he's not; he's just dog-paddling on the surface and not diving deep."

"Huh, how very profound of you."

She growled. "I'm just saying, he's scared of standing up like Logan and saying fuck you all, this is who I love, step up or step off."

"Now you're gangster?"

"God, I hate you right now!"

I laughed harder and she shoved me, which was dangerous with me driving. "Speaking of Koren," I said, "where was he when you left?"

"He wasn't there. Isn't he out of town?"

"No."

"Oh, that's right, if Logan is, he can't be."

I nodded. "Like the president and the vice president, can't have them in the same place at the same time or both not at home. Somebody has to be protected and safe, either the semel or the heir."

"But where was Koren, then?" she asked me.

I had no idea. I had not even thought about him when we were plotting our escape, and why was that? Why didn't I....

"Oh, I know," she said quickly. "He had to go to Avery's mating ceremony, remember?"

"Shit, that was tonight," I groaned, only then remembering that Christophe Danvers, the semel in Reno, had invited Logan and me to attend the mating ceremony of his sheseru, Avery Cadim.

"I know Avery wanted you and Logan there, but since Logan was gone and you were on house arrest, Domin had to go, and Koren would have had to go too...." She trailed off, wincing.

"I bet they're sitting there in silence glowering at each other."

"Or Koren's dancing with all the pretty young things and Domin is just sad."

And suddenly I understood what she had been saying earlier. I didn't want Domin to be sad or alone. He didn't deserve to be waiting or cast aside. He didn't. I wanted him to find the guy, the smart guy, the strong guy, the guy who could deal with his bullshit and not break. I had thought it was Koren, but apparently I was wrong. We all were. And now I wanted a prince for the prince of my tribe.

"I hope he's not sad."

But I had bigger concerns. I knew Domin well enough to know that the man had a self-destructive streak in him a mile wide and that he liked to test his limits. I had talked to Ivan, his former sylvan, and Markel, and understood the level of bad boy that Domin had once been. I didn't want him slipping down the rabbit hole into danger; I didn't want to lose the man Logan had created just because his heart was broken. When I had seen him the few times in the fall, at Christmas, New Year's, and one other time a week or so ago, there was a hardness in him I had seen when we first met but that had been missing for so long since. I had been worried, and then he had come with me and Yuri and Logan to the morgue, and he seemed grounded. I wanted to talk to him, but really, we had never been friends.

"We'll all have to keep an eye on Domin," I told Delphine.

She smiled at me. "Isn't it funny to even be thinking like that?"

And it was.

"You know, if Koren could actually pull his head out of his ass, then all my brothers would be on the right track, although Russ is being a little bit stupid as well."

"It was probably just a mistake."

"Oh, I forgot I wasn't supposed to shift? Oopsy."

I smiled at her.

"He wouldn't have to worry about it being all or nothing if he wasn't trying to turn his back on his entire culture."

"Well, apparently he's picking and choosing what parts to keep." I had filled her in about what I thought had happened while we were together on the plane.

"Which is just fucking brilliant. I mean, Christ, Jin, you don't get to keep the parts you want and say screw the parts you don't. God, I'm gonna beat the crap out of him."

And she was certain, beyond a shadow of a doubt, she would get that opportunity. I really hoped she was right.

Chapter Four

"So," DELPHINE said as we walked toward the Italian bistro where Russ had gone to meet Blake Dempsey two days prior. "Tell me what an aker is, now?"

I did a slow pan to her.

"What?"

"You were serious about that?"

"Yes, I was serious, just tell me already."

I gave her an eye roll and got a swat on the arm as reward. "You're supposed to respect me," I told her.

"I missed the memo," she volleyed.

"Fine, in large tribes, ones with either a big territory or just a lot of members, there is usually a maahes, or prince, and under him are akers. There is normally a manu and a bakhu, always an even number, always ruling as a set. So, like, two people here, two there, whatever. They report to a maahes who, in turn, as you know, reports to the semel."

"So like a sheseru and a sylvan but not reporting to a semel, reporting to a maahes."

"Except it's not a position that's chosen, it's a position that's fought for. The strongest wins, you fight for it in the pit, and it can be challenged at any time."

"So if I wanna be a manu or a bakhu and I think I'm stronger than the guy or girl who has the title now, I just tell my maahes and he puts us in the pit?"

"Exactly."

"That sounds barbaric."

"It's survival of the fittest."

"But the positions of sylvan and sheseru aren't decided that way."

"The semel chooses the strongest when he's picking a sheseru and the smartest when he's choosing a sylvan. If he decides that someone else is stronger or smarter, he replaces them."

She turned to look at me. "Are you kidding?"

"No." I smiled at her.

"I had no idea that Logan could replace Mikhail or Yuri if he decided to."

I shook my head at her, and she playfully shoved me away.

"But then how do you account for the bond between a sheseru and reah? Wouldn't Yuri still have that even if, say, Logan replaced him?"

"But that's hardwired into the animal part of him, so that's not logical, it's primal. Yuri is the strongest after his semel, and as the strongest, he protects the mate of his leader. That's all built into the part of Yuri's brain that has nothing to do with him as a man and everything to do with him as a panther."

"I guess I don't separate it because when I'm a panther, which I hate being, by the way, I'm not really aware of being a panther. I can't look at the experience through my human eyes like I guess you and Logan can, I just become an animal."

"Logan can't."

"Logan can't?" She was surprised. "I thought he could?"

I shook my head. "When Logan's a panther, he knows me, and that's as far as his reasoning goes. I mean, just like any other panther, he won't attack a cat he knows or has scented before, but if another cat tried to get close to me when he's in shifted form—he'd tear them to shreds."

"Anyone."

"Anyone," I assured her.

"Jesus."

"It's why there's a whole laundry list of precautions when dealing with a semel and his true-mate that are different if he has mated with a yareah."

She nodded.

"But yeah, when he's in his panther form, Logan isn't really any more cognizant than you are."

She let out a deep breath.

"What?"

"I—I just thought he was just like you."

I shook my head.

"Then you're even more amazing."

"How so?"

"Jin, when you shift, you're still you. When I shift, I'm like a wild animal with no ties to anyone. I could kill Markel in that state and not even know it."

I chuckled. "No, love."

"No?" She looked so hopeful, like she had been thinking about this. "I wouldn't hurt him?"

My smile made her do the same. "Even though you think you're just an animal when you shift, you're still not."

"I'm not?"

"No. All werepanthers make choices, even in their shifted form. You decide to kill or not kill, attack or not, fight or not, run or not. You would never hurt Markel because you know his scent; you know him on sight in human or cat form."

"Really?"

I nodded.

"But Logan would kill either me or Markel if we were close to you when he's in his shifted form."

"Yes."

"I don't get it."

"Semels and reahs mate for life."

"Yeah?"

"Yeah, so the bond is different, it works on levels that a mating with a yareah doesn't, that matings between regular cats don't."

"Then what you're saying is that if Logan had a yareah for a mate, I could be close to her when he's in shifted form and he wouldn't have a problem with that."

"Probably not."

"But you, because you're his one true-mate, he'll go nuts."

"Yes."

She was taking it all in. "Okay, so back to regular panthers, those cats that attacked Logan back when Domin had a tribe; they made that conscious choice to try and kill Logan."

"Yes."

"And Logan forgave them all how?"

"Because they were following their semel at the time," I told her. "There's no punishment for loyalty."

"And the night you saved me from Markel, that's almost two years ago now, he could have killed me and not even known because he didn't actually know me then."

"Markel was a sheseru, so he's stronger than you, he has more control. He was never going to kill you, he was trying to scare you, and he knew who you were. The target was Logan, not you."

"But let's say Markel didn't know me, he's just out doing his thing in his territory and I came along. Would he attack and kill me then?"

"Even if he never saw you before in his life, it's still a decision he makes, to attack you or hurt you. No panther is pure animal; we can't be. Even when the attack is done purposely, panthers still retain their humanity."

"You lost me."

"Well, some semels, before a scheduled fight in the pit, they will have their khatyu, their fighters, shift to panther form and stay that way for the week before or for however long it is before the challenge."

"That makes no sense. You'd think a semel would want their khatyu to fight smart and fast, not long and bloody."

"You see, you think like a leader and not like a brute."

"God!"

"What's wrong?"

"See, I get why Russ hates all this bullshit. It's crazy. I mean, it's hard enough to live your life as a human being, but then you have to add the whole panther bullshit on top of it? How do you do it?"

"It's different for me, like you said. I don't have the whole animal-versus-human war going on in my head all the time. I'm just me."

"What is that like? You shift and you're still you, still Jin, aware of everything, making sense of—"

"Except when I change into my nekhene form," I told her.

"What?"

I cleared my throat. "In Sobek, I changed into my nekhene form; you saw it."

"Yes. You saved Logan and Markel from the semel-aten's men."

"In that form, I'm not me," I confessed.

"But my God, Jin, you have to either be threatened with Logan's death or with forced separation from him to bring on that form. That's not just something you choose or don't choose to become. Circumstances make you into your nekhene form; it's a purely visceral reaction."

And it was, but I didn't like it.

"What's interesting to me about that is that the form you take changes. The first time you shifted, Logan said you looked more like an enormous werepanther, that form that only a semel or reah can be, and then another time he said you looked more like a dragon, and then when I saw you, it was like you were a cross between a scorpion and a panther, almost like a giant spider with a cat muzzle."

"All those forms sound horrible. I just want to be a panther or a man, nothing else."

"Well, you can have the panther form, I'll just be me."

"If you shifted faster and it didn't hurt, you might enjoy the freedom of being in your panther form."

She smiled at me. "That's another part I don't get, it seriously doesn't hurt you even a little to shift?"

"Not at all."

"But I've seen you shift, and it's amazing. It's like I blink and you're a cat."

"We can increase the speed of your shift if you want."

"We can?"

"It's a skill just like anything else; if you practice, you'll get faster."

"I'll think about it."

"Okay."

We were silent for several minutes, just walking together, enjoying being outside in the cool night air.

"Jin."

I turned to look at her.

"If protecting you is hardwired into Yuri specifically, then why does every sheseru want to protect you, and not just him?"

"It's hardwired in a sheseru to protect the mate of his semel, his yareah, but a reah, that notches up the feeling and pulls it from every sheseru that's encountered. And in Yuri, because he is my sheseru—"

"God, poor Yuri, he must want to sleep with you."

I gave her a look.

"No, I just mean he must want to be with you and protect you all the time."

"Yuri's stronger than people think, and I'm not talking about physically. He's very disciplined mentally."

"Yuri's a brute."

I shook my head. "He's really not."

"I'll take your word for it." She sighed heavily. "So back to these akers, where are they in hierarchy in relation to a sylvan and a sheseru?"

"Like I said, they report to a maahes, and he, the maahes, is on the same level as a sylvan and a sheseru."

"So you think what? You think Russ got taken by a maahes?"

I nodded. "Or a manu or a bakhu. I doubt the semel even knows he's here."

"So, then, what's your plan?"

"This bistro was picked so whoever could talk to Russ. His answers, whatever they were, didn't make them happy, and so they took him. We just need to go in there and talk to whoever approaches us."

She sucked in her breath. "I'm a little spooked, I have to be honest."

I squinted at her. "You're with me, why would you be scared?"

"See, this is what I don't understand. Anybody passing through another semel's territory must alert that semel that they're there."

"Wrong."

"Oh God, could you just tell me?"

I turned, and she stopped walking to look at me.

"If you are going to spend more than a week in another's territory, then and only then must you make that semel aware of your presence, or if you are traveling with more than two other panthers."

"So, like, if you were here with Logan and Yuri and Mikhail—"

"Then we would need to call the semel of Los Angeles and ask his permission to be here."

"But since it's just you and me, who cares?"

"Right."

"I get it."

"But do you also see the problem?"

"Well, yeah, Russ was here for months without telling the semel of LA he was here, so that's why he's in trouble."

"They probably think he's an amenta."

"I'm lost again."

I just looked at her.

"What?"

"You know, really, I weep for your tribal education. Who taught all you guys?"

"Just never mind, what the fuck is an amenta?" she snapped.

"Well, it used to be that a semel would send an amenta into another's territory to live and gather information and sometimes even join another tribe to learn all their secrets before they attacked and took over."

"Like a sleeper cell."

"I guess, sort of."

"And so they could, what, execute Russ as an amenta?" She giggled.

"Yes," I said solemnly.

"Oh, Jin." Her face scrunched up, and I saw the fear finally grab hold of her.

"Honey," I soothed her, taking her hand. "If they were going to do that, they would have to alert his family first, that's the law, and since if anybody called the house, it would forward to my phone," I said, holding up my iPhone so she could see it, "we're okay. They're probably getting a hold of their maahes, and then he will contact his semel…. We have time to figure this all out."

"Okay."

"First things first, we have to make contact with the manu or the bakhu or the maahes."

"Okay," she said again, calming down, "all right."

We started walking again.

"But what keeps them from hurting us once we make contact with them?"

"Love," I said, smiling gently, "I'm a reah."

She took a deep breath. "I forget sometimes."

"Which I like."

She threw herself at me, and I grabbed her and hugged her tight. After a minute, we went on.

The bistro was small and intimate, located close to the Santa Monica pier. There was seating outdoors close to some heaters, and when the waitress showed up after the hostess left, we ordered some flatbread to start and the house wine. It took only minutes for a very handsome man in a Versace suit, no tie, to show up at our table.

"Good evening," he greeted us. "I'm Dennis Jennings, the manager here. Welcome to Bella Mia."

"Thank you." Delphine smiled at him, offering him her hand. "It's a pleasure to meet you."

He took it, kissed it, and gave her a dazzling smile, all perfect white teeth and gleaming blue eyes. "The pleasure's mine."

"I'm Delphine Kovac, and this is Jin Rayne."

He turned to me after reluctantly releasing Delphine's hand.

I offered him mine.

The second he took it, he jolted and his hand tightened involuntarily. The smile was gone, the muscles of his jaw clenching tight instead.

"I'm looking for Ruslan Church," I told him, lowering my voice, narrowing my eyes as I looked up at him. "Tell me, have you seen him?"

His eyes were huge as he stared at me, and I parted my lips, inhaling him, his scent, tasting his power or, as it turned out, lack thereof.

"Are you the manu or the bakhu here?"

"I—" He looked so confused. He understood I was powerful, but he also knew I wasn't a semel. He didn't have the overwhelming feeling to submit to me, so I couldn't be a semel. "I don't...." He shook his head. "Who are you?"

I released my pheromones, because he was fighting instead of answering.

The man grabbed for the edge of the table, clutching at it to keep standing. My hand, he held on to for dear life.

"Jin," Delphine whimpered, her eyes, when I looked at her, heavy with need.

Shit.

I stood and eased the man down into the chair beside me. When I looked at him, his eyes were glassy and unfocused.

"That was fuckin' brilliant," Delphine snipped, taking shallow in-and-out breaths.

"I didn't mean to—"

"It's because you're missing Crane. Right now you don't have 100 percent control over your power, and since you don't know how strong it is to begin with…." She trailed off.

"You're saying I'm like some nuclear reactor or something?"

"Yeah, an unstable one. Think about it. Back when I first met you, we could all tell you were different, but we couldn't quite put our finger on why. The difference was noticeable but not overwhelming. Now your power sort of grabs you by the throat and shakes you."

"Great."

"And maybe this part just has to do with Logan being gone, but, sweetie, what's pouring off you right now is like sex and candy all rolled up together."

I squinted at her.

"You're just oozing this yummy smell, and I just wanna taste," she finished, her voice going guttural for a second as she closed her eyes and rode out whatever it was that was twisting her up inside.

"I'm sorry," I said, my voice low and soft.

"I know." She exhaled, calming, taking long moments before she opened her eyes and smiled at me. "Okay."

I looked at her.

"Before, I used to want to be close to you or hold your hand or just sit with you, but now, it's like I can feel your heart beating in my chest sometimes, and I just want to crawl out of my skin and climb into yours. It's really something."

"I'm sorry," I said again.

"It's not your fault, but you need to be conscious of the fact that if I feel like that, so does everybody else."

"Sure."

"So please, honey, take it easy, and don't add any more emotion to the mix, because that makes you secrete pheromones, and unless you want my lady parts in your face—"

"I get it," I said, and I couldn't help but grin.

"Seriously, I was this close to attacking you."

"Sorry."

"But this guy," she sighed, looking at Dennis Jennings, who was staring at me with besotted eyes, "is just gone. I thought I was always the weakest cat in the room, but compared to him, I'm frickin' Yuri."

I eased my hand from his, and he leaned forward and stared at me.

"Reah," he breathed out. "How may I serve?"

"Are you manu or bakhu?"

He swallowed hard, his eyes on my mouth. "I am manu."

"And your maahes?"

"Would you like me to call him for you?"

"Does he have Russ Church?"

He nodded slowly.

"And is Russ alright?"

Another nod.

"Is your semel aware that you have him?"

"We informed him last night. He wanted us to contact the panther's family, and therefore his semel, but Russ won't tell us what tribe he belongs to, so it's slow going. We will start with claw on skin soon."

"He's mine, a member of my tribe. Please call your maahes for me."

"Yes, reah, at once."

He got up and left fast.

"Jesus."

I turned to look at Delphine.

"You spun him hard."

"I didn't mean to."

"The maahes won't be so easy."

"No, I know, and I was just trying to get him to talk to—"

"It's alright, lighten up," she said as she patted my knee. "We should eat while we have a chance."

It was an excellent suggestion.

Dennis returned a half an hour later, explaining that his maahes had arrived. Our dinner was taken care of, which we thanked him for, and as we followed him upstairs, he said again what an honor it was to meet a reah.

The rooms on the second floor were private and luxurious. We followed Dennis to the last one, and he held open the door. Inside, we found a long table with a man sitting at the head, a woman at his side, and five others clustered around him.

The second the door closed, the man leaned forward.

"My idiot manu thinks you're a reah. Speak your lineage now to me."

"Who are you?" I asked instead.

He scoffed at me. "I'm Blake Dempsey, who the fuck are you?"

"I'm Jin Rayne of the tribe of Mafdet, reah of the semel-netjer, Logan Church."

It was fun to watch his face drain of color, his mouth open, his pupils dilate. I could smell the fear in the room. The others, so defiant moments ago, ready even to hurt me or Delphine, sat there in shock, staring, utterly still.

Every semel who had attended the Feast of the Valley in Sobek had returned with a version of a story about me, Jin Rayne, the panther who was first a reah and second a nekhene cat. Reahs were rare, a million-to-one rare, but a nekhene cat was off the grid. As I stood there and saw their faces, I understood why they were frightened and excited and awed all at once. I was unique among our kind, and I would use their feelings toward me to my advantage.

"Ruslan Church is the brother of my mate. I humbly request his return, and I would speak to your semel if that could be arranged, maahes."

His eyes ran all over me.

When I bowed my head in deference, everyone rose at once. Chairs squeaked on the floor as they were hurriedly pushed back from the table, each man going down to one knee, the woman standing, preparing to kneel.

"No." I stopped her, moving fast, offering my hand.

I watched her shiver as her hand clasped mine. "Reah." She bit her bottom lip. "It's an honor."

"You are?"

"I'm Liza Dempsey, mate of the maahes of the tribe of Deshret."

"It's a pleasure to meet you."

Her dark brown eyes locked on mine. "Reah, may my mate and I accompany you to the home of our semel, Miguel Garza?"

"I would be honored." I smiled at her.

Her indrawn breath was shaky as she nodded. All the men stood after that, and I felt the whole room exhale as I turned back to Blake Dempsey. "May I please see Ruslan Church?"

"Of course," Blake breathed finally, turning to one of the men. "Bring both Russ and his friend Tony," he said sharply before his eyes were back on mine. "Once he joins us, we should go immediately to see my semel."

"Of course," I agreed, offering him my hand.

He took it gently in both of his and tugged me forward without meaning to, just wanting me closer. If Yuri had been there, the impropriety would have never happened, but I was alone, so whatever I offered could be accepted.

I felt his hands around my one, watched him breathe me in, my scent.

"May I introduce the sister of my mate?"

He turned to meet Delphine, and Liza did as well, and then I met the other men, all speaking with lowered eyes that quickly flicked to my face when I took their hands.

"Oh, what the fuck."

I turned to the door and there, with a split lip, black eye, and various scrapes on his knuckles, cheek, and chin, was Russ.

"Jin, why did you come?"

I stalked over to him. "Because, you fuckin' idiot, your girlfriend called me."

"Shit."

I grunted, reaching for him. "Are you alright?"

He sucked in a breath, and I watched him swallow hard.

"This was really stupid," I said, putting my hand around the back of his neck, stepping into him, easing his head down onto my shoulder. He was bigger, but I was older. "You're gonna be all right."

He clutched me tight, and when Delphine put her arms around us both, I felt him tremble. He had been scared, and bitching or no bitching, he was glad to see me.

"Listen to me," I said, leaning back. "You have a very important decision to make, and unfortunately you're going to need to make it, like, right now."

"What're you talking about?"

"The choice you made not to be part of a tribe has blown up in your face. So now you have to either tell Samantha the truth, and she and you come back home with me so she can meet Logan and be initiated into our tribe, or you stay here and keep your secret."

"Jin—"

"If you stay here, then we have to speak to the semel, Miguel Garza, and ask for the status of duat, and you're dead as a panther."

"What does that even mean?"

"That means that you can never shift again on punishment of death."

"Here or at home?"

"Anywhere, ever," I told him. "You never shift again."

"How is that even possible?"

"If you don't want to share your secret with Samantha, then you can live on another's land, but you have to do it as a human and not a cat."

"And if I want to live as a cat?"

"Then you can only do that on Logan's land."

"Why? You can live wherever you damn well want."

"Not if I was taking a human for a mate. If you want to mate outside your species and live as a cat, then you only live on the land you were born on. That's the law."

"But first I would have to tell Samantha my secret and have her meet Logan."

"Yes."

"Why? Why can't I just ask the semel here to accept me?"

"Because you're asking to bring a human into the tribe," I told him. "Only your original tribe will accept a mate outside our species, and normally not even then. It's a huge deal, Russ, but you have more options than most because your brother is a semel. I don't think you get how lucky you are."

"So basically I can either tell Samantha about werepanthers and go home with you and Delphine, or stay here and I'm only human, never a cat?" he asked.

"Yes."

"The semel here, will he let me live on his land as—what is it called again?"

"A duat."

"Okay, so will the semel accept me as a duat for sure?"

"We'll have to ask."

"And if he doesn't, then I basically have to tell Samantha anyway, right?"

"Yeah, probably, because you'll have to move—he'll drive you from his territory."

"But I live here, I work here."

"That's no one's fault but yours. You should have never put yourself in this position."

"Why didn't you tell me this before?"

"Oh, fuck you," I groused. "I told you from day one that you should contact the semel of Los Angeles and speak to him. Before you even moved here, I wanted to come see him, just like I did the semel of Las Vegas, and Crane's not even shacking up with a human, so all he needed was permission to be in the other semel's territory, not special status."

"I fucked this up."

"Yeah, ya did."

"So how do I get to talk to the semel?"

"You start by talking to the maahes, but you really need to know if this is what you want, Russ."

"I know I—"

"Because you're making a promise to the semel of the tribe that has granted you the status of duat that you will no longer act as a panther," I told him. "It's a big deal; breach of terms is punishable by death."

"Jesus," he groaned.

"Hello."

I turned my head, and there was another man there, just as beat up as Russ. "You must be Tony."

"And who are you?"

He was cocky and I didn't like him, and Delphine was right; I was not myself. I breathed out to try and relax, but instead my pheromones washed over him in a drowning wave.

"Ohmygod," he moaned, falling to the floor, his body bent in half as he began his shift.

"Jin!" Delphine cried out, and I closed my eyes, concentrating.

But I didn't have any control to stop, calm, or gather myself.

Crane.

Russ.

I was so glad Russ wasn't hurt, and even though I didn't understand his reasoning, I wanted him to have the choice of what to do, not have Logan or Miguel Garza decide. But more than anything, I wanted to see my best friend. I needed to see Crane.

I wanted to see Crane.

"Jin!"

I looked up at Delphine, saw the pain in her eyes as she went to her knees.

"Jin." Russ gagged before he dropped to the floor at my feet.

His loss of control fed my desire to punish those who had taken him. At once I understood the true size of my ego. What in God's name made me think that I could travel by myself with just Delphine in the state I was in? Why hadn't I called Logan or Mikhail? Why hadn't I reached out to Justin Cho, Logan's friend and the semel of San Francisco, who probably knew the semel of Los Angeles well? And why, ever, would I go anywhere without an escort? I was the mate of a semel; I didn't leave home without bodyguards. No mate of a tribe leader did that; it was considered unsafe, and you were inviting trouble. Why did I think I could or should simply because I was a man?

The truth was that I was furious at Logan, and I had used his brother's kidnapping as an excuse to leave. I was worried about Russ, but I also knew they could not hurt him, not really, without first speaking to Logan. They could rough him up, as they had done, but that was all. I knew that and I had gotten on a plane anyway. It was selfish and stupid because I had not only put myself in jeopardy, but Delphine as well.

"Reah!"

I could be killed. Delphine and Russ could be killed, and no one would ever know because no one knew where any of us were. I was counting on archaic customs and observed ritual to keep us safe, and that was insane. I should have been home, waiting for word on Crane, waiting for word on Russ, not acting on impulse. I was the mate of a semel; I needed to comport myself in that manner. What had I been thinking?

"Reah!"

The scream tore me from my thoughts. When I turned to look for the man who had let loose the blood-curdling sound, I realized Blake and I were the sole humans in the room. Everyone else—Delphine, Russ, Tony, Liza, and all the rest of the men, including Dennis Jennings, the manu— were cats. I was surrounded by panthers.

I took a breath and everyone in the room, including the maahes, collapsed. A wave of guilt washed over me as I looked at the cats sprawled on the floor, panting, some throwing up, others lying curled in balls, shivering with the aftershocks of my power surging through them. I had no idea what apology I could make, what excuse would even be accepted.

"That was obscene."

I turned my head to look at Blake.

There was a stain on his pants: he had come in them, and where he had ejaculated was clearly, glaringly visible. I gave him a lot of credit for standing there, eyes locked on mine, swallowing his humiliation down as he stared at me with burning eyes.

"I'm so sorry." I choked on the words because it hurt to say as much as it hurt for him to hear.

"Fuck you and your power, reah," he roared at me, furious. "I will not suffer this insult; you cannot strip us of our humanity on a whim!"

"No," I pleaded, motioning to Delphine, who lay panting on her side on the floor, and then to Russ, who was heaving and retching, bringing up nothing, his body simply spasming with the need to try. "I didn't do it on purpose, why would I?"

Only seeing Delphine and Russ there, suffering the same fate as the others, both in their panther forms, cut through the veil of his rage. It made no sense that I would want to hurt members of my own tribe.

"You will come with me to see my semel, and he will determine what apology is to be made."

"Agreed." I nodded, wanting to say, or do, something but unsure what that could possibly be.

"I was so honored to meet you," he told me, his voice low. "And now I can barely stand to look at you."

I thought I might be sick myself.

BACK AT the hotel after leaving the restaurant, I realized the experience had proven to be too much for Delphine. She wasn't mad, she said she wasn't a thousand times, but she wouldn't look at me. She apologized as she packed and took deep breaths and sniffled. There was a lot of sniffling, a lot of her blowing her nose and shivering. I tried to touch her, but that was out of the question. I was making her skin crawl. She didn't want a hug good-bye; she wanted nothing to do with me at all. She just needed to go home and see Markel. Her thoughts were only of him.

"I'm so sorry," I told her as she was at the door, a cab downstairs waiting for her.

"It's not your fault," she said, again without looking at me. "You just—it's Crane, I know, but you took away choices from me, and it's like… it felt like… like…."

And she didn't want to say, so she stopped herself. She didn't want to say I had violated her, raped her, but it was how she felt. I had made her feel powerless, done it to all of them, and the only person who could have stopped it once it started was myself—or Logan. I had power but no control, and I was dangerous.

"Please forgive me," I said to her, moving slowly closer to her.

"I have already," she told me, her eyes finally flicking to mine, the green eyes she shared with all her brothers except my mate staring back at me, hers being the softest color, celadon. "It's not in you to hurt anyone on purpose, and while I know that, it was brutal. I felt like I was being turned inside out, and even though I don't hurt anymore, it was terrifying."

I had scared my girl.

I was a monster.

"I want to see Markel."

She must have said it a hundred times, and all I could do was nod like an idiot.

"I should send Artem here, and Ivan, or—"

"No, don't do that," I told her. "Just leave it—"

"Fine," she said, cutting me off, opening the door. "You know best. Bye."

She was gone that fast, and I let the wave of guilt come and flood me. My self-destructive streak I could own having, sometimes it not only tried to drown me but everybody else as well. I needed to be more focused on what I was really doing. I sat down on the end of the bed, put my head in my hands, and tried to calm my racing heart. When my phone rang an hour later, I realized that I had not moved, and answered without checking to see who it was.

"Hello?"

"Where are you?"

I cleared my throat to speak to my mate. "You know where I am."

"I gave explicit orders that you not leave the grounds."

"Russ was kidnapped."

"Taken, held, not kidnapped. I received word from Miguel Garza, the semel of Los Angeles, and Justin was on his way to negotiate Russ's release and to determine if my brother would come and present his girlfriend to me or would accept the station of duat."

Of course my entire trip was useless, and it was my fault because I was mad and so had leaped before looking, as I always did.

"How's Crane?"

"No. You don't get to ask about Crane because now you have—"

"Logan, tell me about Crane!" I shouted, my voice a rasp as the tears blurred my vision.

"Crane is home! I'm home! You're the only fucking one who's not home because you're a petulant child who doesn't ever listen to anyone but himself! I'm the law in this tribe, Jin, not you, for this very reason. A reah is emotion, a semel is logic, and we see before us a clear example of this. You are not allowed to treat my orders like suggestions! You listen to me, and if you can't, I'll make you. Do you *understand*?"

I couldn't breathe. I couldn't even speak.

"If you were here, you could see Crane. If you were where you were supposed to be, you would not be in danger of being scourged yourself for what you did to Miguel Garza's maahes! If anyone did what you did to Domin, I would kill them. Do you get it? And Delphine was sobbing on the phone to me. Markel should fight Yuri in the pit to atone for the disgrace, but because we're family, he's leaving it to me to punish you. Are you getting it? Is it sinking in?"

Of course it was.

"You made Russ's decision so easy! He already asked for and received the status of duat from Miguel Garza. And do you know why the semel granted the request without question?"

"I—"

"Because he felt so sorry for him," he roared. "The semel said that anyone that could do that—hurt not only strangers but his own people— was a fuckin' monster! He was so excited to have you there on his land, a reah, the only nekhene cat in existence, and now he thinks you're a horror!"

And I was, wasn't I?

"So to keep Russ away from you, he granted his request. So now my brother, who I wanted to see, wanted to talk to before he made this life-changing decision, made a rash choice because of you! This was all because of you! It's your fault that Russ left his family, no one else's."

Because my family had been taken from me when I was sixteen, there wasn't anything worse he could have said to me.

"Do you realize that I gave my mandate as much for everyone else as for you? You are volatile right now. Your emotions are all over the place, and because you're a reah, because you have the power of a nekhene in you, you are able to transmit all your pain and anger and rage outward at everyone else."

I wanted to scream; it felt like my whole body was being squeezed in a vise.

"Right now we—and I mean me, your family, and your tribe, all of us—need to be protected from you! I'm afraid for you to see Crane because he's very delicate right now and if you bring all your heightened emotion and flood him with it—will that kill him?"

"You won't let me see Crane?" I asked, my voice not mine, garbled with tears, nasal and low.

"Not right now."

"What did they do to him?"

Silence.

"Logan?"

He took a breath. "They castrated him."

I dropped the phone and ran for the bathroom.

Chapter Five

THERE WAS nothing left in my stomach, and I was shaking by the time I picked my phone back up long minutes later. I couldn't actually speak yet, but he heard me breathe.

"Crane won't shift back," Logan told me. "It's lucky that Martine sent his private jet for me, otherwise I wouldn't have been able to bring him home."

Martine Soto was one of Logan's oldest friends and the semel in Miami, in fact, the semel of the state of Florida. It wasn't usual, and the man had many maahes, princes, who took orders from him, as well as many akers. His sylvan and sheseru also had many men who served under them. I had no idea how he did it, but he was very rich and very powerful. Logan had no desire to take care of that many cats.

"I don't know what he looks like in his human form; he won't show me."

My friend was so traumatized that he could not allow himself to be vulnerable even for a moment.

"When I arrived in Chicago I was met by Derek Jackson and Shahid Alon, who was sent by the phocal on behalf of the priest. Jin, a sepat has been called."

I couldn't breathe.

"Jin." He cleared his throat. "The priest of Chae Rophon has called me as one of his six champions. I have been summoned to fight for the seat of semel-aten, master of Sobek."

Master of Sobek? The priest had wanted Logan to fight Ammon El Masry before, and now it looked as though he would finally get his wish.

A sepat was an honor challenge that was called by the priest of Chae Rophon if he, along with his council, the council of Ennead, felt that the actions of the semel-aten were in violation of his mandate as guardian of the law. The semel-aten ruled the city of Sobek and the first tribe, the tribe of Rahotep, served him. He was second in power only to the priest of Chae Rophon, and only the priest could call for a sepat to unseat him.

Logan took a breath. "Crane was taken to lure you to Chicago, and in pulling you, I would follow. Ammon had some of his khatyu there to kill me."

"Logan—"

"Crane's father, yours, and Archer Pike were granted sanctuary for their part in Crane's kidnapping and scourging as well as in your and my proposed murders."

They had taken Crane to get to me, and in getting to me, would have had Logan. Crane was just a pawn and so was I, with Logan being the real target. "I don't understand. You went anyway. How was the trap not perfectly set?"

"Your cousin Danny," Logan sighed deeply. "He saved me."

My cousin. "Tell me."

"He met Derek and me on our way to the house, where we were to take possession of Crane. He told us about the plan, so Derek's sheseru and Yuri took khatyu there and surprised Archer's men. Ammon's men were there as well, led by his sheseru."

"Roshan was there, Ammon's sheseru?"

"He's dead, Jin. All Archer Pike's khatyu, as well as the men that Ammon sent, were all killed. I had to get Crane; he was my main concern, so I left Derek to hunt down Archer and your father and Crane's. But he was too late; they all fled for Egypt."

"Explain to me why the priest has called for a sepat."

"As you know, if the priest of Chae Rophon can prove that the semel-aten has misused his power, he can call for a sepat, the challenge of lineage, and call six challengers, and their houses, to meet the semel-aten in three challenges of blood, law, and heart."

It was lucky I had already thrown up, because I had nothing else left to void as my stomach rolled and twisted.

"Apparently last month Ammon had some members of his tribe, some of the women, tortured and killed when they refused to submit to him at a gathering. The parents of the women went to the priest and have demanded justice for their children."

As well they should have.

"The priest informed Ammon that he was calling for a sepat at that time. He told him that I would be the first challenger he called."

And that was what had put Crane's abduction into motion.

"The priest has chosen the semel of the tribe of Khertet in Arkhangai aimag to host the sepat."

"Where is that?"

"In Mongolia."

I was having the strangest day of my life.

"So I'm going there to compete against five challengers, and then, when there are finally only two of us, we'll face off, and then whichever of us wins that fight, he goes into the pit against Ammon El Masry, the semel-aten."

I cleared my throat. "A sepat is not just you fighting, Logan; it's your maahes, your sheseru, your sylvan, and your mate."

"I know."

"You won't even compete in the first three challenges when there are still six of you. You don't fight until the one-on-one challenge."

"I know the mate and the semel's household fight but I don't know the specifics."

"There are three challenges, like you said: blood, law, and heart."

"And?"

"The trial of blood is about strength and tests your sheseru. The trial of law is about exactly what it sounds; it's about laws and lore, reciting them, knowing them, and so tests the knowledge of your sylvan. The heart trial is the test of loyalty, and that's for your mate and your maahes."

He was quiet on the other end. "I need you to come and stand at my side."

"That's a given."

"Jin," he said, his voice cracking, "the tribe of Anuket has been disbanded, and the tribe of Mnevis has absorbed it. Derek's tribe is now the only one in Chicago."

The tribe that had cast out both me and Crane and then scourged him was no more. I didn't even know how to feel.

"The priest has promised that if any other man becomes semel-aten, then the sanctuary given Archer Pike, and your father and Crane's, by Ammon El Masry, will be rescinded. Only if Ammon keeps his seat will they go unpunished. The other five challengers have already agreed."

"Okay."

"Your brother Kei has asked for and received permission to join the tribe of Mnevis."

It was hard to hear the word "brother" when it had not been the case since I was sixteen years old.

"Your cousin Daniel, because he saved me, is no longer welcome with those of your old tribe. He's here with me."

And in the midst of everything, amazingly, with all else that was going on, I was jealous. I remembered seeing Danny when he came to my home with my father, his delicate features, porcelain skin, huge liquid-brown eyes, thick-feathered lashes, and dark curls. "Doesn't he have a family to return to?"

"Apparently not."

I swallowed down my heart. "He's beautiful."

"Who?"

"Danny."

"I wouldn't know—I see no other but my mate."

"Logan—"

"Jin, Yuri and Domin are on their way to bring you home. Stay there in the hotel until they reach you. I suspect they'll be there in another three hours. Justin is on his way to you now with his sheseru as well as two of his khatyu. Miguel Garza will have an entire entourage with him. Justin and Sean Li, his sheseru, are allowed in the room with you. Miguel can also be in the room with you along with either his sheseru or sylvan or his yareah, but no other. You know the law, I know I don't need to tell you, but these are special circumstances."

"No, you don't."

"I would come, but I have too many people here. Crane is hurt; Danny is here, and…." He trailed off, seemingly lost in thought.

"Logan?"

"Fuck it; I'll be there to claim you."

"No," I insisted. "I'll be home this evening."

He took a breath. "You're not hurt, are you?"

"No, no one can seem to get close enough to me to even touch me."

There was a silence before: "I'm sorry, what?"

"I'm the same as I was before you left."

"How do you mean?"

"I mean I'm not—myself."

"But you were fine when I—"

"And I was fine until I got here."

Long silence, and I knew he was working something out in his head. "Jin," he said sharply.

"Yeah?" He sounded scared, which was making me uneasy.

"I thought it was on purpose."

"You thought what was on purpose?"

"I—I thought you pulling the others through their shift was intentional!"

"What?" I was hurt that he would even think such a thing. "Why would I do that?"

"I thought you were angry with me and so you were trying out a new power and—oh fuck!"

"What's wrong with you?" I asked irritably.

"Love." He took a breath. "Before I left, you were leaking pheromones. Everyone's reaction to you, when they were in the house… that was not you making them want to be away from you, that was them all wanting you, wanting to have you."

"There's no way."

"Jin, I asked the priest why you would be throbbing with pheromones and he said that nekhene cats, unlike reahs, when they build up power, they exude them to try and draw the strongest cat to their side to mate with. A reah seeks only their semel, but a nekhene, who does not normally have just one mate, sends out a siren call that is impossible to ignore."

"But I haven't shifted into a nekhene form at all, not once."

"You haven't physically shifted, but the power is still growing and every time it makes a jump, every time you tap into it for protection, you radiate this primal call for a mate."

"I only want you," I said, willing him to believe me.

"I know that because the reah in you is comforting the nekhene. It's reminding the wild creature of the bond with me. It's why my scent, having me close to you, calms you down."

"I got that, but the pheromones thing is just—"

"The strongest cats will fight for the chance to be the one who mates with the nekhene, while those unworthy of mating will be rendered unfit. Turning them into panthers, forcing the change so that they are panthers and not human, would definitely render them unsuitable for you to mate with."

"I wouldn't do that to Delphine or—"

"Jin wouldn't, Jin the reah wouldn't, but the nekhene has no family, no friends. The nekhene sees only potential mates or potential enemies."

"But I'm a panther, too, why would changing them into animals render them inadequate?"

"Because you have sex in your human form, Jin."

I cleared my throat. "Might I remind you that I've had sex with you in both your human form and your werepanther form?"

"But never in panther form."

True.

"And I claimed you as a man, and you identify yourself as a man first and panther second, and so on instinct, your nekhene power shifts unworthy men and women into panthers, which makes them unfit, in your eyes, to mate with."

"I didn't change them on purpose."

"I know that, but every panther in the room was, to you, weak, and was thus unsuited to be your mate, so your nekhene power punished them. I get it now."

"But—"

"You did something, started to get upset, and your nekhene power spiked and came pouring out of you, but because you're not in complete control because of Crane, you flooded the room with pheromones looking for a mate."

"I'm not looking for a mate! I already have one."

"You as a reah, yes, and you know that, but the nekhene who lives inside of you searched and couldn't find the reah's mate, and so you lost yourself for a moment in a wave of heat and craving that I can't even imagine. Your power reached out and finding no one worthy, it attacked."

"But the nekhene in me respects, or whatever you wanna call it, our bond."

"If I'm there, if you can smell me, feel me, taste me, the nekhene responds, but if I'm not there to physically remind the nekhene of the bond, then the reah part of you is lost and only the wild creature remains."

I sucked in my breath. "You make me sound like a monster."

"You're not a monster; you're an animal looking for a mate."

"I have a mate," I said again.

"But the nekhene doesn't know that, and I didn't show that part of you my power the other day. I held you, made you stop, but I didn't hold you down and make you mine."

Thinking about Logan, imagining myself submitting to his will, made my heart leap, pulse race, and my skin heat.

"But I will," he promised me, his voice dropping low and menacing, the power and strength and dominant male there, in the tone, making my knees weak.

"Logan—"

"That's why Delphine's so angry. She's mad at her reaction to you and that you didn't want her. It's not logical, but that's it. Russ must be feeling the same way, which is why he's so scared of your power and doesn't want to be around it, that's why the knee-jerk reaction—son of a bitch!"

"Logan, I—"

"I'm so sorry," he told me, and his voice was suddenly quiet, gentle as it had not been since he first got on the phone with me. "Oh baby, I didn't know. I thought you were testing power, like I said— forgive me."

"Of course." I smiled through the tears now filling my eyes.

"Everything I said, forgive me. I'm an idiot."

I took a breath.

"I'm still mad at you for leaving."

"Yes."

"You're still in the wrong."

He always had to remind me, which was Logan, the semel, the leader, explaining why he was mad, showing why it was fair. "I know."

"Oh shit!" he gasped.

"What?"

"Don't open the door for anyone but Yuri, do you hear me? No one."

"Yes, my semel."

He made a choked sound in the back of his throat. "I'm leaving now. Wait for me. I order you to wait."

"Of course I'll wait."

"Stay in the hotel room and do not open the door."

"But Logan, you really don't have to—"

"Honey, you're not getting out of the hotel without me. Literally, you won't make it out in one piece."

"What're you—"

"I'll be there soon, wait for me. Don't run."

"Why would I run?"

"Jin, wait. Please. Don't run from me."

"No, I would never."

"I love you."

I whimpered into the phone, and it was undignified and I wasn't sure where it came from, but it was there, my sudden need. "I love you too."

"I'm coming, sit down." I heard the smile in his voice. "Watch TV."

He hung up instead of saying good-bye, and I found I could breathe better. The man really did have a very good influence on me.

I showered and changed, turned the TV on in the background as the sky opened up and dumped down rain. It was a gift because I loved it and it soothed me. Hours later, having done nothing but think—think about Crane and Logan and Delphine and the maahes and his mate and his men and all of it running around in my head, my phone rang. It was a number I didn't know.

"Hello?"

"Jin?"

"Yes."

"Jin, this is Justin, where are you?"

"In the hotel, waiting for you."

"No, I mean—I know you're at the hotel, where are you in the room? Are you standing by the front door?"

"No, I'm by the window."

"Okay, hold on, I'll call you right back."

He hung up, which was weird. I looked down, out the window, and on both sides of the street there were cars, lots of them, parked up and down. It was like there was a party at the hotel that I didn't know about. I went to the door but stopped before I opened it. Logan had told me to stay inside.

There was a knock on the door, and I called out to whoever it was.

"Jin, it's me, Justin."

"Okay, lemme—"

"Don't come out; I'm on the phone with Logan, just wait."

I moved close to the crack between the frame and the door and listened.

"Yeah, I'm here," he said, and when the door bumped, I realized he was standing against it, leaning his back into it. "And Sean's with me, and my other two men, along with Miguel Garza and his, but Logan, what the fuck? Was he like this when you left? Did you *leave* him like this?"

There was a silence, and I realized he must have been listening to my mate.

"You don't understand. I have never in my life felt like this, I want to be in that room so fuckin' bad I'm choking on it. Miguel went back downstairs because he was that close to going through me."

More quiet.

"Well, the good news is that you no longer have to make amends to the tribe of Deshret or its semel; he understands that Jin wasn't doing it on purpose, you can feel it as soon as you get close—it's raw animal power, there's no gentle pull like it was when I first met him, this is furious and carnal and—God, what…." It was like he was searching for a word. "Throbbing need."

It was quiet again for a moment.

"Yeah, well, the problem is now that there's too many men here. I can't calm Sean down without doing it physically. I will have to make him submit to me, but to do that, we've both got to be in our panther forms. I can't shift in the middle of this fuckin' hotel."

I shivered at the man's voice, the power of him, and the semel that he was called to me.

"You fuck! Why would you do this? Why would you let him out of your sight if he was like this?"

There was more silence, and I knew that Logan was telling him everything. It took long minutes during which I listened to Justin breathe on the other side of the door.

"Okay, okay, I get it, but right now, right this very second, I don't see how I'm getting your mate out of this hotel in one piece unless I can get him to stop filling the air with his fucking scent. I mean you sent me here so I could put him on a plane back home to you but… Logan, do you have any idea what he smells like? What his skin must taste like?"

I wanted to smell Logan, see Logan, taste and touch him. I needed him.

"Oh fuck!" Justin yelled, startled. "Jin, get away from the goddamn door!"

I took several steps back as I heard something bang the wall outside in the hall. After a few minutes of silence, there was a sharp knock on the door.

I moved back close. "Hello?"

"Jin, it's Yuri. Open the door."

He was the only person my semel had given permission to open the door for. When I cracked it, the blue-eyed glare of my sheseru was the first thing I saw. "Hi." I smiled at him, so happy to see him.

He growled at me, grabbed the door, and gestured for me to step back.

I walked away, across the room, to the window, and when I turned, he was following and several other men had come in.

Yuri stepped closer than he normally did, then turned and went down on one knee. He was so big that even when he was kneeling, the top of his head was at my waist. Instinctively, I put my hand on his shoulder. His deep breath turned my head.

"Okay." He took a breath as Domin joined us, stepping in front of me, completely blocking my view of the room, hands on his hips and, from the tip of his head, seemingly bored, though I couldn't see his face.

"I'm Domin Thorne, maahes of the tribe of Mafdet," he announced loudly. "All of you, everyone in this room, speak your lineage to me now."

"I'm Miguel Garza," a voice answered, deep and husky, "semel of the tribe of Deshret; this is my sylvan, Adam Manuel, and my sheseru, Taylor Pang. I have many khatyu in the hall, as is my right."

"I'm Justin Cho," I heard Logan's friend say, his voice resonant and smoky-sounding, "semel of the tribe of Qebui from San Francisco, and I have my sheseru, Sean Li, with me, and two of my khatyu. I am here at the request of your semel."

Domin nodded and cleared his throat before he bowed and stepped sideways. I was suddenly facing the room. I looked over at the man I didn't know, Miguel Garza. He was tall and handsome with dark brown hair, broad shoulders, and warm eyes. I went down to one knee.

"I beg your forgiveness, semel; I did not mean to drag your people through the shift and meant no disrespect to them or you by my actions. I am not myself and apologize deeply."

His jaw clenched as he took one step forward.

It happened fast: a hand fisted in my hair, and my head was yanked back sharply. I couldn't stifle the gasp.

"Would you leverage your power against that of his semel?" Domin asked.

I realized Domin held me, and even though I could shift and get free, it felt too good to fight. I could feel the heat rolling off my maahes and inhaled his delicious smell. I had no idea the man's scent could become warm vanilla and salty sweat all at the same time. And he was so strong, I could feel it, not just physically but inside… he wouldn't break; he would stay, he wouldn't run. The man was powerful, and I needed my mate to be or I could never submit.

"Domin," I breathed, wanting him to hold me tighter, hold me down. I wanted to feel the weight of him and the heat of his body…. I needed….

"Yuri" was all he said.

Instantly, I was lifted and slammed hard into the cool glass of the window. The shock of the motion, the cold surface on my skin, cleared my head.

"If I can control my shift," I heard Miguel say, "then I will be allowed to taste him. You have no say. There are two of you; if the semel of Qebui and his men join you, then six, but even now I see his resolve crumble."

I leaned sideways around Yuri and saw Justin shivering with pain.

It was all my fault.

I was about to put Domin and Yuri in danger, and that could not happen. They would both sacrifice their lives to keep me safe, to honor me and Logan, and it was shaping up to be a very one-sided fight.

Shit.

Without a word, I stepped around Yuri. "Come, semel, I will let you feel my power, if that is what you would have me do, but bring your yareah so she might see."

"You mistake my need as mine alone, reah. My yareah and I will devour you together."

"Is that so?"

"Yes, that is so. Show me your power and then I'll show you mine. I will have you there on that bed, and your men will watch and do nothing."

My stomach twisted into a knot of cold anger.

"I will call my yareah; she'll be pleased. Normally we have other women in our bed; another man will be a nice change. She will take you inside of her while I bury myself in you," he said as he leered at me. "I cannot wait to feel you wrapped around my cock."

"My mate will kill you for this trespass."

"He can try."

Logan.

At the thought of his name, I was all reah again but with the nekhene's simmering anger.

Where was the reah's mate?

"You will be mine, reah."

No one would ever disrespect Logan Church. The rage that had been rising slowly boiled over in an instant, rolling over my skin and exploded out of me like a furnace blast, engulfing the entire room in heat.

Domin went to his knees; so did Justin and his sheseru, falling forward, hands on the carpet, bracing against the flash of scorching power. All the others were on the floor, writhing in pain, the semel, sylvan, and sheseru of the tribe of Deshret already beginning their inexorable shift to panther.

"How dare you think you can touch me? Only my mate touches me," I roared at them all.

"Yes." Miguel's voice was garbled as he sought to control the shift by changing into his werepanther form, but I still understood him.

"Only my mate!"

His scream was horrible, his transformation freakish as his body contorted into an animal. He was not strong enough to hold onto his werepanther form.

"Yuri," Domin cried.

"Jin."

I turned to look at my sheseru when he spoke my name, and found him still on one knee, taking deep breaths in and out.

"I would allow no man to touch you, my reah."

My breath caught with the sincerity of his promise.

"I will slaughter any that even reach a hand toward you."

I knew that, and so I instantly calmed.

"Oh thank God," Domin gasped, sitting up, hands on his thighs, closing his eyes and breathing. "Please, Jin, calm down."

"Yes," Justin agreed, letting his head loll back as he, too, exhaled deeply.

I watched Sean, Justin's sheseru, claw free of his clothes, roll to his paws, and take a seat behind his semel. He was a beautiful, sleek golden panther. There were many in the room. Years ago I had found that my black color was as rare as being born a reah. Every panther I had ever seen was gold.

"You trust me," Yuri said.

I nodded.

He closed his eyes, and I saw the tremble run through his massive frame. My faith washed over him, and his certainty of his place as my guardian anchored me. We were bound together, the two of us, and every day the bond got deeper and stronger.

"Once everyone shifts back," Justin said after long minutes, his eyes on me as he took long steadying breaths, "I think we will all wait here for Logan's arrival."

I nodded.

His smile wavered, but it was there. "You have to be a very strong panther to withstand your pheromones, Jin; I feel very privileged to have passed this test, though had it gone a second longer, I, too, would have succumbed."

"No, you wouldn't have."

His eyes were locked on mine. "Oh yes, I don't think I've ever wanted anything or anyone as badly as you."

I looked away, unable to hold his gaze. My eyes found Domin.

"You are the mate of my semel, Jin," he said tiredly. "I don't think of you as a man, only as my reah."

"Yes," Yuri said, and when I looked at him, he nodded. "Your power is painful to bear, but I can withstand pain; I was made to stand between you and anything, even yourself."

The tears came fast as I squeezed his shoulder.

"Imagine how strong Logan Church is to have such a mate." Yuri smiled, and I saw him glow with pride.

"What now?" I asked Justin.

"Now we all wait for Logan."

"I'll order some food," Domin suggested, climbing unsteadily to his feet. "I'm starving."

I walked over to the window as Yuri rose to his towering height, positioning himself between me and everyone else.

"Tell me how Crane looks," I asked.

His eyes, when he looked at me, were slits. "He's broken, Jin. He won't shift back."

Shit.

"His father was the one with the knife."

I braced myself on the wall.

"If I see him, anywhere, at any time, I'll kill him. Pit or no pit, Crane's father is dead," he said, and his voice was dark with purpose.

I nodded my agreement.

Chapter Six

THE KNOCK on the door came just minutes after nine that night, and Artem Varda, Yuri's second, walked through the door a moment before Logan. I stood, the whole room stood, and my mate waited. It was my place to go to him, and when I moved, everyone stepped back. It was like I was a leper or something; no one wanted me to touch them.

Logan drew me up against his side, tucking me there, and I inhaled him, his scent, put my hands on him and leaned.

"Please."

I opened my eyes and saw Miguel reach for the edge of the table and grab it tight.

"Semel-netjer, I ask your forgiveness for my trespass against your reah and humbly beg you to remove him from my territory. I have granted your brother the status of duat and will offer him no further jeopardy as long as he honors his place and never shifts."

"What trespass did you make against my reah?"

"May I speak?"

Logan turned his head to Domin, who was standing between Yuri and Artem. "The semel of the tribe of Deshret has given to your brother; let us return the favor and depart."

"Can we go home now?" I asked my mate.

"Yes," Logan said quickly, his arms tightening around me. "Are you packed?"

"I never unpacked," I told him.

The nervousness in the room was palpable, and I understood that it was because they were uncomfortable sitting there in clothes from overnight bags or ones that someone had had to go and fetch for them. Miguel Garza and his people had all shifted; ripped through the clothes they came in, and were wearing new ones procured from stores close by. They wanted to leave, wanted to rinse away the night and forget that another panther had turned them inside out, pulling them through their shift, rendering them powerless. It was humiliating, and every instinct screamed at them to simply slink away and hide. But that wasn't the law. The law said that Logan had to be greeted, and so they remained. If Miguel had left to go home and shower, he would have looked weak in front of my mate, so he stayed even though the reek of sweat and come and pain and arousal clung to his hair and skin like a sticky July afternoon. Sitting there, waiting for him to give the word that they could go, had to be maddening.

"I accept your terms, semel," Logan said, stepping away from me, walking over to Miguel Garza, who rose to shake hands with my mate. "And thank you for your care of my brother."

He sighed deeply. "Your reah is dangerous, semel-netjer, and though I would like to seek justice for the shift that was forced on myself and my house, I also saw you in the pit in Sobek and do not want to challenge you."

"May I offer you some other reparation?"

"I would accept any that you would see fit to offer."

"I will have my sylvan contact yours and set terms."

He bowed his head, covering their joined hands with his other. "My thanks, semel-netjer."

I trembled because it was over and I could go home to Crane.

"May I present to you my sheseru and sylvan?"

I crossed the room, away from the others, and looked out at the lights of the pier while Logan met Miguel's household.

"Are you well, my reah?"

I lifted my eyes to Artem. He was tall, almost as tall as Yuri, but leaner, and I liked his dark brown beard and mustache. They were striking on him. "I am. How was your trip?"

"Quick," he said, smiling at me. "I'm glad you're coming home, Crane needs you. He won't shift back, and we can't let him out to run on the grounds because we're afraid of what he might do to himself."

I nodded. "So he's locked in a room in his panther form?"

"He's not locked up, all he has to do is shift and he can get out."

"But he won't."

"No."

I took a breath. "I just want to go home."

He was looking at me, staring, and I saw his brown eyes bleed to cat green a moment before he dropped to the floor.

I had not been there to protect Crane. I had let him be taken and violated and maimed. How could I have done that? He was my best friend, the closest thing I had to a brother.

"No!" Miguel shouted, and it was chaos in seconds, everyone yelling, the fear and panic drowning me, choking me.

"Jin!"

I lifted my head, and Logan was there and I was wrapped in strong arms and held tight.

"Logan!" Justin roared.

"Baby, I'm here," my mate told me.

I clung to him, pressing against him as hard as I could, freezing suddenly, wanting to draw every bit of warmth I could from him.

"You're panicking, and you don't need to," he soothed. "I'm right here. You're safe."

I was trembling, my teeth chattering as he tightened his hold so I could feel his heart beating. I felt a hand in my hair, his other arm around my waist, and his lips on my forehead as he tried to soothe me with his presence, with his body. He smelled like stale air and musk, with a faint trace of the cologne I had bought him for Christmas. I wanted to crawl inside him where I knew it was safe. I clutched at him, my fingers digging into the hard muscles of his back, holding on.

"Logan!" Justin yelled. "Either claim your reah or step aside!"

"He's mine!" Logan roared out his ownership, and the primal sound sent a flush of heat through me, my mouth opening on his throat.

"Show me," Justin challenged.

Logan's low growl was answered by my moan that was part growl, part purr.

I was spun around hard and slammed against the window, only my hands splayed on the glass keeping me from going face-first into the hard surface. My sweater was yanked and tugged, and I heard the ripping and then felt the cool air on my skin as the shredded garment slid off me and fell to the floor at my feet. Logan fisted my hair and pushed my head down, causing a shudder to tear through me.

"Mine," he whispered in a voice more animal than man as fangs were driven deep into my skin, holding me there hard, pinned, under his teeth.

I whimpered and whined, my cock so hard and needy that, that fast, I was leaking in my jeans.

"Clear the room!" Yuri commanded.

I pressed back against Logan, rubbed, and ground against the now-hardened bulge in his dress pants, sliding my crease over his arousal.

"No." Justin's voice was cold and hard. "The law states that any semel may watch another semel take his mate at any time. Miguel and I will remain."

"Yareah," Domin Thorne answered, his voice just as icy as Justin's had been moments before. "Not reah, never reah. No one shall bear witness to a semel taking his true-mate."

Domin knew his law well.

"Get the fuck out," he growled from low in his chest.

"So the maahes of the tribe of Mafdet commands," Yuri said, his voice booming through the room. "On his word—out!"

I was panting with my devouring need and did not follow all the movement behind me, but when the door slammed shut, Logan withdrew his fangs and took a step back from me.

Whirling around, I lifted my face to his, and I saw that his eyes had bled to all gold. He had not shifted to his werepanther form, but he was trembling on the verge of it.

My body responded to the strength in him, his beauty and dominance. I got out of my clothes as fast as I could, kicking off my sneakers, unbuckling my belt, shucking out of my jeans and underwear until I was naked in front of him. He had watched me, not touching his own clothes, gold-slitted eyes instead locked on my body, running over it, never leaving me.

When he reached out a hand, I saw claws where there should have been fingers.

I fell to my knees and went to work on his belt.

"Nekhene," he growled.

I loosened the belt, unhooked the clasp of his suit pants, let them fall, and then eased his briefs down until his enormous cock bounced free. I admired the curve of it, the bronze color, the length and girth, the prominent vein that ran down the side, and the wide, flared tip before I rose up and took him down the back of my throat.

His cry of pleasure filled the room. A second later I felt the sharp claws in my hair, gliding over my scalp as he held me against him, making sure that his cock would remain buried in my hot, wet mouth.

I sucked hard, licked, swirled my tongue around the length of him, pulled back to trace the underside, leaned forward to bathe his balls, using my hand to tug and pull gently but firmly, swallowing the dripping precome before I took him in again from swollen head to base. He pushed in and out of my mouth, holding me there, his hand fisted in my hair.

When he pulled away, I tried to recapture him, but he used my hair like a leash as he lifted me to my feet and hurled me backward onto the bed. I hit it and rolled and he was on me, lifting my ass into the air. I heard him spit once and then again, and when his long, hard, rough tongue pushed into my opening, I cried out.

Normally there was lube, normally there were his talented fingers, but this time, there was nothing, and he did not want to hurt me with his claws. He spit again, and I writhed against him as I felt his thighs brush the backs of mine.

"My reah," he snarled as I felt the head of his cock at my entrance.

But that wasn't me. I was a nekhene cat and I was free; no one owned me.

He felt me tense in rebellion and responded. "Mine!"

I hissed out a moan as claws were driven into my hips, holding me still as he pushed inside me, slowly spreading me open, easing past the tight rings of muscle, pressing deeper and deeper.

The nekhene in me stilled, quieted, waited through the welcome jolt of pain.

My mate.

The man was my mate, and I wanted to be claimed more than I wanted to breathe.

He pressed into me, pushing, never stopping until he was fully seated inside, buried to the hilt. I was so full, so stretched, and the pain was white hot even as it began to change from burn to pulse to aching, throbbing need.

"Logan," I cried as my muscles clenched around him, spasming.

He pulled back, sliding slowly, and then he thrust back into me, hard and deep.

"Oh please," I begged, loving the feel of the man sheathed in me.

The action was repeated over and over, his rhythm set in seconds, again and again, fucking me, the length of him sliding easily in and out of my slick, clenching channel.

It was not tender; it was bruising, and I was held down, like a mating the rutting animals did, until he was coated in a sheen of sweat. What changed it to more was his hand, morphed from the clawed version back to human, on my face, turning my head, lifting my chin so he could take possession of my mouth as well as my body. Our lips melded together, and heat flared between us, his desire and mine exactly the same—to be one. He demanded surrender, and I gave it. When I felt his hand grip my cock, just that much pressure on oversensitized flesh brought my orgasm roaring up out of me in a blinding rush. My muscles flexed around his hardness, tightening all at once, hugging his shaft and wringing his shuddering release from him seconds later.

He collapsed on top of me, pinning me to the bed under him, both of us heaving and spent, panting for air.

"Maybe you should take me with you from now on," I finally said, smiling, turning my head to nuzzle aside his sweaty hair and kiss his temple.

His body was shivering with aftershocks, my channel still rippling around him, holding him tight. "Maybe," he agreed before he started to laugh.

I could feel his heart beating against my back, the rumbling of his laughter, and his throbbing cock still buried deep inside me. Every part of me was sated and satisfied, and even the part that rebelled against the bond of reah and semel recognized the claim Logan had just marked in my flesh with his teeth and claws.

"I didn't hurt you, did I?"

I shook my head as he pressed a hot kiss to the side of my neck.

"You belong to me, Jin; every part of you, every piece is mine."

Yes. "Yours," I agreed.

The deep, satisfied male grunt made me smile.

He eased gently from my body and rolled me over to my back before he lifted to his knees. I was naked, and so was he, from the waist down.

"You look like I had my way with you," he said, smiling wickedly.

"You look pretty much the same." I arched an eyebrow for his benefit.

He pounced on me, and I was laughing as he kissed me, wrapping me in his strong arms, holding me tight as he took possession of my mouth.

I kissed him back, tangling my tongue with his, tasting him, sucking and nibbling, arms and legs holding him tight.

"Say it," he whispered breathlessly, taking a gulp of air so he could kiss me some more.

"Logan," I gasped, panting, "I love you."

"And I love you," he said, his eyes locked on mine, his fingers combing through the long, thick hair that fell to the middle of my back. "I love nothing and no one more."

I pulled him down for another kiss, and he chuckled into my mouth.

"Mine," he breathed, and I was.

Chapter Seven

LOGAN HAD taken a shower after me, and so when he came out, I was again standing at the window, staring out at the night.

"Should I have some food brought up before we leave for the airport?" he asked gently.

"No." I shook my head, my eyes flicking to his honey-gold ones.

"We're going home, we're not staying. Don't be anxious or panic or think we're not leaving, because we are."

I nodded but said nothing, afraid I would dissolve into tears. I felt vulnerable suddenly, naked, because everyone knew what Logan had done to calm me and assert his dominance. I felt as though I was on display.

He crossed the room and took me in his arms. Pressing my face into his throat calmed me, the steady beat of his heart soothing, his hand cradling the back of my head, so gently, so tenderly, drawing the first tear from under my closed lids.

"Baby, look at me."

I tilted my head back and looked up at him.

"There." He smiled at me. "Don't worry about anyone else; you're the reah of your tribe, no one can understand your heart except me, and I'm the only one who matters."

But as everyone filed in and I saw their frightened faces, the wary looks, and the anger, I found that I had to look away. Even Artem, who had not shifted, looked scared.

"Let's go," Logan said after a few minutes, having changed out of the dress shirt and sweater he had been wearing earlier into just the sweater under his suit jacket. He pulled his wool and cashmere trench coat back on over it before he took my hand in his and led me out.

Domin took care of my hotel bill, and I followed Logan outside and into one of four enormous black Hummer limousines. Normally I would have had some sort of snarky comment about how Hollywood it was, but today it didn't matter.

I wanted to see Crane. I wanted to go home.

Inside the car, I sat beside Logan and was quiet, staring at his hand holding mine. The gold of his skin beside the olive of mine was, as always, noticeable. I heard yelling outside, and then Yuri was in the limo with us before Justin and Sean climbed in as well. I noticed that Miguel Garza and a woman were also seated inside.

"We're just waiting for my sheseru," he told us. "My sylvan will ride in the car behind us with my maahes, yours, and your other man."

He meant Artem.

"May I present my yareah, Erin Ralston Garza."

"It's a pleasure," Logan assured her.

Even if he had noticed before, as he had, Logan could never speak to her or even acknowledge her without her mate's permission. The fault that it took so long for him to greet her was Miguel's alone.

"No, semel-netjer, it's mine," she said. Then she turned to me. "I understand you are very powerful, reah, more powerful, even, than my mate."

I didn't answer her, as it was obvious that the taunt was meant as bait for Miguel and not me. Perhaps the women in his bed he had spoken of earlier were not as welcomed by his mate as he would have had us believe.

"Here he is," Miguel said too loudly, in obvious distress.

Taylor Pang, whom I had met earlier, whom I had dragged through a shift just as I had so many others, climbed into the car and took a seat beside Miguel. The man who had gotten out of the passenger seat to open the door, one of the khatyu, returned, and then I heard all the locks click as we pulled away from the curb.

It was quiet for long minutes, and when Logan finally broke the tension and silence, I would have startled if he had not moved his arm before he spoke and put it around me, drawing me in tight against his side.

"My mate is no longer making you ill, is he, semel?"

"No," Miguel said quickly, "I don't think so."

"And you?" Logan questioned Taylor.

"No, semel," he addressed Logan. "I feel different now."

"Protective," Yuri offered, his voice kind, as it normally never was.

"Yes." Taylor's dark eyes flicked to my sheseru.

"My reah's scent is now as it normally is."

"Oh," Taylor said softly.

"For you, semel," Logan said softly, "if you just breathe past his smell, past the need to protect and dominate him, your head will clear."

The silence returned but was broken seconds later by Miguel.

"Fuck." He exhaled sharply, looking across the space at Logan. "That's what a reah feels like regularly?"

Logan nodded.

"And he's not my mate," he said, squinting, "but I can feel the—that's crazy. I mean, just for a second there I wanted to—"

"Kill me," Logan provided calmly.

"Yes."

"I know."

"How do you—"

"All my friends told me I should be afraid of you, reah," Erin said sharply, ending all conversation in the car, "and I don't know why."

I didn't have the time or the energy to discuss what a reah was compared to a yareah. I especially didn't feel the need to speak to a trophy wife.

She was perfect. Nails, eyebrows, tan in the middle of winter, clothes that cost more than my car; her hair, with a pouf, was immaculate. The Chanel purse sitting at her feet matched her diamond-encrusted watch. Her makeup was flawless, and her jewelry was big and flashy. She reminded me of a rich, pampered housewife, and though I was normally much kinder, less judgmental, I was depleted of my normal goodwill.

I turned my head, burying my face in Logan's shoulder.

"My reah is exhausted," Logan began, and his voice, his really wonderful, smooth, mellifluous voice, hushed the car. "If you would allow me, I would answer your question, yareah of the tribe of Deshret."

I turned my head a fraction of an inch so I could see her.

She smiled at him. "Please."

Every woman smiled at Logan. It was a given; he was gorgeous. The man was gold all over—gold hair, gold skin, gold eyes—and the way he walked and carried himself, you knew you were looking at strength and virility and delicious soul-singeing heat. But there was more to him than just what you felt and saw. It was the calm you felt in his presence and the way the laugh lines in the corners of his eyes deepened when he smiled. He took in pain and confusion or anger and rage and breathed back out soothing quiet. It was what was needed in the semel, the leader of the tribe, but not often found.

"Your friends probably feared for you because an unmated reah, if they were to come across a semel mated to a yareah, could possibly end up being that semel's mate. There is always the chance that a semel mated to a yareah could still find his true-mate, his reah."

"So somewhere in the world could be Miguel's reah."

"Yes."

She let that sink in. "That is really scary," she told him. "I mean there you are, a yareah, and you've put years in with your mate, maybe had kids, and then one day he's walking down the street and he just runs into his reah and your life is over."

Logan nodded.

"I mean, that's what you're telling me, my life could end tomorrow if he finds his mate."

"No, you would become taurth, second-mate."

"It sounds horrible."

"Some female werepanthers refuse to even be considered as yareahs for that very reason," he told her. "Better to never love a semel at all than lose him."

She nodded.

"But they're foolish," Logan told her. "The chance of a semel ever finding a reah is miniscule at best."

"Spoken like a man." She pointed at me. "Because there sits your reah, and even though my mate is straight, he has not taken his eyes off him since he got into the car."

"What?" Miguel snapped.

He had obviously not gotten around to telling her what he had planned between him and her and me, back at the hotel.

"I understand," she said as she nodded, smirking at him before returning her eyes to Logan. "But a mated reah, why do I care about a mated reah?"

"Precisely." Logan smiled. "A mated reah is no threat to any yareah and should be seen only as a friend."

She looked at Logan hard. "Were you mated when you met your reah, semel-netjer?"

"No, I was not."

Her smile was huge. "That's good, so no lives were lost in the forming of your partnership."

"No," he said, chuckling at her wording. "I was very fortunate."

"I'm sure an unmated reah would be someone that a yareah might even want to kill."

"Yes, but most yareahs will never even see a reah in their lifetime."

"It's hard to imagine a reah being so rare when I can see one right in front of me."

He was quiet.

"I am curious to see if the power is really as great as I've been told."

"Unfortunately a display of my mate's power in this car would get us all killed in the ensuing chaos."

"He is that powerful?"

"Ask your mate," Logan said, which basically brought all chitchat to an end.

At the airport, Logan thanked the semel for his hospitality and told him that Mikhail would be in touch about reparation and the arrangements for the transfer of funds that would be decided on. The semel seemed uncomfortable, and I was certain that now, late in the night, when the anger and pain and humiliation had dissipated, the idea of having Logan pay him for his own weakness and that of his men seemed petty.

"Perhaps instead I might be allowed to visit, with my household, and we could hunt with you. I have not been on a hunt in years."

"Your tribe must hunt together," Logan said, "or one of the most basic of bonds is lost. And I would be honored, semel, and so would my house."

Miguel's face lit up, and he bowed, and then Logan bowed and everything felt better. I noticed Miguel still could not meet my eyes, and unlike his yareah, he didn't want to touch me.

Erin offered me her hand, which I took. Eyes that had been combative had softened, and when I smiled at her, it was returned.

When they, the semel and his household, were gone, Domin and Artem joined us for the walk toward the doors that led inside the airport. Logan was ahead of me, with Yuri and me behind, my sheseru's hand on my shoulder.

It was nice that now we were mated, Logan allowed others of his own household to touch me and be close to me. I reveled in his trust.

Logan promised to call Justin if he needed help with the challenges he would face during the sepat and, of course, to tell him if he became semel-aten.

"It seems like a dream to even be talking about this," Justin sighed. "Do you even want to be semel-aten and live in Sobek?"

"I don't, no, but there are probably choices I don't know about yet that the priest will make me aware of if I actually win."

"I have no doubt that you'll win," Justin told him. "You're the strongest semel I know, and all your men, your maahes, your mate… you'll win."

Logan stepped into him without permission, all the rules gone suddenly, just two old friends saying good-bye. Justin smiled as he was grabbed tight and hugged Logan back just as hard.

I cleared my throat, and all eyes were on me. "May I make apologies to your sheseru?" I asked Justin.

In answer, he stepped aside, and I was faced with Sean Li.

"I'm so sorry, sheseru of the tribe of Qebui, I did not mean to—"

"Reah," he interrupted me, having lifted his hand. "I learned a great deal about myself this night. When I shifted, I didn't lie on the floor gasping and flailing as did others; I did not have to be held down by my semel. I shifted, yes, but I held to my duty even in the shift. I have far more control than others have credited me with having. Thank you for showing me that there is still more to learn and ways I may better myself. We all have power inside that needs training."

"Yes." I smiled, bowing low.

When I rose, I saw him smile in return. I watched him shake hands with Yuri and Domin and Artem, and realized again, as I had in Sobek when I had first met Justin Cho, that Logan's friend was very similar to him, and the men he chose were much like my mate's, strong and kind and gifted. Watching Justin and Sean walk away together, I saw the same easy camaraderie Logan shared with his sheseru and his sylvan in private moments.

"Where's the damn gate?" Yuri grumbled. "I wanna go home."

"Me too," Domin said with a nod, yawning as he lifted his head to scan the list of departures.

Yuri smiled and put a hand on his shoulder. Domin's in return, warm, gentle, was a surprise.

"This way." Artem pointed before he led us toward the gate.

It was like the whole horrible trip had never happened. We all ate together at the airport and then sat in the boarding area and waited. My mate spoke to his brother on the phone, wished him well, hoped they would still hear from him upon occasion, and told him that if he ever wanted to return to the tribe, the door was always open.

"You didn't want to see Russ?" I asked Logan afterward.

"I don't anymore," he told me honestly as we were boarding. "I'm the semel of my tribe, and basically Russ has told me that not only does he not want to belong to me, but he doesn't want to belong anywhere. The part of me that is related to him will accept his decision, but it's a slap in the face, Jin, and I can't pretend that it's okay. A tribe is your family, and his choice is not to have one. What use can I have for him?"

It was cold and harsh, but I understood it too. Logan was the leader of his tribe, and Russ didn't want to belong. What more could there be between them?

Even when Crane and I had been traveling together from one part of the country to another, neither of us had ever thought to ask for the status of duat. I could not imagine never shifting, and Crane had never given up his dream of belonging to another tribe. I had wanted nothing to do with being a panther, but even then, I had still peeled off all my clothes and gone running in the night. I had lied to myself years ago when I had told myself that I hated being a werepanther. I had never hated the shift; I had hated being an unclaimed reah. Ruslan Church truly wanted to be nothing but human; I hoped his decision made him happy.

"I hope one day Russ will embrace his heritage like you did once you found your place in the tribe, but he is allowed to make the decision to never return if that's what he wants. I would never ask anyone in my family or my tribe to live by a law that they didn't believe in. My purpose is to guide and nurture and keep everyone safe, not to punish."

I stared up at his profile, looking my fill of him.

"What?" he asked, noticing my fixed regard after a moment.

"I love you very much," I told him, my eyes swimming.

"Yeah, I know." He smiled, hand on my shoulder as he followed me into the cabin of the airplane. "And I love you back."

Chapter Eight

I WALKED through the front door of my house and suddenly had an armload of sobbing Delphine. Apparently, from what Markel said minutes later, first they had been angry tears, then sad, and then humiliated, and now, finally, they were relieved. I hugged her so tight that she calmed, and when I asked her if we were okay, if she still loved me, she started crying all over again. Of course she loved me, always would, had never stopped even for a second. I was relieved and told her so over and over. Everyone walked away from us in disgust.

I wanted to see Crane, but it was very late, and I was told by Mikhail, who had been watching him, that Crane was finally asleep. In the morning I could see him. Domin was on his way to his car, parked with many others in the snow, when Logan ordered him to use the room that was still his and spend the night. The lure of family and warmth was a hard temptation to fight, but Domin shook his head and thanked his semel for feeling sorry for him, but he was no charity case who needed pity. He was leaving.

"No," Logan barked, brows furrowed, his scowl intense. "I want you here, and tomorrow we're gonna talk about you moving back."

Domin staggered up the steps, as exhausted as the rest of us. "Do you really think—"

"Yes, I think it's a very good idea," Logan said, reading the argument in the head of his maahes. "I hate you not being here, and I've lost one brother, I won't lose another."

I watched Domin absorb the word.

Brother.

Logan had called him his brother. Russ was gone, and Logan wanted Domin close. No one turned down the semel-netjer; no one argued and tried to wiggle out of things except me. I was the only one allowed a voice.

"Come," Logan ordered.

Domin moved forward until his semel could reach him, and when he could, Logan put a hand on the bicep of his maahes and dragged him close. I watched my mate lean in, press his nose into Domin's thick brown shoulder-length hair and inhale. The tremble that followed, the flutter of lashes, the clench of Domin's jaw, was all very telling. Oh, how the man needed to be held tight and told he was beloved. The need was etched in every line of his long, lean frame. It was hard not to notice the beautiful picture the semel and his maahes made: the golden, chiseled, muscular leader and his dark, lithe, sleek second-in-command.

"Okay." Domin gave in, walked into the house.

I smiled at Logan, so very pleased with him for seeing that Domin, too, needed a slice of Logan cake, needed his attention, validation, trust, and to be told, once and for all, that he mattered, that he, too, was necessary.

"Jin," he called, and I moved fast.

Logan had e-mails to answer and needed to check on his actual business and so left me with a kiss to lock himself up in his office for a while.

Yuri was exhausted, and I followed him and Domin upstairs after receiving a welcome home hug from Markel and a shoulder squeeze from Mikhail. When I asked where Logan's parents were, I was told they were still happily on their cruise in Europe. They would be home before we all left for the sepat in eight weeks.

Yuri gave me a smile before opening the door of his room, and then at the other end of the hallway I saw a door open, and Koren appeared in jeans and nothing else. He stood there watching, waiting, in silent invitation. Domin walked by without a glance, disappearing into his room seconds later. We all heard the lock.

Koren slammed his door hard, and I put on a really good show of going to my room to go to bed. Once there, behind closed doors, I threw everything on the bed, kicked off my shoes, and slipped back out. I was outside Crane's door in minutes.

The idea that I would wait and just go to sleep while my best friend was right there where I could see him was ridiculous. Surely Logan knew me better than that.

I stepped into the room and locked the door behind me. I heard a low snarl and turned to look toward the bed. He was in his panther form, curled up by the headboard, and every light in the room was on. I got that. If he accidentally fell asleep, when he woke up, he would be in his cat form, and he would instantly be able to see, to make sure the nightmare was not reoccurring.

He must have shifted at least once to light the room, but that was it. He was making himself comfortable with being an animal. I knew panthers that had done it purposely, shifted and then never returned, for whatever reason. I would not let that happen to Crane.

"I know you," I told him, walking slowly, carefully, into the room. And I was basically talking to myself since he was in his shifted form, soothing him with my voice, the words more for my benefit than his understanding. "You've always been so strong, and if you stay as you are, then no one will ever see that your body's been mutilated."

His ears went flat and he hissed at me, mouth open, flashing his fangs.

"But it's only a mutilation to you," I said firmly. "Logan told me what the doctor said, that for human men, sometimes as a result of what you've gone through there are side effects, bad ones, and for others they don't affect them at all. Everyone's different, Crane, everyone has a different system. Just because you've heard things doesn't make them so."

Panthers other than semels and reahs, when they changed, were animals. But that was not to say that they did not know they could change back, that they stayed in their bestial form. And even though Crane was now, for all intent and purposes, a wild animal, he still had the familiarity with me that any creature would with a human who fed it or who they continually saw. He knew me but didn't. It was dangerous to be in the room with him as he was in his panther form and I was human, but the risk, for me, was of no consequence. I needed him back.

"Shift," I commanded.

He charged forward to the edge of the bed, growling, snarling; his hair rose, and it looked like he was going to rush across the floor and rip me to shreds.

I went for the heart of his fear. "You're scared that you won't be able to get it up. You're terrified that women will laugh when you take them to bed, tell you that you're not a real man anymore, or half a man, or no man at all. I know you; I know exactly what you're thinking."

He came at me, stopped a foot in front of me, and roared.

"Shift!" I ordered.

He ran back to the bed, halfway up the wall, and then crashed back down. The picture rattled and fell. Glass shattered; the lamp on the nightstand, bone china, smashed into a hundred pieces, only the fixture intact, the light still on but rolling back and forth on the floor. In a frenzy of anger, he destroyed the down comforter and the sheets, left them in shreds along with the mattress underneath.

"Shift!" I screamed.

He ran at me and pounced, slammed me hard to the floor, and stood over me, heaving, his muzzle inches from my face, teeth bared, a low growl curling up from his throat.

"They did this to you because of me, to hurt me—Crane!"

He leaped away and crouched by the window, and slowly, he shifted. When he was sitting there, shivering, I sat up.

I was not prepared for the way his hair had been shorn off so close to his scalp, the skin dug into in places, leaving matted bloody patches. To see the black eye, the torn lip, and the bruises that mottled the left side of his face brought hot tears welling up in my eyes. His hands were over his genitals, covering them so I couldn't see.

"My father did this to me," he said, and his voice was not his, broken and rusty instead. "And I know what you're thinking, but he didn't do it because of you; he did it because he hates me. He let them hold me down, he let them spread my legs, and then he took the knife himself and cut me."

I felt bile rise in my throat and fought back the urge to vomit with everything I had.

"He did it, and when it was done, he rolled me over and told everyone that I was no longer a man, no longer a panther, I was nothing at all. He left me bleeding to death on the table."

Trying to imagine it, I found that my brain could not dredge it up; there was just no way—the betrayal was far worse than even my father's of me.

"All I could think to do was shift. It's what you always do when you're hurt, it's what you always told me, and I could hear your voice in my head telling me to do it."

My voice.

"And when I did, oh God, Jin, it hurt so bad, but when you shift, you know, you can feel your body heal; you can feel it use what it needs to fix itself."

But I didn't. I had never known that sensation. Only those who shifted as Crane did, in intervals of time, felt the change. Even Logan, whose own shift was slow in comparison to mine, shifted too fast to feel the metamorphosis of his body. Semels and reahs never had that understanding. Me especially, I had never even glimpsed it.

"The semel-aten is the one who had Archer kidnap me, he's the one who turned me over to my father, and he's the one who's going to have to face Logan at the sepat."

"I know all this," I said gently, sliding a centimeter closer to him. I was careful, moving slowly, not wanting to startle or spook him.

"Then why did you come in here?" His voice cracked.

"Because I wanted to see you," I told him.

"Why?"

"That's the stupidest question you've ever asked me. Why do you think?"

"Jin, I—"

"You're mine."

His tears welled up and overflowed fast. One second he was just staring; the next his head was back against the wall and water was rolling down his cheeks.

"It's my fault."

"It's not!" he screamed, raw eyes back on me. "It's my father's fault, and Archer Pike's, and the semel-aten's! They did it. They all did it!"

"I won't let you be a panther."

"I could be your pet." He laughed suddenly, and it was heartbreaking and sad and utterly defeated and slightly unhinged. He was teetering on the edge of a complete breakdown.

"The doctor told Logan that for a normal human man, the loss of testicles can cause all the side effects you know about, but for you… you're a goddamn werepanther, you ignorant piece of crap! The shift is fueled by testosterone; even female werepanthers have an ungodly amount of it in their bodies. Use your head, Crane, please."

Logan had talked to me on the plane, told me every detail his doctor, our doctor, Jefferson Smith, a werepanther himself, had told him. He lived in Reno but was part of our tribe, and even though Christophe had made the man very generous offers, he refused to renounce the tribe of Mafdet for the tribe of Pakhet. He was a good man and had given Logan the facts without sugarcoating. It was time Crane heard them.

"I can't have kids," he whispered.

"You can have all the kids you want, Crane. Just because they won't share DNA with you doesn't make them any less yours. Logan can't have any of his *own* kids, either. You think he gives a shit?"

He dragged in air.

I moved closer and closer.

"I'm not a real man anymore."

"Being a man has nothing to do with anything between your legs and you know it. Anyone in their right mind would be blessed to have you. Anyone."

He watched me move closer. "If you touch me, I'm gonna be done."

I shook my head, almost able to reach him. "No, you're gonna take my strength until yours builds up again."

"I should have never gone to Vegas. I should have listened to you."

"I never told you not to go."

"But you didn't want me to."

"Because I was being selfish, thinking of me, not you."

"I think, for a while, I'm gonna move back to the house. I can't face going back there."

He had no idea they had torched his condo, and I wasn't ready to tell him all his things were now ash. "I think that's a wonderful idea."

He nodded, squinting hard, his eyes filling but not overflowing. "I wanna be safe."

"I won't let anyone touch you."

But the haunted look in his eyes, to my surprise, didn't go away.

The knock on the door startled us.

"Jin."

Logan was in the hall.

I turned to Crane. "Do you want him in here?"

"He's the semel-netjer. What does he want?"

I rose and walked to the door, and when I opened it, I was faced with my scowling mate. "You asked too much of me to wait."

He just stood there until I moved, holding open the door for him. He walked into the room, and I locked the door behind him.

I was surprised that instead of moving toward Crane, he strode to where the desk and chair were. Slowly, silently, he took off his clothes. He started with his wingtips, put his socks inside of them, and then pulled his sweater off over his head. I had no idea what he was doing, just watched as all his golden skin was revealed, as everything was draped over the chair. When he was completely naked, he shifted into his golden panther glory, took a step, and then, in one powerful leap, he was on top of the ruined bed. He lay down, paws in front, head lifted, and growled.

I looked at Crane and saw him tremble, saw the tears dripping down his cheeks, and then saw the beginning of his shift. It took long minutes, and then he was a panther, standing there, still shaking, head lowered.

Logan opened his jaws and made a chirping noise at Crane. It was high-pitched, the call, and seconds later, when he called him again, it became a churr. I had never heard him make the sound; as leader, he didn't have to invite anyone to him, coax anyone but me. But he was calling Crane, and I watched my friend react.

He bolted to the bed and then sprang up onto it, sinking down instantly beside his semel, leaning against him, pushing his muzzle forward to touch Logan's. Slowly, carefully, my mate lifted his head only to lay it gently on the back of Crane's neck. I heard the whine come out of my best friend, and I was flooded with relief and sadness all at the same time.

Clearly Crane did not believe I was powerful enough to keep him safe. No matter what I was, nekhene cat or no, Logan was the semel and I was the reah. He was the tribe leader and I was his mate. He would always be stronger than me. I was thrilled that Logan knew exactly what Crane needed—to feel utterly and completely safe. I heard Crane begin to purr, and I knew he would finally sleep. I turned to go.

The low churr caused me to turn around.

Logan lifted his head, waiting.

"I don't wanna do anything to upset him."

Logan rubbed his head against his own shoulder and then called to me again.

"But he doesn't need me, he has you."

There was a whine from my mate, and I finally got it. No, Crane didn't need me at that moment; it was Logan's strength and dominance that was necessary. But for my mate, to have me at his side, that was vital.

I moved around the room, picked up what was left of the broken lamp, and turned it off. I flipped off every light but the desk lamp before I stripped out of my clothes. My mate watched me with hungry eyes, and when I was done, I shifted and padded over to the bed. I was up and lying down beside him seconds later.

He ran his chin over the top of my head and down the back of my neck, rubbing and nuzzling until I rolled over, my back to his side, and wiggled around until I got comfortable. He licked the side of my head before gently biting my ear. The message was clear: I needed to settle, already. When he put his head down on his paws, he began to purr. We were a warm pile of fur, the three of us snuggled together, and I was glad Logan could be there for Crane and I could be there for him. I went to sleep content.

Chapter Nine

DANNY HAD saved Logan. He had warned him and Derek Jackson of the trap to kill both semels. Danny was a hero, he had risked his life, and everyone was treating him as such. I had been jealous because I loved my mate desperately, so when he had told me Danny, my cousin, had come home with him, I had been unsure. The following morning, I understood everything.

I woke to find Logan gone and Crane wrapped around me. Lifting my head, I shifted and smiled at him.

"I'll take a shower. You take one, 'cause you stink, and come down and eat with me."

His shift took longer, but he did it, for me, so we could talk.

I waited while his muscles elongated and reformed, twisted and pulled, and the feline gave way to the man.

"I wrecked the room," he said quietly.

"We'll fix it."

He cleared his throat. "I can't go back to that apartment in Vegas, Jin, I—"

"It's gone, honey," I told him gently and waited while understanding sank in.

"What'd they do?"

I cleared my throat. "They torched it."

After a minute he nodded. "Okay, so, I need stuff."

"A lot of stuff."

He just looked at me.

"If you don't want to leave the room, we can stay here."

"It's trashed; it looks like I had a killer party in here. I need to get out for a while." He exhaled, and I got just a trace of warm eyes and a smile.

"I know Delphine packed whatever you had left here at the house for Logan to take you when he went to Chicago. Do you know where that is?"

"Yeah, it's there"—he tipped his head toward the opposite side of the room—"in the bathroom. I have clothes I can change into."

He sounded so good; he looked so good. My stomach flipped over. "Okay, so you shower and I'll meet you downstairs."

"Okay."

Yes!

"But if I wanna go, then you need to go with me and not try and make me stay there."

He wanted me with him. Was he kidding? I would do anything he wanted. "Absolutely."

There was a quick nod, and he rose off the bed in a fluid movement I was thrilled to see. The back and forth shifting was healing his body.

"And put on some damn clothes," he teased. "No one wants to see your bare ass 'cept Logan."

I smiled as I watched him cross to the bathroom. I was pulling on my clothes, underwear, jeans, when I happened to look up at him again. It was then that I saw the marks on his back.

It took everything in me not to be sick.

He had been flogged, and the man wielding the whip had missed no part of the broad expanse of skin. The welts, and there were many, were angry; the cuts, crusted but still oozing, spoke to how deep—bone deep—they had been. My best friend had been set upon by vicious men; it was a wonder he was alive. Violence even I could not conceive of had been done to him. It was monstrous.

"My hair looks like shit."

He had been mutilated, but he was grieving his hair at the moment. Jesus.

"Doesn't it?"

They had cut his thick waves of blond hair to tufts; even his scalp was covered with scabs.

"I'll get you a hat," I said instead of crying.

"Excellent idea," he called back, turning to look at me. "Would it be too weird if you came over here and held me as tight as you can?"

I ran.

I hit him hard, harder than I should have, but he whimpered deep in his chest and clutched me tight. We stayed like that until he could breathe without me.

Logan was in the kitchen with the others and Danny when I finally came down.

"Good morning, Jin." Danny beamed at me the second he saw me. "Thank you for giving me sanctuary in your tribe. I am very grateful."

He was smaller than I remembered, slighter, his features delicate and fragile. Compared to him, I was a damn Viking. He was easily the prettiest man I had ever seen in my life, with his big almond-shaped brown eyes; short, straight nose; long, thick lashes; and porcelain skin. His hair fell to his shoulders and was the same color as mine, jet black. Looking at him, I felt my power rise with the need to crush him.

Logan's warm laughter turned my head.

"Come here."

I crossed the room to him, and when I was close enough, he reached for me, drew me close, and kissed me breathless, until my skin was on fire and I had a steady pulse of need surging through my body. When I broke the kiss, we were both panting.

"What was that for?"

The noise he made was all male as he dipped his head forward, his lips against my ear. "So you know that there's only one man I ever want in my bed," he told me, his tongue licking down my collarbone, nibbling at the base of my throat. "You are my miracle, Jin Rayne, do you think I don't know that? Do you think you're the only one who feels lucky?"

Logan always knew what to say.

The beast in me stilled, quieted, and forgot about doing violence to young Danny as my hair was nuzzled and my earlobe sucked inside a hot, wet mouth.

My mate.

"Would you do something for me?" I asked, looking up into the honey-colored eyes. "Or lots of things?"

"Whatever you want."

So I explained about redoing Crane's room.

"Take him into Reno today, get him whatever he needs or wants, and I'll have his room done by the time you guys get back."

"Thank you."

"You're welcome."

I stood there close to my mate and just breathed.

"Hey."

My eyes returned to Logan's topaz ones.

"What about both of your jobs? You guys work for the same man, and now…." He sighed deeply. "Jin, with the sepat and Crane and…. I mean, is it fair to Ray to ask him to continue to keep you employed when he really needs someone there full time? How are you supposed to manage his restaurant when you have so much going on here? And if I fail in—"

"You will not fail," I cut him off sharply. "I need you."

He nodded. "Just talk to Ray, tell him that Crane had an accident and that you're not sure when either of you will be back. Put the ball in his court. Sometime soon your life will balance out, but right now your tribe has to come before your work."

I opened my mouth to speak.

"Don't tell me about being a burden and not pulling your own weight financially," he told me. "Since you've been here helping me with distribution and marketing, business has gone through the roof. I had to hire two new managers and brought Delphine on full time. Because of you, I am making more money than I ever have before. You don't have to work, and neither does Crane, until he's ready to."

"And I appreciate that, but it's not your place to—"

"Of course it is, who else's but mine? You belong to me; I want your focus on me, your family, and the tribe. It's all I've ever wanted. When I get home and you're closing the restaurant and you're not home until two…." He sighed. "I climb the walls, Jin."

And I knew that. Male panthers, all of them, were a very Neanderthalish lot. They liked their mates at home when they were, around, underfoot, close enough to touch at all times. Semels were twice as possessive, twice as protective, and three times as caveman-inclined. Logan wanted me there where he could see me, eat with me, talk to me, and touch me at all times. Me working had always been a source of contention, and it looked as though I was about to finally lose the argument.

"I'll talk to Ray," I told him, because it was time, and it was fair. My boss was a good man; I did not want to take advantage of him.

"Really?"

The light that infused my mate's eyes was something to see.

"Yes."

His hand went to my throat, and his thumb tipped my chin up as he bent and brushed his lips over mine. He was very pleased.

"Morning."

The whole room turned to look at Crane, who had just walked in.

"Hey," Danny greeted him, crossing the kitchen fast to reach him. "How are you this morning?"

"Better." Crane forced a smile.

"Oh," I said softly, turning to look at my mate. "Danny didn't just save you, he saved Crane."

Logan shook his head. "I don't think so. He feels sorry for Crane and he wants to help Crane, but it's not what you think."

But I knew interest when I saw it. My semel had no idea what he was talking about. "Logan, I—"

"Listen," he began as the door opened again.

"Good morning," Logan's sylvan said as he came into the room.

"Mikhail." Danny swallowed hard. "Come eat. I'll make you a plate. What do you like?"

I watched Mikhail, my reserved sylvan, as he thanked Danny but told him he could get his own food. Danny flushed and stammered, taking a step back, lacing his fingers together so those restless hands would not flutter around like frightened birds. He very badly wanted to touch Mikhail, it was so very obvious, and just standing there breathing in his scent was making the younger man breathless with anticipation.

I coughed softly. "Oh."

"Take back what you were thinking about me."

"What was I thinking?" I teased.

"That your mate was clueless."

That had been my conclusion, but I saw the truth very clearly. "Danny saved Mikhail."

"And the rest of us," Logan said, smiling warmly, "but yeah, first on his mind was Mikhail."

"Interesting."

"Apparently," Logan coughed, "he remembered him from when he was here with your father."

"Really?"

Logan nodded.

"That's very interesting."

"I thought so."

"Did anyone happen to mention to him that Mikhail's straight?"

Logan tipped his head, and I watched my sylvan reach out and curl a long piece of hair around Danny's right ear. He then squeezed his shoulder and smiled. And when you got the real deal from reticent, aloof Mikhail Gorgerin, when you were gifted with a sparkle in the shining midnight blue eyes and saw the wicked curling lip along with the arch of the dark brown eyebrows… you were good and gobsmacked. The man glowed, and Danny nearly swooned as Mikhail brushed by him. I watched for a minute before I checked to see what Crane was doing.

He was smiling at everyone, and then he turned funny and winced.

"You okay?" I held my breath.

"I'm fine," he sighed, stepping around Delphine to walk over to me. Without thinking about it, he rubbed his chin over my shoulder before he sat down at the table with a huge plate of eggs and steak and biscuits. "Is anyone gonna talk to me?"

They descended on him like locusts: Delphine and Markel and Yuri and Koren. When Mikhail sat down, he took a seat on Crane's right and put a hand on his forearm as they spoke. The closeness soothed Crane; the sylvan touching him was good. They were friends, and I had no idea when they had become close. Koren stepped up behind him, hands on his shoulders, and Crane patted his hand as Delphine put a large glass of juice down in front of him and Markel followed with a steaming mug of coffee. Taj came in last, having been outside checking the grounds as was his routine.

His eyes lit up when he saw Crane. He pulled the beanie off his own head, walked over to Crane, and put it on him, rolling it up so it fit, so all you saw was my best friend's bruised face, not where the thick wavy mane used to be.

"Thanks, man." Crane smiled up at Taj, one of the members of the Shu cats, the deadliest panthers in the world, those that reported directly to the priest of Chae Rophon.

Taj patted his back, and I realized that in a very short time we, the household of the semel-netjer, had mauled the distance out of him. He was no longer standoffish, no longer cold and quiet; he was a part of our tribe. I doubted he would want to return to Egypt even if he was called.

Logan cleared his throat softly, so only I would turn and look at him.

"He can't scent-mark you, I won't allow it."

He had noticed Crane scraping his chin over my shoulder.

"I'm his, too, Logan, we—"

"No." He cut me off, kissing my forehead. "When cats catch your scent, after yours, they should only smell me."

I watched as he slid his cheek over the same shoulder Crane had marked. "Don't pee on me, alright?"

He chuckled as he turned to leave the room.

My hand on his bicep stopped him.

"You gave me a task," he reminded me.

"I wanna sit down with you and talk about the sepat. We have to make plans and strategies, and we have to start training and—"

"Love," he said, smiling at me, hands sliding up my arms to rest on my shoulders, "you need to focus all your energy on Crane, because as your beset, he must accompany you. In two months you're going to have to decide if it's going to be him or if you'll appoint another."

I nodded quickly.

"Along with Domin, he's going to be in the pit with you during the trial of the heart."

"I know."

"Come here."

He slowly turned me around and walked me out of the kitchen and into the living room, where a fire blazed away, warming the large polished wood and leather furniture-filled space. When it had been his mother and father's home, apparently the house had looked much different, but now there was a strong masculine feel to every part of Logan Church's home. I loved that the man's presence could be felt throughout the mansion.

"Look at me."

Tipping my head back, I met Logan's amber-colored eyes.

"We're all learning this as we go, Jin. I can't remember even hearing of a sepat being called, can you?"

"No."

"See, so, Ammon's father was never challenged, or his grandfather, but now he is, and the priest is giving me these rules that are supposed to be finite but make no sense at all."

He looked worried, and I put my hands on his chest, resting them there, to comfort him.

"I mean, there's a law that no reah may ever fight in the pit, and yet the law of Bast, which you yourself have called, allows a mate to take the place of their semel during a challenge. And now the priest tells me that having a nekhene cat in the pit would be an unfair advantage, so he may need to blindfold you or—it's a mess. And the sheseru is supposed to do the trial of the blood, but the law also states that no sheseru who is protector of a true-mate will be placed in the path of danger. So that means Yuri can't stand as my champion for the trial of blood, but—"

"You're going in circles."

"Yes, I am," he sighed heavily. "It's—I mean, sometimes I understand Russ's old argument with me, because some of the rules are completely antiquated and barbaric, and someone does need to update them, and—"

"Did you ever think maybe that's why all this?"

"What are you talking about?"

I shrugged. "Logan, maybe it's you. Maybe you're the man who's supposed to bring the panthers that have been lost back into the fold by accepting that a semel could take, even as a yareah, a male for his mate."

He squinted at me.

"Maybe you're supposed to do that."

"Jin—"

"And maybe panthers who love people, regular human people—maybe they should be allowed to do that without fear of reprisal."

"What're you—"

"I've traveled all over the country, and I've met a lot of panthers who have left their tribes, run from them for one reason or another, but the one thing they all have in common is how much they miss being a part of a community. Panthers need other panthers, and maybe this is what you're supposed to do."

"Jin, honey, there's no way that—"

"Maybe you'll be the semel-aten who appoints a council to rewrite the law, making it, finally, understandable for everyone."

"But I'm not anyone special."

"You are, though, Logan; you have gifts that others don't."

"Oh yeah?" He leered at me. "I have gifts, do I?"

"Knock it off," I snapped. "You're the strongest panther I know, and I don't mean physically, Logan. I mean your heart."

The look I was getting was all love.

"You could be semel-aten."

"I never wanted to be anything but yours."

"I know."

"I just want to be the semel who found his heart, Jin, that's all. Just semel-re."

I shook my head. "You're supposed to be more."

"Love, I am not the—"

"How do you know?" I took his face in my hands, staring into his gorgeous amber eyes. "Really, Logan? How do you know? The laws are ancient, they need changing, and who's to say that you're not the man to do it?"

He stared. "Do you realize what you're talking about? You're talking about me being semel-aten. Me. Do you have any idea what that means?"

"I think so, yeah. It means that you rule Sobek and the people who live there, and that you're in charge of relationships with every tribe in the world, and that you and the priest of Chae Rophon are best buddies for life. You would be a king."

"Which I don't want to be."

I smiled up at him. "Which is probably why it *should* be you."

He took a deep breath and grabbed me, holding me tight. "Whatever happens, as long as we're still us, I'll be okay."

I hugged him back, laying my head over his heart. "We'll always be us."

"But you can't get tired; you never get to say that this isn't what you signed on for, because right this second, you're promising to stand by me, as my mate, forever."

"I already did that," I groaned, shoving away from him. "For crissakes, Logan, it's you and me until one of us is done here and the other follows. I don't plan on being here without you."

He nodded fast. "Me neither; I'm not strong enough."

I stared up into his eyes, and he held my gaze without wavering. Always, I saw the love there, always his granite resolve, the strength and will. But there was also that piece no one else saw: his absolute, drowning need. Blessed with finding the other half of his soul, he could not be expected to live without me.

I was the same.

It was the only scary part about finding your true-mate: the inability to live without them. Others who weren't semels or reahs could never be expected to understand.

"Okay, so." I took a breath. "What? When do we have to know about Crane?"

He reached for me, and I took a step back just beyond the tips of his fingers.

"Come here."

I shook my head, smiling, retreating behind the couch.

"What are you doing? I'm not gonna chase you around the living room."

But he lunged at me, making his words a lie, and I moved away just as fast. His expression was priceless.

"What?"

"I don't know," I teased, putting more space between us. "I'm just trying to talk to you; you're the one that's all touchy-feely after you said you weren't gonna be."

He scowled, crossing the room so there was only a loveseat between us.

"Tell me, who's going to Mongolia to be with you?"

"You." He went to grab me, but I was faster, looking for it, walking backward and hitting the wall between two windows.

"And?"

He came around the piece of furniture, stalking me, ready to bolt any direction I did.

"Yuri."

"And?"

"Mikhail and Domin."

"Who else?"

My mate closed in on me, and I noticed his eyes had heated, changed to a beautiful warm gold, just that trace of a hunt firing his blood. The man so wanted to run me down and make me submit. Just the idea of it, I knew, flushed heat through his blood.

"Stay there."

"Why? You so want me to take off just so you can catch me."

I saw the muscles in his neck cord, saw his jaw clench.

"You're kinda twisted there, Church."

His brows furrowed.

"What?" I asked.

"I want something, but it has to be okay with you, and I don't want you to say yes unless it's really okay."

"What is that?" I waited for him to explain.

He stepped in front of me, and his hand went to my throat, closed, and his thumb slid under my chin, tipping it up as he bent toward me, his breath featherlight across my face. "I want you to take my name."

My eyes flicked to his.

"You can't wear a ring because of how fast you shift and—"

"No panther can wear a ring, Logan; everyone shifts too fast to remember to take it off."

"I'm talking about you right now."

I was silent.

"You already bear my mark, but it's not enough. I want everyone to know, not just werepanthers, that you belong to me, with me. It's important."

I could see that it was, from the look on his face. "You want me to be Jin Church?"

"Yes, very much."

Our eyes locked as he waited.

"I need to think about that."

He nodded.

"Is that okay?"

"Yes."

"Good." I smiled up at him.

He made a sound in the back of his throat.

"What's wrong?"

"When you see me again, I'll be this wild creature that you'll have to tame. Eight weeks in panther form will take its toll."

"I know," I told him, pressing forward, my hands sliding up under the lightweight cashmere sweater to touch hot skin and rippling muscles. The man was so beautiful, utterly edible, and I was ready to make a feast of him.

"It's part of it, part of the trial of the heart—the mate taming the semel."

"Yes."

"If you can't even do that, then you—"

"We both know I can do that," I told him, lifting my eyes slowly to meet his. "Logan."

"I don't want to hurt you. The priest says that in the history there are accounts of semels ripping the throats out of their mates in their werepanther forms before being ordered to shift back to panther form, never being semels again, never knowing they slaughtered them, nev—"

I chuckled. "Ripping their throats out, really?"

"Jin, this is—"

"Stop, you know I can tame you, Logan Church. In whatever form you are, you're mine."

"But we're not even allowed to shift back into men until after the trial of the heart is concluded. So when you're done with your trial, I get to be me for a day before I meet the semel-aten in the pit. We go from panthers to our werepanther form. I won't even be able to talk to you. They lock us up at night and—"

"It's okay."

"And if Yuri fails, or Mikhail, or you, then I never get to talk to you as a man ever again!"

"Logan—"

"Jin, if the semel kills his mate, he is immediately ordered back into panther form and never allowed to shift back again," he said, his voice strained and cracking. "You spend your life as an animal that dreams of being a man."

"Kiss me."

"Jin." His voice cracked on my name.

"Please."

He exhaled sharply before he bent and kissed me.

There was the press of his lips, his mouth melting over mine, slow, sensual, utterly claiming, and so hot. I trembled in his arms, lifted mine, wrapping them around his neck to hold him tight and close. I wanted my mate. The desire to strip away all his clothes, have him naked and heaving in bed, both of us slick with sweat and come, was almost overwhelming.

He whimpered in the back of his throat.

"I love you," I told him, easing back for a moment before I reclaimed his mouth.

The kiss was endless, and breathing became a secondary consideration.

"Your scent, Jin… you're gonna make me forget all my plans today."

It was what I wanted, but not what was best for my mate. He would be leaving soon, and he needed to make sure that everything was set before he left. For his own peace of mind, I had to let him go.

"It's gonna be soon."

"What is?"

"They're coming for me and Domin at the end of the week."

I reached up for his face, and he closed his magnificent eyes as he gently shivered under my touch. "That's okay, everything's okay."

He nodded, put his hand over mine, and pressed my palm against his cheek as he opened his eyes. "You're gonna be okay, right? You seem okay."

"I'll be fine, I promise."

The sepat for me would begin in eight weeks, but for Logan it would start on Friday. Members of the Shu would arrive to take him to Mongolia. He would spend the next two months in grueling training meant to strip him of his humanity and leave only the animal. The maahes of each semel was there to intercede if a semel was close to death and report to the mate of their semel. He was also the one to report if the leader was killed during the preparation for the sepat. The maahes had no other function, no voice.

"The trial of the heart has more or less two parts. So when you first see me, in my werepanther form, after I've shifted back from panther, that's supposed to test the bond between the semel and his household."

I just smiled at him.

"I'll be a savage the next time you lay eyes on me; I'll be altered and angry."

"I know."

"The priest said that there is strength training and punishment, and that you shift into panther form when you arrive and are not allowed to become human again until the day your household joins you after the trial of the heart."

I nodded.

"I'll be more animal than man when you see me next."

"I know."

He took a breath, taking both my hands in his. "The point is to test the bond even if I am not the same man you know."

"Yuri and Mikhail and I won't fail you."

"I know you won't, especially you, but you have to forgive me now for whatever I do then. It won't be me, and you have to remember that."

"You would never hurt me, Logan. It's not in you."

"But I'll be so hungry for you by then." He took a breath. "You have to forgive me."

I had more faith in the man than he had in himself.

"Please, Jin, don't abandon me, no matter what."

"I won't, I can't."

"Eight weeks without me," he sighed, "and you leaking power. The timing is shit."

"I'll be fine."

"I want you to miss me because that will smother the nekhene instinct to run or to look for another."

"You're the only mate I'll ever have."

"I know that," he said matter-of-factly, "but the wild creature that lives inside of you doesn't."

"Then I'll teach it."

"I *will* educate the nekhene cat," he promised, bending to kiss me.

It was not gentle; he ground his mouth down over mine and ravaged my lips, put his hands on me until I was writhing in his arms, pressing against him, whimpering with need. When he shoved me back, I yelled at him.

"You see that," he told me, his voice low and sultry. "I'm what you want, only me. Don't forget it."

He turned and walked away, and I had a tremendous urge to follow, but my desire died a second later when Crane poked his head out of the kitchen and said he was ready to drive to Reno. The need to nurture and protect drowned all else, but still, I needed my mate too. It would have to be a shorter trip than what I had originally planned. I didn't want to miss spending any time I could with Logan.

Chapter Ten

THE PRIEST had told Logan a week, but when Crane and I returned home, I found out Hamid Shamon, the priest of Chae Rophon, had purposely lied, part of the sepat to catch us off-balance. Yuri explained, haltingly, that my mate was gone, along with my maahes. The Shu had come for them both, and all I had to hold me was the kiss I had given my mate when I left for Reno.

"I'm so sorry you weren't here," Crane whispered.

"It's not your fault," I told him even though my heart hurt.

"We need to concentrate on getting ready for the sepat," Mikhail told me and Yuri and everyone else, including Danny, in the living room. "Jin, you need to tell us everything you know."

I explained about the challenges and asked Danny to please chime in if I missed anything. He seemed pleased at being included.

The first test, the one of blood, was for the sheseru. Yuri would be placed in a locked cage with between five to ten shifted panthers he had never met or even seen before, and with only the strength of his station, he would have to make them submit. They would have to roll over and present their stomachs, their midlines, and only then would Yuri be allowed out of the locked cell.

"Am I in panther form?" he asked.

"No, you're you."

His brows furrowed. "Jin, they'll tear me to shreds."

"Not if you're stronger than they are," Danny told him. "You have to show your panther blood in human form. It's hard."

"No shit," he growled, annoyed by the obvious.

"You'll do it," Mikhail told him. "I've seen you."

Yuri shook his head. "Don't you remember when Jin was attacked in the kitchen by those cats last summer? If I was so strong—"

"That was before Sobek," Mikhail reminded him, "and before Jin was discovered to be a nekhene cat. He's different, and so are you because you've had to adapt to him."

I watched them stare at each other.

"You'll do it."

Yuri nodded. Always Mikhail was the voice of reason, and because he made sense, Yuri heard him and absorbed his words.

The second test, or trial, was that of law. Mikhail would recite any law he was asked and would have to interpret it and defend it.

"And the last test?" Crane asked.

"It's heart," I told him, turning. "Logan will be tied down or shackled, or, I dunno, but he won't be able to move, and other khatyu led by someone will try and get through me, and you, and Domin, and one other."

"Me?" he asked.

"You're beset of a reah," I reminded him. "You stand with me. We just have to decide who, along with you and me and Domin, will be in the pit."

"Domin."

We all turned to look at Koren. All the color had drained from his face.

"I thought the only reason he was going was to watch over Logan until the sepat."

"No." Danny shook his head. "Domin is in the pit with Logan and Jin. If the semel is killed, then, in essence, his household dies, but not his house. The mate is put to death, and the maahes, because the new semel would want to choose both for himself."

"I—"

"At least that's the logic behind it," I told him. "You would only be able to claim whoever else was at the sepat—Crane, Yuri, and Mikhail."

"But if Logan is killed," Danny told Koren, "then Jin and Domin are killed immediately after."

Koren took a breath, and I saw his eyes bleed to the dark olive green that normally only his irises were. "You're telling me that, that man walked out of here, without a word to me, knowing that he might never, ever see me again?"

"Yeah," Yuri said flippantly. "But why the fuck would you care?"

"I care!" he roared, and we all saw, finally, some passion from him where Domin Thorne was concerned. "I care more than you—"

"He was not allowed to tell you he was leaving." Danny tried to soften it for Koren. "Just like Logan was not allowed to call Jin. They just have to leave."

"They both yelled at me from downstairs," Yuri snapped at Koren. "Logan called me." He took a breath. "And so did Domin."

"But you were in the house, I was out."

Clearly Yuri was too disgusted to say another word to Koren and stalked over to the fireplace. He was brooding and silent, and I wasn't sure why.

"Does Domin know?" I asked softly, stepping in closer to Logan's younger brother, "or does he still think that you're holding open auditions for the love of your life when it's obvious to all of us that the man's been right in front of your face this whole entire time?"

"I—he—"

"Oh," Crane said, nodding. "You broke up with Domin. I wasn't here for that. What the fuck for, man? How are you doing better, heir of the tribe of Mafdet, than the prince of the tribe of Mafdet?"

"Oh." Danny sounded so sad.

"What?" Koren snarled.

"No, just—if Domin Thorne were your mate, maahes or no, he would not have been allowed to attend the sepat. Mate to the heir trumps maahes."

And I remembered that. "Shit," I groaned, my eyes on Koren.

He was shaking just a little. "You're saying if I'd just claimed him, he would have had to stay."

"Yes," Danny assured him. "The mate of the heir is bound to your side just as the mate of the semel is bound to his."

"Fuck!" Koren yelled, the fury rolling over all of us as he charged across the room, striding to the window to stare out at the falling snow.

After a minute I joined him. It took many more for him to speak.

"I'm an idiot."

"Yes," I agreed.

"He's perfect for me, he's everything I'm not, dangerous and strong and loyal…. God, Jin, I really fucked this up this time."

I was silent, letting him work it out and talk to me.

"And I don't think I should try and fix it, but I want to, so bad."

He was ready to pull Domin back into the tornado with him, and no one wanted that for our maahes, not any of us.

"The shit of it is," he said as he turned to look at me, "even now, I still don't know what I want."

"Meaning?"

"Meaning that I want him, but I don't know if it's love. And it's not fair to be with him until something or someone I want more comes along."

No, it wasn't.

"God, this is such a mess."

I looked at his profile, which was so close to Logan's and yet so different. The intense regal bearing his brother had was not present in Koren. Logan was strength and power and heat, and just his presence in a room made the air spark and sizzle with vibrant electricity. Koren had none of that, and I was beginning to wonder what it was Domin saw in him at all. Maybe the maahes of my tribe had been infatuated, and now, finally, after easily four years of their back-and-forth bullshit, which had started way before I had even arrived, it was waning. And so maybe he had not punished Koren with a silent departure, but it had simply not crossed his mind to even gift the man with a good-bye. Last night in the hall, perhaps he had missed Koren's invitation because he had not been looking for it.

"Someone else will want him, Koren, and whoever that is, you have to step aside."

"I know."

"It's a mistake, I'm telling you. You're gonna grieve for the rest of your life when somebody else, some other panther, claims him."

"Or I won't," he said, turning to me, looking pained. "And that's the problem, right?"

Never in my life had I been the indecisive sort, and sometimes it had been bad. I always did something, and a lot of times those choices were selfish, but Koren was not even that guy, not even me, thorns and all. Koren was the waffling guy, and because we were so different, I was having trouble wrapping my brain around who he was.

"I figured you wanted him," I said, looking for the man I thought I knew. "Before the Feast of the Valley, before I was kidnapped… didn't you?"

"He gave me an ultimatum." Koren sighed deeply, raking his fingers through the same thick blond hair he shared with his brothers.

"He said, 'choose or leave me the fuck alone.' I wasn't ready to let him go, so... but being with him, I look at other people."

"But when you're with other people you think about him," I said, because I knew it was the truth.

"Yes."

"And then you want to go on the prowl the minute he's back in your bed."

"Yes," he groaned. "And I know that makes me seem like a total shit."

"It's honest, and until you find the one person that makes you forget everyone else, you have to keep looking. I understand it, but it's not fair to Domin, and he's too important to the rest of us. We're too invested in his happiness to watch you dick him around. It's time to cut him loose, Koren."

"I already did."

"Are you sure?"

"I am."

"It stopped going back and forth?"

"Yeah. We haven't reconciled since the last time." He sounded so sad. "He won't let me, and now, as you saw the other night, he doesn't really even see me. He's over me."

"Which is killing you."

"Fuck yeah." He exhaled, carding his fingers through his hair. "Because I want him back and I want to make him promises and.... But the minute I do, the minute he's there in my bed...."

He would want someone else. "Sure."

"You think I'm an idiot."

I did and didn't. "You can't make your heart want something just because you think you should. I get that."

"I thought when we were together when you were all away at the Feast of the Valley... fuck, Jin, I thought that was it. I thought I was done looking anywhere but at him."

But he wasn't, and Domin knew that, and his earlier ultimatum had changed to resignation. Koren would never be his, and at some point he had stopped caring. The problem was, without anyone to love him... what did Domin Thorne have for an anchor?

I studied Koren's face for a moment before I walked back to the others.

"I have a question," Artem said.

We all turned to look at him.

"Besides Crane," he said, his eyes on mine, "who else goes into the pit with you and Domin when you defend Logan?"

"I can pick one other."

He nodded. "Then pick me, Jin, please."

"No," I told him. "You have to stay here and act as sheseru while Yuri is away."

"If I die," Yuri said, his hand reaching for Artem's shoulder, "then you're the new sheseru of the tribe of Mafdet."

Artem took a shuddering breath.

"You have to remain to guard Koren."

His nod was decisive though not happy.

"Take me with you, Jin."

I turned to look at the man who had come from Sobek with us six months ago and was now truly part of our household. "I can't do that, Taj; you're a member of the Shu."

He shook his head. "I resigned my place," he told me. "I am now a member of the tribe of Mafdet."

"I'm sure Logan will consider you for the place of sheseru, then," Yuri told him. "You're much faster than—"

"But I'm not stronger than you," he told Yuri. "And I discussed it with Logan a while back, and he said that if I stayed, he would make me a manu and Ivan a baku."

"Ivan?" Markel was surprised.

"Me?" Ivan said, and I realized I had forgotten he was there with us. I always called him; I never left him out, as he lived in the house with us.

"Yes. Logan said that Markel and Artem would also be granted those positions when he returned from the sepat."

I looked around the room at all four men: Markel, Ivan, Taj, and Artem. They were stunned—all but Taj, who had been the only one privy to the plan—and pleased, I could tell. Ivan and Markel were especially touched, as they had been Domin's sylvan and sheseru when he was semel of the tribe of Menhit.

"Logan trusts you all implicitly," Taj continued, "and the tribe is growing so fast that Logan needs his household full of those he deems most worthy." He turned to Artem. "You're the only one not living in the house, Artem, and you're to move in at once."

He swallowed hard, overwhelmed, I could tell. As they all closed in around each other, talking, I walked to the window and looked out at the snow.

"My reah."

The room went silent behind me, but I didn't turn to Mikhail's call.

"I'm happy for you all," I told him, facing the gray January sky. "But before anything else, we have to think about the sepat. Because no matter what you all think, without Logan Church, the tribe will suffer. Without him, I won't be here; without me, Yuri won't be himself, and so on, and so on.... The priority must be making sure that Logan comes home safe."

"Of course," Mikhail agreed.

"Yes, Jin," Yuri agreed.

I felt a hand on my shoulder, and when I turned, Crane was there.

"I need you to help me get strong so I can go with you."

The fact that he wanted to go, even though I knew he had to be terrified, spoke volumes about his strength. "Okay."

"First thing tomorrow, let's go talk to Ray and see about resigning our positions."

"You don't have to do that, Crane, just me."

"No, we both do. I just wanna be here, Jin, at the house, on the land. Yuri said he would teach me his business, he said I could go to work for him, with him. I think that would be best."

It was strange to think about everyone outside of their roles in the tribe, that they had lives that didn't include Logan or me.

Yuri owned and operated a security business where he installed high-tech alarm systems for commercial as well as residential clients. Mikhail had a demolition company that knocked stuff down—buildings, bridges—and then hauled the debris away and disposed of it. Markel was an artist, Ivan taught fifth grade, and Domin owned many very lucrative pawn shops, two in Reno and three in Las Vegas. Koren owned a real estate company in Lake Tahoe, and Delphine worked for her brother, for Logan, at the glassworks he owned. She was the on-site manager. Everyone worked, and I was worried about not doing my share even though Logan said my concern should have been him and the tribe and nothing else.

"You already have Taj here patrolling, being the guardian of the house and the grounds. I want to do my part, but I have no idea when and if I'll ever feel like leaving."

Which was fine with me, even though I knew it was selfish. If my best friend was always where I could see him, I would never have to worry ever again. But how fair was that to him?

"Come on, come sit down and talk to me."

I followed, as always, without question.

IT WAS hard talking to Ray the next day, with Crane. He was a good man and didn't understand why we were leaving him. I finally lied and told him that Logan's business needed us both, and that, finally, made sense to him. He himself ran a family business, and that loyalty clicked for him. I said I would give him two weeks to hire and train a new manager, and I felt bad when he told me it wasn't necessary. Basically, people had been doing my job for months; he just needed to pick one of them to take over permanently. He extracted a promise from Crane and me that if either of us ever wanted back in the restaurant business, we were to call him at once. We both hugged him really tight before we left.

During the following month, Yuri practiced by making himself the quarry of hunts. Artem and his men chased him down, all of them in panther form, and once they reached him, pumped up on adrenaline and bloodlust, he practiced calming them and forcing them to shift back into men. It was grueling and hard, and Yuri returned night after night bruised and bloody from his exertions. One night I saw an old face I had been missing for a while, Andrian Basargin, and while we caught up—he had gone away to grad school in Boston—I finally realized there had to be a reason I was seeing him.

"Where's Yuri?"

"He's hurt, my reah, and spending the night in a cave with Taj to watch over him, but he begs you to not come, let him be, and he will join you for breakfast in the morning. This is part of it. He has to learn to dominate others not through fear or brute force, but only by power. Please understand and grant him his time."

I wanted to go, every impulse told me to go, but the look on Andrian's face stifled my instinct. He was the first man I had ever met from Logan's tribe, and the ease he had first shown me, the kindness, had never dissipated.

"Alright?"

I nodded.

"Good." He smiled. "I'm returning to them with food and water. I'll tell them that you expect both of them in the house in the morning."

"And you," I told him. "I wanna see you too."

"I would be honored, my reah."

As promised, they were all there in the morning for breakfast, and when I smacked Yuri on the back of his head, he rolled his eyes at me.

"Never again," I snarled.

"Jin—"

"Who's going to protect me? Who should do that?"

And I realized my safety had never crossed his mind. It shouldn't have, not really—I was scary now; no one in their right mind wanted to mess with a nekhene cat—not after my display in Sobek—and Artem was there, and the others—but still… Yuri was my sheseru.

"No, my reah, I forgot my place."

"Don't do it again," I cautioned, my voice hard.

To have me say it, speak my need for him, I saw how his eyes filled, watched the muscles in his square jaw clench; it was what he needed, had to hear. That I counted on him, that I slept better knowing he was in the house—the confession gave him strength and filled him with his own self-worth. Mikhail bumped my shoulder on the way out, and I saw his smile. They all understood what I had done, and it was nice.

Logan's poor parents came home to a world gone mad, and after the whole house sat down with them and explained, Eva was distressed and Peter was very proud of Logan for being chosen and terrified for me.

"He really could kill you, Jin." He caught his breath.

"No," I told him, utterly positive, "he won't."

Even then, even after everything, Peter Church could still not quite wrap his brain around the fact that two men could love as hard and as *'til death do us part* as a man and a woman. But his wife could and did.

"You'll bring us home a semel-aten," she said as she patted my hand. "God, will I like living in Sobek?"

I squinted at her.

"Well, we'll cross that bridge when we come to it, won't we," she sucked in a breath. "Now come on, tell me about Russ before I call and yell."

"No one will ever speak to Russ again!" her husband ordered, still so angry for Russ not wanting to be a panther, so hurt, the feeling of betrayal making his temper flare momentarily.

"Logan said," Koren chimed in gently, "that any of us may speak to him by e-mail or phone or whatever else, webcam, you name it, but we are all forbidden from visiting him. If he wants to see us, he comes here."

"Yes," Peter agreed, taking a deep breath, calming, walking over to me and putting his hands on my shoulders. "Thank you for going, Jin, and protecting my son."

It had been a trip I didn't have to make, but I accepted the thanks from a man who felt like his sons were all alien creatures to him. I patted his hand, and he squeezed mine gently. My arrival had changed everything, altered Logan's path as well as Koren's, because if the semel-re was gay, then his brother could be as well. And even though I had nothing to do with Russ's choices, I was still the catalyst for everything else. That Peter could still like me at all was a testament to the tolerance in the man. He didn't understand Logan and me, what Koren and Domin had begun and ended, but he loved us all regardless. It was more grace than a lot of people were granted in their families.

Because he knew Logan needed help, Peter helped Yuri master his beast and offered Mikhail the resources of his personal library to help him study. Mikhail himself was all for drowning himself in the old texts, committing chunks to memory, but both Danny and Peter cautioned against that. It was better, they said, and I agreed, to have a working understanding of the text as a whole, to be able to interpret it and explain it back to someone else, teach it to another. So they took turns sitting with Mikhail, quizzing him during the day, reading to him at night, and even listening to him during meals, always just talking about one law or another. The three men had endless conversations, and Danny, whom my father had been training as he had me, to be a sylvan, showed him citations, Peter showed him illustrations that would spark his memory, and both men corrected Logan's sylvan gently and patiently.

We were two weeks from leaving for the sepat when I came downstairs because I couldn't sleep. It was getting harder and harder for me, Logan's absence weighing heavily on me. I stopped before walking into the great room, though, because I saw them in front of the fire. Mikhail had obviously dozed off, and I watched Danny, his hands fluttering close but not touching, leaning close to the man's lips, inhaling his scent, finally, after weeks of just looking, reaching out to lift a strand of dark mahogany hair from his eyes.

"That's quite the crush you're nursing," I said as I stepped around the corner, making my presence known.

"Oh, I—I just—"

"It's okay." I smiled. "I get it, Mikhail's a good man."

"He's beautiful," Danny breathed, his bottom lip quivering. "Have you looked into his eyes? There's so dark and deep and blue and—"

"I've looked at him," I assured him.

"He's amazing, Jin."

"Agreed, but what do you want from him?"

His eyes hit mine. "Everything."

It was not my place to tell him what Mikhail was or was not. I felt that Mikhail was straight, like Crane was, and Taj, and Artem, but how did I know? The one man I could speak for implicitly was my best friend. For him, for Crane Adams, only a woman would ever be his mate. For the others… I would wait and see.

"Jin?"

"You should talk to him when this is all over," I soothed Danny, "but not now."

"No." He nodded. "He would not appreciate me thinking about anything but Logan."

"No, he wouldn't."

He reached a hand toward me. "May I?"

I gave him a slight smile, and he put his hand on my shoulder.

"I've always wanted to touch you."

It was part and parcel of the whole reah gig.

"Your father must have loved you so much, Jin."

Strange start to a conversation. "What makes you say that?"

"Because he hates you so much now." He took a shaky breath. "I mean, I never told him I was gay. I was too scared of what he would do to me, and that was before what he let happen to Crane."

And I had known, of course I had, that my father could have saved Crane but had not.

I took a breath, squeezed his hand tight on my bicep, and smiled at him. "My father is not important. Tell me where my mother is."

"She stayed with Kei in Chicago. Both of them were accepted into the tribe of Mnevis."

I nodded.

"Her and Kei—they just don't understand who you are or what you are, Jin. Did Logan tell you that he met them?"

I shook my head. "No."

"I figured."

"What happened?"

He shrugged. "Kei and your mother, Ayumi, they were on their knees, and Logan asked them if they wanted to see you."

I waited for what I already knew.

"Kei said you were dead to them, and your mother told Logan to cleanse the wickedness from his house."

I closed my eyes. There was a time when it would have hurt, but I was far too insulated by Logan's love for it to touch me anymore. "And what did the semel-netjer do?"

He cleared his throat. "He said how sorry he was for both of them, and the way he looked at them…. Jin, it was like they were both dying there in front of him. When he walked away without a word, like they were nothing, everyone was stunned, you know? I mean, to a panther, to have a semel look at you like that, not even acknowledge you or dismiss you… God. It was so horrible, and he did it, just removed his regard, you know? And he's the only one, the only semel-netjer in the world, but I think it's like Yuri said."

"What did Yuri say?"

"He said that they cannot comprehend that you are a reah and a nekhene, and because they don't really see you, Logan can't fathom their existence at all."

I sighed deeply. "Sounds like Yuri."

"I was just floored. I mean they could have—they could live here with you and Logan, they are both related to the only nekhene cat in a thousand years."

"But all they see is a gay man," I told him. "And that's fine, because gay is a word that can be used to define me. It's not all I am, but it is a facet of the whole."

"They don't understand," he said, shivering.

"And that's okay," I sighed, patting his hand before I stepped away from him. "Because I have a family of my own that accepts and loves me."

"It still has to hurt, Jin—be honest."

"I am," I assured him. "They left me for dead, and the only one who came for me was Crane."

"Crane?"

"Yeah. He replaced them all—mother, brother, father, there's only him now."

"Your father said that he was glad your grandmother didn't live to see the abomination you grew into."

I chuckled. "Well, it would be funny for him to know that my grandmother, his mother, is the one that told me it was okay that the first person I ever had a crush on was one of the khatyu in the tribe."

"She knew you had a crush on a guy?"

"Yes, she did, because I told her."

"What did she say?"

"She said what she always said—that my love was a gift, and whoever was lucky enough to get it should count themselves blessed."

"She sounds like she was wonderful."

"She was."

He cleared his throat. "Can I ask what happened to the guy you had your first crush on? I might know—"

"He died a long time ago."

"How?"

"I mean, to me." I smiled gently. "He was one of the men who beat me when I turned into a reah for the first time in front of others."

"Oh God, Jin, to have someone you—"

"My parents are the bigger tragedy," I assured him. "My brother.... But you're getting upset over ancient history."

"You're lying if you say it doesn't bother you."

My eyes flicked to his, and he shivered.

"I'm sorry, my reah, I forgot my place for—"

"It's fine; you can believe what you want. But what's true is that I'm the reah of my tribe and I don't have time to live in the past. I have people to take care of, a best friend to help heal, and a mate to defend. I have people who love me now; I don't have time to worry about people who wish I was dead."

He studied me, looking for a lie on me. But he wouldn't find one. I had closed the door on my past, finally, when my father had first visited me after Logan and I were mated. The door had been sealed in Sobek after both my father and Crane's had spoken to the priest. I wished that after I knew the hatred that lived in both men's hearts, Crane had not fallen into their hands. I would give anything to have kept him safe.

"Oh God, Jin."

If I had only been able to safeguard him... what I wouldn't have given to protect my friend.

"Jin!"

My head snapped up, and I turned toward the kitchen as Yuri emerged.

"Yes?"

"Your power," he said, scowling, squinting before he tipped his head behind me.

Turning, I found Danny in his panther form, wrestling with his clothes, trying to get free.

"Oh shit," I groaned, going to my knees, reaching for him.

He hissed at me, and I flicked him on the nose.

"Jin, be careful," Yuri growled, crossing the room fast even as Danny went limp under my hands, having rolled over on his back, paws in the air in complete surrender.

"Of what, the deadly housecat here?" I scoffed, rolling my eyes at my sheseru.

"All cats are dangerous," he told me, dropping down to one knee, rubbing Danny's chin, hard, then his cheeks, and finally his ears. "Even sweet little kittens like this."

I heard Danny's loud purring, watched him run his chin over Yuri's hand and finally curl his body around the man.

I squinted at Yuri.

"What?"

"He's all cat right now and can't understand a word, so I'm gonna ask you, what's with all the attention?"

"He's cute." Yuri gave me a lopsided grin.

"Is he?"

"Very."

"So, uhm," I said, chuckling. "What are your intentions here?"

He ended by rubbing Danny's ass, which of course made him lift it, wanting more. He was a panther—I had forced his shift out of my frustration, which had translated to sexual heat, and now Yuri had spent long minutes petting him, which had overstimulated him. My sheseru was also bigger and stronger, and Danny was showing him the depth of his submission.

Yuri stood up, and Danny let out a whine of protest that came out as a very resentful meow. My sheseru was right, he was very cute.

"He doesn't want me," Yuri told me, his eyes on mine. "He wants Mikhail. I get that, he's handsome, I'm not—it makes sense."

"Yuri, you—"

"Stop." He smiled at me. "You are my reah, you see me as no one else does. I know my value to you and to my semel. I have a good family, great friends, I lack for nothing. I don't need you to extol my virtues; I live well in my skin."

"Yes, but—"

"I've had women in my bed; I've had men as well. Someday I'll find my mate, and he or she will love me as I am. Until then I am content. Someone should tell Danny here, though, that as much as Mikhail doesn't give a shit that his semel is gay, or his maahes, he himself is as straight as Crane is. Mikhail's lust runs only to women. Danny's gonna get his heart diced up if he's not careful."

"I think it's like you said, Mikhail's not caring what people do in their own bedrooms is giving Danny the wrong impression."

"Agreed."

I rose and, as always, even on my feet, had to tip my head back to meet Yuri's eyes. "I think if you let him know what—"

"I have no illusions about what Danny thinks of me," he said, smirking. "You shouldn't either."

I didn't want him to think of himself as lacking, because he wasn't, in any way.

At six five, the man was massive. He didn't have the rippling muscular build that Logan did; his body was not cut and chiseled. He was built, instead, like a tank, like a mountain. Yuri's biceps were as big as some men's thighs, so that what you noticed first was the space the man took up, how he seemed to fill any room he was in. Second, you saw his face. He had deep-set eyes, dark cobalt, a long straight nose, and dark, full lips. I had always seen the beauty in the man, but from seeing the reaction of others, I understood I was in the minority. I saw Yuri clearly, but most people saw only his size and strength.

"You—"

"Besides," he said, giving me a sly grin, "I don't want a boy. I want a man."

And the way he said it made me squint at him. "Do you have someone in mind?"

"I might."

He might? "Who?" I asked, being a total girl at that moment and not giving a damn.

His eyes narrowed, and I knew I was going to have to dig, but we were interrupted.

"What happened?"

We both turned to Crane as he came walking into the room.

"I fucked with Danny," I said, grimacing.

His smile was endearing because he was looking at me like he always did, like I was a total idiot. "Brilliant."

"Yeah, well," I said with a shrug. "It was an accident."

"Come here."

Mikhail, who slept like the dead, finally woke up as I was crossing to Crane. I asked him to herd Danny up to his room, as Yuri was already striding across the room toward the front door.

"Where are you going?"

"I've got another hunt tonight," he told me. "Christophe very kindly sent up six of his panthers who have never met me to help."

"And told them to do what?" I was concerned.

"Kill me, if they could," he told me from the door.

"Yuri—"

"Jin." He was exasperated, and some of it was at me, but some was because of what he had almost confessed, and all of it together was making him snarly. "I need to practice, and I can't do it with any of the panthers in our own tribe because Logan makes sure that everyone comes to our gatherings, so no one hasn't fuckin' seen me."

I knew that. The last gathering we had, over the long Memorial Day holiday, had seen more than four hundred people coming and going at different times. It was like a fair. There were booths for food and drinks—all free, of course—and dancing, and, of course, hunting. Yuri had led most of the hunts himself, and everyone knew the sheseru and sylvan of the tribe of Mafdet as they strolled the grounds. Normally, they traveled together, Yuri loud, the extrovert, and Mikhail reserved at his side, the introvert. Taj was there, too, always with a woman on each arm. I had watched it all from my balcony, content to breathe in the smells, see everyone enjoying themselves, instead of trying to walk the grounds of my home when it was open to the entire tribe.

At the gathering before that, back in August, I had tried to take part, but I had been stopped every five feet, sometimes ten, by people who wanted to talk to me and touch me. I had enjoyed seeing my tribe, wanted to know them all, see them all, but it had gotten to a point, after the discovery that I was a nekhene cat, that it was too much. Logan didn't like me being constantly pawed, Mikhail didn't like the grabbing at me, and then, on the final day of the gathering, on that Monday night, I got stuck in the middle of people pushing and shoving to reach me, and when my hair got yanked and my clothes torn, I lost my footing for just a minute and was pulled to the ground. Yuri's yell had been frightening. Everyone froze, and he lifted me free, set me on my feet, and took my face in his hands to look at me. Even with me assuring him that I was fine, I was thrown over his back in the fireman carry and taken to the house. Logan had appeared when I got out of the shower.

"No more."

I was towel-drying my hair, having changed into sweats and a T-shirt and warm wool socks Delphine had made me. They were bright fuchsia and neon lime green. "So I don't get to see my tribe anymore? I don't get to attend gatherings?"

"People can come to the house, stand in line if they want to see you, and offer their regards. We'll make it so all the gatherings from now on are three days long, start them all on a Friday, but, Jin—I won't have people so frantic to put their hands on you, so excited to see you, that they end up hurting you. I won't."

I went to my armoire and opened the door, took a brush from the shelf, and walked it to Logan. Turning, I presented him with my long, thick black hair.

"Why're you being nice to me?"

I turned to look at him over my shoulder. "Because I want you to change your mind. One bad encounter does not—"

"It does," he said, cutting me off, hand in my hair as he gently tugged with the paddle brush. "I won't have you hurt, Jin, because your tribe loves you so much that they can't stand to not touch you."

"A reah needs to be accessible."

"A reah stands at the side of their mate and doesn't question him."

I scoffed and heard the answering groan.

"How did I know that wasn't gonna fly?"

Standing there, letting him brush my hair, I closed my eyes, reveling in the ministrations of my mate. When he pushed my hair aside and I felt his lips press down onto my shoulder, I shivered hard.

"I can't have you hurt, Jin, I've failed you once already. I—"

"You've never failed me," I told him, turning in his arms to look up into his golden eyes. "I'm a powerful werepanther, Logan. I don't need anyone to protect me; I just need you to love me."

"And I do, you know that," he said, putting his hands on my hips, pulling me close, his thigh pressed to my groin, leaning forward until our foreheads touched. "But I know you won't use any of your considerable power to extricate yourself from members of your tribe. So because you don't want to hurt them, they're going to end up hurting you. Do you get the problem?"

"Yes." I smiled, enjoying the closeness, his hands digging into my hips, the sound of his breathing getting shallow, and the way he pushed against me with the now hardened bulge in his vintage jeans. "I think the semel-netjer needs to claim what's his."

"I'm not some mindless brute that just wants to fuck his mate when—"

"If you take me, you'll know I'm fine."

"I—" He took a breath, and I saw his pupils dilate with need. "Jin."

I loved him flustered, torn between duty and desire; he was so serious most of the time that distracting him was all kinds of fun. And of course I would never try if what he was supposed to be doing was important—I was the mate of a tribe leader, after all—but to keep him from the last gasp of a gathering was really not that big of a sin.

My pheromones filled the room. "Fuck me."

"Jin," he growled, and I smiled before I lifted my head, and he claimed my lips in a rough, mauling kiss.

He was all hands, my sweats and underwear stripped away, the T-shirt yanked off over my head. Only the socks remained as he hurled me down on our bed, face-first onto the comforter. I lifted to my hands and knees, and when he touched my ass, spread my cheeks, I moaned out his name.

"My reah," he rasped before his tongue slid over my puckered hole.

"Logan!"

"Again?" he teased.

I had made a mistake. I thought I was seducing him when it was really the other way around. "You let me think I was corrupting you," I managed to get out.

"Yes."

My whimper was embarrassing, would have been if this were anyone but my mate. As it was, I was myself, honest with what I needed, wanted, and held nothing back.

"I love the way you taste," he told me and plunged his tongue inside me deeper, licking and sucking, swirling, thrusting, the long languid stroking slowly driving me right out of my mind. When he added his fingers, pressing, pushing, grazing over my gland, scissoring inside over and over, relentlessly, words were lost to me. Only grunts and growls and whimpers and whines escaped me as my muscles clung to the invading flesh. No one but my mate had ever taken such time and care to open me up; no one but Logan had ever wanted to.

It went on and on, and I knew without even giving voice to the question that Logan Church loved exercising his power over me, loved watching me come apart.

"Logan," I gasped, writhing under him, panting, begging. He fisted my leaking shaft, tugging and pulling, and I warned him that I was close, so close, and needed him inside me.

My muscles were relaxed and loose, I was dripping precome, and my entrance was slicked with saliva, but still, I felt the chilled coating of lube over my skin before he thrust into me, burying himself in my ass in one easy forward slide.

He felt so good, and my channel clenched around him, the suction strong and tight.

"Oh fuck," he groaned, easing back only to plunge in harder, deeper, the pressure of his hands on my hips sure to leave bruises.

"Don't stop," I pleaded, nearly shouting. "Just keep—Logan!"

He had lifted up, changed his angle, and driven down into me. His long, thick shaft slid over my gland, and I came without either of us touching my spurting dick at all.

"Jin," he gasped before he filled my ass, the muscles rippling around the length of him as he pushed in and out of me faster, riding the trembling release, my own aftershocks flushing my skin hot and cold at the same time.

He gave himself completely over to me every single time. When our flesh was merged, he belonged to me body and soul, and there was no denying it and no hiding it. He was mine.

"I'm never moving," he said as he pressed his chest to the long length of my back, licking the sweat from my skin before kissing down my spine.

"Okay," I murmured, not caring even as he eased from my body so tenderly, so gently.

"Did I hurt you?"

"You never hurt me," I told him, collapsing down onto the bed, rolling over on my back to look up at him.

The smile he was gifting me with made his gold eyes molten with heat. "Should I lick you again to make sure?"

And amazing as it was, as sated as I was, the thought of his wonderful, talented tongue back in my ass made my cock throb and my ass twitch all over again….

I wanted him; the nekhene ached for him… where was he?

My desire finally permeated my thoughts, dragging me back from the past to the here and now.

The yelling was a surprise.

"Jin!"

I blinked hard, the last of my daydream dissipating from my thoughts. I forgot I had been thinking about Logan, about being loved by Logan. I had started off in another place and wound up back at my mate. Always my mate.

"Jin!"

My head snapped up, and Mikhail was there in front of me, angry, breathing hard, trembling with fisted hands.

"Stop!"

I squinted at him and heard gasps in the room.

He sank to his knees in front of me, and I watched him puddle to the floor.

"Fuck," Yuri groaned, and I looked for him.

I was surprised that the great room was filled with panthers. Delphine had shifted, as had Markel, Ivan, Koren—which surprised me—and Taj, which shocked me even more.

"What happened?" I asked Mikhail as he knelt at my feet, hands on his thighs, looking like he was doing yoga as he took deep in-and-out breaths.

"Your fuckin' pheromones happened," he growled as Danny padded over to him, rubbing his chin over the man's shoulder, licking behind his ear. He was cute, the size of an ocelot, but gold, maybe more of a small cougar.

"Crane," I gasped, terrified, as I whirled around to look for him. "Where—oh."

My best friend had not shifted to his panther form, but what was amazing was his enormous grin as he lay there on the floor, spread-eagle.

"Are you all right?"

"Fuck yeah," he sighed, and I realized from the look on his face that I was looking at a very satisfied Crane Adams.

"You came in your jeans." I scowled.

"I can't come," he told me as he rolled his head to the side to look up at me. "I don't have balls full of jizz anymore, idiot."

I was horrified at my stupidity, but his smile blindsided me, and then I got it. "You were hard and you had an orgasm."

He took the baseball cap off his head and scrubbed his still-shaved head—he had decided to keep it military buzz short for the foreseeable future—and then let out a deep breath up from his soul.

"Yes orgasm?"

His eyes were back on mine. "Fuck yeah."

The recovery time for a human man was long; apparently the recovery for a werepanther took six weeks. And not that he was cured, not that physical and emotional scars could be so quickly dealt with, but to know he could still have sex—that would go a long way to helping him heal.

"And?"

His gaze stayed fastened on me.

"How do you feel?"

"I feel better than I have in I don't know how long," he said, and his eyes were soft.

He looked like him. The fear wasn't there anymore, the broken shadow in his face was gone, and the smile was all wicked and wild. I made a sound in the back of my throat.

"I missed you too." He waggled his eyebrows.

Only Crane came back from the horror that had been visited on him to be the man now sprawled out in front of me. Only him. He was so strong inside and out, and—

"Oh shit," Mikhail said slowly in disbelief.

"Oh shit, what?" Crane yawned, sitting up and then rolling to his feet.

"Crane."

He looked at my sylvan, waiting.

"You didn't shift."

His squint was fast. "Why would I shift?"

"Jin's power."

"And?" He was confused.

"Crane," Mikhail said, "Jin's power is nothing to scoff at."

"Yeah, but it's still just Jin," he said as he gestured at me. "I wouldn't have even had the, uhm—" He coughed and smiled at the same time. "—reaction to his scent if my body wasn't so damn weak."

"Danny shifted earlier with just a hint of Jin's power. *Taj* shifted, so did Markel and Delphine and Ivan. Only you and me and Yuri are still in human form. Even Koren shifted."

We all looked over at Koren, who was purring loudly as Danny rubbed his muzzle up under the larger panther's chin.

"Shit," Yuri grumbled, walking to the front door and throwing it open as Koren charged out of it, Danny seconds behind him. They flew out into the night together.

"I'm sor—"

"Oh for crissakes, Jin," he groused, "I don't give a fuck who Danny fucks—I care more about Koren."

Koren?

"Wait. That didn't come out right. I—"

"What am I missing?" Crane asked.

"Crane didn't shift." Mikhail's voice rose on purpose to try to get us all to focus.

And we all turned to look at Crane at the same time.

"What?"

"Even in your weakened state," Mikhail began, studying him for perhaps really the very first time, "you didn't shift. How?"

Crane shrugged. "I dunno. I've had a lifetime of feeling Jin's power run over me. Given, it's a helluva lot heavier now than it used to be, I can actually feel it sort of push its way inside, but it's still Jin, so I take a breath and let it do whatever it wants."

"You're talking about Jin's power like it's a living, breathing thing."

"Which it's not, and I get that, but it's still Jin, right? I mean, you guys like him a real lot, but I love him and so does Logan, and I think that's why the power doesn't bother us. Even the nekhene form likes me, I've felt it."

"You've felt my power change to nekhene?" I asked.

"Sure. It's like your reah power is gentle, soothing, makes me feel good. The nekhene power, it's like prickly heat on the back of your neck. It comes at me, and I think about you and how I feel about you, and then it calms and feels like reah."

I was staring at him.

"What?"

"I fight it. I fight the power welling up; I fight feeling out of control… I fight every part of it."

"Yeah, don't do that." He yawned before he smiled at me.

"Don't do that? This is your sage advice?"

"Yeah." He burped and blew it out the side of his mouth. "Sorry, the burritos we had for lunch are kinda comin' back on me."

The man was unbelievable. Effortlessly he dealt with my new form, my changed energy, because he simply accepted everything about me. Without the fight, there was nothing for the nekhene to rebel against, and so my power, when it encountered Crane, simply gave up and played nice. What the hell?

"So if everyone just stopped fighting, they wouldn't shift." I turned to look at Mikhail.

"It's not that simple," he assured me. "Crane has how many years' head start knowing you, knowing your power? The rest of us don't have that luxury, and we're cats, our first instinct is not to submit, not to just allow your power to render us helpless."

"Is that how you feel when you fight my pheromones?"

"Yes."

"I'm sorry."

"It's not your fault, but you do need to learn to control it. Maybe in the next two weeks before we fly out of here, you should let Crane tell you how to not fight."

"Maybe," I said, turning to look at my best friend.

"So…." Crane smirked, gesturing to all the other panthers in the room. "How much apologizing do you gotta do now?"

Shit.

Chapter Eleven

THE FLIGHT from Reno, Nevada, to Buyant Ukhaa, the airport in Ulan Bator (or Ulaanbaatar, I wasn't really sure which was the correct spelling; the tour book I had said one thing and my plane ticket another), took twenty-five hours and twenty minutes. We flew from Reno to Los Angeles and then flew United from there to Beijing and Air China to Mongolia.

The flights were comfortable, and I was glad Peter had insisted on first class. He said savings were for rainy days and that Logan would appreciate riding in luxury on the way home after the sepat. I appreciated Peter's unshakeable faith that his son would be home. When I had been almost to the door, my mate's father had surprised me by grabbing me tight and pulling me close for a hug. After long moments, he had let me go, stepping back to look down into my face.

"Bring my son home to me, Jin," he had said hoarsely.

I had promised him, as well as Eva and Delphine and Koren, that I would bring Logan back, along with Domin. They wanted their maahes back too.

Now, as I stood in an international airport of a very modern-looking city—I had stared at it from the air as we landed—the enormity of the task was starting to bear down on me. I was a world away from my life, what I knew, and my power base. The task seemed terrifying.

"Deep breath," Crane soothed, hand on my shoulder as we stood in the line after getting off the plane to go through Immigration. "Where's your passport?"

I dug into my messenger bag and came up with it for him.

"And the entry and exit visa?"

"It's in there."

"Where's the customs declaration form?"

"They don't need that to let us in the country. We're just supposed to keep that 'til we leave."

"How long is the visa for?"

"Two weeks."

"Okay." He yawned, and because he was calm, I was.

I realized for the millionth time in my life that I could look at Crane and gauge how I should feel. I trembled quickly, trying to think of what I would have done without him.

"We're up," he said, bumping me with his shoulder as we walked forward.

Once we had our passports stamped and were in the actual airport proper, we had to claim our luggage and then stand in line again, the noncitizen line, to have our luggage clear customs. We had only brought clothes, so there were no duties or taxes to pay, but the whole experience was nerve-racking for me. Just the idea that I could be kept out of the country, kept away from Logan, scared the hell out of me. It was illogical, but I was terrified.

"See, we're fine," Crane announced, and just him stating the obvious made me feel better.

The airport was busy, the zoo they all were, and because it looked like almost every other one I had been in, my sense of unease dissipated.

There were supposed to be people there to meet us; the maahes of the tribe of Khertet, Chuluun Borjigin, was the man we were looking for.

"Jesus, it's even cold in here," Yuri groused from behind me, looking like he was ready to go dog sledding instead of just leaving the airport.

We were all swaddled up in parkas, beanies, gloves, boots, long underwear, and scarves.

"It's gonna be worse outside," Andrian assured him.

"Jin."

I turned to look at Yuri, and he tipped his head for me. Looking to where he had gestured, I saw the three men cutting through the crowd toward us. Even from where they were, the scent of cat clung to them. The power rolling off of them was daunting.

They stopped five feet from us, and the looks we were getting were less than kind. "Snide" was the word I would have chosen.

"Sain bainuu," the first man said.

I had no idea I was supposed to have learned Mongolian. Holy crap.

No one said a word until there was a faint clearing of a throat. Turning, I looked at Danny. He smiled faintly.

Was he kidding?

"May I?" He gestured to where I was. "My semel asked me to learn as much as I could of the language."

Logan had asked Danny to study up. The man thought of everything. "Sure."

Moving up beside me, he then looked at the man who had spoken. "Sain ta sain bainuu?"

The man was surprised that he was being responded to. "Sain banaa," he said in return. "Ta yamar ulsaas irsen be?"

"Bi Amerikiin Negdsen ulsaas irsen," Danny replied. "Ta angular yairdaguu?"

"Yes," the man replied. "You did well."

"Thank you so much," Danny said as he smiled. "Tand ikh bayarlaa."

The man who had been addressing Danny grunted. "So which one is the mate?" He sounded like he was bored out of his mind.

I stepped forward. "I'm the mate."

"Oh," he grunted. "The reah."

Normally I got a little better reception than that.

"Not a big deal to you guys, huh?" Crane smirked. "See reahs every day, do you?"

"We have our own."

This was news.

"Oh yeah?" Crane chuckled. "Who's that?"

"Amirah Fehr."

"Amirah." I squinted at him. "We were told that Amirah Fehr had been killed by her semel."

"No," he told me, and I heard it finally, a trace of an accent as he spoke. "She asked for sanctuary with my semel and was granted it."

"Does the priest know?" Taj asked.

"He knows now."

There was a silence.

"Well, even if you have a reah in your tribe, this is our reah," Crane told him, "and you need to show him the proper respect."

"Or?"

"Or…." I parted my lips, let my power out, let it uncoil and hunt. "You can feel the difference between reah and nekhene."

"I—"

"Jin," Crane cautioned.

But we had been working on things, he and I, and my control was better, could be directed.

"Uuchlaarai!" The stranger wobbled and went to his knees, the other two following fast.

His head snapped back, and he met my eyes.

"I am the mate of the semel-netjer," I told him, my eyes narrowing. "Don't mistake me for anything less."

"No, my reah," he said quickly.

I was proud that unless I wanted it to be, my power was no longer sexual at all. Now it was pure, breathing strength, discipline, and will. Crane being with me had changed everything.

"Stand."

He rose, and I tipped my head back to meet his gaze as he stepped closer, offering his hand now in greeting. It was a pissing contest, and I had won. American, Mongolian, it didn't matter, we were all cats, and it only mattered who was alpha. Normally it was Logan, but here it was me.

"I'm the maahes of the tribe of Khertet, Chuluun."

"Borjigin, right?" I asked, taking his hand.

He smiled suddenly. "That is the clan name of Genghis Khan, Borjigin; it's not a real last name, just something to use. We don't have surnames like you do, as they were illegal here for a very long time when the communists came to power."

"Quick history lesson there," Crane muttered under his breath.

"Stop," I told him and then smiled at the man I had just met. "So just Chuluun, then?"

"Yes."

"Then just Jin." I took a breath.

I felt his hand clutch mine, and that fast, Yuri was beside me.

"Ataide," he snarled.

The word that had come out of my sheseru was one I had never heard before, and since I doubted he had been studying Mongolian along with Danny, I had no idea what I was hearing. But Chuluun must have, because he released his grip. He didn't move away, though, and that was not making Yuri happy. I could feel his anger rising.

"What was that?" I asked.

But he wasn't looking at me, all his attention instead riveted on Chuluun.

"Ne trogai," my sheseru growled.

"Oospakoisya," Chuluun snapped back, but I watched the maahes take a step away from me, respecting Yuri's wishes.

I took a guess at the language. "Russian, right?"

"Yes," Mikhail told me, moving close before addressing Chuluun. "I understand that it's a whole day's ride, like, nine hours to Tsetserleg in Arkhangai aimag from here."

"That's a close approximation."

"And how far from Tsetserleg is Vanchigdash, where your tribe lives?"

"Not far. We will pass the nature preserve, and then we'll be there. Our home is in the side of a mountain, and there is a small valley that sustains us during the winter."

"So you don't live in the traditional ger? You—"

"The home of Orso Bataar, semel of the tribe of Khertet, was carved out of stone. It has a hot spring that runs underneath it, but the home itself is without electricity or running water," he said, and his voice, the way he was standing suddenly, all of it suggested irritation.

Yuri said something else in Russian, and I wondered why until I saw the amazing transformation his words wrought on Chuluun. The man was visibly stunned.

"That's really smart," Mikhail said under his breath.

"What?"

"Yuri gave him commands in Russian so he'd know they have a common language between them—his accent is Russian, after all."

"I thought that was a Mongolian accent."

"No." Mikhail gave me a hint of a smile.

"You did?" Chuluun speaking to Yuri in English brought my attention back to him.

He nodded.

"Good." His dark black eyes locked on Yuri. "I'm glad you realized that to visit us would not be a resort vacation. We are a tribe that lives the same way we have for hundreds of years. Others have been less than appreciative of our home and culture and language."

"We, unlike some of the others, are honored to be your guests," my sheseru assured him.

I watched the tension, animosity, and defensiveness run out of not only Chuluun but the other two men with him. And I understood then. Everyone else they had picked up at the airport had not been thrilled with the accommodations. We didn't care; we were just happy to have a roof, or a cave, as it were, over our heads. The maahes was pleased with us already.

Yuri then asked for the names of the two men with Chuluun, and he apologized for his lack of manners, and the long introductions began. They didn't speak the lineage because we were all aware of what tribes we belonged to, so that extra posturing wasn't necessary. But between all of us, it still took a while, and by the time we were ready to go, I was antsy. Just getting started, just driving somewhere, would make me happy. I wanted my mate, and just being in the same area as him, just knowing he was close, would help ease my rolling stomach, fluttering pulse, and jittery, like-I-was-on-crack demeanor. I knew I was a mess, but as soon as I saw Logan, in whatever form he took, I would be better. Just being in the same country as him had taken away my nausea. Things were already looking up.

"Can we go?" I asked after an acceptable moment of silence had passed.

"Of course."

There were five Jeeps parked outside of Arrivals, waiting there at the curb with a driver in each. They looked just like the one I had at home, and when I told that to Chuluun, that pleased him as well.

"When you visit me, you can ride in my baby," I told him.

"Thank you," he said hoarsely, and the smile was genuine.

Crane and Yuri came with me in the first Jeep, and Chuluun got in to drive, replacing the man who was there, sending him to another. Mikhail and Danny were in the next vehicle back, and Andrian and Taj were in the third. All the luggage was piled into the fourth one, and the last had the rest of the khatyu Chuluun had brought with him. Once everyone was seated, we got on the road.

"Are you hungry at all?" Chuluun asked us.

"Starving," Yuri said from the passenger seat.

"No one is allowed to see their semel until tomorrow night, so we should get you all fed, since we're not in a hurry."

"Sounds good," my sheseru agreed.

I wanted to say something, to ask why I couldn't see Logan, but before I got my mouth open, Crane's hand was on my thigh. When I turned to look at him, he gave me a slight shake of his head before he widened his eyes. And I got it. It was time to listen, not speak.

"Can you give us the timeline?" Yuri asked.

"For the beginning of the trials, you mean?" Chuluun wanted to clarify.

"Yes."

"Well, as your sylvan said, it will take us all day to reach our home. Tomorrow morning when you rise, all mates of the semels and their entourages will meet with our semel and the priest of Chae Rophon. He is here with his phocal and his Shu warriors to officiate the sepat, but he will only interfere if he sees a rule broken. The trials themselves will be performed by my semel, myself, and our tribe. It was a great honor to be chosen to host the sepat, and my semel has had the priest here for eight weeks preparing him."

"Why did the priest choose your tribe, do you think?"

"The security of the location," Chuluun answered, glancing over at Yuri. "And because my tribe won all the tests of strength at the last Feast of the Valley, and two of our number became Shu warriors. I myself was asked to take the oath of the Shu but prefer to stay as the maahes of my tribe. My semel asked me to remain as well."

I had known he was powerful, I could feel it rippling off him.

"You must shift very fast." Yuri smiled at him.

"Yes."

"I don't," Yuri confessed.

"But I remember you in the pit in Sobek," Chuluun told him. "A stronger, more powerful panther I have never seen."

Yuri nodded but said nothing.

"So after meeting your semel and the priest in the morning," Crane chimed in. "Then what, maahes?"

"Then the day is for the mates to prepare themselves to see their semels, and that evening they will."

"When my reah sees his mate," Yuri began, "what happens?"

"Our pit is attached to the cells where we keep prisoners when—"

"You lock up members of your tribe?" I asked.

"Of course, don't you?"

It was an outdated, archaic practice, and I was beginning to understand why Hamid Shamon had chosen the tribe of Khertet. They were not modernized and seemed ensconced in old practices and antiquated ideas.

"Sorry," I said quickly. "So your prison, you said, is attached to your pit?"

"Yes."

"So there's a door," Yuri clarified.

"An enormous grate that lifts and lowers," Chuluun explained. "All the semels will be released through it to find their mates, and we'll see who comes out alive."

"So the preparation that the mates are doing during the day—that could be them preparing for their deaths."

"Yes," Chuluun said solemnly. "I am sorry."

"Not to worry," Yuri said with a shrug. "The mate of our semel is his reah; there's no reason to even worry."

"Of course."

"So we'll be above them, we'll be able to see."

"Yes, our pit was built like most, like a coliseum, with entrances on the top and bottom so you can walk around the rim of the room and see everything that's going on below."

"I look forward to seeing it."

I watched Chuluun nod and turn his head just enough to catch a glimpse of Yuri out of the corner of his eye.

As he drove, I studied the maahes of the tribe of Khertet.

He was just as tall as Yuri, but he wasn't as wide through the chest or shoulders. His hair was black like mine, but whereas mine was so dark that Logan always said he could see blue highlights in it, Chuluun's looked like there might be streaks of brown in his. He had sharp, chiseled features and dark bronze skin that set off deep-set sepia-colored eyes. Striking man, and his voice complemented him, low and husky.

"Since you're going to have nothing but traditional food soon, lots of mutton, goat, maybe we should stop for some Thai food for now or—"

"Whatever you choose will be great," Yuri assured him.

"I—" He coughed. "—apologize for earlier and—"

"Zaboot." Yuri smiled, cutting him off gently.

"Spasiba," Chuluun whispered.

We drove for an hour, and slowly, cautiously, my sheseru prodded the maahes with questions about the trials. Yuri's would start on the third day; the test of blood was first, then Mikhail's, the test of law, and finally mine on the fifth day, the test of heart. He then prodded about the reah, where she had come from, why his semel would allow her sanctuary and not simply return her to the semel-aten.

"We don't know yet who the semel-aten will be," Chuluun told him. "Might we simply be gifting the semel-netjer with another reah?"

"No." Yuri smiled, stretching languidly, and I saw the maahes open his mouth to take a breath, taste my sheseru's scent in the air. "You misunderstand. My reah was not simply taken as my semel's mate because Logan Church chose to do so; my semel is semel-re first, semel-netjer second."

Chuluun looked at me in the rearview mirror. "You are the true-mate of your semel? You're not simply a reah that he decided to take for his mate that was born on his land?"

"I'm his true-mate, he is semel-re."

He grunted. "Then my semel's...."

"What?" Crane asked after he realized Chuluun didn't want to say. "Your semel's what? Does he have a plan to use Amirah as an added bonus test?"

It was obvious the other man was flustered.

"He's using her," Crane said as Chuluun took a turn off the highway into what looked like a busy metropolitan area. "Does your semel have a plan, maybe? Use the reah to screw with the other tribe leaders?"

Chuluun couldn't say; it would be dishonorable, disloyal. The way he wiggled in his seat, uncomfortable suddenly, was enough of an admission.

"I doubt it was his idea," I said, relieving Chuluun's semel of any wrongdoing, putting the blame firmly where I was sure it deserved to be. "I'll bet you that Ammon El Masry found her and made Orso take her in just for the purpose of using her as a diversion in the sepat."

"Yes," Chuluun agreed, sighing deeply. "The reah is to be used as a diversion. No semel can ignore a reah, the semel-aten said."

"So he brought her with him, or she came before him?"

"Before," he told us. "She came asking to join the tribe at his request. As you know, he could not ask Orso to take her unless she belonged to his tribe, and she did not. She belonged last to the tribe of Ariat."

She had belonged to a semel who had killed himself over her betrayal. And she had not forced him to take his own life—no one could force anyone to do that—but she had been the catalyst.

"It's a shame that she joined your tribe just on the semel-aten's word," Yuri said, changing the subject. "Because she's missing out."

"How do you mean?"

"I mean I can't think of anywhere more secluded or safer than this."

"You think it's safe here?"

He nodded. "Even though I haven't seen your home yet, the wide open spaces, the fact that your ancestors built into solid rock—I'm sure it's like a fortress."

"And that appeals to you."

"It does," Yuri told him. "You know how a sheseru thinks; we crave a castle to defend and hole up in to protect the people we love."

"Yes, you are all the same."

"We're simple."

"Which is a blessing."

Yuri nodded, and I saw Chuluun's first real smile.

Inside the restaurant, we all sat down on the floor with pillows and a low table. There was hot tea with milk, and then Chuluun ordered many dishes for us all to share. He started talking about Amirah again, and how many of the semels were already distracted.

"I don't know which semel is which," he told us. "Only the priest knows, even our own semel does not. Only when and if the semel can claim their mate in their werepanther form will we know who belongs to which tribe."

"But you'd be able to tell which semel was which by the maahes with them," I pressed him.

"No." He shook his head. "The princes are not allowed to speak their lineage, are not allowed to speak at all to anyone. They take a vow of silence when they enter with their semels."

"They haven't been allowed to speak for two months?"

"No."

"But they stay with the semels?"

"If they can." He looked sad suddenly. "We have lost one maahes already, and even though he has been dead now for two weeks, we can do nothing, as we don't know who he belongs to. When they join you tomorrow, only then will we know who is missing."

Domin could be dead.

I turned to Yuri, who gave me a quick shake of his head. "What?"

"You actually think that your maahes was the one to die?" Yuri scoffed.

I thought about it. "No, actually."

Yuri nodded. "There's no maahes here stronger."

"Are you certain?" Chuluun asked Yuri, taking offense, as he was one as well.

"I am," he told him. "And I mean no disrespect, but you cannot be stronger than Domin Thorne." He looked back at me. "Think about *your* maahes, Jin."

And I was trying to, not really understanding, until Crane bumped me with his knee. Only then did it hit me. Yuri meant because only Domin had been a semel as well. Logan Church had given another semel the place of maahes in his tribe because he knew he was strong enough to rein Domin in, if need be. Normal leaders were not secure enough to take a chance like that, but because Logan had, that made Domin superior and strongest, as he had his werepanther form.

"I understand," I told Crane.

"Good." He nodded before turning back to Chuluun. "So what's been happening to the semels?"

Chuluun was watching Yuri instead of listening, so it took a minute for him to look back at Crane. "Sorry?"

"The beset of my reah wanted to know what the treatment of the semels has been up to this time," Danny told him.

I had nearly forgotten he was there.

"Hello," Danny snapped, and I was surprised. This was not the respectful man from earlier; something was wrong.

I turned to him and was surprised to find his eyes locked on Yuri as well.

"Are the semels beaten?" Crane wanted to know, and he asked his question softly, with more finesse than Danny had.

Chuluun turned his head to look at my best friend. "My semel uses a whip to communicate with them, so yes, they are struck daily."

"And they're all in their panther form now?"

"Yes. It's why their mates are not allowed to see them until tomorrow night. Today completes the full eight-week cycle of the semels as animals. In the evening, they are allowed to shift into their werepanther form, which they will remain in until they either kill their mates or recognize them. If they kill their mates, or any other but their mates in the pit, they are instantly ordered back into panther form, where they will remain and someday forget they were ever men."

It was horrible, the idea you could kill the person you loved and then forget not only loving them, but your humanity as well.

"That's barbaric," Danny said, getting up. "Where's the bathroom?"

He was being combative and surly, and I had no idea why.

One of the two men with Chuluun pointed toward the back. I had tried to catch all the men's names but only remembered Krem and Berhna, who had come with Chuluun to the terminal.

"Your boy needs manners," Krem turned and told me.

"I'll teach him," I assured him.

He nodded.

When Danny came back, he took a seat between Crane and Yuri, explaining that where he had been sitting before was uncomfortable.

There were questions for Mikhail. Both Krem and Berhna had many for him, as he was a sylvan in America, and they wanted to know about living in tribes there. He was more than happy to explain. Apparently the punishment for crimes was severe in their tribe: branding and marking were common practices, as well as death. As Mikhail explained, quietly, confidently, I watched the men listening attentively. Parts of what he was saying were very appealing to them, perhaps mostly the system of having a trial.

"Our sylvan does not speak for us as you do for your cats, he merely recites the law."

In every tribe I had ever known, sylvans were advocates for the members, not merely the yardstick to be judged by. The enormity of the tribal differences seemed daunting, so it was nice that we all enjoyed eating together.

The food was good, and it didn't hurt that we were all starving. But Thai food was one of my favorite things, anyway. After a while, Yuri got up, and moments later, Chuluun leaned toward me but didn't speak.

"Yes?"

"Reah," he said, swallowing, "in my tribe, we must ask permission before we take something that belongs to another."

Take was a term that encompassed many things, and I understood that. "What of mine would you like to have, maahes?"

"I would taste your sheseru if he would allow it."

I took a breath. "In my tribe, my people make decisions for themselves. The choice would be Yuri's alone."

"Thank you," he said, and he got up fast, jogging across the restaurant.

"Wait," Danny gasped, leaning forward. "Jin, you can't just give Yuri to that—"

"I didn't give Yuri to anyone. I don't own my sheseru; he's a member of my tribe."

"Yeah, but—"

"Like that guy could make Yuri do anything he doesn't want to," Mikhail scoffed. "Yuri could break him in half if he wanted."

"Or fold him in half," I offered. "Which is probably more along the lines of what Chuluun was thinking when he asked for permission."

"Oh God, what's with you and being a crass piece of crap?" Crane scolded me.

"Sorry."

But they didn't come back, and Mikhail had to order Danny to stay where he was instead of getting up to go look for them.

"Yuri wouldn't just—that would be so disrespectful to Logan."

"How so?" Taj asked Danny. "Yuri's been working like a madman, been training harder than all the rest of us combined, and now, on the eve of seeing his semel, a day before his leg of the trial, he gets to maybe fuck and drain off some of the tension. C'mon, he deserves it."

"If that's even an option," Crane chimed in.

Taj scoffed. "Are you kidding? Did you see how that guy was looking at him? So an option—I could smell his scent change from here."

So had I, but as crass as Crane thought I was, I had not mentioned the change in Chuluun.

"Isn't it rude to just go off and screw somewhere while the rest of us—"

"Panthers usually copulate together in large rooms or after meals," Berhna said, interrupting Danny. "Do you not practice this in your tribe?"

"No," Danny sneered. "That's disgusting."

"It's something that only a tribe shares and is a way for tribe members to ensure that their semel and his mate are truly a mated pair and not in name only."

"It's revolting and vile," Danny said, shuddering.

I turned to two of our hosts and saw how humiliated they looked and the hatred they bore my cousin. He was not making friends. "His ideas about things will change once he attends the heru-ur in Sobek, huh?" I grinned, waggling my eyebrows for them.

Krem's face broke into a wide grin, and after a moment Berhna's did as well.

"Oh yeah, that rocked," Crane cackled, and both men joined him, laughing hard.

Danny, who knew the heru-ur was called every year in Sobek after the Feast of the Valley, knew it was basically a huge orgy, flushed dark red and dropped his gaze to the table.

Mikhail cleared his throat, and I looked at him.

"You should send him home," he mouthed to me.

"I can't," I said out loud, "but we'll all take turns coaching him."

He nodded and then stretched, smiling. "None of you know Yuri very well if you think he's fucking in the bathroom."

And his statement brought all table conversation to an end.

"No?" Crane asked.

"No," Mikhail said, chuckling. "I've known Yuri Kosa since I was eight and he was seven." He turned to look at me. "He's my best friend."

I knew they were close, I just didn't know how close.

"They're talking, maybe doing more, but beyond that—he's your sheseru first, Jin. Screwing his new friend in the bathroom wouldn't disrespect Logan, but it would make it hard for him to protect you from a position of defenselessness. He would never allow his ability to guard you to be compromised."

I knew that.

"So Chuluun is gay?" Danny asked Krem.

He squinted at Danny. "I don't understand this question. In our tribe, panthers are not considered to have a preference until they find their mate and then are simply considered to be mated."

"You're all bi?" He was dumbfounded.

"One cannot know the sex of one's mate until the mate is discovered, so if you only sleep with men or women, might you not miss your mate by limiting your choices?"

Danny just stared at him.

"Doesn't it make more sense to taste all that you would so that you may find your mate?"

"It makes perfect sense," Mikhail agreed.

Krem turned to my sylvan. "Only a semel must choose a female mate, as he must procreate, and that has always seemed, to us, unfair."

"To me too," Mikhail agreed.

"So your tribe has no problem with Jin being Logan's mate and him being a man?" Crane asked him.

"No. A male reah seems like the natural progression of finding your mate. It never seemed fair to me that semels alone are locked into the sex of their mates because they must procreate, but now, with the coming of your semel and your reah, I see that this is not the case. We were all pleased to hear that there was one semel among the six who had a male mate."

"I should have been born here," I told Krem.

"And we grieve that you were not, if you were met with anything but joy when you were discovered to be a reah."

My smile, I was sure, was bittersweet.

THE DRIVE down the endless two-lane highway did not have enough to look at to keep me awake. I dozed, fading in and out, listening in intervals to Crane talking to Yuri and Chuluun, Yuri and Chuluun talking, and Crane and Chuluun talking.

True to Mikhail's word, Yuri and the maahes of the tribe of Khertet had been speaking privately out on a balcony and not having sex in the bathroom. Yuri's scowl after Mikhail leaned close and whispered to him was blistering. Apparently that I had even entertained such a thought did not sit well with my sheseru. But I could tell from Chuluun's actions, the way he crowded into my sheseru's space, grazed his cheek over the back of his shoulder, and draped his arm across his seat, that he was more than interested in getting Yuri in bed.

Chuluun drove and mentioned sights as we passed them in the dark: Ögii Lake, Tsenkher Hot Springs, Bulgan Uul Nature Preserve. He explained the history and the importance of each as we drove on. But I didn't care. I was cold, so cold, and even though my blood ran hotter because I was a panther, it was still a frigid thirty-six degrees below zero outside.

"When does it warm up here?" Crane asked through chattering teeth.

"We're in the second of the nine nines," Chuluun explained. "Unfortunately, you've come here during the coldest eighty-one days of winter that start right around the winter equinox."

"Is that why you left the Jeeps running the entire time we were inside?" Yuri asked.

"Yes, it gets warmer after Tsagaan Sar."

"That's your New Year, in February, right?"

"Yes, reah," he answered me indulgently.

"And the first day of the New Year festival is called Shiniin Negen."

He smiled into the rearview mirror. "You've done some reading."

"Yeah."

"It's frickin' freezing out here." Crane shivered again, crossing his arms tighter. "How do you guys even leave your homes?"

"With great effort," he said, smiling at my best friend before turning to me. "Tell me, reah, who will fight in the pit with you?"

"My beset and me, along with Domin and—"

"No."

"What?" Yuri was confused about why he had cut me off, and so was I.

Chuluun again met my eyes in the rearview mirror. "Jin, I mean no disrespect to your beset, Crane Adams, but unless I was misinformed by the priest as to the severity of your beset's scourging at the hands of the disbanded tribe of Anuket, then he was gelded, was he not?"

"He was," I said flatly, turning to look at Crane's profile as he stared straight ahead, jaw clenched, not moving, barely breathing.

"Then he cannot fight in the sepat and may never step foot into another tribal arena. I understand that this is not the case, but by law, he is no longer fit and may not enter the fighting pit. He is not allowed to defend your tribe, as he is considered unclean and not even, as was done in ancient times after a challenge, fit for sacrifice."

I heard Crane catch his breath.

"Take off your glove," I told him, closing my eyes as I took off my seatbelt and leaned sideways into his lap.

"Jin," he whispered.

"Take off your glove," I repeated, ordering him, the first time having been a request that he had not obeyed.

If Crane's hands were uncovered and I was anywhere near him, he had to touch me. It was far too ingrained in him not to.

"Jin." His voice cracked.

I turned my head, baring the side of my neck, and put my arms around his hips, nestling in against him. "Crane, do you know who you are?"

After long minutes of waiting, I felt his fingers thread through my hair.

"Tell them who you are."

He stroked my hair from scalp to end, over and over, and then I felt the tips of his fingers slide down the side of my neck.

"Crane," I whispered, turning my head, laying my head in his lap so he could press his palm to the base of my throat, feel my pulse beating there. "Tell the man who you are."

It took a while, but I was not surprised that no one spoke. Finally, he cleared his throat. "You have a reah with you, maahes, but she apparently has no beset, or you would know," he began hoarsely. "Being chosen as beset of a reah is the only station that changes only at the discretion of the reah," Crane told Chuluun as well as Yuri. "Any other man—gelded—you would be correct, but not me. My station of companion to my reah supersedes all others. I can always fight in the pit as long as I hold the title of beset."

All I heard was the sound of the rushing wind outside. All the Jeeps we were in had the soft tops on them; otherwise we would have frozen to death, I was sure.

"I mean no disrespect, Crane Adams, but I will ask my sylvan if your words are true."

"Of course."

"Don't mistake me checking with him as me not believing you."

"No, I wouldn't," he told him, and I felt him fist his hand in my hair, tugging gently.

"I don't wanna." I yawned loudly, the idea of sitting up not appealing at all.

"Screw you; I ain't your fuckin' pillow."

He was grumbling, which was a very good sign. I sat up and turned to look at him.

The smile I got broke my heart. The gentle slap in my face made me smile before he replaced the glove on his hand.

"Ass," he grumbled under his breath. "You makin' me take off my glove is gonna give me fuckin' frostbite."

I arched an eyebrow for him.

"Move over, you're crowding me."

Settling back, I was not surprised when, after several miles, he put an arm around my shoulders and drew me close, leaning me against him.

"Thank you for reminding me."

I wouldn't let anyone hurt my best friend ever again. Nothing else would be taken, in any form.

Never.

Chapter Twelve

THE HOME of the semel of the tribe of Khertet was breathtaking in the morning. At night, in the dark, after an entire day of travel, I was exhausted. I passed out on the pile of furs in the ger that was ours, reserved for the delegation from the tribe of Mafdet for the duration of our stay.

I had thought we would be inside, in the home built into the rock. I had misunderstood. We were guests, so we would sleep in a ger, or a yurt, a large, round wooden-framed hut covered in waterproof canvas that was extremely durable and able to stand up to the snow and wind. The gers, all six of them, one for each house of the challengers, had been erected along a small river that cut through beautiful pastureland. In the summer, or anytime it wasn't winter, I could imagine how green it must have been, but now everything was covered with heavy white snow. The river water was still clear and turquoise because it was reflecting the magnificent color as far as the eye could see. The travel books called Mongolia the country of blue sky, and as I stood, turning in every direction, I understood why. It was just endless. I felt like I was on another planet, as alien as everything felt.

Absolutely nothing was like I thought. We were outsiders, so we stayed, literally, outside. There were no sleeping quarters for us. We were allowed only into common areas, the pit, corrals for animals, food stores, and a large main hall where the semel received visitors. It was where we were supposed to go after we were brought our morning meal of tea with milk and rice congee, which was porridge with pickled vegetables and tiny freshwater fish.

I was standing outside the ger I shared with the six men who had made the trip with me when I saw Chuluun walking toward me with two men I had not met. He himself looked exhausted.

"Good morning," I greeted when he was close to me.

He squinted, and his brows furrowed. "Good morning, my reah. May I introduce my sylvan, Naran, and my sheseru, Sükh?"

I bowed quickly as they both went to their knees. I had forgotten their tribe was much more formal than my own.

There was a grumble of sound before Chuluun, too, went very slowly to his knees.

What was I… oh. "Please," I prodded, "rise and be at ease in my presence."

They both stood. Naran helped Chuluun up and then shook his head.

I smiled at the maahes. "Uhm, I'm gonna guess drinkin'?"

He groaned, and the sheseru, who was trying really hard to hold on to his glower, had to give me a trace of a smile. "It seems that your own sheseru can hold his liquor better than the maahes of our tribe."

I nodded.

Sometime in the middle of the night, I had woken to hushed voices whispering in the dark and had gotten up, gone around the partition that stood to give me, and only me, some semblance of privacy, and walked toward the front of the ger. It got colder the farther I moved from the wood-burning stove that gave off the only heat, but when I discovered the source of the sound, I doubted the two men were concerned with the freezing temperature in the least.

Chuluun's pants were piled on the ground beside him, and the man himself was on his hands and knees, moaning softly as Yuri, fully clothed, his own pants shoved down just enough, took him from behind. It was raw and hot, and as soon as my brain wrapped around what I was seeing, I turned around and went back to bed, too tired to let the muffled whimpers and cries keep my eyes open.

Hours later, Yuri woke me when he came stumbling back toward the main area. I pushed my head up under the small silk curtain to see him. He was shivering and wet and had, he told me through chattering teeth when he noticed me, washed himself in the river beside the ger. It was morning already, and even though he smelled mostly like him, there was still alcohol on his breath.

"At least you don't smell like come," I teased.

He grunted and Mikhail woke up.

"What are you guys doing?" he grumbled irritably.

"Just freezing to death," Yuri said shakily.

"Come here," Mikhail snapped.

I thought Yuri would have preferred to lie down by me and Crane, or Danny, or even Andrian, but he went instead to Mikhail and crawled under the blankets with him, and when I checked later, he was wrapped tight around his friend. But even watching them sleep, I understood how devoid of sexuality it was. They slept like cats, for warmth, companionship, and when Mikhail moved, there was that annoyance I got with Crane, not the sensual invitation any movement from Logan would have signaled.

When he rose before Mikhail in the morning, Yuri was careful not to disturb him. As he shed his shirt, I saw the marks.

"Your back is covered in scratches," I told my sheseru from where I was sitting up on the furs, reading, waiting for the day to begin.

"I'm sure," he said, not turning.

There was a bite that looked deep on his shoulder.

"You gonna shift and run so you can heal that?"

"It's nothing."

"If another panther gets a fang in it—it could be bad."

"Alright." His voice rumbled in his chest.

"I saw you guys. Sorry."

He shrugged, still not turning to look at me. "Had to be there, nowhere else. I can't be inside his home at night, the tribe doesn't trust me, and I don't trust him any closer to you."

"If hc was gonna kill mc, he would have already."

"I take no chances after Abbot George and you almost being killed in your own kitchen." He sighed. "Fuck. I still can't believe I let that happen."

"Like you knew that guy was a psychopath."

"I don't take chances anymore."

"And?"

He finally turned to look at me, and I saw the scowl. "And what?"

"Are you going to keep the maahes?"

"Are you insane? I wouldn't live here on a bet. There's no—"

"We both know you love it here. Your idea of heaven is living off the land up high in the mountains. You fuckin' love this."

He smirked at me. "Yeah, but it's not my tribe."

"And Chuluun, does he wanna keep you?"

"I think he wants me to keep fucking him until I leave, beyond that… I doubt it."

"Well, after he sees you in the pit with other sheserus, he might change his mind."

"Perhaps."

And now, later that morning, I was looking at Chuluun, smiling because he looked like he was in a lot more pain than Yuri.

"What did you drink?"

"Just airag, it's a traditional drink, it's nothing."

I looked over at Naran, the sylvan.

"And vodka." He smiled. "Let's not forget the vodka."

Which my sheseru drank like water when he did have it, so it was not surprising that of the two of them, Yuri looked better.

"Are we going to see the priest?"

"Yes," Naran told me. "All of you need to come with us; the priest is addressing everyone at once."

And my brain stopped. Luckily for me, when Crane walked out of the ger, he understood from my face and so stepped up next to me and went on full alert.

"Did you hear—"

"I heard you," Crane told Naran.

Chuluun winced. "I received permission from my semel to speak to the priest, and the station of beset is as you said. You remain the reah's companion, and as the title cannot be stripped from you, neither can the duties. You will always be able to face challengers in the pit."

I didn't necessarily even want Crane there, but he needed to be. He had fought in the pit in Sobek and would stand at my side in the sepat as well. Nothing had changed for him, and whatever his father had thought to take by maiming him, he had been unsuccessful. He remained a panther in his tribe, beset of his reah, and a member of his semel's household.

"Good," Crane breathed, secure in his place, content that everyone knew who he was and what he was to me and, more importantly, to Logan Church.

Logan.

I had to see him. I was dying to see him. I was going slowly out of my mind with the waiting.

I had been able to put it out of my mind, shove it back, shove it down, fill my head with anything and everything else: the lush scenery, the new and different-tasting food, the smell of the air, the mineral taste of the water…. I had let all of it clutter my brain, anything not to focus and obsess, but now….

I didn't need to eat anything else, I didn't need to see Hamid or meet the semel of the tribe of Khertet or do one more task that was not seeing my mate. Didn't they understand? We were supposed to be….

And it hit me that they didn't. No one understood the pulse-pounding, blood-racing, heart-pumping need to be with their mate, because only semels and reahs ever had that soul-searing desire. Only semels and reahs mated for life. Everyone had jumped on board with awe and reverence that I was a nekhene cat, but they forgot about the reah part, the part that craved my mate, hungered for him, could barely breathe with the weight of the wanting riding him.

"Jin," Crane snapped out my name.

I lifted my head and looked at him.

"Your scent's changing." He widened his eyes, signaling the danger. "Stop."

His hand on my shoulder grounded me.

"Let's go," he told the sylvan of the tribe of Khertet. "We'll follow you."

Each mate of each semel had been allowed four companions along with their sylvans and sheserus, and we joined the others walking silently toward the entrance of the semel of Khertet's home.

"Why the quiet?" Danny asked Crane as we trudged with the procession.

"All but one group of these people will lose their semel," Crane answered. "Some of them will lose him today. Some of them will lose their sheseru or their sylvan or their yareah, and one tribe has already lost a maahes. This is a very solemn occasion, and no one here wants to care at all for anyone outside their circle. Only the people from the tribe of Khertet are candidates for friendship, as they're the only ones that aren't a threat."

Danny nodded as he fell into step beside Mikhail.

It was a maze inside, tunnels carved deep into the side of the mountain, rock on all sides, dirt covering it at our feet, the air smelling damp and like something else, sandalwood incense and fire and burning wood.

Finally, after easily a half an hour of walking, we were led through a corridor into an opening that turned out to be the pit. We gathered there, assembled, to be addressed by the priest of Chae Rophon, Hamid Shamon. He stepped forward to speak, and Jamal Hassan, the phocal, head of the Shu cats, stood on his right.

I tried to listen, I really did, but the speech, the posturing of the semel-aten, Ammon El Masry, as he stepped forward on the Hamid's left, was too much. We all knew what hung in the balance. Hamid was leveraging his power against Ammon's. If the semel-aten emerged victorious, it was within his power to appoint a new priest and have Hamid Shamon, who had served for over forty-three years—the man was in his seventies—exiled or ritually executed. It was the price the priest paid for challenging him. But if the semel-aten was killed in the pit, then the strong, vital priest would continue his reign and be partnered with a new semel-aten, together enacting law for the werepanther world.

Hamid spoke on, and all eyes moved from him to Ammon and back. I looked at the semel-aten and wondered for the millionth time why he would ever try and hurt Logan. If he was so terrified of losing his power, surely, even from running my gaze around the room, there were more men than my semel who would try to seize power.

"Jin, you need to focus," Crane cautioned, because he knew my mind was drifting.

But I was close now, hours instead of days away from seeing Logan. He was being kept in a cell close by, caged separately, as were all the semels, from one another.

"And now let us please thank our host, Orso Bataar, semel of the tribe of Khertet."

Only Genghis Khan himself could have possibly lived up to my expectations. As it was, the man was tall and broad with hair that was graying at the temples but otherwise thick, black, and straight. His yareah, Khongordzol, at his side, was elegant, queenly, and smiled at us all and waved. Their sons—they had three—all bowed low from above us. His khatyu, those who would test us, were headed not by his sheseru, whom I had met, but by Dval Quach, the new sheseru of the tribe of Rahotep. Roshan Tabir, whom I had met when I was in Sobek, had been killed trying to carry out his semel's orders to ambush and kill my mate.

Now, as I looked up at Dval, I knew Ammon would have told him the story, told him specifically to make sure Logan didn't live, and all the men Ammon brought with him would have the same orders: to kill my mate.

The task at hand was overwhelming, and for a moment I let all the fear and uncertainty flood me.

"Stop," Crane ordered hoarsely. "Don't forget who you are, Jin. Yeah, that's the semel-aten up there and the priest of Chae Rophon and some guy who gets his rocks off hurting his own kind, but you're the only fuckin' nekhene cat in existence. Get it in your head."

I centered and calmed.

"We will now return to all but one tribe their princes," Hamid said, gesturing toward a side entrance.

Every other entourage turned to look, holding their breath. None of us worried. We all knew Domin better than that.

He was the second maahes through the archway, and his smile was wide and all him, wicked and warm all at the same time. I was surprised that Yuri moved around me and ran toward him. Domin lifted his arms, and my sheseru collided with him, filling them and hugging him hard. Crane bolted next, and then Mikhail. When finally he was in front of me, I smiled big even as the cries of the entourage that had lost, by his absence, their maahes filled the air.

"I knew you'd be okay." I sighed deeply. "After Crane reminded me."

Domin turned to Crane and gave him a grin of pure evil. "You told him I was too mean to get hurt?"

"Pretty much." Crane smiled back.

"I missed you," I said instead of lunging at him. As a rule, we didn't hug.

"Me too."

Staring at him, I realized how shaggy he looked, the full beard and mustache, his hair pulled back into a queue longer than he ever let it get. But eight weeks of introspection, of solitude and silence, had maybe been good for Domin Thorne.

I just stared at him.

"Logan's fine." He answered the question I hadn't even asked.

"Did you talk?"

"I talked to him," he teased. "I figured things out, and before he shifted, remember, we had a whole day alone just getting here."

And the way he said it was funny. "You guys did what, plotted together?"

He arched an eyebrow for me. "Something like that."

"What did you talk about?"

"That's between my semel and me," he said playfully, but I heard the thread of seriousness in there. They had decided something, figured something out, but what?

"He's worried about what will happen if he dies." My brain jumped there.

His brows furrowed. "No, Jin, Logan doesn't think he'll die."

I was surprised. "He's not scared at all?"

"No, he has bigger concerns."

Bigger than death? What the hell?

"Domin—"

"The priest is talking," Crane cut me off, turning me around so I could look up at where everyone else was.

Hamid was asking that the mates separate themselves from their retinues, as they had to be taken and cleansed and changed into the ceremonial robes.

I turned and looked at Crane. "He means sacrificial robes."

He glowered at me. "Knock it off."

I saw the other yareahs turning and hugging people, and so I lunged at Crane. He clutched me tight, face buried in my hair. Ever so slightly, I felt him tremble.

"I'm not worried about this now, or Yuri's part or Mikhail's. I'm worried about you and me and Domin and Andrian keeping those assholes off Logan in three more days," Crane told me.

But that concern had not even crossed my mind.

"My reah."

I turned to Yuri. He hugged me first, and then Mikhail did. Domin patted my shoulder. The others I smiled at, and even though Danny wanted to touch me, Mikhail wouldn't let him. Inside the home of the semel, there were strict rules, and so the noncaste rules I had in my tribe were not relevant. Only those one step lower than my station—Yuri,

Domin, Mikhail, and Crane—and one higher, Logan, could I touch. Everyone else was off limits inside Orso's home.

Tribe members came forward, and my people formed a circle around me, all of them facing out as I stripped out of my clothes. A fur cape was passed to Crane and then to me, and I wrapped myself up in it from head to toe. Everyone moved at the same time, and the priest instructed us to form a line and kneel. Following his order, we all moved quickly.

Hamid Shamon descended with everyone who had been above us on the tier, what looked, from the floor, like a portico carved directly from the rock. He stopped in front of the first yareah.

"Katrina Kozel, yareah of Anatoly Kozel, semel of the tribe of Ptahket from Kiev in the Ukraine. We grieve the loss of your maahes."

She bowed low, thanking the priest for receiving her and for his sympathy before she offered him her hand. He squeezed it briefly before stepping aside. The semel-aten took her hand next; then his new sheseru, the man who would be testing her mate; the phocal; and the semel of the tribe of Khertet, and his mate, Khongordzol.

The small procession moved down the row, one after another. They moved from one yareah to the next: Narae Yusuke, yareah of Narae Hiroshi, semel of the tribe of Reshep from Hokkaido, Japan; Teresa Medina, yareah of Gavin Medina, semel of the tribe of Nebthet from Santa Cruz, Bolivia; Juliet Payne, yareah of Wallace Payne, semel of the tribe of Taweret from Drake, Pennsylvania; and Oyuun Kushi, yareah of Oyuun Aldar, semel of the tribe of Girdaht from Guangdong, China.

When Hamid reached me, he took a breath before he spoke.

"Jin Rayne, *reah*"—his voice rose on the word—"of Logan Church, semel-netjer of the tribe of Mafdet from Incline Village, Nevada."

"Thank you for receiving me, Your Grace," I told him after I bowed low, offering him my hand.

He took it in both of his, and his smile was radiant. "Jin," he said, and his voice was infused with warmth. "It is my honor to see you again."

"As it is mine," I assured him.

He nodded and moved to stand beside me, which, from the sounds in the room, no one missed.

"Reah," Ammon El Masry said, his cat eyes gleaming, watching me but not lifting his hand. "I have a surprise for you."

I waited, and he turned his head to look at Orso.

"You promised me she would appear."

The older man squinted at Ammon for a moment and then called across the room to Sükh, his sheseru.

"Why do we wait?" Hamid asked Ammon.

"The reah must meet his equal."

"There is no equal for a mated reah," Orso's yareah, Khongordzol, said, gliding forward, extending her hand to me. "And as the priest has presented you, I have no need to wait." She smiled at me, and I was struck again by her regal bearing, the dark, beautiful glittering eyes and the warmth of her smile. "It is an honor, my reah."

Women who wanted to mother me, really, I just couldn't get enough of them. I took her hand and held it tight. "The honor is mine. Thank you for our accommodations outside. I would love to see more of your home when the sepat has concluded."

"And it would be an honor to show it to you and your mate."

I felt hot tears fill my eyes fast, but they didn't spill. She just went blurry for a second. She had basically told me she thought Logan would win and that it made sense to her. But it did to me as well.

There were gasps all around, and I turned as a woman started toward us. She was stunning, and I had no doubt that she knew it. Her walk was the fluid grace of a dancer; she flowed across the floor, and the air almost sparked with electricity. She was radiant, her huge brown eyes with thick feathery lashes, her skin the color of warm cinnamon, flawless and glowing, her features delicate and fragile, and when she spoke, calling out a greeting to Hamid, her voice was lilting and mellifluous. Here was a reah, the embodiment of feminine beauty and mystery. There was not an eye not riveted on her… except….

"Such airs," Khongordzol said under her breath.

"You dare speak to me, yareah filth."

"You are not mistress in this house." Khongordzol's voice rose loud and defiant. "And as you are not my mate's reah and I will not be taurth, you will get on your knees."

All yareahs hated unmated reahs because the potential was there that they could take a semel from them. But once the semel acknowledged the reah was not his mate, then the yareah, as mistress in her home and undisputed mate of the semel, had all the power. Normally, unless the semel in question was the semel-aten, the reah was sent away. But the semel-aten was the only one who could claim a reah as a consort—as wosret. Ammon El Masry's yareah, Ebere, had had no recourse but to live with Amirah Fehr in her household. It was why, when she had met me, she had treated me so poorly at first. She had forgotten that I was a mated reah and had just seen me as a reah.

We had mended things between us, and even though she had cancelled her trip to visit with us in the summer, it had been, she confessed, because she had moved with her children back to Cairo. She and her mate no longer shared a bond; it had been shattered years ago, and she was tired of pretending it still existed. I wondered vaguely if she was there for the sepat.

"I will never bow to you," Amirah snapped, bringing me from my thoughts and pulling my attention back to her.

"I think you will," Khongordzol said, her tone icy.

Amirah's head lifted. "Your husband gave me sanctuary, and I was called here by the semel-aten to speak with the mated reah, and that I will do."

Khongordzol growled, and I realized at that moment that I had been right and Orso had nothing to do with receiving the reah into his tribe. Ammon must have found out Amirah was alive and sent her to Orso after Hamid called the sepat. He was going to use her, her allure, to stack the odds in his favor. Even happily mated semels still might want to have a reah on their land, in their house, ensconced in their bed.

It made my stomach roll to think that she would allow herself to be used, but she had made choices I did not understand before.

According to the law, all reahs, upon discovery that they were reahs—so at the time of the first shift—were to be presented to the semel-aten. So basically you flew to Sobek, met the semel-aten, and once you were of age, eighteen, you were sent to Sobek if the semel-aten wanted. Amirah's parents had presented her to Ammon El Masry when she was sixteen, and when she was eighteen, he had requested she return. She then became wosret, his consort, until she found her mate. Every year at the Feast of the Valley, she walked at his side and saw semel after semel.

The thing was, every semel was supposed to make the trip to Sobek every year, but this was life, real life, and not everyone could go to every feast. Logan had missed many before he saw me, only wanting to go to the last one we attended because he wanted to present me to Hamid Shamon, the semel-aten, and as many semels as would be there. The fact that all had not gone as planned was not his fault.

But Amirah, who had not wanted to remain the consort of the semel-aten and did not want to live her life as basically his mistress, had pretended that she had found her mate. The power of a reah was heady to begin with, and coupled with pheromones and the promise of a true-mate, Terrance McCord had succumbed and taken a reah home to his tribe from the Feast of the Valley a year ago.

"May I speak?" I asked suddenly, and the argument that had risen in decibel level while I was thinking came to a stop.

The priest granted me permission. "Yes, reah."

"The semel-aten was mistaken," I said, turning to look at Amirah. "Because he told us all, even His Grace, that you were dead."

Her eyes flicked to mine. "The sylvan of my tribe found my semel, my sheseru, and me. He's the one who allowed the lie."

"Is he still alive?" I asked her. "The sylvan?"

She squinted at me. "As far as I know, why would you—"

"Is he?" I asked Ammon El Masry.

His eyes narrowed as he regarded me. "He is not."

I looked back at Amirah. "So maybe the sylvan was looking after you at the request of the semel-aten, huh? And you're here… why?"

Her eyes studied my face. "I want my freedom."

"And so because you want to be free of the semel-aten, the price is to help him here at the sepat and try and tempt any of the mates of the yareahs you see here besides me, is that it?"

Her eyes were hard as her chin snapped up. "I do not answer to any of you mated chattel."

She saw mating just like as I used to, as a prison, as a death sentence.

"May I have permission to speak?"

I turned my head to look at Narae Yusuke, yareah of the tribe of Reshep. We all did.

"Speak," the priest told her.

Her eyes met Amirah's. "I tell you now, reah. If my mate becomes semel-aten, then he has dominion over you, and the day he does, I will take your head myself for what you visit on us this night."

Amirah smirked at Yusuke. "You will be dead in the morning, as will your mate."

"We'll see, reah."

"Oh," Amirah spat back, "you would leverage your power against mine!"

"Silence!" Hamid's voice rose, and no one dared say a word. "The mates will retire to prepare for the opening of the sepat. There is nothing in the law that says that a reah may not enter the pit with the other mates of the semels. It is done; she may attend and change with the other mates."

He moved in close to Amirah, and his eyes looked right through her.

"Thank you, Your Grace."

"Your choice of path is a mistake," he told her, his voice dark and low.

"I will be consort no longer. I will be free."

Hamid nodded. "Well, then, do now as your master bids you and meet Jin Rayne."

She stepped close to me. "I have heard of you."

"And I have no use for you," I told her, leaning sideways, "or your master. May I greet the phocal now?"

"You may," the priest said, and Ammon, as angry as he was, and Amirah, as fuming as she was, had no recourse but to step back because the priest allowed me to disrespect both of them. After a moment, Jamal took their place in front of me, and I lifted my hand for him to take.

"Jin." He smiled.

"Have you seen Taj?"

"Not yet, but we'll have time while you prepare for the beginning of the sepat."

"Good."

Khongordzol introduced me to her mate then, and I met the semel of the tribe of Khertet and thanked him for his hospitality and for the kindness of his maahes, sheseru, and sylvan. He nodded and then stared at me.

"You pride yourself, as does my semel, on the treatment of a tribe like a family. It had to have gone against your sense of *maat* to allow Amirah into your tribe. The actions of the semel-aten are regrettable." I bowed when I finished, and he bowed back, deeper, longer, and I understood he appreciated what I had said. It wasn't that he needed forgiveness or would ever ask for it; the whole encounter was simply, as I said, regrettable.

"You speak out of turn, reah," Amirah snarled.

"Mind your tongue, bitch," Kushi, yareah of the tribe of Girdaht, warned her, dark eyes flashing as she looked at Amirah. "We may all die tonight, and that would be regrettable. You die tonight and no one will mourn you."

Amirah took a breath to speak, and I lifted my hand. "We need to follow Khongordzol now," I cut off her venom. "Let's go."

And with that, Khongordzol took my arm in hers and led us in our fur capes from the pit. When we returned, the sepat would begin.

"Jin!"

But I didn't turn around to look at Crane. I wasn't that strong.

Chapter Thirteen

THERE were candles everywhere and braziers set up in each corner of the huge space of the pit of the tribe of Khertet. One end, I realized when we returned, had an enormous grate that rose and lowered on a winch. It was just like a coliseum in that respect. The heavy grate lifted, animals came bounding through, and you fought them. But this time, creatures did not escape out onto the floor—werepanthers did.

We stood in a row, looking, just as I had quipped to Crane earlier, like sacrificial lambs. Above us, seated, looking down from a safe height, was the entire tribe and everyone each mate had brought with them to the sepat. When I looked up, Crane, of course, was the first to lift his hand to show me where they were. The second hand lifted to me was Ebere's, and I nodded at her as she smiled down at me. It answered my question: yes, the semel-aten had brought his mate.

All of us, every mate who stood in the pit, had been bathed and scented with oil. The point was for purification but also to confuse the semels. We all needed to smell the same. We were also all dressed in white silk robes cinched at the waist with a tie. Even Amirah, who had walked in with us and taken her place in line, was outfitted the same.

"This is very brave of you, reah," Teresa, Gavin Medina's yareah, told her as we all waited for the grate on the other end of the pit to lift. "You might be torn to shreds along with the rest of us."

"You forget," Amirah sneered back, "I've been here as long as they have. I've stood outside the cells of each of your mates, just beyond their reach, torturing them with my scent for weeks. I've had sex in front of them and watched them spill their seed with wanting me. None of them will hurt me, they all want me, and any of them that come near me will tear you to shreds when you try to claim them," she purred. "I'm a reah, and mated or not, mate or not, I can take them from you."

"But why would you want to?" I asked.

"My deal was struck with the semel-aten. If I help him turn semels into panthers, he renounces his claim over me as wosret. I have no desire to return to being his consort."

"There are other ways to secure your freedom," I assured her.

"I disagree, but I see only animals anyway. It's a simple task to turn your semels from you."

"They're men first," Yusuke said, and I realized how much I liked her voice. It was strong and husky and confident. "And men love those that make their homes a sanctuary. We'll see what we see."

"Oh," Katrina gasped, and we all heard the groan of metal at the same time.

The roar of panther was next, followed by snarling that made my blood run cold as six werepanthers came running into the pit.

We couldn't shift and flee; I couldn't turn to my own werepanther form and fight if I was cornered by anyone that wasn't my semel. The only form that we, as mates, could take as monsters descended upon us was human. To disregard any rule was instant death for the semel and his mate.

I ran to the side and saw Yusuke do the same, putting a brazier between any werepanther and her. My brain screamed at me to shift, the nekhene sensing danger and flooding my senses with adrenaline, ready to attack. I looked for Logan and saw him running fast, sniffing the air, searching for me. He had no idea what he was supposed to be doing. He had been a panther for two months, living as an animal, eating as one, been caged, beaten, run, and hunted. He had been tortured by Amirah, tantalized with her closeness, and then, finally, minutes ago, had been ordered into his werepanther form and released into the arena. I had no idea if he was even sane. Only my faith in him as my mate, as a man, kept me on my feet.

The first yareah killed was Juliet. She went to her knees, arms open to receive her mate, only to scream seconds later as his claws closed on her throat and punctured her jugular. I had never seen so much blood. Her mate, Wallace, drank some of it before running toward Amirah. She received him joyfully as he tore the robe from her body. I looked away before the final violation of faith and trust between him and his dead yareah was committed.

Kushi was next, her mate tackling her to the ground, shifting to panther as he mauled her. I looked away, her screams dying fast as she drowned in her own blood.

Logan was circling Amirah and Wallace, not sure if he should fight the other semel for the reah. She called to him, arms out, but he stepped back, lifting his head, looking, inhaling deeply, unsure.

Calling him would be a mistake, and I knew that. Words were meaningless, and adding my pheromones to the already saturated-with-adrenaline and sweat-scented arena would only confuse him. Running would draw others, so I waited and made myself small.

Logan's presence was too distracting for Wallace, and he turned from Amirah and launched himself at my mate in a frenzy of tooth and claw. The two semels went down in a tangle of snapping jaws and bloodlust, and I followed them before my attention was drawn to Katrina as she ran by them, sobbing.

She flew toward Amirah, who had been shoved up against a wall by another semel who was preparing to bury his cock in her. When she reached him, she leaped, but he caught her in midarch, savagely grasping her face, twisting it sharply, snapping her neck like a doll's. She was dead before she hit the ground.

Another semel leaped at Katrina's mate, hurling him to the ground before he lunged at Amirah, who was laughing.

"No!" Yusuke yelled. "I forbid it! Narae Hiroshi, remember who you are!"

His head turned, and he ran at her. I saw her change her stance, prepare to defend herself, but my vision was suddenly blocked by a huge werepanther towering over me.

It was a dream. Everything had all happened so fast, the entire scene playing out in minutes; all the savagery and carnage had become a blur. As the clawed hand shoved me back, lifting at the same time, I found myself pinned against the wall, held immobile several feet off the ground.

"No," I growled, and the nekhene in me braced for battle.

There was a loud roar of warning, and before I could process the motion, I was on the ground, dropped hard, confused for a second as I was grabbed a second time and slammed into the stone wall, the impact rendering me breathless with pain.

The rock cut into my back, and my vision swam as every gasp of air was torn from my chest. As I was still reeling from the first attack, I wasn't able to respond like I wanted to the panther/man hybrid who held me immobile in his grip.

"Come to me!" Amirah screamed at the semel who had released me as well as the one who was holding me now.

But she wasn't getting the one who was looking at me hungrily; never would she claim what was mine.

I coughed, my lungs on fire, as I focused my eyes on the man I loved.

In his werepanther form, Logan Church was still beautiful. He was covered from head to toe in fine gold fur. His face was larger; all of him was huge and massive, his head that of a panther, with ears flattened back, eyes, nose, and mouth transformed to feline. The muscles were pumped big, but even in this form, Yuri still would have been bigger. The shift altered features but couldn't add size or weight, just lengthened some muscles and bulked others. I was the only cat who changed completely, and no one knew why, the answer always being the same: nekhene.

As my eyes ran over my mate, I calmed, dragged in air, and finally lifted my hands to his face.

He shivered, taking a step back, and I fell again as he dropped me down the wall, abrading my robe, scraping skin as I crashed to the ground.

"Logan," I got out, even as he was on me, claws driving into my shoulder as he held me trapped in his grip.

I heard a snarling growl close, and he turned his head and moved, giving way to the other panther, allowing him close. It was the way of cats, the dance of dominance. Another cat would growl at Logan and bare his teeth, and Logan would retreat, allowing the other cat close until he decided he wanted to investigate me again and would drive the usurper away. I had seen it at many gatherings, with panthers, the circling, the flash of fang, the swipe with claws. It would go back and forth, because Logan wasn't certain of me, wasn't sure who or what I was. So he retreated and let the other dominant male near. It would go on as each semel struggled to realize what he could claim, what was his, and who belonged to him.

Normally Logan knew me at all times, but he had been an animal too long and been allowed to shift only partway back, to his werepanther form. So now he wasn't sure of me, and the noise and the smell of blood and Amirah's suffocating, cloying pheromones… all of it swirling together was driving him mad.

Scrambling to sit up, I sat there, frozen, as the other semel leaned forward to sniff me. It was hard to smell anything in the chaotic pit, but he tried, pressing his nose against my throat even as I turned my head away.

Seconds later, the semel flipped me over onto my hands and knees, and I made a noise that I wasn't proud of, part anger and frustration, part sick, cold terror. In my human form there was no fighting whatever he had planned. I was completely at his mercy unless I shifted—but if I became a nekhene, I would lose everything. But to be raped… Logan would hate himself, hate that it had happened to me, that he had allowed it to occur, and so I would lose him anyway. I wasn't sure what to do, and I had seconds to make a choice that would affect the rest of my life.

It turned out I didn't have to.

I had never heard a noise like the one that followed my own. It was a strangled, roaring cry, almost a howl, and it was filled with pain and outrage and fury. The sound blew through me, made me shiver with dread. I was released instantly, and the entire room went silent and still. No one moved, not even Amirah.

The hush was almost as frightening as the sound had been. When I turned my head, Logan was crossing the floor to me, eyes huge, mouth open, snarling low as he came so all I saw were fangs and claws and his hard, obvious erection. The semel who had thought to claim me scuttled away, and I was aware that the space was frozen around me. No one was even breathing as Logan dropped down, crouching on the ground beside me, panting, heaving, nostrils flaring as he inhaled me.

I understood at once, because he smelled like her.

He had been on the other side of the room, prepared, from the looks of him, to fuck Amirah, the scent of arousal clinging to him, when he had heard me whimper.

That sound he knew, my resonance, coupled with my familiar posture of submission when he turned to look for me, had combined to clear the fog from his brain. For a split second, he had been the semel of the tribe of Mafdet, and he knew who I was, what I was, knew I belonged to him and that another was about to claim me. He had warned the other semel fast that to touch his mate would bring swift death. I would remember the sound for the rest of my life and pray that he would never have to make it again.

I rolled to my knees and faced him. "My semel," I said softly, leaning forward, my lips parting, finally releasing my pheromones. I wrapped him in the aroma that was mine alone, letting him taste my desire, my overwhelming, devouring need.

He reached for me with a clawed hand, and I slowly, gently touched the underside of his wrist, my thumb sliding back and forth over the pulse-point as his eyes slowly narrowed and his mouth closed.

There were sounds around me; life resumed, but I was only vaguely, peripherally aware. This was my mate in front of me, and he had to claim me and I had to tame him.

"Do you know me?" I murmured, reaching back, moving my hair, baring the side of my neck so he could see skin, smell skin.

He was thrumming with power and sizzling heat and was, as always, a gorgeous specimen of male beauty. I wanted to eat him. The whine I released was deep and throaty and full of longing as I squirmed in front of him. When the clawed hands grabbed me, hauling me forward into his lap, I wrapped my arms around his neck and held on.

It was his turn to whine.

His engorged, leaking shaft was caught between us, wedged against his ripped, muscular torso, and when he began to pant, I reached down and stroked him. He shuddered beneath me, pushing up, trying to get more of his cock into my hand, and I fisted the long, hard, thick length of him, beginning the slow, tight pull and slide that I knew from experience would bring him release.

As I watched him, I realized I would let him bury himself in my ass, even dry, even though it would have torn me up, because my logic had drowned in emotion by that point. But I couldn't move, couldn't even lift to maneuver him beneath me; the sharp, clawed hands anchoring me to his thighs left me no wiggle room. And he could still hurt me, even inadvertently, by slicing through an artery if he gripped me too tight. So I tugged and slid my hand over him instead, opening my robe to reveal my own throbbing shaft dripping with precome, pressing it along the length of his, using both hands now to jerk us off together.

The velvety hardness of Logan's dick next to mine, the smell of him, of me, of us together, made me writhe in his lap, buck against him, and ache to be filled.

He moved fast, leaning forward, his jaw open before I realized it, coming for my throat. And the thought leaped into my mind that if I died in his arms, it was worth it to have loved him at all.

The sandpaper tongue grazed my collarbone, licked up the side of my neck, and then tasted the spot behind my ear. His long, sharp fangs came next, pressing to the spot where my shoulder joined my neck before he nipped at the skin and trembled under me.

I squeezed and yanked, felt his cock swell further in my grip as I pumped harder, faster, and felt my own release build.

One hand moved from my thigh, his right tangling in my hair, yanking my head back as I cried out, just that much of his dominance bringing me to orgasm. I cried his name as I pumped out thick streams of semen onto his muscular, taut abdomen. I shot over my wrists, my fingers, and over the purple head of his swollen shaft a second before he found his own roaring release.

We shuddered through our aftershocks together, and when I lifted my hand to my mouth, he watched with heavy-lidded eyes as I began to lick semen from my fingers. He leaned forward, tongue out, wanting to taste, and I pressed light fingertips to the sandpaper surface, smiling, purring at the same time. He whined in the back of his throat, and I extended my own tongue, rubbing it along his, slowly, decadently, over and over until he leaned forward, wanting more. I opened my mouth, and his tongue slipped in and explored. He whimpered as his hands returned to my thighs, yanking me forward, needing me closer, tighter.

I wrapped my legs around his back, my chest now plastered to his beautiful sculpted one. Even under golden fur, the definition was still there, and as I closed my lips on his questing, thrusting tongue and sucked hard, I lost myself in the taste of him. He growled and clutched at me, one hand on my ass, kneading, squeezing, the other holding the back of my head, cradling, but his claws trapped me, rendering escape impossible. Not that moving even flickered through my consciousness.

I licked and sucked and wriggled in his lap, and when he winced at the contact of my stomach pressing against his sensitized, flagging penis, I took that moment to take a breath and nuzzle my face into the soft fur at his throat. I sighed deeply, and I heard him begin to purr. He was content, and I let the feeling flood my senses.

We were safe because we were together. Always.

Finally, I lifted my head and took in the blood and gore in the pit but also the beauty. On my left, Yusuke held her semel as he lay draped over her, heaving with aftershocks of what had to have been a bone-numbing orgasm from how exhausted he looked and how scarlet her face was. The quivering smile she gave me was embarrassed and sated at the same time.

On the opposite side of the room, Gavin Medina was in his mate's lap, head back, eyes closed, and his flaccid cock dripping with come as he lay, spent and boneless, in her arms. Teresa was stripped naked, as Yusuke and I were not, covered in scratches, but smiling down at him as they lay together in the dirt. When she turned her head and shuddered, I looked to see what was wrong.

Amirah had risen from where she had been lying close to the wall. Apparently she had been struck unconscious at some point and was now awake. The three other semels who had killed their mates circled around her but didn't come any closer; she seemed to be holding them at bay with her power.

"It's not over," she yelled before she opened her mouth and breathed out her pheromones. Hiroshi jerked in Yusuke's arms; Gavin groaned, exhausted, but his primal urges were too strong to deny; Logan, only Logan, didn't stir or move to rise, instead just tightened his arms and rubbed his chin over my shoulder, scent-marking me.

Amirah came toward us, intent, it seemed, on Logan, because he was the only semel who had not immediately responded. She strutted forward and stripped off her robe as she came, a vision as she closed in.

My first thought was that she had to be freezing. You could hang meat in the pit, and as I shivered, my mate snuggled me tighter, grunting softly, comforting me.

He only wanted me, would, if he were allowed, curl around me and go to sleep. He was exhausted—we all were—and still the horror of a reah came to try and separate us.

I was angrier than I thought.

Lifting my head, I released an angry, wild, desperate shot of nekhene power to intercept her.

She screamed and dropped to her knees, fighting, her wail unhinged and terrified. If she shifted in the pit, she was dead, and everyone knew it. That was the law.

"No!" Her shrieking got louder, and Hiroshi settled, rolling off his mate but not leaving her side. There was no allure in terror, and so he stayed where he was.

Gavin curled closer to his mate. I spared Teresa a glance as I had Yusuke, and I saw the desperate thankfulness in her gaze.

"No!" Amirah wailed, and I let it recede, inhabiting once again the mantle of reah, of love and shelter and peace.

"Yield." I found my voice, my eyes flicking to hers even as Logan took a deep breath of me, licking a long line up the side of my throat, the small whimpers making me tighten my arms and legs, the desire to climb inside his skin nearly overwhelming. "You have done your duty: three semels are only panthers, three yareahs lay dead, and three tribes will have new leaders. We're lucky, as the priest had Khongordzol inform us, that he chose no semels with children, that you have left no orphans crying for dead parents."

"I don't care!"

"But we care!" I yelled back, indicating Yusuke, Teresa, and myself. "And you can stop; you've done what was required and are now free. Is she not free?"

I lifted my head to Hamid and saw that everyone was clustered close around the edge now to see the slaughter and the sex.

"She is free," the priest said, rendering his verdict, "and no cat may ever touch her again without her leave."

I returned my eyes to her. "You're free, Amirah Fehr; you do not even have to make account of your actions to the tribe of Ariat or to the family of your semel, Terrance McCord."

She rose stiffly and smiled suddenly. "Attack me again, reah. I'll be ready this time."

"Where is your beset?" I called to her. "Let her, or him, offer you comfort and counsel now."

"Never did I need the same crutch that I have heard you have; I've never been that weak."

But needing Crane had never been anything but a blessing, and again, I felt so sorry for her to not even have a companion, not one person to always look for as a grounding force. And not that Crane was mine anymore, Logan having taken over as my touchstone, but she had no mate, no beset, and no tribe, she was utterly alone in the world. I ached for her and the pain it all must have caused.

"Attack me!" she yelled.

"Don't leverage your power against mine," I warned her. "If I pull you through your shift, you're dead. You'll be wounded and left to die outside, at the mercy of the elements and animals. It is not a death I would wish on anyone, even you. A reah is a precious thing—please don't force my hand."

"You think you can do it! You think I can't turn all these semels to slaves that will still turn on their yareahs, and their reah, and carve you into pieces?"

She was so drunk with her own power that she wasn't even listening to me.

"Please," I begged as she advanced.

"You're trembling, reah," she said snidely, "frightened of losing the man you hold clutched tight to your chest. Because whatever you think in that deluded brain of yours, he would pick a reah who is a woman that is not his over a true-mate who is a man, because, really, all you are is a sick, filthy abomination. Your bond is unnatural and unclean, and you will die now and see the semel of the tribe of Mafdet drink your blood even as he fills me with his hot seed."

"You can come live with us," I offered, meaning every word. "You can be a part of our tribe and travel the world but know that you'll always have a home to return to, where you'll be protected and cared for and loved."

She put on a show of being shocked, eyes wide. "Live in your tribe? Live in sin with the rest of your disgusting panthers? Are you kidding?" Her voice rose. "You're a monster, and you've polluted and disgraced everything you've ever touched. You should have killed yourself the moment you had your first thought to go to bed with a man. It's vile and so are you, and the bond you share with your mate is a—"

"That is your final word," I cut her off, shaking not with anger or fear but with the need to break down and sob. She was so angry and broken, and I wished, with every part that was reah, to heal her and protect her and that she would accept my offer of a place in my tribe.

She laughed at me as she exhaled heat and desire in a wave of throbbing, pulsing power.

There were gasps from above us as even the gallery was hit hard with her pheromones. Logan leaned back, looking at me, I knew, because my scent was changing. I pushed out of his grip, and he looked at me before his head swiveled fast to Amirah.

I saw the hair rise on his back, the ridge of fur that ran the length of his spine, as he bristled, became wary, ready to fight. She smelled like danger to him because I was his mate and she was threatening me. But if he killed her, he would be a panther forever just as if he slaughtered me or one of the other yareahs. I could not allow his desire to protect me to endanger him.

"Jin!"

I looked over at Yusuke, saw her dark eyes on me.

"You can't save everyone. You want to, I know you do, reah, but sometimes," she said, and her smile was full of aching sorrow as she glanced around the pit, "you can't."

"Protect your mate," Teresa called over to me. "Honor those who love you, and guard your tribe, reah of the semel-netjer."

My eyes flicked back to Amirah as she let out a call to Logan, to the other two semels, the lure of her scent and flesh drowning and overwhelming.

I exhaled and released the fury of the nekhene. It was a wild, untamed thing, but Logan Church had claimed it, held sway over it, and the energy that lived and breathed inside of me was curious about him, wanted to run with him, see if he was really strong enough to mate with. Amirah wanted to take the semel from the nekhene, and so the power blew out of me in a scalding jealous rage, exploded so that my back bowed and I gasped with the release of the ancient annihilating wrath.

If it had been two months ago, Amirah might have countered, but Crane had stripped the temptation from my power, taken away the lust and the seduction and the glamour and the allure. He could not curb my will—the essence itself was feral—but he had trained me not to call others, to instead keep them away. In the past, the energy shifted those not worthy to mate with me into panthers but still wrung sexual submission and climax from them. Now, it brought them to their knees and attacked. If I was allowed to shift, the power transformed me, worked through me, and assailed only those I could physically touch. If I couldn't shift, it blasted through whoever was in my way.

Amirah Fehr was threatening that which the nekhene found tempting and trying to steal the true-mate of a reah. She screamed when the energy hit her.

She was strong, but my moment of regret, of nurturing reah, had passed, and now I saw her with my nekhene eyes, saw only a rival for the affection of the tantalizing creature beside me.

I stood, and Logan rolled forward to his knees, sitting back on his thighs, his legs folded under him. As I pushed my fingers through his hair, he leaned into my touch.

Amirah screamed, and I heard voices from the gallery yelling, screaming.

"She chose!" I heard Hamid's voice drown out all protests. "You heard him, we all heard him—he gave her a choice! Be silent!"

Amirah collapsed in a heap, and I watched as she whimpered and whined, her body moving inexorably through the change from human to cat. Only I and members of the Shu had the ability to stop the shift once it began. It was a strength only a handful of panthers in the world possessed. I realized for the millionth time that my blink-of-an-eye shift and the mastery over it had nothing to do with being a reah and everything to do with the gift of being a nekhene cat. I was both humbled and thankful and closed my eyes as the rise in power made me tremble hard as fury slammed through me.

Crane had taught me not to fight. Embrace the ebb and flow, back and forth, the roll of the wave. And even though I was afraid, because it would hurt if he was wrong, I relaxed and let the wall down inside and exhaled my fear.

The reah I was rose up, and I felt it instantly, the change, and I was me again. The nekhene in me went still and quiet, because the fighting was unneeded, as the mate of the reah remained and all was well.

"This trial is concluded." The priest's voice boomed, and when I slowly opened my eyes, I saw Amirah heaving, yowling, curled into a ball on the floor of the pit, shifted into a golden panther.

"All of you, on the wall!"

The snap of the whip of the sheseru of the tribe of Khertet moved my mate and the other two, and when Logan rose, his hand went tight around my neck, snapping my head back, lifting my eyes to his.

"Reah," he rasped, the voice rough, hoarse, and more snarl than speech.

"Yes," I managed to get out. "Yours."

He growled low and menacing. "Mine."

I nodded even as he gripped my throat. "Yes, my semel."

He let go at the same minute he swept me up off my feet and crushed me against his broad, rock-solid chest. I was carried to the side of the pit, and he shoved me back into the wall as he, too, pressed his shoulders there.

The priest was in the pit moments later, twenty khatyu armed with traditional spears having run in before him, forming a phalanx of protection. Not that any of us had the energy to even lever off the wall.

"Remove the panthers; inform the tribe of Ptahket, Taweret, and Girdaht that the heir is now semel. Scourge the reah, and at nightfall stake her outside at the base of the mountain. These are my orders, carry out the law!" Hamid shouted.

"Surely—"

"Silence!" he yelled at Ammon. "No one may question the law; even you, semel-aten, and Amirah lost all rights for claiming when she chose not to submit to the reah of the tribe of Mafdet but to instead engage him. That is an individual challenge, the rules for which are finite. To change in the pit without permission is scourging, followed by staking and death. This is *maat*."

"Your Grace," I called over to him.

He turned to look at me.

"I beg you to contact the tribe of Ariat, speak to their current semel. Let him decide if he wants Amirah staked or sent to him to answer for the crimes against his house."

"Jin, the rules are—"

"She would still be staked, perhaps, just not this night. Find out what he wants; the justice is owed to the tribe."

"Agreed," he said, turning to Jamal. "See it done and speak to them that only on the word of the reah of the semel-netjer is this choice given to them."

We were all silent then, waiting.

"The semels will now return to their quarters until they are called for the tomorrow's trial of their sheserus."

More khatyu filed in, the priest obviously expecting the semels to resist being put back in their boxes.

They did.

When Dval Quach came for Logan, he placed iron shackles on his wrists and ankles. All his khatyu looked at me warily, feeling the hot, prickly power that swirled around me like stinging desert wind. Logan didn't want to be restrained, but because I was calm, so was he. When they began leading him toward the grate, only then did he balk, struggling to see me, calling with a stuttering, whining purr. I moved forward and he stopped, and I saw the bullwhip then in the sheseru of Khertet's hand.

"No, please," I begged, moving between him and Logan.

"He's resisting, reah, he will be flogged."

"He just doesn't understand," I said, taking hold of the shackles, leading Logan toward the gate.

Yusuke and Teresa both led their mates as well, and when we reached the open door, where I couldn't go, I reached up and put my hands on Logan's face.

"I love you and I'll see you in the morning, alright? You go eat something and sleep and wait to see me, okay?"

He leaned forward and ran his chin over the top of my head, inhaling me deeply before he bent and licked up the side of my neck.

Suddenly it was me who needed calming. I leaped at him, not caring that the robe fell away and I was naked, clutching at him, arms and legs holding tight.

Claws dug into my buttocks; teeth grazed the cord in my throat as he purred loudly. I knew then that with each day, the parting would be worse, would get harder for both of us, and that that, too, was part of the test. It was a horrible thing, parting mates that mentally, physically, chemically, and emotionally were supposed to be together. Nothing intuitive about forced separation. It was obscene, and the nekhene in me didn't like it.

"Jin" came Crane's call.

I lifted my head, and Logan snarled loudly.

"No, no," Crane soothed, and I had no idea why he was in the pit. He went down on hands and knees and let his head drop down between his shoulder blades.

Logan walked back over to him, knelt with my weight in his arms, and ran his nose up the back of Crane's neck. And my best friend smelled like him, and me, and the others, and they were all scents Logan knew. When Crane sat up and then back on his knees, Logan knelt and put me in his arms. He then nuzzled my hair, gave me a low growl, rose quickly, and walked without a backward glance to the grate.

After he was gone from sight, I turned to look at my friend's face. "How did you know?"

Crane took off his parka and wrapped me in it, since I was naked and starting to shiver. "He's a semel, Jin, and since he claimed you, he's not a wild creature anymore, he's a werepanther. He gets that you're his, and he wasn't about to leave you in here unguarded."

"He could have killed you."

I got an indulgent smile. "I smell like you, Jin, and since he knows that you belong to him and that I belong to you—he's okay with leaving you with me to care for."

"Shit, Crane, when did you start seeing things so different?" I said, slipping out of his arms to stand up.

He rose beside me. "When you took a chance on becoming a reah," he told me, signaling for the others to come close.

"Did you get permission to be down here?"

"It's over," he told me, tipping his head at Yusuke and Teresa, who had both been engulfed by members of their entourage. "Now we gotta get you showered and warm."

"Yes, please," I said as my legs went out from under me.

I didn't want to lean on Crane, because he was still not 100 percent healed himself.

"Jin."

I turned to look at him.

"I'm good," he said, nodding.

And all the emotion came flooding out of me as he shook his head before he grabbed me. As I felt the others around us, crushing us, pressing, holding tight, I gave up and let them care for me. For once.

Chapter Fourteen

IT WAS horrible. The tribe of Ariat, though very appreciative of my offer, wanted Amirah Fehr dead right then. It made sense that Orso Bataar owned an Iridium satellite phone, otherwise he would be truly out of touch with the rest of the werepanther world. His Internet connection was of similar origin but it hardly mattered to me. Only the judgment mattered. The tribe of Ariat didn't want to see Amirah ever again, at least not alive. The semel, Terrance McCord's brother, Angel McCord, wanted a picture of what the reah looked like in the morning after all her blood had run from her body and the animals had been at her.

I found the practice of staking utterly vile and cruel and obscene. But I had done all I could, tried to delay and give her that hope. But in the end, Dval Quach ripped a hole in her side, and he and his khatyu took her outside in the sub-zero temperature and left her, screaming her pain into the howling wind. The only comfort was that there were no animals around at all, and we all knew she was going to freeze to death before long.

Inside the ger, I lay between Crane and Yuri, shivering with horror and cold. Staking went against every reah instinct I had.

"Get your ass up and let's go sit by the stove and talk," Crane told me after an hour of trying to get me to close my eyes.

Once I was there, all the others joined us.

Mikhail boiled water for tea, and we sat there huddled together, no one saying a word.

"What the hell are you all doing?" Domin asked as he came in from outside, shaking snow from his hair and beard.

I was glad he had been allowed to join us; every maahes was reunited with his tribe now that the sepat had officially begun.

"Jin's sad about Amirah," Crane told him.

Domin crossed the felt-covered floor to me and squatted down. "What were your options, my reah?"

"I know that logically, I—"

"Jin," he cut me off. "She took away your choices. And yeah, maybe if we'd have gotten hold of her, us, your tribe, maybe we could have healed her, but, Jin… how things stood in that pit—it was her or you, and if Logan had reached her, he would have killed her. There was no lust riding him, only fury, and if he had eviscerated her, then he would have been next, and then you. I know you feel like shit right now, but I want you and Logan alive more than I wanted Amirah Fehr to keep breathing."

I nodded.

"I promise to try and save everyone else I can from now on, okay?"

"Yes." I smiled at him.

Domin rose, and my eyes followed him until my head was tipped back so I could still hold his gaze. "And so you know, she's dead already. It didn't take long. The cold is merciful. If this was summer, she would have been mauled and mutilated. Everything happens for a reason, Jin. You gotta believe that."

I put my head in my hands and cried silently for the only other reah I had ever heard of, and Domin's fingers in my hair were comforting.

"I have an idea."

Slowly, I lifted my head to look at my maahes.

"Let's go for a run. The speed and our fur will protect us. C'mon, see if you and Taj can outrun me."

Taj scoffed and Domin laughed, and Yuri was already stripping as Mikhail stood up to join him.

"I'll stay here." Crane yawned, giving me his lopsided grin. "And feed the stove."

"Me too," Danny told us, annoyed with all of us for reasons I didn't understand.

"Oh fuck no," Crane groused. "You go with them."

"Agreed," Andrian told him. "I'll keep Crane company, the rest of you get the hell out."

So all of us except Crane and Andrian shot out the door of the ger and flew out into the deep snow. It was like running into a wall of icy wind for a moment, until I let myself stop thinking and just feel. The others were already running, sprinting across the icy terrain, and when I joined them, streaking by, only Taj catching me, I felt the thrill of being in my panther form.

The only thing that compared to running, which as fast as I moved across the ground felt more like flying, was being in bed with Logan Church. I was as addicted to being under the man as I was to the freedom of shifting into the animal that lived curled around my heart.

I ran on and on, and when Taj and I were joined by others, I knew from the scent that I was looking at Jamal Hassan, the phocal of the Shu, the protector of the priest of Chae Rophon. The Shu, the fastest, strongest cats in the world, were the only ones who could match my speed. It was a pleasure to have company to run with, and I felt the singing joy infuse my entire being.

We climbed so high we could see the whole valley stretched out below us. There was no way to see where earth stopped and heaven began, and the midnight blue sky, the black clouds, the diamond-cut snow were breathtaking. I shifted fast, a man again atop the precipice, hair blowing in the wailing wind, head back, eyes closed, arms outstretched; I felt like I could fly. Stretching my arms wide, I jumped.

I soared through the air, and as I neared the ground, I shifted so I could turn the falling dive into a leap and touch the snow. I got my feet under me and bolted forward, and the surge of speed took the velocity and channeled it so I was again streaking across the valley floor. No one had followed, could follow. I was the only nekhene cat in existence, and while that should have been sobering and sad, I belonged to my mate and my tribe, and so I could never be unclaimed and float away.

But I didn't want to be alone, so I ran sideways and leaped high, landing in the powder, falling into it and going still. There was only the wind and the blue sky and the snowflakes that fell like tiny diamonds, each sparkling in the light. The others appeared beside me after long minutes, and Jamal, because he was the only one who could shift fast enough not to freeze in the snow, even stronger than Taj, stood for a second to say that I was breathtaking.

I shifted, naked as he was, and smiled at him.

"Your speed is phenomenal, Jin," he yelled at me over the wind. "You might see one day if you could run over water—I bet you could."

I had been wondering about that myself but would never confess to it.

Jamal shifted and so did I, before we both froze, and we took off toward the ger. As I charged back, I saw Crane open the front door and lean out, looking for me.

He smiled when he saw me, and I saw a shadow move at the same time. Something was close to him, and I couldn't reach him. I was too far away.

I couldn't save him. I wouldn't be there.

Again.

He would die, and it would be the second time I failed to protect my best friend, the man who held a piece of my heart.

My vision went white, and there was nothing.

INHALING DEEPLY because the smell, a mixture of pine, wet earth, and fire, was intoxicating, I let out a deep purr of contentment before I opened my eyes. Instantly, my bleary gaze met the golden one of my mate. Lifting my head, he growled softly, still petting me, stroking my muzzle with his razor-sharp clawed hands.

"Oh thank God," Crane breathed.

Turning my head, I saw him through the bars of the cell and wondered why he was locked up.

"Not me, idiot," he snapped irritably, reading my mind like he could sometimes.

It took a minute before I realized I was in Logan's cell.

"Jin."

Looking to the left, I saw the priest of Chae Rophon, and then I finally registered the others. Apparently in the dungeon of the tribe of Khertet, the cells were free-standing squares, not interconnected, and on all four sides of Logan's were people and more people, jockeying for position to peer in at me. My mate and I were on display.

I whimpered, and Logan was suddenly there, leaning against me, the claws buried in my fur, face pressed to the side of my neck as he simply breathed. His warmth, his scent, all soothed me, and I put my head down on my paws before returning my eyes to the priest. Logan crawled on top of me, arms and legs hanging down around me, and just let me feel his weight.

"Listen to me," Hamid said gently after several minutes. "Ammon El Masry sent two cats to your campsite tonight to kill your beset, as we had all heard that he was the one who had helped you with the control of your nekhene power. He had not thought, none of us did, that you could run up the side of a mountain and simply leap off and return so quickly."

There were whispers and murmurs from those crowding around us, and I got the idea that what I had done was a bigger deal than I had registered at the time.

"You and you alone arrived in time to save Crane Adams, though as beset of a reah, I truly believe that he could have easily handled two assassins."

"Agreed," Crane groused, and when I looked at him, I saw his scowl. "We are so gonna talk about this."

And it was funny, really. Here was the priest and everyone—all the people who come with the semels, the semel of Khertet, the tribe of Khertet, everybody except Ammon—and Crane was there, like normal, giving me grief like it was just the two of us and he was pissed off. It was nuts.

"Regardless, you eviscerated the assassins, and after they were killed and the alarm was raised, we found ourselves faced with a nekhene cat that none of us could control."

I waited for what came next.

"Ammon has been placed under guard in seclusion, and he, too, has been ordered to change into his werepanther form. He has also requested that the final one-on-one trial between him and the challenger include the maahes so that now, your maahes will be unable to compete in the challenge of the heart. You must choose another to stand beside you."

He was acting like it was bad news. I would much rather have Domin with Logan in the final challenge than standing beside me in mine.

"You must shift and tell me who will stand with your beset, Crane Adams, Andrian Basargin, and yourself."

I looked at Crane and saw the concern on his face.

"Nekhene."

My eyes returned to the priest.

"You were following the scent of the assassins back to Ammon and would have disemboweled him, as well, had you found him."

I was scared to hear what I had done.

"Many of Orso's khatyu were wounded before the counsel of your beset was heeded."

Again, I was looking at Crane.

"It's why you find yourself here, Jin; your beset had us release your semel, and he found you quickly and brought you here."

I had no memory of anything.

"You would follow your semel anywhere, it seems."

Of course I would; the man was my mate, and I loved him.

As soon as I thought it—*mate*—I was me and being pinned to the dirt floor under two hundred pounds of shifted creature that was my semel.

"Oh blessed be Ra," Hamid gasped, and even though I knew he was right there, knew everyone was watching us along with him, I just didn't care.

"Logan." I breathed his name, laughing because I couldn't help it. He was squashing me.

He moved fast, and I felt a hand on the small of my back telling me not to move, not to run, before both clawed hands were on my hips, lifting my ass in the air. The swipe of tongue over my right cheek gave me an idea of what he wanted.

The first purr was involuntary, as was the second one, when his fangs traced down the curve of my buttocks to the back of my thighs. He inhaled deeply, my musky scent apparently just as alluring as his was to me, and even as I wondered at his agenda, I realized I didn't really care.

"Jin."

Crane's voice cut heat like nothing else, and the fog of passion cleared enough for me to lift up and look over my shoulder at my mate.

His eyes were golden slits of primal, carnal need, and his mouth was open, panting. The urge to submit had me teetering on the verge of begging.

He let his pheromones loose between us, and when he heard my deep, dark moan, he came forward, his sweat-damp fur sliding over my own slick skin until his engorged shaft notched into the curve of my ass. I leaned forward to angle down so I could take him inside me.

"Jin."

Logan bristled instantly at the intrusion, and claws scraped my skin.

"Honey."

I lifted my head so I could see over Logan's shoulder and find Crane.

Honey.

He never called me honey. The last time he had used it had been in Sobek after I had a panic attack.

"Can you come out?"

Out? Why the hell would I want to leave my mate? The nekhene in me was uneasy with the thought.

"No," Domin commanded, and all eyes were on him.

"Do not let your power rise, you spoiled fuckin' brat. Get the hell out of there; we've got a sepat to finish, and you're not allowed to fuck your mate right now. Think about Logan seeing you and then having you taken away and then given back—how screwed up do you want him to be?"

He was talking about my mate, whom I loved. My semel... and I was his reah.

I took a breath, steadying myself, before I leaned free of his grip, crawled forward, and stood up. I was looking down at him for only a second, and then he was mirroring my movement, rising, staring at me. I took a step back and he followed instantly, stalking me. This was, after all, his favorite game.

"Shit," I whispered, knowing there was no way I was getting out.

"I can go in and distract him," Mikhail suggested.

"He'll tear you apart," Yuri assured him.

"Jin."

I glanced at Crane.

"Just put him on the ground, on his knees, and let him know it's okay and then walk out."

How could I explain that even when Logan was a man, he liked this game? There were private things between my mate and me that no one else should or could know.

"Just wait," Domin said, and we all heard the creak of the cell door as he came inside with my mate and me.

Logan's roar of outrage as he turned and charged his maahes was horrible.

I yelled for Domin to run.

The priest cried out in fear.

Hundreds of voices overlapped, and I caught Yuri's in the mix, the terror hard to hear. But Domin only went to his knees and tipped his neck sideways, offering.

Logan reached him, and there were screams from the assembled crowd, but he only grasped Domin's shoulder hard, tight, put claws deep into it, embedded, and bent his mouth to the vulnerable flesh. I held my breath and then took one when everyone else did as only my mate's nose grazed over Domin's skin.

He breathed in the scent of his maahes, and Domin lifted his hands and put them on Logan's face.

"Your control, semel-netjer, is greater than any of these people can even guess. You and I, how many times have we done this, practiced this, knowing as we did that this day would come?"

They had? When had Logan and Domin become so close? How had I missed it? Maybe, just maybe, Domin leaving the house had hurt Logan more than he told anyone, even me. Maybe he was angrier at Koren than any of us knew, for driving away not only the prince of his tribe, but his friend.

Logan turned his head and pressed his nose into Domin's palm.

"Go to Yuri, Jin."

I stood and moved toward them.

"Don't touch either of us," Domin ordered.

And even though I wanted to, I knew that reaching for Logan would serve no one, especially not my mate. I needed to go.

When I walked through the cell door, Yuri was there to receive me with a heavy wool blanket that he wrapped me up in from head to toe.

"Fuck," he groaned, rubbing my arms, my back, tightening the blanket around my neck. "You scared the shit outta me."

I turned to look back in the cell and saw Domin rise, leaving Logan on his knees, head lowered, in pain, I could tell.

He wanted to be a man, not a beast, and it was slowly tearing his heart out of his chest.

I felt tears well up hot behind my eyes as I took several deep breaths.

Logan was on his feet fast, not chasing Domin but rushing to where I was. He thrust a clawed hand out toward me through the bars, reaching, grasping, and pressing as hard as he could, trying to get hold of me.

I had to go.

"No," Crane warned me, barring my path as Logan screamed out his rage.

The nekhene did not understand, and I felt my skin flush with heat as the power rose. I needed to get to my mate. *Had to.*

Yuri's hands tightened on me so I couldn't move.

"Listen to me." Crane's voice washed over me right before I started to shift.

My head tipped up, and all I saw was blue.

"Soothe him, he's your mate, my reah. Give him solace, not pain."

Solace.

Love.

I stepped around him and looked into the tortured eyes of my mate. He looked wild and hurt and angry, in a frenzy now, bashing himself against the bars with his need to claim what was his, have what was his beside him, wrapped around him.

He would tear himself apart trying to shove flesh through metal.

Reah.

I belonged to my semel; I was his true-mate, and even as I let the love I felt for the man flow out of me, thought of how much he meant to me, my touchstone, I watched his struggle subside, saw the gentle calm creep over him, engulf him, and give him peace. His melted-gold eyes closed, and I could hear him take a last heaving breath before he took a step back from the bars, shivering hard.

My mate was my other half, and while that was beautiful, it was also terrifying, because we had so much sway over each other that it bordered on a control that could be crippling if misused. He was strong and virile and proud, and I could reduce him to a shattered husk if I wanted.

And he could do the same to me.

"Jin."

I turned my own wounded eyes to Hamid as he closed in on me.

"I apologize for insisting that you and your mate take part in the sepat, for to inflict a forced separation on true-mates is cruel. I forgot what enduring it looked like on both of you and had thought only to have the semel-netjer as semel-aten when I spoke Logan's name to the council of Ennead. Forgive me."

But I couldn't do it with my heart breaking. "You asked earlier for a name, and I tell you now that Taj Chalthoum will join Andrian, Crane, and me in the pit to defend my semel."

He nodded. "As he is a member of your tribe, and soon to be, I understand, an aker, he will be allowed into the pit."

I nodded.

"We request permission to retire," Yuri growled, and without warning, he turned and grabbed me and threw me over his back. He didn't move until the priest gave him leave, but the second it came, he turned and strode away from the cells where all the other semels were held, up toward the pit.

"This is very caveman of you," I sighed, "but the blood is rushing to my head."

"The priest shouldn't be sorry he did this to you and Logan, he should be ashamed of himself. It's a fuckin' ordeal," he snarled. "And all those people looking, watching like it's a freak show, not understanding that it's killing him, that this is eating his heart out—fuck!"

He was angry, furious for Logan and for me, and I felt it rolling off him. "Put me down and let's walk together, okay?"

Once he set me on my feet, we were joined by Domin and Crane.

"Are you alright?" Crane asked me.

I swallowed hard, trying so hard to keep my power from rising, to stay in control, contained, and not let my pain show.

"Jin."

I turned my head to Domin.

"My reah," he said, and his voice was low and husky. "Everything's gonna be okay."

He blurred, and I understood I was falling apart.

"God," he sighed, smiling suddenly before he grabbed me tight and wrapped me up in strong arms. "We didn't think we were gonna get you back, and then Crane had that brilliant idea to get you to Logan. I envy him the power he has in you, Jin, but that bond, the one between a semel and his reah, must really be crazy, because shit—the power is something."

I let him hold me and tried to breathe.

"Jin."

My gaze lifted to Taj as he and Andrian moved where I could see them.

"I've never experienced a run like the one you took us on tonight. Thank you for that and for allowing us to be there to show all of us what the love between a semel and his mate should look like."

I pulled away from Domin and bowed to Taj.

He returned the bow, and when I straightened I felt better, more me.

"Jin," Taj murmured.

I could barely speak.

Taj was the same but managed to get out a very rusty-sounding thank-you.

"You can't ever go back to the Shu," I told him. "You understand?"

There was a quick nod from him. "I do," he said, his voice gravelly and low. "And I thank you and Logan for making me part of your tribe and showing me what a true home is. I will not fail you, you know I won't. I'll stand with you and Crane and Andrian and kill anyone that tries to hurt any of you."

"It's just Logan."

"It's never been just Logan," he assured me, giving me a trace of a smile. "And he would agree with me if he were able."

I really didn't want to fall apart right there with people starting to close in on us, milling around, looking at the freaky reah. Domin had said I was in my nekhene form for a while, so that meant I had been gawked at and pointed at and basically been on exhibit with my mate. It was horrible and it wasn't over yet, and now on top of it, Taj's heartfelt confession was going to make me cry.

I wanted to run away.

"Listen," Crane said, draping an arm around my shoulders. "We're gonna get you cleaned up, okay? You're covered in the blood of dead men."

I nodded.

"But Yuri's gonna hafta carry you again, because you don't have any shoes, and you'll get frostbite if you walk in the snow, even with your body temperature. You and Taj talking out in the snow in human form tonight was not bright."

My gaze flicked to him.

"Domin told me. Not smart, Jin."

Apparently I was making all kinds of poor decisions lately.

"Don't do the poor-me bullshit. Just let Yuri carry you, and I'm gonna wrap your feet in another blanket, alright?"

I didn't argue.

Once we were outside, I felt so much better even though, really, the cold sucked all the air from my lungs.

Behind the ger was a shower enclosed with clear plastic walls on all four sides, a protected, sealed heater on the top and warm, flat, smooth river stones on the bottom. It was like stepping into a sauna. You had to pour hot water into the base and it cycled and was pumped up a pipe, and then it rained liquid down on you from the shower head. The water had been brought from the home of Orso Bataar, from the hot spring that ran under the cave, on the order of his yareah. It was carried out to us in huge insulated tubs by several members of the tribe of Khertet.

"What exactly did happen?" I asked Crane as I stood under the water.

"Wash the blood out of your hair, Jin."

"Talk, then."

"Fine, wash."

I did as he asked while he explained.

Two cats had come to kill Crane because, as Hamid had explained, Ammon wanted my best friend dead. With Crane gone, he felt my control would slip, and with me gone, Logan would not be far behind. It was smart, it was a good plan, but he had counted on Crane being broken, which he wasn't, and me being much less in control of myself than I was. His information on both counts was faulty.

"Did I really tear them apart?"

"Yes," Crane assured me. "It was fast, faster than anything I've ever seen, it was like they were yanked into thin air and blown up. There were only scattered pieces left."

I started retching.

"Stop," he ordered. "You saved me, even though two guys, Jin— c'mon, I've faced five before and been okay, just me."

"You're still hurt," I barely got out, my voice garbled, my eyes watering like they did after a bout of heaving.

"I'm pretty strong, Jin," he insisted. "You have to stop letting your heart stop every time you think something might happen to me."

I nodded.

"Less talking, more rinsing," Yuri said as he poured another huge tub of scalding hot water into the basin in a continuous stream, letting Crane concentrate on pumping only. By the time it reached me, it was only warm, the air cooling it that fast, the heater making sure I didn't freeze, as well as the rocks at my feet.

"How long was I in my nekhene form?"

"A long fuckin' time," Yuri grumbled, sounding angry and hurt at the same time.

"You shift so fast for Logan," Crane told me. "But not for the rest of us."

I heard his voice tremble. "You guys were worried I wasn't shifting back."

They didn't need to answer me for me to know it was true.

"Did anyone else see me in my nekhene form?"

"Everyone," Yuri told me. "All those rubberneckers you saw. And you scared the crap out of all of them, the entire tribe of Khertet, their semel, all the other yareahs and their retinues, and Danny," he finished with a heavy sigh.

I looked at him through the plastic as warm water sluiced over me. "But not you guys, right? You weren't scared, were you, Yuri?"

"No, my reah." He smiled at me. "You never scare me or any of those that truly know you and your heart."

"And no one from my tribe was—"

"No," Crane answered, passing shampoo and shower gel in through the folds of the shower wall to me. "Now hurry up before we all freeze."

I showered as fast as I could, but there was still ice in my hair when I stepped inside the ger twenty minutes later.

Everyone was there, sitting, sipping hot tea, bundled up. After I changed behind the partition, I joined them, taking a seat beside Mikhail in the circle.

"God, it must be late." Danny yawned, sharing a heavy quilt with Andrian, leaning against him.

"It is," Yuri agreed, also having changed, ready to take a seat.

Domin looked up, and I saw my sheseru's cobalt eyes hit those of my maahes. He lifted the quilt, inviting, and Yuri sat down beside him, letting Domin put the cover around him before he scooted close, pressing into the smaller man's side.

The muscles in Yuri's jaw flexed, quivered, and I wondered about that for a second before Crane dropped down beside me and wrapped me in a heavy quilt, getting comfortable, shoulder to shoulder with me.

"Yuri."

My sheseru looked over at Danny.

"Are you ready for the challenge today?"

He nodded, his eyes drooping. "I am, I just—I need to sleep, and even though I'm exhausted, I don't think I can."

"You can," Domin told him. "And we all should."

"Agreed," Mikhail said, and as he was the sylvan in our midst, we all deferred to him.

I asked Yuri to take the partition down because I didn't want to be separated from the others even by a slip of silken gauze. He smiled at me as he removed it.

A half an hour later, snuggled between Crane and Mikhail, I fell asleep fast, exhaustion blindsiding me.

THE SCENT of arousal woke me, hard and aching, three hours later. I sat up and looked around and instantly was pulled back down. I was faced with eyes glinting in the darkness, those of my sylvan.

"What're you doing?" I whispered.

"If you make a fuckin' noise and do anything to mess this up for him—reah or no reah, I swear to God I will smother you to death with your pillow."

I was still asleep, I had to be.

"Did you hear me?"

"What are you talking about?" I said under my breath, being quiet enough that no one but him, or Crane on the other side, could have heard me.

He made a sign for me to lift up a little.

I moved just enough to see over the top of his head, and there, in the flickering glow of the lanterns, on the furs closest to the stove, were Yuri and Domin.

Yuri was positioned facedown with his ass in the air. His hand was on his enormous rigid shaft, jerking, tugging, pulling as he strove for release at the same time Domin pistoned inside of him from behind. Domin's hands were braced on Yuri's flanks, and if the look on the face of my sheseru was any indication, he was teetering on the edge of a shattering orgasm. I had never seen the look of absolute bliss on the man's face before, ever.

My head thunked down as I turned to look at Mikhail. "Since when?"

"Since when what?" he answered, which was impressively done because I "heard" every word without him making any noise at all. He enunciated perfectly.

"Yuri likes Domin?"

He pointed beside me, and when I turned, I saw that over Crane's left shoulder was where all the luggage had been stacked. It was quite the pile, and at that moment it could not have been more perfect.

It took long minutes of maneuvering to get us both over my best friend, who luckily slept like the dead, and down on the other side of the suitcase, duffel bag, and backpack mountain. As I faced a grinning Mikhail, I realized that in all the time I'd known the man, I could count the times he'd smiled at me. He was not a man given to shows of affection.

"Talk."

He shrugged broad shoulders as we huddled close together, whispering. "Yuri Kosa has been in love with Domin Thorne since he was sixteen years old."

"What? How?"

"Why would Logan just allow a man that tried to kill him to be his maahes? Why would he care about that man's tribe?"

"Logan cares about all tribes, he cares about everyone."

"Not enough to allow a viper into his home."

"He let Abbot George into the house, and he nearly killed me," I reminded my sylvan.

"He let a sheseru in training into his home, but he never thought for a minute that someone wouldn't be there with you at all times. He was certain that Yuri would never leave you unattended with Abbot."

"That wasn't Yuri's fault," I defended him.

"It *was* Yuri's fault," Mikhail told me. "But that was when he thought that everyone was as mindful as him. He thought that you would be fine because the burden of the protection didn't just fall to him. Now he knows better."

"But then—"

"But we're talking about before that, we're talking about when it was brand new—Logan would have never let anyone he didn't know live in his house. Abbot was visiting; I'm talking about a permanent fixture in the house. Why would he do that?"

"Why would he do that?" I echoed the question.

"Think."

"Because Logan and Domin had history," I said, the truth hitting me.

"Exactly."

"Why didn't he explain?"

"It has nothing to do with you."

"Tell me."

"We all went to school together: me, Logan, Yuri, Domin, and Christophe. We've known each other forever. But Domin never saw Yuri, only Logan and then Koren."

"Domin had a crush on Logan?"

"We all had a crush on Logan; it's the lure of the semel. When they first shift, their pheromones—you know, it's crazy; all anyone wants to do is roll over and submit, men and women alike."

It was true; a semel's first shift was a heady thing for the entire tribe.

"You don't know until later, until you sort things out, whether what you're feeling is real or not. Me and Christophe figured out that we were straight, Yuri that he was bi, and Domin that he was gay. But then when Domin shifted, Yuri knew who he really wanted in the whole forever-and-ever way."

I nodded. "And when Christophe shifted?"

"Christophe's shift came so long after Logan's and Domin's that by then Logan had asked me to be his sylvan and Yuri to be his sheseru, so we were all separated already."

"How did Domin choose Ivan and Markel?"

"He met Markel at a club, and they got in a fight that ended with Domin holding him down and asking him to be his sheseru, and Ivan was the son of Domin's father's sylvan, so it made sense."

"I see."

"It's great that Logan's going to make Markel and Ivan both akers when we get home, they deserve that."

"Yes, they do."

He waited for what I would say next.

"So because Logan and Domin had a history, that's why he made him his maahes."

He widened his eyes, gave me a subtle nod of his head.

I heard breath catch from the other side of the ger, there was a hiss of pain/pleasure, and then purring, whining, and soft, urgent whimpering. Scents came as well, the telltale smell of semen and sweat.

Leaning sideways so I could see around the mound, I saw Yuri's head twisted back, over his shoulder, and Domin kissing him hard, grinding his mouth down over my sheseru's, claiming him. Yuri's tears surprised me, as did his trembling and the low moan that escaped as Domin fisted his hand in the bigger man's hair, holding tight. The angle, the pressure, Domin's weight—the entire action was suggestive of a kind of domination I would have never guessed my hulking, scary sheseru wanted.

Low growl, and I turned back to Mikhail. "What?"

"Stop that," he scolded.

"But they're so pretty together." I smiled at my sylvan. "And hot."

His scowl was dark.

"You knew, all this time."

"Of course." He squinted at me. "Like you know Crane, I know Yuri."

"And so Yuri's been what, pining away?"

"Not pining, hoping."

"Hoping that Domin would get over Koren?"

"And every other guy," Mikhail grunted, and even in the quiet I could hear the bitterness in his tone. "Yuri's been breaking his heart over Domin since he was sixteen, like I said."

"Sex changes nothing."

He shook his head. "It will, you'll see. Domin's not stupid anymore, when he feels the love that's there, ready, waiting, he'll claim it. Before, when he was a semel, he was a self-destructive, vain, egoistical piece of shit. But when Logan beat him in the pit, made him maahes, he started to change. I mean, Yuri died a little when he started up with Koren, but I knew it was only a matter of time."

"What?"

"I knew it wouldn't last."

I studied his profile in the darkness.

"Jin?"

"Domin wanted Koren for a long time."

"And my guess is that it was mutual."

"But?"

"But this is Koren we're talking about."

I thought about that.

"What?"

"I was so happy when Koren finally stood up for Domin, when he took a stand and said that Domin was the one he loved."

"He never said that," Mikhail corrected me. "He showed the man affection in front of the rest of us, but there were never any words. You told Logan's father that if Koren became Domin's mate it would be cause for celebration, but Koren never chimed in that that was what he wanted. Think back, it wasn't."

And he was right, but I didn't want him to be. I still wanted to think of Koren as wanting Domin at least at one time.

"Koren's always been like that, Jin. He's different from Logan and Russ and Delphine; he's never had any backbone at all. They all look alike, even her, but that's as far as it goes."

"You don't like him."

"No, I never did, but I didn't start hating him until he was dicking Domin around, because while he was doing that, he was killing Yuri too."

I stared at Mikhail and realized that we never talked, just him and me. I had really been missing out.

"But this time, Koren made it permanent. He finally cut deep enough to sever the bond between him and Domin."

I had felt that too.

"Domin's finally over it. He grew his spine back, and for once I'm glad."

"Yeah."

"Did you see him that last night with Logan before we came here?"

I had, I just didn't think anyone else did. "He seemed like he wasn't bleeding over Koren anymore," I whispered back.

He nodded.

"So maybe he can finally see Yuri."

"God, I hope so," Mikhail sighed softly. "I want it for him so fuckin' bad."

"You want what?"

"I want Yuri to get what he deserves."

We were silent and heard the rustling, the movement, as two bodies that had been involved in something that resisted cold were finally at a stopping place and so were assaulted by the frigid air.

I held my breath, and so did Mikhail.

When it was quiet again, both of us lifted up because, shit, we had to look. We had to see.

Domin was on his side and Yuri was spooned around him, his face nuzzled into Domin's hair, his bicep under the smaller man's head. I watched Yuri's nostrils flare, Domin's scent causing him to sigh contently.

I sat back down at the same time Mikhail did.

"You know, you worrying about Yuri's happiness—that's kind of great."

"It's what you do for your friends."

And when he turned and smiled at me, I fell in love with him just a little.

Chapter Fifteen

THE TRIAL of blood was vicious. Everything I thought it would be was wrong. I had pictured a sheseru in the center of the pit standing still using only his pheromones and willpower to basically calm the raging panthers that came at him one after another. From the texts, from everything I had ever read, that was my understanding.

What I sat and witnessed was simply an attack. The sheseru was put into the pit and eight panthers were released, and he used brute force to either wrestle them into submission, render them unconscious, or kill them. When I realized that all it was, was a brawl, I was thankful that Yuri had worked so hard, day and night, building up his stamina, his muscles, and his agility. It did not make it easier to watch.

The khatyu were all from the tribe of Rahotep, and I was thankful at least that these were men loyal to Ammon and not members of the tribe of Khertet. I didn't like the idea of the host tribe losing members because of my household, even if it was a trial. Normally any cats participating in a challenge where they attacked another were paid menat, or tribute, and this was passed to their families. So if Ammon's men were killed, their families would be compensated. I hated the practice that seemed, in my opinion, a way for the semel in charge of the challenges to feel better about the fact that even if men were dying, their families would be cared for. And while I liked that, liked knowing that the tribe itself would care for its own and take responsibility, I understood that the trials themselves were antiquated and, as Logan's little brother was fond of saying, barbaric.

Watching Yuri fight for his life amidst snapping jaws and shredding claws, feeling the bloodlust that filled the pit, was brutal. I held my breath knowing that one slip, one wrong turn, a second of hesitation, indecision, would allow my sheseru to be slaughtered. I was nauseated watching it, but to look away, even for a second, would shame Yuri. My regard was as important as his defense of Logan and the display of his power so that others could see that the tribe of Mafdet had a fearsome sheseru.

When it was finally done, Yuri Kosa still stood, washed in blood, his and others', but the important part was that he was on his feet. The second Hamid called the challenge done, they released Logan into the pit with him. This was the final stage, to see if the shifted semel in his werepanther form would tear his bloody, bruised sheseru to shreds.

Logan flew over to Yuri, who slowly went to his knees, and when he was there, staring up at Logan Church, he simply waited for whatever came.

My mate slid a clawed hand down his sheseru's throat, leaned in, inhaled the scent of blood and sweat, nuzzled the wet hair, and then turned away, looking for me. When he saw me, he called out, and the long painful roar was hard to listen to after the carnage I had just been forced to witness.

I wanted Yuri the hell out of there, I wanted Logan out of there, and I wanted us all on a plane flying home. When the priest proclaimed the trial concluded and Yuri victorious, I ran from the edge so I could throw up without anyone seeing.

It was Yuri's trial first, and then the sheseru of the tribe of Nebthet, and then the sheseru of the tribe of Reshep. It would take all day.

AS IT turned out, I was not the only one who was sick. People fled at different intervals, and some didn't make it out in time.

The spectacle was ghastly, and no one was unaffected. When I was finally able to return to my quarters, dragging in after dark, numb and exhausted, still shaking, I found everyone there but Yuri and Domin.

"Where are they?" I asked Mikhail.

"Yuri had to shift and eat and drink, so Domin went with him once he had gorged on meat and drank more water than I even thought was possible."

"You saw him, though? You sat with him?"

"I fed him," he said, smiling at me. "And he's sore and he needs to sleep and—"

"He'll probably have nightmares for weeks," I said, flopping down beside the stove. I was tired of being cold too. I just wanted to go home.

"Why would he have nightmares?" Mikhail seemed surprised.

"Because he was attacked by panthers," I said like it was obvious.

"It was a trial, Jin, and Yuri can separate that in his head. He did what he did for Logan, for our tribe... for you. It's over, and if he dreams about it at all, it won't be the horror part, only the victory part."

"You're so sure."

"Very. I'm very sure."

I was silent for a few minutes. "So he went to shift?"

He looked at me. "That's what he told everyone."

"But they needed to be alone."

"They took bedrolls, so the chances of you seeing your sheseru and your maahes before the morning are very slight," Mikhail said with a chuckle. "Yuri is gonna do his damndest to make the man his before we go home. I'm sure he wishes this trip would never end."

"And all I want it to be is over."

"Agreed." Mikhail sniffled, glancing around the room. "We're all wrung out and ready to turn on each other."

"Who wants hot chocolate?" Crane asked as he walked over to us, beaming, eyes glinting china blue in the low light.

"Most of us," I said to Mikhail even as I smiled up at my best friend, accepting the steaming mug as my sylvan got dibs on the next one.

Andrian and Taj and Danny could not have been more appreciative of Crane Adams making it feel a little less like a nightmare we were living through and a lot more like home.

"I got my portable DVD player fired up to watch *The Hangover*, figured we could all use the laugh, ya know?"

So I sat there in a heap with the others, and they were all laughing as I used Crane's thigh for a pillow and he stroked my hair as I passed out. It was the only good part of the whole shitty day.

CHULUUN HAD come looking for Yuri, and when Crane told him that he was not there, he smiled knowingly and trudged back the way he had come, toward the rock-carved home of his semel.

"Mikhail talked to me."

I rolled my head on the pillow to look at Danny.

"You were right."

"I didn't need to be," I said.

"I know."

"Hero worship is okay, and I get thinking Mikhail is amazing, because he is."

He nodded. "I've just been so scared, Jin, and I'm grasping at everyone, Mikhail, Yuri, even Logan, to try and make me safe."

"Well, that actually is your semel's job, you know, to keep you safe."

"But I've been so frantic to find a mate and thinking that if it couldn't be Mikhail, then it should be Yuri, because he actually is gay—"

"Bi," I corrected. "But since we both have eyes, you know as well as I do that the only thing Yuri really is, is into Domin."

He grinned at me. "Yeah."

"So what's your plan now?"

"I have a lot of things I wanna do, and I think that I should do them before I think about finding a mate."

"Like what?"

"Going to school, for one," he said, "but I'm gonna need to talk to you and Logan about a loan so I can start."

"College is a good plan," I assured him. "We can make that happen."

"Thank you, Jin."

"Of course. My father took so much time grooming you to be a sylvan that he forgot to let you live at all."

He didn't argue.

THE FOLLOWING morning Mikhail and I were summoned alone to the pit when it was still dark out. Dval Quach came with some of his khatyu to summon us, and they were careful and quiet, which I didn't like. The fact that it was almost like we were sneaking out made me wary. Why was it a secret that we were leaving?

When we reached the pit, I found that each sylvan was there with only the mate of their semel. I understood when I was stripped, along with Teresa and Yusuke, and secured to a saltire cross, that Mikhail's answers were more important to me than I had originally thought. The semels were shackled to the wall in front of the cross so that I could see Logan and he could see me, but only he could see Mikhail. My sylvan stood behind me. Apparently the semel was to be able to see the face of their mate when they took a lick of the lash. It would not have been as frightening if not for the stipulation that went along with every test: there was no shifting in the pit. We were not allowed to heal the damage until the trial of law was concluded.

It was more frightening than I thought it would be, being spread-eagle on the cross, wrists and ankles immovable, waiting, anticipating the feel of the whip on my skin.

Once the trial officially began, before the first question was asked, the gallery was allowed in.

There were rules for the spectators. If they made a noise, they were dismissed. If they spoke to one another, they were dismissed. If the name of the mate was yelled out, or the sylvan, or the semel, they were dismissed. There was to be silence so that the questions could be heard, the person who answered quickly identified, and the crack of the whip audible.

What went through my mind was that it was like *Jeopardy* if it had been played in Roman times with gladiators. Basically, the priest asked a question, and the mate of the semel of whichever sylvan answered first and correctly avoided the sting of the lash. The other two were flogged for their sylvans not being the one who answered. If the sylvan took a chance and answered wrong, the mate got two strikes instead of just one. I took a deep breath as I realized how long the day was going to be.

The sylvan had to yell out the name of their semel to be called on, and that, too, was designed to drive their leader right out of their mind. The mate took a lash, or didn't, right after their semel's name was called. I could only imagine the therapy we were all going to need once the sepat concluded.

The sylvan was allowed to speak to the mate of their leader before the trial began. When Mikhail walked around in front of me, I realized how pained he looked.

"Listen," I told him. "There's no way to avoid me getting hit. Even if you know all the answers, someone will get picked before you, and I'm gonna get hit. Remember that I can heal whatever damage I take; I've come back from more than this, Mikhail, you know I have. This trial is just like Yuri's: it's not about winning, it's just about enduring. We just have to make it through until it concludes. That's all."

He nodded, tight-lipped, his eyes lifting to the people above us sitting around the edge.

"Look at me."

His gaze returned to my face.

"Please don't beat yourself up about this."

He gave me a quick nod before he heeded Hamid's order and slowly moved out of my range of vision. I took a breath and the questions began.

The first lash of the whip took my breath away before it felt as though my back was sliced open with a razor blade and alcohol was poured on it. I absorbed it, breathed through it even as Logan's wail of pain tore through me. The sound of his anger, frustration and helplessness was worse than anything else… at least at first. By the tenth lash, Logan's torture, I was sorry to say, was secondary. Each lick of pain was indescribable; I could feel the blood running down my back, and the sting had blossomed from white hot to aching to screaming, tensing agony.

I could see Logan through blurry tear-filled eyes, and even though I still hadn't made a sound, Logan made enough for the both of us. Each snap of the whip that hit me sent a jolt of fear and anger and fury through him. He looked like he had been electrocuted.

Every part of me screamed to shift, to make the horror stop, free Logan, and annihilate the man beating me. It made no sense to remain still and do nothing.

I didn't move. I lost track of the strokes.

There was no food or water, and still the day wore on. There was the crack of the whip and more questions, and time slowed, dragged, and finally, simply stopped.

And then exploded all at once in red and white, and each time it took a little longer to come back, swim up through an ocean of pressing, smothering oblivion until I was again looking into the raw and ragged eyes of my mate.

The hatred in him was palpable. If he got loose, even for a second, the man flogging me was dead. When my legs finally went out on me, the shackles had cut into my wrists as I hung there on the cross. It was undignified and I felt weak and unmanly, like I should have held myself up, but I was drenched in blood, muscle and bone feeling as though they were exposed, and each new fissure that opened in my flesh caused more shivering.

My tongue was swollen in my mouth; my head was pounding with dull, aching, relentless pain; and I could not control the retching caused by the nausea. I was in shock, and my body was shutting down with the need to eat and drink and shift.

"The trial of law is now concluded."

It took long minutes for the words to register, and I realized I was tensed and waiting for the next stroke of the lash that was not coming. I found that I could not unclench my body.

When I felt hands on me, I looked up at Mikhail. He was flecked with blood, covered in sweat and dirt, and his eyes were dead.

I shook my head. I didn't want to see the hurt there on him, in his gaze, but I couldn't fix it right that second. I couldn't even stand. I would have reached for him, but my arms would do nothing but hang useless at my sides.

"It's over, Jin," he told me.

I was a panther a second later, rolling, twisting, clawing free of the restraints. There were gasps as I lifted my head and surveyed the pit.

Teresa Medina was on the ground, panting, her hair soaked with sweat, looking more dead than alive.

Narae Yusuke was shifting, but not so fast that I couldn't see her ruined flesh. We had all been horribly beaten. I walked stiffly over to Yusuke and stood over her as she finished. I helped her out of her restraints, shredded them with my claws to free her. When I bent my nose to hers, she touched it with hers. It was dry and hot, and that was dangerous. She needed water to cool her feverish temperature. I purred, and it calmed her, allowing her shift to quicken. Once she was lying beneath me, all sleek golden panther, she rose and walked with me to Teresa.

The yareah of the tribe of Nebthet was not moving. She had been released and laid on the ground, but her chest was not rising and falling. When I called to her, it took long moments for her eyes to flutter open and focus. She looked like she was hovering on the verge of death, her skin ashen, covered in sweat, as she began to shiver.

I called again, a warning, and she tensed before I sent my pheromones hurtling into her.

The spasm made it look like her body had been snapped in half before she convulsed with the shift. Others tried to close in on us, my tribe, Yusuke's, even Teresa's, but Yusuke's warning snarl, her bristling stance, hair raised, made everyone keep their distance.

She was all panther; there was no yareah in there at the moment, just animal, if anyone was stupid enough to test her.

"They're out of their minds with pain," Hamid told the room. "Everyone stand back."

It took long, exhausting minutes, but when Teresa, too, was beside me, I bolted for the door with the two yareahs close behind me.

I could smell the water and the meat, and so led them to it.

It was toward the entrance of the semel's home, in the long hall, three enormous platters of raw meat and a trough of fresh mountain stream water.

I drank first, gulped down liquid until my tongue no longer felt as though it were cracking in my mouth. Yusuke did the same; Teresa ate first. We switched then, us eating, Teresa drinking. And the three of us didn't move, just tore through the meat, drank and drank and drank, filling ourselves, until each one of us could breathe.

I shifted then, back to man, and then back to panther, and I watched the others look at me, Yusuke shifting twice in the time it took me to do ten, Teresa only once. By the fifteenth time, the skin on my back was tender but new. On her fourth shift, Yusuke no longer had open, seeping welts on her skin, but scabs. Teresa was having more trouble.

Finally, I returned to panther form and lay down. Yusuke came forward, head down, and I gave her the growl of welcome. She was instantly curled into my side, tail wrapped around her as we watched Teresa eat. She had to stop when she started retching, and I lifted my head and called her. She was eating and drinking too much, and because she wasn't shifting, her body wasn't metabolizing, and she was going to be sick.

She moved fast, padding over to me, came forward with her head lowered until I began to purr, and then she dropped down on the other side of me, her head sliding over my paws so she could rest her head close to me. My scent, the heat rolling off me, both were needed, wanted, and seconds later, feeling safe, sated, I heard her take a last shuddering breath before she passed out.

Yusuke pushed against me on the other side, rubbing her cheek on my shoulder, wiping her scent all over me, and then ran her nose back through her own smell now on my fur. She trembled in pleasure before she, too, let out a huff of air and surrendered to unconsciousness. Normally I liked only Logan this tight against me, but at that moment, being sandwiched between the two panthers was finally chasing the cold from my limbs.

The final trial seemed far away.

Chapter Sixteen

THE HAND stroking my fur, gently scratching my ears and under my chin, felt good, and when I let my eyes drift open, I found Crane.

"Hey, you," he said, smiling at me. "How ya feelin'?"

I lifted my head to look at him and found that the two yareahs were gone and only I was there, alone in the dirt in the cold, dark, cavernous hall.

"You think you wanna come back to our quarters with me? Can you stand?"

When I rose, I found that my muscles were sore but solid. I noticed, too, that he was there with everyone I had brought with me.

Mikhail was beside Crane, down on one knee, studying me. "You were so brave, Jin, and I'm so sorry that I couldn't—"

"You did everything you could," Danny said, cutting him off, moving forward, turning from my sylvan to look at me. "If the others hadn't chimed in with shit they didn't know, you would have never taken one lash, Jin."

I waited.

"Danny helped," Mikhail said, his hand in the younger man's hair. "Each time I looked up at him, I remembered something he had said." He looked into Danny's face. "You helped me save my reah and my semel. I'll never forget this."

Danny nodded, unable to speak, only reaching up to wrap his fingers around Mikhail's wrist. He never wanted the attention to end, of that I was sure.

"Jin."

I turned my head, and there was Yuri, smiling softly.

"Can I carry you back to the ger? I would love to if you'd let me."

I shook my head, looking for Domin. When I saw him, I shifted fast, startling Andrian and Danny as I walked the few feet to stand before my maahes.

"Is Logan alright?"

Domin was a study in contrasts: his awe at my shift, his concern for Logan, the furrow of his brows as he delivered bad news. "Jin, Logan needs to shift soon, alright? He was really close to it earlier, and if he had…."

I knew what would have happened if he had: he would have been executed in front of my eyes.

"Watching you take those lashes was more than he could bear."

I nodded, turned, and shifted. Padding around Domin, I headed toward the entrance of the hall toward the enormous cave opening.

"Wait."

I turned and looked over my shoulder and saw Taj stripping out of his clothes.

"I'll go with you, my reah; just don't outrun me tonight."

As I waited, I saw how uneasy I was making everyone. They were all worried about me, even scared. I was usually more communicative; that I couldn't be was frightening.

Once Taj joined me, we ran out into the icy wind and swirling snow together.

I RAN leisurely and enjoyed being free instead of lashed to a post. Once we got back, I slipped into the ger in my panther form, rushing to the area by the stove and lying down. When Danny came close, I got up and moved to the other side, away from him.

"What did I do?" Danny asked Mikhail when he called him over to him.

"Nothing, he's just in pain, leave him alone," my sylvan answered from where he was sitting, crossed-legged, off to one side of the sleeping area.

"I thought the shift healed him?"

"Not all of it, and not on the inside."

Danny rose and walked back over to Mikhail, sitting close, his hand on Mikhail's thigh as he looked at him.

"You have to understand that it's different for Jin and Logan to be apart than it would be for you and your mate."

"I know that the bond between—"

"It's supposed to be this beautiful thing, right? But what they don't tell you is that the bond between true-mates is rough if they're separated, if one of them dies…. Right now Logan is slowly going out of his mind. He can see Jin, smell him, even taste his scent, but he's not allowed to touch him or talk to him. It's like sensory deprivation."

"Oh." Danny looked over at me sadly.

"You don't know, but Jin—he needs Logan too. His tension level is just rising every day, it's continual, and pretty soon the running and all the things he's doing to externally defuse it aren't going to work. We need them back together before one of them caves."

Danny went very still. "Who do you think it will be? Jin or—"

"Logan," Mikhail assured him. "If this sepat goes on even one more day—he's ready to break, and if he does, the tribe is done, but it won't matter to him anymore, because for a moment, before he's destroyed, he'll have his mate."

"Shit, it's cold," Crane groused as he came in, the others trailing behind him.

I watched them all shed their jackets and boots, watched Yuri feed the stove coal and Domin sit down, rubbing his hands together.

"Come here," he said, gesturing to me. "I wanna see you."

I stayed where I was, eyes narrowed.

"Please, Jin."

But I couldn't move. Everything hurt, inside and out. I was raw and vulnerable, and the only man in existence I needed was my mate.

"Jin," Yuri said, soothing me with his voice, "you want to lie down by me?"

I got to my feet and moved away, toward the door. My panic started to rise, flickering low but constant.

"Shit," Taj said under his breath, turning to Yuri. "Make him heed you, sheseru."

"Jin," he called me. "Come."

Fuck. Him. I was not a dog.

"Just… everybody," Crane grumbled, clearly annoyed, flopping down, lying on his side, shivering hard. "Fuck, I'm freezing."

I was across the room to him so fast it could not be followed by the naked eye, and the catches of breath, gasps, and whispers told me I was scaring the hell out of everybody. I didn't belong with them inside. Nekhene cats belonged—

"Oh, that's better, huh?" Crane yawned, not touching me, just lying close, stretching languidly. "Hey, remember that time in Yuma when you fell out of that tree? Badass stealthy panther, my ass," he scoffed, chuckling.

What? Why was he—

"Or when we were supposed to be all stalkery when we were working as detectives in Nashville, and you fell through the skylight into that guy's apartment?" He was laughing now.

I turned my head to look down at him, and he was smiling so big before he lifted his fingers to scratch under my chin.

"Remember that time we were waiters in San Antonio and you tripped over the side down by the River Walk?" He was amusing the hell out of himself.

Why were we taking a trip down memory lane? And he was forgetting a lot of times when he had been the one… to….

And then I understood, because I had been reminded, in a very roundabout way, that I was a man, apparently a very klutzy man on occasion, but a man nonetheless. I was not a wild panther. I was the best friend of the annoying ass lying beside me.

He washed normal all over me. I put my head down on my paws and listened to the husky, deep sound of his voice.

Yuri crawled across the floor and stretched out close, head propped up on his palm, looking at me. "Tell me the stupidest job you guys ever had," he prodded Crane.

"We tried to be ranch hands."

Yuri snorted out a laugh. "You and him?" He pointed at me. "The guy who has to ride with Logan because he falls off otherwise?"

Crane snickered. "Yeah, just try and picture it."

I growled, which sent Yuri into a fit of coughing, before I stood up, stepped over Crane, and lay down on the other side of my best friend, nuzzling my nose into the back of his hair.

I was hiding, and I knew that, but I just needed quiet and solitude but warmth too. I *needed* Logan. I craved the shelter he provided, the strength. I wanted my mate, and even though the following day was the trial of the heart, I couldn't wait, because at least I would see him. As my eyes closed, I could still hear Yuri and Crane talking, as well as the others. They all wanted to be close to me, and while I appreciated that, I had to simply rest. With Crane talking to them and me close to him, I felt included without having to exert any energy at all. I didn't remember closing my eyes.

Chapter Seventeen

"THE TRIAL of the heart begins now," Hamid announced loudly, giving the command to begin.

I felt like I was in a dream.

Each semel was bound to an actual wooden cross, tied tightly and painfully with rope. It was to be endured. The sooner it was over, the sooner your semel went free. The point was to fight efficiently and release your leader.

If the house failed to protect the semel or shirked their duty in cowardice, the semel was disemboweled by the "knife-wielder," who was the sheseru of the semel-aten. The semel was then cut to pieces until there was "a river of blood," the law said. It was far too horrible to contemplate the death of my mate from having his organs devoured and then being drawn and quartered.

If the assault was foiled, the semel was released and he and the three chosen from his household to defend him, as well as his mate, attacked the other semels. It was kill or be killed during the final trial of the heart, and whatever I had shared with the other yareahs the night before was meaningless as the test began.

We all had to make it out alive.

Dval, Ammon's new sheseru, entered the pit with fifteen men. They could shift, if they wanted, into panthers, just as we could, but I was not allowed to employ my werepanther form. If I shifted into either my werepanther form or any nekhene form, I would be disqualified, and Logan and Crane and Andrian and Taj and I would be executed. Logan, of course, would be killed in the proscribed fashion, the rest of us beheaded.

Dval stood in the center of the pit with the three semels trussed up along opposite edges. Five men each ran to attack the households. The problem was in the numbers. If one semel fell, then all those left who had attacked him would join the others. Whoever fell first would be facing a fair number; the others would not. The trial proceeded until there was only one challenger remaining to stand against the semel-aten, with his maahes, the following day.

We were in a trial today, but there was also the following day to consider. The priest had cautioned us against simply defending our semel and not thinking to attack others as well. If you killed another semel, yes, that would mean more khatyu to fight, but at least you would be that much closer to becoming semel-aten.

I had told Andrian, Taj, and Crane that no one was to leave Logan's side. We would slaughter anyone who came near him. It had been my last order before we all shifted to panther form, having agreed that morning that we would take that form.

As we made the phalanx around the cross, I was unprepared for the bullwhip that wrapped around Andrian's throat and yanked him off his feet into the dirt a few feet from us. Normally there were no weapons in the pit, so I was surprised. Taj moved fast, faster than any of the khatyu were prepared for, and with a snarling roar, landed all over Dval. Even if he had been warned by the semel-aten that Taj was a former member of the Shu, he had not been prepared for such a blurring attack.

As soon as the tension released, even for a second, Crane was there at Andrian's side, having shifted to his human form, as was legal, getting him out of the whip. Andrian rose, coughing, retching a moment before he and my best friend were swarmed by ten panthers.

If I shifted into my nekhene form, I could kill them all, but I couldn't. And I wasn't big in my black panther form. Watching Crane and Andrian fight for their lives, seeing Taj in a fight to the death, I realized the futility of my situation. There were more cats advancing on us, and even without looking, I knew that one of the other semels, either Gavin or Hiroshi, was dead. What could I….

"Reah!" Logan screamed.

When I turned to him, I saw his eyes. Even where we were, as close to horror, to the end, to the edge of the precipice, still, there was love there in his eyes, not fear. He was so full of desire and want and need, and… he was my mate.

He was the mate of the reah of the tribe of Mafdet, but not the mate of the nekhene. The nekhene had no mate.

I couldn't outwardly shift to anything but a panther, that was true, but the power I released could be whatever I wanted it to be. And while my nekhene power was feral and angry, my reah power would not touch my tribe, would not hurt what was mine or what I loved.

I had felt cursed. I had wanted to be free of the selfish, wild nekhene, wanted the power to submit to the reah I truly was. But at that moment, I was thankful, so deeply, desperately thankful.

I let down all my barriers, all the careful checkpoints in my head Crane had helped me build, and let the nekhene burst forth wild and wanton. This was not the moment to punish, it was the time to lure and then exact the toll. My power, which I had worked to empty of heat and seduction and raging carnal appetite, I allowed to embody all those qualities once more. I called every panther in the home of the semel of Khertet to me.

Where was the mate of the most powerful cat in the world? He needed to show himself!

The challenge was there as I felt electricity crackle around me, ripple the air, split it, charge everything, and spark over my skin.

The instant the panthers wanted me, the second they thought to respond to the call, they were sucked through their shift.

Screaming roars came fast as the pile that had covered Crane and Andrian sloughed off and revealed the two bloody and beaten panthers.

The air heated, got heavy, sticky, and oppressive, making it hard to breathe. I watched some of the khatyu run from the pit in panic, not even wanting to taste my power, and saw the cats that had been attacking Taj leap away from him as though burned before they fell to the dirt, their fur looking as though it were bubbling. As Taj lay panting, he could have been attacked anew. But no one got close. No one dared; instead they just stood there in wide-eyed shock and dread.

The ones who ran were smart.

A moment later, everyone who remained who did not belong to me was on the ground writhing in pain.

What had started as a search for a mate—I knew, because it had been my thought when I started—had become punishment.

Painful, debilitating punishment.

The nekhene power became a fist of judgment, and I dragged them all through their shift, turned them inside out in a horrendously painful, wrenching action. It was like having skin flayed off, bones broken, muscles torn, and all of it happened in a scalding, burning, squeezed-in-a-vise second.

Logan. I had to see him, reach him, and touch him. Turning, I saw him straining against his bonds, desperate to get free, to get to me.

Taking a breath, shifting back to human, I took two steps to Logan and put my hands on his chest. Looking down into his eyes, I saw how pained they looked, how full of longing.

"My mate," I said and realized that my voice was not my own. It was low and full of gravel, broken.

He whimpered and tried to lift up, and I felt my pulse leap at his struggle. Here was what I needed, and it was being kept from me. The frustration rose in me, and instead of trying to gentle it, as Crane had been coaching me to do, I let it out and drowned the room again in blistering, scorching power. I would annihilate them all if my mate was not released.

"Jin!"

How dare they restrain the mate of the nekhene!

"Jin Rayne!"

I shifted back to my panther form and faced every panther in the pit.

"Reah of the tribe of Mafdet!"

My head lifted, and I saw Hamid Shamon, the priest of Chae Rophon above me. I saw no other man or woman close to him, only panthers. Turning my head, panning right, I took in the gallery. There were so many panthers; the entire tribe of Khertet, it seemed, had succumbed.

As I followed with my eyes, I saw Domin. He was on his knees, and beside him was Yuri and then Mikhail. No one else was there, only animals.

"Jin!"

I looked back to the priest.

"The trial of the heart is over; your semel is free!"

My eyes never left him even as he balled up his fists and began to tremble ever so slightly.

"Your semel returns to you, reah, and to his human form."

What? I must have misheard.

"All semels are relieved of their werepanther form."

How? They weren't supposed to be men until after the final trial, semel-aten against semel to determine the new master of Sobek.

"The contest is moot if no one can participate."

The nekhene had rendered the exercise obsolete.

It was over.

I exhaled, and when I did, then all of it, my power, my pheromones, the thrumming, searing energy, was suddenly sucked from the room, leaving the cold and the damp and the suddenly clear, fresh air.

There were moans and gasps as a collective sigh of relief was released. I shifted and screamed for Yuri, for Domin and Mikhail, as I rounded on Logan, on the man I loved.

I moved fast, standing beside him, hands in his hair, on his face, touching, tracing, and mapping territory I knew with my fingers.

"Jin." His voice was hoarse from disuse, his eyes ragged with dark circles under them; he had grown a golden beard and mustache I had never seen before, his hair standing in tufts, gnarled with sweat and dirt.

He was breathtaking.

I bent and kissed his forehead, his eyes, his nose, his cheeks, ravenously, deliriously, beyond happy to see him, enraptured.

"Jin," he whimpered, tears rolling down the sides of his face toward his ears. "Me—baby, kiss me."

My lips sealed over his, gently, tenderly, because for all the desire, we were both frayed and raw and sensitive. He was vulnerable and so was I. So even though I was hungry for him, I claimed what was mine without the urgency, with only the love.

"Jin!"

I turned, and Yuri was there with the down comforter from our bed at home, the one thing I had brought that had both our scents on it, Logan's and mine. Yuri wrapped me up in it before he, Domin, Andrian, Taj, and Crane lifted the cross Logan was lashed to. They leaned it against the wall before Yuri hefted the ax he had been given before the trial began. Each sheseru had one, no one knowing who would be using it, who would be allowed to free their semel.

Yuri swung it three times, and the pain it caused Logan, the jolting, pounding vibration, was acute, but he was silent until he was suddenly on the ground under the cross, finally free. Both of his shoulders were dislocated, he had broken ribs, and his skin where the ropes had been looked like raw meat. But still, he rose up and staggered forward.

I went to my knees, and he dropped down into my arms, finally, utterly, safe.

He was safe.

With his head notched under my chin, his arms wrapped around me, his skin pressed to mine, I could breathe again.

It was so good to breathe.

When I felt a hand on my back, I lifted my eyes to find Crane's.

"I felt the pressure of your power, Jin, but none of the heat or the anger."

"Me neither," Taj chimed in, and my eyes flicked to him. "I saw the others going through their shift, and it was just hard to drag in air, but nothing else. I was okay."

"Me too," Yuri agreed. "How did you do that? It never happened like that before. Normally you just have to take it."

Domin had felt the same, as had Andrian and Mikhail. Danny had changed to a panther, and I was sorry for that and not sure why it had happened. Crane thought it was because I didn't think of Danny as belonging to me yet, my power didn't recognize him.

Besides Logan and me, the only other humans in the room were Hamid, Crane, Yuri, Domin, Mikhail, Andrian, and Taj. Everyone else, phocal, semel, maahes, yareah, sheseru, sylvan—it didn't matter. They had all been turned to panthers.

"You're like the goddess Circe," Crane said, chuckling. "You turn men to beasts."

But I didn't want to be compared to a witch. I would have argued with him, but the priest was speaking.

"It is unusual for us to judge a winner when the trial has not concluded, but as every panther in the pit was rendered immobile, pinned to the floor in pain, it could not go on. As a result, the semel of the tribe of Reshep may now challenge Logan Church to one-on-one combat to determine who will face the semel-aten."

I turned to look for Hiroshi and found him gasping, trying to rise from the fetal position he had obviously been locked in for several minutes. He was attempting to get up off the ground. I saw, too, that there was only his yareah with him; the three other khatyu of his household were dead. On the other side, Gavin, his yareah, and all in his household lay mutilated. It was why there were more panthers on us so fast; they had not been able to keep the marauders from their semel and were simply overrun and killed. I had no idea how quickly they had fallen, but it had to have been fast.

A high-pitched scream turned my attention, and I saw that Hiroshi had shifted back to his werepanther form, probably to give him strength, and was now attacking his yareah. Yusuke was being held down by several panthers, other members of her tribe who had rushed to the pit, as her semel mauled her.

"No!" I screamed, and Logan jolted in my arms, lifting his head.

The panthers, Hiroshi's sylvan and sheseru among them, stepped in front of their frenzied semel, shielding his actions from our eyes, even though we knew he was biting and scratching and tearing at his mate.

"Yuri," Logan roared, his voice carrying like it always did, the embodiment of power and strength even in his weakened state. "Bring me the yareah!"

"Stay back!" the priest warned Yuri, Mikhail, and Domin as they moved toward the cluster of the tribe of Reshep. "The semel will not kill his yareah, only mark her as apophi. We all saw her hesitate to attack Jin when she had the chance before he let loose with his power."

"No," I rasped, struggling to rise, to go to her.

"Listen," Logan coughed out and pulled me back to look at my face. "He's not killing her, Jin; he's giving her the mark of apophi."

Marking her? "Why? She did not disgrace herself," I whined, struggling to get free, so tired but needing to get to her, to save her.

"Stop," he whispered. "You can't do anything. This is the law. She had a chance to kill you, I saw it—she was close. I turned my head and saw her maybe twelve feet away, but her mate screamed and she ran back to defend him."

He blurred as my eyes filled with tears. "He's marking her as a disgrace because she chose to protect him instead of kill me."

"He might have been able to take care of himself, and so he feels her duty was to attack and kill you before going to his aid."

"Domin!" I screamed for my maahes.

"No!" Hamid yelled over me from above. "Call no aid for her, Jin Rayne!"

"You can't," Logan told me, tightening his grip on me. "Baby, you can't. It's his right, just as it would be mine to mark you."

My eyes locked on the shining amber ones in front of me. "You would never, ever mark me."

"Not like that," he agreed, hands on my face. "But I'm not him."

I was exhausted, overwrought, and the soul-rending screams of the terrified, wounded, and heartbroken yareah were eating me alive. Tears rolled down my cheeks as I began to shake. Logan was in pain, too, excruciating pain, but he grabbed me anyway, as he had his strength as a semel to tap into, and held me tight.

The sound went on and on for what felt like hours but could not have been more than a few minutes. Members of my tribe stood hovering over me and Logan. The tribe of Khertet, having recovered from my turning them all to beasts, had returned, changed and clothed, and brought robes for the members of other tribes who were naked. Thus Danny was wrapped in a fur cloak.

When I could catch my breath, Logan eased me from his lap, and Yuri put his hands on my shoulders as my semel shifted into panther form, and then man, panther, and finally back to man. Logan looked better after he shifted twice more, and as he flexed his muscles, he put his right hand on his left shoulder and stretched, repeating the action on the opposite side, I understood everything that had been dislocated was healed and he was well on his way to recovery. He needed food, though, meat, lots of protein, lots of water, and sleep.

When he stood up, Yuri slid a fur cloak over him, and Logan pointed at the now-bloody and mauled body of the yareah of Reshep. I had watched with horrified eyes as every remaining member of her tribe, including her semel, had spit on her. She had lost her right eye as well as that side of her face. The ripped flesh would heal, but never completely. The scarring would be heavy. Her eye was gone forever; she would never be the beauty she once was.

Logan declared, "I claim, as a member of my tribe, Narae Yusuke. She will be a member of my tribe."

"You cannot!" Hiroshi snarled at Logan before looking up at the priest. "She will be staked for her cowardice and—"

"To me, what she showed you was the depth of her love," Hamid told the semel. "But you have marked her, shown her your displeasure, and by your wish to have her staked, released her from your tribe, and so she may be claimed by another."

"She will have nothing! Her clothes will be burned; I will not have them given to her! She will not be allowed to contact her family, as they are members of my tribe! She is dead to me and to the tribe of Reshep. There is only khet."

He was in a fury; he was completely out of control, as he had just been through the same ordeal Logan had. But whereas my semel had retained his humanity, Hiroshi had not. If only he had food and sleep, if only he had waited and not been so rash, if only he had taken a breath before attacking, his head might have cleared and he would have remembered how much he cherished and adored his beloved yareah. Instead, he had maimed the woman who had been his mate.

"Logan Church," Hamid called to my semel. "You will have to feed and clothe and care for the former yareah of the tribe of Reshep. She might someday try and kill you for what has transpired here today. Are you aware of the danger that—"

"She will not," Logan said, cutting the priest off. "I apologize for my impertinence, Your Grace, but she cannot blame me for anything that was brought on her this day. Her semel, and her semel alone, has mauled her and marked her for death. I will claim her and give her life."

"So be it," the priest agreed, and he raised his hand, palm up, to present her to Logan.

Hiroshi stepped back from the bleeding, inert body of his yareah. Her tears had mixed with blood, and she was trying to cover her nakedness from prying eyes, and her modesty in the face of the horror that had been visited on her made my heart hurt.

"Crane," Logan said.

He moved fast.

My best friend was met at the fallen woman by a member of the tribe of Khertet, who offered him a soft fur robe. He thanked the man, spread the cloak gently, slowly lifted Yusuke, and then tenderly wrapped her up. He stood up with her in his arms as though she weighed nothing, and as he walked back to us, he began speaking to her.

"Take her to our quarters," Logan told him, and Crane gave him a slight nod as he walked by, holding her tighter, her head turned now, tucked under his chin.

I took a stuttering breath and leaned into Logan's side.

He clutched at me, and I felt the tremor run though him.

"Tomorrow at noon the challenge for the seat of semel-aten will commence. Logan Church and Domin Thorne of the tribe of Mafdet will face Ammon El Masry and his maahes, Rector Vincent, of the tribe of Rahotep, in the pit to decide who will be master of Sobek. May the semel most deserving be granted the grace of Ra."

I already knew who that was.

THE SYLVAN of the tribe of Reshep, Morimoto Arai, and the sheseru, Kenichi Fuwa, both came with all of Yusuke's belongings that she had brought with her to Mongolia. They both bowed low to me, asking that I please keep her out of their semel's sight, as they had been told to burn all her things but could not, in good conscience, do so. They had done their duty, as honor demanded, and followed the orders of their semel to hold her down as he gnawed on her face, gouged her flesh with his claws, and bit through her right eye and cheek. They could do no more to her; it had already crossed the line into torture and abomination. As I looked at them, I realized they had both very recently been violently sick.

She had only one suitcase; they would send other things when, and if, they could.

I bowed low. "Thank you."

They bowed back and then were gone. There was no time to linger lest someone see them. I took the suitcase inside the ger to where Yusuke lay sleeping. Even when she had drifted off, she had not released Crane's hand. As I looked at him, I realized how content he looked as he studied her face.

She was strong, and she shifted as fast as Logan could, which was to say pretty damn fast. She had been able to morph back and forth six times before she was too exhausted and passed out. There was now a slash across the patch of pink skin covering her right eye. The entire right side of her face was crisscrossed with scars, but they were not grooves, as I had thought they would be; instead they were raised lines that cut across otherwise smooth porcelain skin.

I had heard her begging at first to be allowed to take her own life, whimpering softly, urging Crane to hear her. She even lifted fingers to his face. He covered her little hand with his, pressing it against his cheek, smiling down at her. She began to shiver, and he tucked the blankets around her chin before he lay down in front of her so they were facing each other. I watched as she stared at him and listened to him talk. He had already told her that he had been scourged; it was the piece of information that had allowed him to be close to her. He was maimed, so was she, and the horrifying tale he confessed to her had brought fresh tears. After all she had been through, that she could still weep for someone else said so much about the size of the woman's heart.

"She'll find her place," Yuri said from his place beside me.

I turned to look at him.

"And so will your boy."

"My boy?"

"Who's the only boy around here?"

He meant Danny. "Oh yeah, I know."

I got a smile then.

Looking at my sheseru, I realized that in the time I had known the man, he had changed so much. "And you?"

"Me what?"

"Will you and Domin find your way?"

"I figured you knew."

"Only because Mikhail told me," I confessed.

"You've been dealing with your own shit."

"But I should have seen that you were hurting. Forgive me."

"Nothing to forgive."

"And now? Is there a happily ever after for you and my maahes?"

He sighed heavily. "I hope so. Jesus, Jin, have you ever wanted anything so bad that just thinking about maybe getting it made you sick?"

I nodded. "Yes."

"Then you understand."

"I do," I said, glancing over at Logan, who was sleeping on my bunk, his face buried in my pillow, absolutely dead to the world.

We had fed him, talked briefly, put gallons of water down him, and listened as he thanked each man who had come on the odyssey with him. He had hugged everyone, even Danny, had sat with Yusuke and accepted her tearful, heartfelt pledge of fealty, and then Yuri and I had taken him outside and scrubbed him.

He had been delirious over being clean, absolutely giddy afterward, and then when dumb things like shaving had been finished—I had told him the beard and mustache were hot, but he wasn't buying it—he had felt like a new man. Things we took for granted, like deodorant, hair gel, clothes, he had appreciated so much. When he had been sitting inside in long underwear, jeans, heavy wool socks, a long T-shirt, a flannel shirt, a wool cardigan, and a parka, he had finally been able to look at me, sigh, and ask me how I was.

"I'm good," I had said, chuckling. "You?"

He had grabbed me and thrown me down on the bed and confessed that all he really wanted to do was take off all his clothes and hold me in his arms.

"Maybe when you wake up," I had told him.

His eyelids had fluttered. After the food, the water, he had been sated, and he was clean and warm. As he stretched out, head on my thigh, his eyes had drifted closed.

"Will you stay right here?"

"Yes, sir, I will," I had said, smiling down at him.

"I love you," he had said, wrapping his forearm around my thigh. "And the tribe means so much, and my family and Yuri and Mikhail and…."

He had been fighting sleep so hard.

"Rest, love," I had said, threading my fingers through his hair, loving the feel of it, the warmth of his scalp, inhaling his scent, musky and sweet and smoky all at the same time.

"But, Jin," he had muttered, sighing deeply, "it's you, you know that, right?"

"Logan—"

"Just you. I would never give up, for you. I have to have my mate; you're the only thing I can't live without."

"I know, me too."

And now, three hours later, I sat with Yuri in the ger with everyone either asleep or close to it around us.

"Where's Domin now?"

"He's out running, trying to clear his head."

"You didn't want to run with him?"

"I did, but I didn't think it was a good idea. I need to be smart enough to give him his space when he needs it and be there when he needs me."

I looked into his eyes. "Mikhail says you've been in love with the guy since you were sixteen."

He shrugged his massive shoulders.

"You don't deny it."

He just looked at me.

"Jesus, Yuri," I sighed. "When it was going to be Domin and Logan in the pit—you had to have been terrified."

"Yes. Either way I would have lost."

"But Logan, he thought of making Domin his maahes."

"Because he didn't want to destroy him, either," he said softly. "I mean, there was the feud, you know? That bullshit that Domin's father kept alive, but once he died… then it was over, and Peter welcomed Domin into their house. Everything was good for so long until Domin was old enough to lead, to take the seat away from his uncle, who held it until he turned twenty."

A new semel was "made" the moment they turned twenty. As soon as the firstborn son, the heir came of age, if there was an heir of age, the semel in power stepped down. Logan had become semel as would his son after him. When Logan had turned twenty, his father had passed him the mantle of command; it was how it had always been, another antiquated leftover from when people only lived to the ripe old age of thirty. There were so many of our laws that needed to be revamped or tossed out completely.

"So Domin took over being semel from his uncle and what?"

"Discovered a tribe full of corruption, plagued with debt, and basically just falling apart at the seams," Yuri told me. "It was a mess, and the only thing he could think of to do was to unite against a common threat."

"And that threat was the tribe of Mafdet."

"Yeah. I mean, he knew Logan, knew his weaknesses and how far he could push him. If you hadn't ever come, I don't know what, if anything, would have ever changed."

"They were just dancing around each other, Logan and Domin."

"Yes, they were."

"And all that time, you just waited and hoped."

"There was nothing else to do," he assured me. "I wanted Domin, but Logan was my semel."

My heart went out to Yuri, who had spent years holding out for Domin even as the relationship between the two tribes, between the two men, disintegrated.

"And then Domin fell in love with Koren."

"He was infatuated with—"

"It *was* love, Yuri, on both sides," I corrected him. "And Koren may be too stupid to know it, but someday it'll hit him like a sledgehammer, and when it does, he's gonna die a little over what he gave up."

"Or not," Yuri said.

And he was right. This was Koren we were talking about, who apparently never knew his own mind, so the chances were good he would never, ever realize what he lost. "What if," I began, "Domin picks you, and then six months, a year later, Koren wants him back. What happens then?"

"Then I have faith in Domin," he told me, "if he even chooses me to begin with."

I stared at him. "So even if you lose in the end, you'll take him for however long you get."

"Hell yeah," he said, smiling at me. "Whatever I can have for however long I can have it."

I grunted. "Your heart is much stronger than mine."

"Oh, I don't think so. You fell in love with Logan and you weren't even sure if he was gay or not. That's pretty damn brave."

"It's not brave," I argued. "The man is my mate, the only one I will ever have. I mean, I know you guys don't really get it, but tomorrow, if he dies… Yuri, you might as well kill me too. I won't live through it."

"But you expected him to; if you had died that time you called for the law of Bast and planned to take Logan's place in the pit."

"He can live without me, Yuri, he's the semel. He's the strongest, the reah the weakest."

"That's a lot of shit," he scoffed. "Logan is physically stronger than you, but I'm tellin' you right now, if you die, he's done. You don't know, you weren't with him when that psychopath Laurent Bruyere kidnapped you. I have never seen him like that, and I've known him since we were kids."

"What was he like?" I asked before I could stop myself.

"He was hard and cold and mean. I had no idea Logan could ever be like that, but he—it was like he was someone else, someone angry. The change once he found you was amazing. I got my semel back."

"I—"

"Here's the thing," Yuri sighed. "I'm not brave. I just fuckin' want what I've been waiting for, for half my damn life, and you and Logan need to never be apart again for any reason other than choice."

"Agreed."

"Amazing, huh?"

"What is?"

He tipped his head, and following where he was looking, I saw Yusuke's right arm slide around Crane's waist as she snuggled closer. "That she can even be alive and isn't a complete fuckin' basket case. Her whole life ended today, everything about who she is, what she is, just done in the time it took her psychotic mate to maim her. I saw it, the way he just terrorized her and bit her, and she was struggling so hard, and even when it was done, she was just so shattered, so shocked that the man she loved would turn on her like that."

"Yeah, but we're panthers," I told him. "We know that being scourged or marked or sent into exile or accepting a title is part of the duality of our nature. All these things are our reality. I'm not saying that the horrible things that happened to Crane or Yusuke or the yareahs that died in the pit or the semels that will never again be men are okay. But for us... they're part of being a panther. The betrayal of her semel may be hard for Yusuke to wrap her brain around, but the rest, his actions, I mean, she's known all her life, we all have, that we live and die at the command of our semel."

He nodded.

"I mean, a regular man does not in his life imagine himself in a large room with eight panthers trying to kill him. But you made the decision to step into the pit for Logan, to show others that he is strong because he has a strong sheseru. It's fucked up, Yuri, and Russ is right, a lot of it is outdated barbaric crap."

He smiled at me. "It is, and it's time for someone to change it."

"Which is what I told Logan," I said, exhaling. "I think he's supposed to be semel-aten because he won't just be about the power, like they've all been for the last hundred years, but actually about bringing the laws into this century."

"That would be brilliant," he agreed. "But Sobek?"

Egypt. I felt the same way. "I know, I kinda just want to live in my town for the rest of my life."

"Me too," he agreed.

"Although," I said, smiling at him, "wherever Domin is—"

"Whatever he wants," Yuri said hoarsely. "I'll do whatever he wants if he'll just keep me."

"You're killing me with this, you know."

He smiled at me, and I saw the feeling there, what I meant to him. "You were amazing today, Jin. You controlled your power, you protected Logan, and you didn't hurt anyone from your own tribe. I'm so proud to stand with you and my semel."

I felt my eyes swimming suddenly, and he leaned forward to hold me. All of us were overly tired, overly emotional, and just completely overwrought. Yuri normally never hugged me. He protected me, he was my champion, we sat together a lot and talked, but hugging was not an activity we participated in. But all of us were raw and vulnerable and needy. So he held me tight, and I let him.

I woke up in the night to the beautiful sight of my sheseru smiling, eyes closed, head back, as Domin sat in his lap, kissing under his jaw and down his throat. Yuri was in heaven with Domin straddling his thighs, and the soft whimpering moan made me sigh. When my maahes leaned back, looking into the face of my sheseru, Yuri's eyes slowly drifted open.

"What do you want?"

"You know what I want," Yuri told him, his voice husky and low. "I want you to keep me. It's all I've ever wanted."

Domin's dark brown eyes looked black in the low light. He had shaved at some point during the day, and the strong chiseled features were again visible, no longer hidden under a thick beard. Yuri was enjoying the feel of the smooth skin if his fingers continually grazing over the man's face were any indication.

"And I'd really like you to mark me," Yuri confessed breathlessly.

"You're insane. You'd never survive it."

"I think I would."

Domin exhaled sharply. "Listen to me. Between a semel and his true-mate, the mark hurts but heals. Between two regular cats... the semel's mark is never given, because you could bleed to death," he finished, obviously shaken. "Besides, what makes you think I would even want to do such a thing?"

Yuri's dark eyes, not quite the cobalt Mikhail's were, more a warm royal blue or sapphire, just melted. God, he was so gone it was painful to see all the need there on display. "Please."

"Fuck you, no," Domin snapped, moving to get up, intending to roll off the bigger man's lap.

Yuri was strong, though, and he wanted Domin there, right there where he was. His fingers dug into Domin's thighs to hold him. "You're still a semel inside, and I know that."

Domin's head snapped up, his gaze locked on Yuri's.

"I know that just because you're a maahes now doesn't take away all the things you wanted and what you're built for, physically, emotionally, and mentally. I know that you wanted to find your true-mate, mark him—"

"There's no way that I would have found a male reah like—"

"But that's why you were so pissed." Yuri took his face in his hands. "What the fuck did Logan Church need with a male mate? The man was straight. So when you saw Jin, you thought he was the answer to everything, and when he wasn't yours, it made no fuckin' sense."

Domin brushed Yuri's hands from his face but didn't move away, instead pushing forward, closer.

Yuri caught his breath, hands back on the smaller man's thighs. "Dom, I know, okay? I do. Please lemme be the guy you need, please mark me."

"It could kill you."

But I knew it could also kill Yuri not to take the mark. Before we got home, Yuri needed to have a piece of Domin to carry around with him. It was necessary.

"Please" was all Yuri said.

"What makes you think I even want that?" Domin snapped, asking for the second time so that even I knew he wanted to, since he couldn't stop bringing it up.

Yuri smiled at him. "I know you."

And Domin was going to argue, I could see he was, but it was there in his eyes, how badly he wanted to bite into the other man's flesh and taste Yuri's blood on his tongue. "What if you bleed to death?"

"I don't shift as fast as Jin, but I can shift fast enough not to bleed to death. I'm the sheseru of my tribe, Domin; the only one stronger than me is Logan." He was matter-of-fact as he stared into Domin's dark brown eyes.

"For a reah, the pain becomes pleasure, for you... it won't change. It will only hurt."

"I think that depends on what you're doing to me as you deliver the bite." Yuri smiled slightly, his eyes heavy-lidded.

I saw the muscles in Domin's jaw clench as he made a noise in the back of his throat.

"Get up and let's go to the cave where we spent that night."

"Yuri—"

"I want this—please."

The last, with his voice breaking just a little, was too much for Domin. He got up, grabbed his parka, hat, gloves, and lube—couldn't forget that—and headed for the door. Yuri was right behind him.

I was smiling as I watched them go.

"You're happy about something."

I looked down at my mate. "Yuri and Domin."

"Oh? You like that even better than Koren and Domin, do you?"

My scowl made him smile, his eyes gleaming in the low light.

"You're an ass, Church." I shoved him away from me as he tried to grab me and pull me down beside him. "How come you never told me that Yuri was in love with Domin?"

"It wasn't my secret to share; besides, you always think I'm oblivious anyway."

What was he... and then I knew. "I thought you didn't know about Domin and Koren's relationship when that was going on, but you did, didn't you?"

He nodded. "I knew they were having one, I just didn't know how far it had progressed. I do see things, Jin."

As I stared down at him, his smile turned wicked. "Come here," he said, patting his chest.

I lay down beside him, snuggled up tight, and listened to him breathing. It was a really good sound.

"It's why I'm so pissed at Koren all the time," he told me, threading his fingers through my hair as he kissed my forehead. "He can't keep jerking Domin around, it's not fair."

"I feel so stupid for missing that Koren was clueless."

"But all of us, me, Yuri, Domin, Mikhail, we all grew up with him; you didn't. He's just annoying you lately," Logan said, chuckling, tilting my head up and kissing the edge of my jaw. "He's been annoying me way longer."

I smiled at him before he leaned close and took gentle possession of my mouth. I loved the kiss, his mouth on mine, and so moaned out my happiness softly, intimately. He clutched at me, the kiss becoming hotter, deeper, and endless. It went on, was urgent and needed but still drugging, languid, not explosive.

"I missed you so much," I told him when I had to take a breath, panting, with my forehead against his, the air heavy between us.

"Me too," he confessed, leaning in to kiss me again.

When I felt a hand on my ass, squeezing, kneading, the other fisted in my hair so I couldn't get away, I put two hands on his chest and pushed. He let me go but stared up at me as I rolled free, breathing hard, his warm gold eyes locked on my face.

"What?"

I arched an eyebrow for him. "What do you think you're doing?"

"I'm trying to get laid."

There was no way to hold in my grin. "No."

"No?"

"Go to sleep."

"Can't," he said, rubbing his very obvious erection. "I could die from this."

Which was funny, considering the things he could have died from over the past few days and hadn't. "Is that what you told the girls in high school?"

"Only you do this to me."

"Really?" I snickered. "Did you use that too?"

He whimpered, which made me smile and made him crack a grin in return.

"You're full of crap. Go to sleep."

"But your scent is driving me crazy."

"Then I'll go sleep somewhere else."

It was really something to see the warm golden gaze turn molten. "You sleep with me, only with me."

The man was so possessive, and I reveled in it. "Yes, my semel."

His groan was pained. "Oh, baby, please, take all that off and lie down with me. Put your skin on mine."

"I'll take off everything on top, but—"

"No," he whined, "all of it. I need to be… inside."

The man's eyes were golden slits; watching him swallow hard, licking his lips as he stared at me, was enough to make my blood run hot.

I rolled up to my knees and began to strip. I was pretty sure everyone else was asleep, only the sounds of the fires in the braziers scattered around the ger, the wind howling outside, soft snoring, and the rustling of bedding.

As I shed my clothes, Logan unzipped his parka and pulled off his sweater and the many layers underneath. When I was naked, I grabbed one of the heavy lined wool blankets beside him, opened it, and came down on top of him, straddling his hips. He moved fast, dumping me down on the furs on my back as a soft purr rose from his chest.

I squirmed under him, but instantly he lifted my hips, and I felt my cheeks spread and his tongue slid between them. As I bucked up off the berth, his rough tongue swirled over my fluttering entrance. "Logan," I gasped, "someone will see."

"They're all exhausted, and Yuri and Domin are gone," he told me as he nibbled up my buttocks, making my breath hitch. "And I need you. I need my mate," he finished and made me understand the breadth of his desire as his tongue slid inside my puckered hole.

He licked hard and long, that talented muscle of his going deeper each time, sucking harder, tasting me over and over until my cock was dripping with precome and my ass with saliva. I was writhing under him as his body arched over mine, begging softly, my whispers desperate. When he thrust two fingers into me, capturing my mouth at the same time, letting me taste myself on his tongue, I shuddered with how close I was to release.

His fingers scissored apart, slid over my gland, and I bit his bottom lip as my back bowed and he caught my leaking cock in his hand.

"Logan," I panted, "I'm gonna come."

He moved fast, changing position above me, my knees in the crooks of his elbows as he lifted my ass and drove down into me.

I came from the first hard thrust, his cock filling me, spreading me, and I cried out even though we were trying to be quiet as I spurted come over his rippling torso. As I rode the waves of my orgasm, he fucked me, pushing in and out, sheathing himself, burying himself fully inside so I could feel his balls pounding against my ass.

"Oh fuck, baby, you're so tight," he ground out, and I could feel my muscles clenching around the length of him, rippling, clasping as he rode me.

My orgasm flushed me with heat; I was slick with sweat as my mate pounded his enormous cock into me. The tears bathing my face were of no consequence. "Mine," I growled.

His breath caught with my declaration of ownership, and I knew that me being possessive of him had sent him right over the edge. He grabbed hold of my thighs and yanked me forward at the same time, ramming the long, hard, thick length of him into me. I felt his hot release fill my ass, pour into me as he pumped and pumped. I wrapped my legs around his back and held on.

We were a single sweat-slickened creature when his hand fisted in my hair and he lifted me, bringing me up to him so he could remain buried to the hilt in my ass and claim my mouth at the same time. I wrapped my arms around his neck and ground my lips over his, our tongues tangling, breath mingling as we trembled with aftershocks, trying to press closer together, tighter, joined.

When he could finally move, when I could, he eased gently from my body, and we lay down together under layers of blankets.

"Jin." He whispered my name as he kissed behind my ear and nibbled down the side of my neck. "I want a promise."

I rolled over in his arms so I could see his face.

His hands were clutching me tight, pressing me closer. "Swear that if I die tomor—"

"Logan." I caught my breath. "You—"

"Promise," he growled, dragging me under him, staring down into my eyes, pinning me there, reminding me that he was all big, hard, virile, muscled man and outweighed me by a good hundred pounds. "Jin."

I closed my eyes, just savoring the feel of his warm, sleek skin against mine, the strong hands holding my face so tenderly and his hot mouth as he sucked on the side of my neck. I would be covered in marks in the morning, and I was so glad. I loved carrying evidence of our lovemaking on my skin.

"Jin."

With effort, I got my eyes back open and met his beautiful amber gaze.

"If I die in the pit tomorrow, I want you to go home and start the process with the surrogate that Delphine knows to have our baby."

I clenched my jaw tight so I wouldn't cry.

"Before this all started, I was going to tell you that I think it's time to start having children. Everything's ready, we've just been waiting for the perfect time. It's time now, Jin, and if I die tomorrow, you have to promise to follow through, because the thought of you holding a baby, our baby… I need to carry that with me, okay?"

There were no words.

"I need to know when I walk into that pit tomorrow that no matter what, you'll be okay."

"I won't be okay," I told him even as he blurred.

He brushed my tears away with his thumbs, bent, and kissed my lips, his big body absorbing my shudders, holding me still.

I tried to breathe around the lump in my throat, my hands holding on to his wrists.

"You have to live, Jin, and know that I've never been prouder of anything than being the owner of your heart."

There were so many things I wanted to say, but I couldn't get anything out.

His hands fell away as he hugged me tight, crushing me to him. "It's gonna be okay, baby, I promise."

I dragged in air. "Then you gotta live, Logan," I said, wrapping my legs around his hips. "That's the only way I'll be okay. You need to know that."

"Love—"

"No," I said, my voice hoarse. "I did everything I was asked to, so did you, and now I'm telling you, I need you to live for me."

"Jin," he rasped.

"I do," I told him, making sure he could both hear and feel my desire.

"Oh God," he groaned, because when he had given me room to move, breathe, I had twisted around under him, lifting up, wanting him again and letting him know it. I had gone months without him; once would not quench my thirst. "Jin, you can't still—"

"Show me you want to live."

He slid inside me easily, as I was still slick with his semen, and I instantly felt the tingling, breathless excitement that always took hold of me when Logan was buried in me. My body, accompanied by my heart, never failed to be touched by the contact.

"Say it, so I know."

"I want to live."

I purred with contentment as he pressed me tight to his heart.

Chapter Eighteen

I WAS a sticky, sweaty mess in the morning and so took Khongordzol up on her standing offer to use the hot springs that ran under their home to bathe. I slipped out without waking anyone, even Logan, went to the entrance of the cave, was allowed to enter by the guards, and was then led to the bathing area by two men.

It was still early, and I was the only one there. The water was warm, and the enormous natural basin was huge, carved into the rock over thousands of years, smoothed by another hundred years of use. Even though I wanted to stay and soak up the warmth and comfort, I made myself get out, dry off, and wrap myself up in the fur cloak to return to the subzero temperatures outside. I pulled on the traditional thick, unbending leather boots Chuluun had brought me the second night we were there. I liked them; they were red, made of buligar, the hardest leather I had ever felt in my life. It had absolutely no give to it at all. The toes were upturned, and when I had asked him why that was, he said that if they were flat, there was no way I would have ever been able to walk in them. It made sense, and I was feeling a little like Genghis Khan in my fur cloak and boots as I made my way back to the ger.

At the entrance, I was suddenly yanked forward hard and ended up grabbed and tucked to Logan's chest as someone screamed.

I was confused, shaken, and I would have been frightened, but I was in my own quarters, and my mate was there, as well as my sheseru. Nothing could hurt me.

"How dare you!"

I had never heard Yuri's voice sound like that, menacing and cold, completely animal.

"Bring him to me!"

I needed to see, but Logan had my head tucked under his chin, and he was clutching me tight.

"Domin! Mikhail!"

It took a minute because Logan was so damn strong, all power, but I wiggled free enough to lean sideways and see that Yuri had one hand wrapped around the neck of a man I had never seen… before….

But I had seen him…. Who was he?

"It's the sheseru of the tribe of Nebthet," Mikhail said. "Armando Mojica."

He was turning blue from lack of oxygen.

I prodded my mate. "Logan."

He just stared, watching as Yuri slowly strangled the man to death.

"Logan!"

"Yuri," he said, his voice barely above a whisper.

My sheseru opened his hand, and the man fell to the floor of the ger. Instantly, the coughing and hacking and wheezing began.

"What—"

"Fuck!" Logan snarled, grabbing me, lifting me up off my feet and walking me backward to my bunk.

He dropped down with me and wrapped me in his strong arms.

"What's wrong?" I asked, my arms up under his, my hands on his shoulders. Bunched muscles in his back and arms flexed against me as he tightened his grip. He had been really scared. "Logan?"

It took several breaths with his face buried in my hair before he leaned back to look down at me. "I didn't think I was going to reach you." His voice was a raspy whisper.

And it had scared him to death. "I'm fine," I soothed, pressing into him tight. "But do you feel that, inside, that moment?"

He closed his eyes, breathed through his nose, and when he opened his glorious gold eyes, I knew he got it.

"So you talking about how I'm supposed to live if I lose you? Fucking stop, okay?"

After a moment, he nodded. "Okay."

I lunged at him and he grabbed me, and we were both on our knees, wrapped together, when Domin squatted down beside us.

"Does anybody care about what just happened? Or do you need to go somewhere and fuck?"

Someone was cranky.

I turned my head to look at Domin. "That was the sheseru of the tribe of Nebthet, and he's pissed because if I had only used my power earlier yesterday, then his semel would still be alive. I'm sure both he and his sylvan blame me."

Logan let me go, leaning back to look at me with the same expression Domin had, like he was confused and shocked at the same time.

"It makes sense. I would blame me too. But they don't get that I was only partly in control of what I was doing yesterday. I'm working on getting command of it, but I still don't know, and since there aren't any other nekhene cats around to ask, I'm sort of screwed."

Domin nodded. "That's exactly why he was here. He wanted to kill you."

"Please return him to his sylvan after you warn him not to come af—"

"No!" Logan roared. "He dies!"

I rolled forward, my hands on his face. "No more blood, no more killing, please…."

"Jin—"

"Just warn him, let him look at Yuri and Crane and Taj and know that he can't touch me. And then let him look at you, semel-netjer, and your maahes, and send him on his way."

He was deciding, thinking.

Let him understand there can't be any blood because of me. Never because of me.

I stared at him, willing him to remember what it was I stood for in his life: the love, the irrevocable trust, and the vow that was always between us.

He could never punish in my name.

It took long moments for the golden eyes to go from molten anger back to warm amber-flecked understanding. When he could, he nodded, stood, and walked away. Domin followed, leaving me alone.

Crane was there seconds later to look me over.

"I'm fine," I told him.

He studied my face.

"Knock it off, I'm fine."

He punched me in the arm.

"What the fuck?"

"Don't be a prick," he cautioned. "I know you're tired of fuckin' being here, we all are, but don't get all annoyed that I was worried that you were almost killed. I will kick your ass."

He so would.

"Didja hear me?" he asked, flicking my forehead hard.

"Ass," I grumbled, rubbing my skin, and then I noticed the surprise of Yusuke as she sat beside Crane. She moved quietly, I would give her that. "What?"

She looked at me and then Crane and then back to me. "Your tribe is different, Jin Rayne."

Like I had never heard that before. "Yeah, I know." I smiled at her. "How are you doing?"

She bowed her head. "I will go and speak to Logan, if you will excuse me."

"'Course," I told her.

When she joined the others—Logan, Domin, Mikhail, and Yuri—I turned back to Crane. His smile, the way he lit up, revealed everything.

"She's so strong, Jin, and she's so resolved to her life, and she still wants things like kids and a home and to create her art. She's a painter, you know."

"Well, Markel needs someone to share his studio with him, foot half the bill for the space downstairs. You should tell her."

"Oh shit, that's right," he said as he gave my arm a swat. "You're brilliant!"

"I try."

As I was following the procession toward the pit hours later, I felt a hand on my arm and turned to find Ebere El Masry, the yareah of the semel-aten. I was surprised to see her, even more startled to have her close to me before the start of the challenge, so when she tugged me after her, I told the others to go on without me. Yuri was going to stay, but Crane urged him on and remained.

I grasped Ebere's hand, and her eyes filled fast.

"Rector Vincent is not from our tribe, Jin. He's a hired killer from another tribe. He's the maahes only in name and is there solely to kill

Domin Thorne so that then he and Ammon can kill Logan. You must warn your mate, because two panthers on one, no matter how powerful your semel is, is too many."

"He's fought more than—"

"But not like them," she went on worriedly. "My mate is very powerful, and Rector Vincent is brutal. I watched them preparing for this challenge, Jin, and even sparring in the pit they killed many."

"It'll be all right," I assured her, even though my stomach was twisted into a knot.

"Logan's weakened," she told me. "He's been through a physical and emotional trial, and Ammon has not. And your maahes is no match for Vincent."

"I appreciate you telling me," I said solemnly, not as scared as she so obviously was.

She cleared her throat. "If Logan dies… I will do what I can."

I nodded.

"If Ammon dies… will your semel speak for my children? My girls?"

"For your children, and for you, Ebere El Masry, Logan would speak."

She launched herself into my arms, which wasn't proper, but I didn't give a damn. We hugged tight, and then she was gone, back into the shadows, disappearing the way she had come.

"God, I'm really glad Yuri didn't stick around to hear that," Crane told me, eyebrow raised.

So was I.

If I never saw the inside of a pit again it would be too soon. The way people were looking at me, frightened, wary, keeping their distance, that was difficult too. I was a reah, but they were treating me like a pariah. I should have been warmly welcomed instead of reviled. Only Hamid and Chuluun came to greet me before we were all seated. Even Jamal kept his distance, and I saw the look on the phocal's face. We were no longer friends. I had pulled him through his shift, as well, his power, apparently, was not as great as he had once thought.

I was sorry that I had wounded the man's pride, Shahid's as well, because as they were members of the Shu. When Logan won, I would need to make peace with them whenever I had dealings with the priest. Sitting between Yuri and Crane, I looked around until I found Hiroshi. His face said everything, and when our eyes met, he gave me a slight bow of his head. Every line of his face showed regret, and I knew if he could turn back the clock, he would. In a frenzy of heated anger and bloodlust, he had changed his life forever. He had to take a new yareah, and maybe, just maybe, the one he'd had was the only woman he would ever love. To know how close she was, simply in Logan's quarters, and yet never be able to speak to her again had to be an inconsolable pain. I hoped one day he would heal.

"Here we go," Crane breathed.

The priest called the challenge to order, had us all look down as the four panthers came into the pit: Ammon El Masry and his maahes, Rector Vincent, bounding fast, Logan and Domin padding in slowly, holding close together.

"The victor is the semel who lives," Hamid announced. "Normally the challenge is one on one, but the semel-aten wished for his new maahes to stand with him."

And I knew why. Ammon was going to kill Domin fast and make Logan suffer.

"Should the semel-aten be triumphant, he may put under the knife all those who have challenged him."

Which meant the priest as well as Logan, myself, and anyone else he felt should be executed.

"Should another semel prevail, he will be the new semel-aten, master of Sobek. The semels in the pit are allowed to shift to their werepanther form, as this is ordained by law."

"Your Grace," Danny said, rising. "May I ask for clarification?"

Why?

"You may."

"The semel who kills the semel-aten, he then becomes semel-aten; this is the law, is it not?"

Hamid looked confused. "It is."

"Thank you, Your Grace."

When Danny sat down, I looked at him questioningly.

"As my semel asked of me," he said with a smile, "so I have done."

He was speaking in that way we all did when we read the law: formally, with purpose. What the hell?

"The challenge for the seat of power begins now!"

It looked like every challenge I had ever seen in the pit. The panthers flew at each other, snarling, roaring; the clash of tooth and claw came fast and furious, slashing, biting, power and bloodlust filling the arena.

I held my breath, terrified, knowing that whatever happened, my life would change. As I had stood with Logan outside the ger before he left, I had kissed and hugged him with every drop of love and desire I had in me. He had to know that he was everything, my whole life, and when he nodded, unable to speak, I was certain he did. But now, as I watched him bleed, I felt my heart squeezed in a vise of pain.

"Logan's stronger than both of them, Jin," Crane assured me under his breath. "Don't doubt it for a second."

I took a breath and heard Yuri do the same on my right. I didn't turn to look, couldn't, my eyes riveted on Logan even as I was sure my sheseru's were riveted on Domin. I had not seen the mark Domin had put on him, but I had watched him reach behind his neck and touch what I was sure was a hell of a scar, raised and silver with scar tissue, on the back of his neck. He could not keep his fingers from tracing over it, and if it hurt, Yuri didn't seem to care. I was scared for him, what it would mean for him if Domin died. I felt my power rise, and that fast Crane's knee was against mine, his hand on my back.

"Hold on, Jin, this is gonna be alright."

But if Logan died, what would I do? What would I become?

Ammon shifted to his werepanther form, and I was breathless with anticipation for Logan to do the same.

Seconds ticked by.

Why didn't he shift?

He had to shift!

What the hell was he waiting for? Ammon would tear him apart! The half-man/half-panther form was the strongest of all!

Logan!

"Wait," Crane said suddenly. "What's going on?"

I was as confused as he was. As the four panthers circled one another after the last vicious attack, instead of Logan squaring off against Ammon, he had taken a small half step back so Domin could rush forward to meet the semel-aten. They hadn't even looked at each other, but it was like… it was planned.

"Oh shit," I whispered as Domin shifted to his werepanther form and the entire gallery gasped at the same time.

Domin.

"What the fuck?" Cranc exhaled, and when I turned to look at him, I saw how big and round his eyes were.

"Logan's not going to do it," I gasped.

"Logan's not gonna do what?"

I looked back at the ring, saw Domin and Ammon rush forward and meet, Ammon tearing at the werepanther that Domin was, and Domin fighting back with his fangs and claws. Ammon's maahes, the formidable Rector, the hired gun, the ringer, went to the ground fast under Logan's superior strength and power. Any cat versus a semel was no challenge at all, and even though Logan had not shifted, had remained in his panther form, it didn't matter. Had he been fighting Ammon, the shift would have been necessary, but now I understood. If he had fought Rector in his werepanther form, the challenge would have been forfeit, but since he hadn't, the challenge was valid. Once Logan had the large panther pinned to the floor of the pit, he held him there, immobile, and looked over at Ammon and Domin, as we all did.

The priest had thought there were only two semels in the pit; it was why Logan had asked Danny to make sure the law was clarified….

The semel who killed the semel-aten then became the new semel-aten, that was the law. And Logan had made sure it had been spoken to ensure Domin's claim. Because there were not two semels in the pit of the tribe of Khertet: there were *three*.

People forgot that even though Logan Church had ended the lineage of the house of Menhit, had disbanded Domin's tribe, he had not, could not, make Domin Thorne any less of a semel. No one remembered who Domin Thorne really was. When tribal leaders fought, semels were killed, and they changed often, no one truly caring about another tribe but their own. And maybe Hamid, as the priest, could recall Domin had once led his own tribe and maybe he couldn't, but he, and everyone else in attendance, were being reminded.

You were either born a semel or not, and Domin had been born to lead, with all the power and strength and the true form of the station, the werepanther.

Ammon screamed in rage; he had wanted Logan, and here, in the final act, still he would be denied. Because unlike nekhene, which meant I was different and that power lived in me, semel-aten was just a title. It did not make Ammon stronger than any other semel. It definitely did not make him stronger than a man who had changed and grown from the proud, scared, vicious creature he had been into the kind and gentle prince of his tribe. Losing his tribe had been the best thing that ever happened to Domin, and now he was ready to lead, and Logan, it seemed, agreed, because he wanted Domin to be semel-aten.

Ammon flexed his muscle and power through others, through orders; Domin used his own. I knew the second the killing stroke was delivered. I saw the surprise flicker over the semel-aten's face, saw the hatred and rage and disbelief before his mouth opened and blood leaked out. He was dead when he hit the ground.

The quiet was frightening as Domin turned, blood dripping from his claws, smeared across his fur, and looked up at the priest.

Domin shifted back to human form, as did Logan and Rector, and each man knelt down on one knee.

I had no idea so many people could go silent. No one even breathed in the room.

"I had thought," the priest finally began, rising to his feet, "to proclaim the semel-netjer as the new semel-aten, as I had thought that the man who ruled the nekhene was most fit to be semel-aten, but it seems that Logan Church and I never had the same agenda."

"No, you did not," Domin answered, his voice strong and resonant as he rose from where he had been kneeling to his full height. "My brother wants to lead his tribe on his land and care for his reah and his family and his people. It is all he has ever wanted. He has remade me in his image, as I will always have his counsel as well as the counsel of his reah, Jin Rayne, and I ask that you now proclaim me semel-aten, as I have won that right in combat by my victory in the sepat."

Hamid looked down at Domin Thorne. "What of Ammon El Masry's household?"

"I claim Ebere El Masry as mastaba, mistress of my house."

I had thought it was strange that Ebere was sitting one tier below me as our mates were facing off in life and death combat in the pit, but now I was glad as I leaned forward and put a hand on her shoulder.

She curled her fingers around mine. "Bless you, Jin. I know this is your influence, and bless your maahes, my new semel. I will make him proud."

But it wasn't my influence; I didn't even have a chance to speak to Domin. He had claimed Ebere so fast, seemingly without thought, as though he had already decided. I had no idea why. And while the act itself was good, I could not for the life of me grasp the reason.

"Will you name your sheseru and sylvan?"

"I will name them from the household of the semel-netjer but will need to ponder the choice before making my claim, Your Grace."

Hamid stared at Domin, at a man he had not thought to share his home in Egypt with. He had wanted Logan because of the kind of man he was, but also because Logan was mated to me. He wanted the only nekhene cat in existence close to him. But as he gazed down, the strength in Domin, the rippling energy that sparked off him, was impossible to ignore.

"Let us all hail the new master of Sobek, the semel-aten, Domin Thorne."

The applause was deafening, and I let my head fall back on my shoulders as I closed my eyes. It was over. The sepat was finally, completely, finished. And my mate was coming home with me.

I couldn't have stopped the tears if I tried.

THE RECEIVING hall of the tribe of Khertet was massive. Carved out of the rock, it managed to be both elegant and rustic at the same time. There were furs on the stone floors and on the walls, and wrought iron chandeliers hung from the beams of wood crisscrossing the ceiling. I had seen it the first day when I had walked through the home of the semel of Khertet with the other mates of the semels. So I knew what I would be missing when I sent Crane with my regrets that my mate and I would not be attending the priest directly after the close of the final challenge. We needed to be alone. He told everyone I was sick, and really, I was. Just the smell of the damp air in the cave threatened to flip my stomach over.

I had waited with everyone else right outside the entrance to the pit after the final trial was concluded, but unlike the others, I was alone. No one came near me, all of them more interested in talking to Domin. And that was fine with me.

The priest was disappointed, I could tell, and his eyes never fell on me. Jamal and Shahid would not look at me, and to every other panther there, I was the monster who had pulled them through their shift the day before. I had never felt more like an outsider.

So I was standing apart from the group when Domin and Logan came to join everyone after they had bathed and changed.

There was applause from every corner, Hamid was there to greet my former maahes, and Jamal was close at his side. Their exchange was warm and genuine, and when the others asked permission to approach, it was granted.

Yuri was being patient, not wanting to muscle his way through, but the second the priest allowed others close, he moved quickly through the crowd and flung himself at my former maahes. I watched Yuri's jaw clench before he buried his face down in Domin's shoulder, trembling only slightly. Mikhail was there, then, and Danny, Andrian, and Taj, and Yusuke, with her hand in Crane's. My tribe embraced Domin, and I was happy and sad. I would miss him; I had just gotten around to truly liking him.

It was Domin's moment, and I was glad, because he was restored to his birthright of semel in splendid, legendary style. But me being there, adding my voice, was meaningless. It didn't matter, not really. I was only critical to one man, and he was all I saw.

Logan squeezed Domin's shoulders as he walked by him, giving him that affirmation of closeness before he left. He didn't pause to speak to anyone else.

The sepat was over, and so was anyone else's dominion over the semel-netjer. We were both free.

His eyes were warm gold as he came forward, and I noticed the fluid stride, the play of flexing, rippling muscles, and the clench of his jaw.

He didn't speak, and as he strode toward me, I noted the silence that fell over the assembled throng. There was not an eye not on Logan, and in that second, I understood what the priest had wanted.

Logan looked like a king. He had the demeanor of royalty; you noticed strength and power, a virile, pulsing energy that took your breath away. The man was a rock. He looked like shelter and home and safety. It could not be taught, the look, the bearing, the charm… it was pure intuition, and Logan had it. Everyone there but the man's own tribe had only ever seen him in panther form or werepanther form, or bound and wounded, before that moment. They had never been treated to the breathtaking golden man before them.

Normally my mate did not put himself on display. He usually downplayed his own power, beauty, and magnetism. But he was free of the madness, free of the threat of Sobek, of becoming something he never wanted, free of rules and tradition and law. He was going home, and everything that had been taken was returned to him. So he was glowing with pride and happiness and overwhelming relief. It was rolling off him in waves. People were transfixed, and even though Hamid Shamon, the priest of Chae Rophon, was there, and the phocal and the newly made semel-aten, for a moment in time, the only thing anyone saw was Logan Church. And he didn't have eyes for anything or anyone but me.

The crowd parted for him, and he covered the space between us in long strides.

I lifted my arms to receive him and heard his breath catch as he reached me.

"Jin," he growled, and I moaned my pleasure into his ear as he reached me, grabbing me tight and crushing me to his chest.

"Oh God." My whimper was torn from me.

"My mate," he breathed down the side of my neck, which raised goose bumps on every inch of my skin.

When he lifted me, hands on my ass as he walked me away from the others, toward the mouth of the cave, I wrapped my legs tight around his back. "This isn't seemly," I told him.

"I don't give a fuck," he told me, increasing his pace, the temperature dropping the farther we got. "We're no longer important to anyone but each other, and that's how I like it."

"I wanna go home," I whined into his shoulder, nuzzling into the crook of his neck, my lips seeking skin, wanting to kiss and lick, suck and nibble.

"Fuck, you feel good," he groaned, tightening his arms, savoring the closeness, inhaling my scent, holding me so tight.

"Wait," I ordered when I realized we had passed through the gate that led outside. The cave was deep, and so from the sentry point, the entrance was another hundred yards away. There was snow on the ground that blew in before you actually hit open air. "You can't go outside in just your ceremonial robes, you'll freeze to death."

He was wearing white silk and brocade pants and an intricately woven tunic that would offer no protection at all. The boots, like the ones I had been given, were the traditional Mongol ones with the upturned toe, but whereas mine were red, his were black. But still, the wool socks would offer only minutes of protection from the frigid arctic temperature outside.

"I'll be in our ger in a few minutes. If I'm carrying you, I can't freeze. You'll keep me warm."

"Logan—"

"No," he told me. "If I don't get to be alone with you, I'm gonna lose it. I need everything to be over. I'm barely holding it together."

I shut up, held him tight, and let him tramp through the powder with me wrapped around him. And he was strong, but he was still quaking with cold by the time we reached the ger.

Inside, I put him by the stove, grabbed blankets, and wrapped him up before I stripped out of my parka and hat and dropped down into his lap, straddling his thighs.

He snuggled me close, and we just sat there for a long time, just breathing together, sharing body heat in silence. When his scent finally started tickling my nose, my hands burrowed up under his shirt, sliding over the washboard abs.

"You want this off?"

I nodded.

He reached over his back and pulled the shirt off, his eyes locking on mine when he finished. "Touch me."

Immediately my fingers trailed up his rippling torso to his chiseled pectorals.

"Now you." His eyes narrowed, became slits of molten gold as he stared at me. "I want skin too."

I peeled myself from my cocoon of warmth slowly and enjoyed watching him lick his lips, swallow hard, and stare at me with pleading eyes as I stripped off my layers of clothing. Anyone who came in would have thought the look was carnal, but it was comfort he was starving for, and closeness, and simply me. He craved my body wrapped around his as tight as I could be, like a second skin. He fisted his hand in my hair and pulled it forward, burying his face in it, inhaling deeply.

"I always know I'm okay when your hair is in my face and I can smell you all over me."

"Logan," I said breathlessly. "Promise me."

"I will never, ever leave your side again. I swear it."

I was holding him to that.

"I need you... closer," he almost snarled, but it was low, frustrated, not menacing in any way. He was uneasy.

"What's wrong?" I asked gently.

He shook his head.

"Talk to me."

But he couldn't, or wouldn't, say what was troubling him.

"You need something more?"

His gaze lifted to mine.

"What do you need?" I stared into all that gold. "To claim me?"

His thick gold brows furrowed, and I started to have a flicker of understanding.

"Do you need to know that you're mine?"

"Yes," he said, his voice breaking with relief that I understood.

"Shall I show you?"

He wasn't sure what I meant.

"Do you trust me?"

"Of course."

I rose then, walked to where my things were, and returned, lube in hand. I could tell just from the subtle change in his gaze that he understood. I recognized the uncertainty on his face, but he didn't give voice to it, and I was touched by the depth of his faith in me. "Will you give yourself over to me, to my care?"

He took a quick nervous breath and nodded.

I had done it in the past, topped other lovers, but never had it meant anything to me, having been instead something asked of me that I had simply complied with. It was not instinctive for me; I was built emotionally and mentally to be submissive, but that didn't mean I had to be. And this was my mate who had asked with beseeching eyes to be claimed. We were men first, but we were also animals, and because of that, sometimes words were not enough to mend the soul. Sometimes it required action and the joining of flesh.

Logan always gave so much of himself to me—love, compassion, whatever I needed, he provided—and now I wanted to return to him and do for him as he had always done for me.

Slowly, carefully, I untied the drawstring on his pants, and when I tugged on them, he lifted so I could slide them off. Immediately, I bent and took the tip of the flared head of his cock into my mouth.

"Jin." He shivered, inhaling my scent, the flood of pheromones rolling through him, soothing and arousing at the same time.

As I took in more and more of him, inch by inch, sucking, licking, I heard him call my name many more times. I slid my hand up his chest, pushing him down with gentle pressure until he was flat on his back making groaning, whimpering noises that left no doubt that he had given himself completely to me, to whatever I wanted to do.

His cock popped out of my mouth at the same time I lifted his knee, showing him what I wanted. He bent them both as I opened the tube and squeezed the icy liquid into my palm. Before I coated my fingers, I rubbed it in my hands, warming it, and then leaned over and took his cock down the back of my throat. Normally it was Logan preparing me, loving me, making me burn with need for him. I realized in that instant how deeply I wanted him, the craving to make the man mine almost overwhelming. I knew it was the same for him, because I had felt it when he made love to me, every single time.

My name was a hoarse whisper as I slid up and then sank down, sucking his cock hard, his hand in my hair as he moved it aside so he could watch.

Tenderly, I slid the tip of a finger around his furled entrance. He tensed, but he didn't pull away, and as I swallowed the long, hard, thick length of him, tasting precome before my cheeks hollowed out with the force of the suction, I felt him relax against my tender onslaught. I used my other hand to stroke his balls, lift and play with them, and he whimpered as I pushed inside. He was so tight; never had the man been breached before, and I was determined to reward his trust in me even as I marveled at the faith.

His muscles pulled me deeper inside, and as I pressed forward and up, curling my middle finger, I felt him shudder.

"That feels so good."

I smiled around his pulsing shaft and eased out slowly before adding a second finger, going just as slowly as I had the first time, this time making measured circles, pushing in, easing out, over and over, pegging his gland, and finally scissoring my fingers apart as he began to pant. I was gentle but insistent, relying on past experience as well as the memory of the many times my mate had brought me to release in this exact same way.

When I again allowed his heavily dripping cock to slip from my lips, I looked down at him, checking his gaze for signs of anything but heat. His eyes were heavy-lidded, he looked drugged, and I noticed his hands fisted at his sides in the blankets.

"Are you okay?"

His wet parted lips, the slow rise and fall of his chest, and his beautiful ass with my fingers buried inside of him to the knuckle—the man was giving me heart palpitations.

"Shall I ride you?" I asked, giving him his out. All he had to do was take it.

"I...." He swallowed hard and just looked at me, and I understood that my question, suggestion, was not what he wanted or needed.

"Logan," I said, running my finger over his gland, watching him go rigid under my hands, one now sliding from balls to head of his cock, the other inside of him.

"Please, Jin."

I drew back, added more lube before I stroked a third finger into him. When I bent once more to the cock that was straining for me, he stopped me before I deep-throated him, only my tongue catching the drops of precome.

"Am I yours?" he asked.

"Yes, only mine."

He eased forward then, off my fingers, and I could tell that sliding free was á hard decision to make, because they had felt good. Rolling over onto his stomach, he then lifted his ass for me, spreading his knees at the same time, offering the virgin pink puckered hole.

"I want to see your face," I told him.

"I wanna be marked and fucked and taken," he rasped back. "Make me yours."

I didn't wait for him to change his mind. I leaned forward, not caring about the lube, and licked over his entrance with my hot, wet tongue.

He trembled hard, and the moan was loud.

"No one but me," I told him.

"Only you."

The second time, I spread his cheeks and pushed inside of him, past the tight rings of muscle, deep, scouring him, pushing in, licking, sucking, nibbling, tasting him, feeling the effect that my ravenous assault was having, the relaxing of his inner walls.

When I was sure he was close to climax, I coated my own throbbing cock and straightened up, leaning back, my thumbs spreading the cheeks of his beautiful taut ass before I pressed against him.

"Oh God, Jin, I don't wanna come without you inside me… please."

His hole was lubed and stretched and ready for me, I had made sure.

"Push out," I directed and then slowly but without pause pressed into him.

He was still so tight, and his muscles resisted me, clamped around me like a fist, fighting the imminent breach, but when I took hold of his cock and stroked him, all at once they relaxed, and I was suddenly buried to the balls in his ass. He felt amazing. All that slick velvet heat wrapped around me was almost too much; it took everything in me not to come.

The tremor that ran through him stopped me from moving even though I wanted to pull out just enough to slam back inside and thrust until I came.

"Logan, you feel so good," I told him before I let my fangs fall, upper and lower, curled over that beautiful, broad muscular back, and sank my teeth into the soft skin where his shoulder met his neck.

It could never be the mark he had given me, for that was the dominion of only a semel, their birthright to brand their true-mate, and my bite would not even leave a scar, but still… he needed to know I wanted to. All the simmering, thrumming desire that had built in me, he had to know it was all because of him and that he belonged only to me.

"Oh fuck!" he roared, bucking under me, driving my cock in deeper, my balls plastered to his ass.

I had to move; I would die if I didn't. And I would die if I hurt my mate.

"Oh God, Jin, please."

Lifting my mouth, I sucked at the wound I had made, which brought on the sweetest whine I had ever heard, before I grabbed hold of his hips and eased out of his clasping channel.

"No, don't—"

I plunged back inside of him, thrusting hard and deep, and his head fell back as he begged me to do it again.

The pounding I delivered was merciless, and from the grunts and whimpers and moans, I knew that this, me claiming him, was exactly what he needed.

"Mine," I growled before I demanded he jerk himself off.

He took a quivering breath before he came, splattering the blanket under him, convulsing with his orgasm.

I shot hot come deep inside his body, filling him until it dripped down the inside of his thighs, hammering him through his release and mine as he normally did to me. Nothing was so primal as coating my mate's inner walls, branding him inside and out, and I felt the emotion rise up in me. The feeling had to be the same when the roles were reversed, Logan must have enjoyed possessing me just as much.

When I collapsed on top of him, because he was bigger and stronger, he didn't fold under me; instead, he held there until I eased from his body and sat back.

He dropped down onto the blankets and rolled over on his back. The hooded eyes, flushed face, and sweat-covered skin were enough to make my mouth go dry. The man was a vision of sated passion.

"Did I hurt you?"

He shook his head.

"I claimed you, you're mine, and you belong only to me."

"Only to you," he said hoarsely, reaching for me, catching my hair, and pulling me close enough so he could fist his hand in it. I was wrenched forward, and when our lips met, the kiss was scorching and devouring as Logan mauled my mouth.

He had submitted to me, trusted me, loved me enough to give himself to me, but there was also never to be a doubt of who was in control. Logan was power and strength and heat; I was his mate, his other half, and so returned softness and soothing calm. He took what he wanted, and I willingly gave, and that truth lived and breathed between us. I would treasure the moment for what it was, a gift, a time when Logan had wanted me to take, and I had. We fit seamlessly, and as I was rolled to my back, I wrapped my arms around his neck and held tight.

"I love you," he rasped against my lips before the second round began, the blistering kiss, the grinding motion that made my skin so hot I thought it would simply brand him when we touched. "My mate, my reah."

I wanted to melt into him, so I tried.

WE REMAINED alone for as long as we could, Mikhail finally coming to find Logan to have him return to the hall to attend the priest before the funeral rites were performed. I told Logan I couldn't go back inside and he understood, making me promise to stay there and not leave our quarters. I told him I needed to go for a run, and even though he wasn't thrilled with the prospect, he understood the need.

Later that night, I shifted and watched from a safe distance as they all stood in a circle under the falling snow and watched the pyres burn. Panthers were never buried, always cremated for safety and secrecy, and the pyres were an ancient practice that somehow, with all that had transpired, made sense.

All the fallen were placed side by side: the yareahs of Girdaht, Tawaret, and Ptahket, the semel of the tribe of Nebthet, his yareah, and his two men. Ammon El Masry was burned apart from the others, and only Amirah's body was not present at all, having been burned and the ashes discarded two days prior. It turned out she had no family, so there was no one anywhere to mourn her. That was, for me, the saddest part of her story.

Once the fire engulfed everything, I watched everyone retreat back inside except for my mate. From where I was, in a shallow cave barely big enough to shelter me, I could see him and the whole valley. It was quiet outside, and peaceful, but what was happening outside had nothing to do with the whirling emotions inside my head. I wanted to go home and be grounded. I was suddenly so thankful to Logan for making that possible. He'd known he could kill Ammon in the pit, but more importantly, he'd also known Domin could. I suddenly wanted to hear the entire story.

I couldn't hear him from where I was, but I could see him. And when he lifted his arms for me, I was on my feet in seconds.

He had not seen me run up the side of the mountain days ago, so I made sure to show him. I pushed myself faster, leaped high, and performed the midair arc, the dive that turned to running across the new fallen snow. When I reached him, still in panther form, and landed all over him, pinning him under me to the snow, he was laughing.

"Holy shit," he yelled, petting me hard, rubbing, the rumbling sound that came out of him making me purr as I licked the base of this throat. "How the hell did you do that?"

I was never sure; I just thought things and my body responded.

"Damn," he sighed, scratching under my chin. "What can't you do?"

But I knew, and so did he: I could not live without him.

"Don't worry, okay? That'll never happen, not with you looking out for me."

I shuddered hard and would have shifted, but his gloved hands were suddenly clutching at my fur. "Don't shift out here; you'll freeze. Be a good kitty and follow me home, alright?"

Whatever he wanted.

THE GATHERING was informal, but Hamid was present, so it was still governed by the laws of hospitality. The semel of Khertet had invited everyone who participated in the sepat into his private quarters, and they were much different from the rest of the cave.

It was like being inside an enormous tent with partitions behind silk curtains, thick wool rugs that covered the stone floor, another enormous fireplace that warmed the room, lanterns that burned perfumed oil, and down pillows that looked soft. A feast was laid on each table, wine was poured, and in the warmth and ease of the evening, inhibitions were shed.

I had asked Yusuke if she wanted to attend or remain in our quarters, and she was so thankful for the choice that she grabbed my hand tight. She had no desire to ever lay eyes on Narae Hiroshi again, and if I were given the choice, she never would. Crane asked to stay with her, and even though she bowed low and said he should not remain at her side, her face, when she rose, told a whole other story.

She looked at him and lit up. Her face, her gaze, her smile, the flush on her skin, the way her breath caught, all of it was mesmerizing. His eyes crinkled in half when he looked back at her, and I liked it.

"Don't be grateful to him," I had told her earlier that night, when I had followed Logan in from the cold.

"I'm grateful to you and my semel," she said and added that she had already replaced her mate with Logan, which made me warm inside. "I'm not grateful to Crane Adams. He didn't save me."

I was glad. I didn't want her grateful to him; I wanted her to love him, if that was what her heart could still fathom. He deserved to be loved, and so did she.

A snicker from beside me drew me from my thoughts back to the present. I turned to look at Mikhail, whose attention was diverted. Following his gaze, I found Domin sitting beside a reclining Yuri. Domin was chatting with the priest while his hip and thigh pressed into my sheseru's side. Sitting on Yuri's right was Chuluun, and both his posture and hooded eyes suggested he was offering more than the wine he was pouring.

It was a mistake. I watched Domin do a slow pan to the maahes of the tribe of Khertet, lean sideways over Yuri, and say something that drained all the color from Chuluun's face.

"I think," I said with a chuckle, turning to Mikhail, "that maybe Domin's done with sharing and waiting to claim what he wants."

Mikhail nodded, his smile the rare one that curled the corner of his lips and made his eyes glitter deep midnight blue. "Yuri's thrilled."

I had to agree. The way Yuri was built, wanting equaled ownership, and he wanted more than anything for Domin to claim him, put his mark on him, as he had, and for Domin to just announce to everyone that Yuri was his. The show of possessiveness made my sheseru unbearably happy. But still, because he was kind, he caught Chuluun's wrist before he could leave, pulled him down so he could whisper in his ear, and as Chuluun rose, he didn't look startled anymore, but resigned. When Yuri sat up and leaned against Domin's back, I saw him smile even as he continued talking.

"Shit," I muttered under my breath.

"What?" Mikhail turned to me.

"Domin's going to Sobek, Yuri's staying with us. How the hell is this supposed to work?"

"Everyone's alive and safe, Jin," he said and then sighed, reaching up to gently pat my cheek. "Let's just sit here and be thankful, alright?"

I couldn't argue.

It was interesting to see people approach Domin, the new title changing everything. Everyone was reverent. Even Jamal and Shahid, when they came in, both came forward and bowed to him. When Shahid, who was more than an acquaintance of my former maahes, leaned forward to speak to him, I watched Domin tilt his head away, making certain simply from his body language that Shahid being that close to him was not welcome. Things had changed, and whatever anyone thought they knew of Domin Thorne was no longer correct. In the morning, Hamid had said, Domin would need to name his maahes, his sheseru, and his sylvan. He would not go back to Nevada with us; his duty was to the tribe of Rahotep. They needed to meet their new leader, and the semel-aten needed to put his house in order.

"You do understand," Mikhail said softly, "that this will change your life, Jin, no matter what."

I wasn't sure what he meant until Logan put his hand on my thigh. I turned to look at my mate.

"Baby, you do realize that Domin has to have people he trusts around him."

I was still lost.

"And where do you think those people will come from?"

It hit me like a sledgehammer in the gut. "Oh shit."

Logan threw an arm around me and hugged me to his side.

"Who will he take to Egypt with him?"

"We'll just have to wait and find out."

I was afraid to know.

Ebere presented herself to Domin, bowing low before he bid her rise and took her hand as was the custom, to show she was claimed by him and under his protection. The priest pronounced her, again, mastaba, mistress of Sobek, as Domin had claimed her. She was considered the widow of the semel, but in giving her the title, he had declared her his until she chose to marry again or died. She could not be forced to take another mate, as she, as well as any children that were hers, had been claimed by the semel-aten. Domin had granted her and her daughters safety.

It was not as though Ebere even lived in Sobek anymore, but wherever she was in the world, she was mastaba and so was safe. The reach of the semel-aten knew no bounds. She came to sit with Logan and me afterward and thanked us both again.

"I'm sorry for the loss of your mate," Logan told her. "Please make sure your daughters understand."

"This was tribal law, semel-netjer," she told him. "And we all live with the duality of our lives. We're human and not, and so my daughters will grieve the loss of their father, but they will understand the law. Every semel can be challenged; every mate put to death or marked; every man, woman, and child brought before their semel and judged." She took a breath. "We all live by the same rules, and perhaps some of them, now that Domin Thorne is semel-aten, can be changed, but to say that my daughters would somehow not understand tribal law is impossible."

"It's all well and good to know why something happened. It's something else to be okay with it. They can still hate Domin for being the instrument of their father's death."

"Or perhaps love him for releasing their mother from a nightmare," she said, smiling through her tears.

I had no idea what kind of horrors Ammon El Masry had visited upon his mate, but from seeing the face of his widow, I no longer feared she or her daughters would ever hurt Domin.

When she left, I hugged her, and she made me promise to visit her if I was ever in Cairo. It was a vow I made wholeheartedly.

After another hour, Domin rose, lifted a hand to Logan and me, and then pulled Yuri to his feet. They both bowed to the priest—it was the etiquette—and were gone seconds later. Yuri knew better than to ask Logan to leave; that was not how my semel ran his tribe, with bowing and scraping and rigid observance of tradition. And I was so glad: the rigid rules were one of the things Domin had already promised he would change. I had seen the look of concern on the priest's face when Domin had been talking to him at dinner about the list of laws he would be tackling first. His plan was to see the council of Ennead weekly, whereas Ammon had seen them only once a year when it was mandated.

"You have changes to the law you wish to make?" Hamid had asked him.

"Oh yes." Domin had smiled his wicked smile that made his brown eyes glow. He looked dangerous, like some sort of pirate king, and the priest shivered just once.

Wine was swapped for vodka and airag, and the talking got louder and more boisterous before people started migrating into dark corners of the warm sandalwood-scented room. The lanterns were dimmed, musicians were ushered in, and the semel of Khertet thanked us all for honoring his house with our presence and thanked the priest for honoring him with the sepat.

Many of the people, both men and women, who had been serving had returned and were now offering more than food and drink to the guests of their tribe. Andrian and Taj each had a woman in his lap, and Danny was almost in Mikhail's.

"He's drunk," my sylvan said to me even as he smiled up at my whimpering cousin. "I'm gonna go put him in bed." Mikhail smiled at me, shaking his head even as Danny leaned forward and wrapped his arms around his neck.

"I thought Mikhail told me he and Danny talked," Logan told me as we watched Mikhail carry young Danny from the room.

"They did, but," I said with a shrug, "come on. Between the alcohol and the pheromones in here, hearing other people screwing, smelling it, seeing it—are you kidding?"

He made a noise, and I laughed softly before he fisted his hand in my hair, yanking my head back sharply so he could kiss a line up my throat.

"What're you doing?" I chuckled even as he pushed me down under him.

He stared at me with his warm gold eyes, and I felt the relief and peace wash over me.

It should have been heat, being that close to him, with his big hard body pressing down on me, trapping me, with the scents and sounds all around us... but all I could feel was joy.

"I'm supposed to be making you hot."

I started laughing.

"Shit," he grumbled as he rolled over on his back, bringing me along with him.

Leaning over, I kissed him gently, tenderly, letting him feel how much I loved him. "When the priest introduced each of the mates of the semels before the sepat began, he said Jin Rayne."

Logan was searching my face, and I watched as he stilled, like he was holding his breath, waiting for what I was going to say.

"And I thought," I said as I inhaled his delicious scent, "that I wanted to be just like those yareahs. I wanted to have my name be the same as yours."

"Oh."

"So I thought," I said as my breath fluttered over his face, "that if it was still on the table, I would really love to take your last name."

His hands lifted to my face, and the look in his amber eyes made me breathless. They were glowing with pride. "You would?"

I nodded.

"Because you know that's what I want," he assured me. "And it would make me... I mean, you're not Jin Rayne anymore, are you?"

No. I wasn't. I had not been since I met him. He made me different, stronger, better, kinder, all the things that a mate was supposed to do. All the good things, at least.

"So, then," he whispered, easing me down until I was lying on top of him, my hands flat on his chest, "when we get home, we'll change your name."

I nodded.

"And begin the process with the surrogate."

"Yes," I managed to get out.

His eyes searched mine. "I never wanted it to be my sperm and a woman I didn't know, you know? I always wanted it to be you and Delphine. It's how I dreamed it."

"But you deserve to have—"

"My line, *and* you," he said, squinting hard, his eyes reddening, softening as he stared at me. "Do you even get how bad I wanna see your big gray eyes on someone I can protect and never let get hurt and take care of?"

My vision blurred as my eyes filled.

"I want my own family with you. The second I met you, when I knew you were mine, I swear, Jin, I could see my whole life in that one moment." He eased me closer, my lips hovering over his. "Thank you for taking my name, it means more than you can imagine."

I bent and kissed him, and he opened for me so I could taste him, slide and rub my tongue over his, take thorough possession of his mouth. When he rolled over on top of me, arms wrapped around me, holding me tight, I moaned deeply, loving the feel of his big hard body on mine. As the kiss changed, grew more heated and carnal and urgent, Logan broke it off, rose and grabbed my hand.

He tugged me after him, passed many people engaged in various sexual acts, some couples and a few in threes and fours, until we reached the priest, and both of us kneeled before him. I saw how heated the older man's eyes were as they raked over Logan. I understood then that yes, he had wanted Logan to be semel-aten because he was semel-netjer, but he also simply enjoyed looking at my mate. It made sense; he was gorgeous.

"Semel-netjer, will you and your reah grant us the honor of watching you and your—"

"I request permission to take our leave, Your Grace," he said as he rose. "I will see you all in the morning when the semel-aten chooses his household, but for now… I need my reah."

"But we would be honored to have you claim your mate here."

The priest wanted to watch; he was curious, and it was very human, but also, in this instance, something that was not in his power to demand. Not with a semel and his true-mate.

There were laws that could be changed and others that were finite, like the one that protected Logan and me, always, from prying eyes.

"It would do my reah no honor, nor me." Logan bowed, and I did as well. "So we will take our leave and bid you good-night, Your Grace."

No one said another word as we left.

Back at our quarters, Logan started stripping out of his clothes.

"What are you doing?" I asked, as Yusuke was trying not to look, Crane was chuckling, and Mikhail was confused.

"I'm going to go for a run with my mate."

I was stunned. "But, Logan," I said, starting to take off my parka, which I had put on just to get from the mouth of the cave to the ger maybe a hundred yards beyond. It was so damn cold. "You were in your panther form for so long? I didn't think you'd want to—"

"I'm not afraid of being a panther, Jin, and running with you is one of the great joys of my life. I know who I am."

I caught my breath.

"And I know what's mine."

I nodded because I couldn't speak.

"Hurry up." He smiled at me before he shifted.

Crane was laughing as I tore off my clothes.

Chapter Nineteen

WE ALL stood near the entrance of the cave late in the morning, having convened after breakfast. There were Jeeps outside to take us to the airport and a helicopter that would take the new semel-aten and his chosen household, along with Hamid and the Shu warriors, to a secluded airfield where a private jet stood fueled and ready to make the long trip first to Beijing and then on to Cairo. We would be making a similar trip, except we would fly first back to Beijing and then on to Los Angeles. Logan had been on the phone that morning booking Yusuke's flight back, even though he had no idea yet if everyone who had come with me would be flying home with us.

Whatever happened, he was prepared. I was not.

It had taken hours for everyone to say their good-byes to the priest. He and Logan had met at dawn, as it was the priest's favorite meeting time, and they had spoken at length. I had not been included, which was fine with me. I had become, to Hamid, a worrisome creature to be feared. That was unfortunate, but I hardly cared. I was happy Jamal had sought me out and that the two of us had talked, and though he still seemed wary of me, he was no longer openly resentful of my power. When I had dragged him through his shift, he had been at first surprised, then furious, and finally ashamed. He was supposed to be stronger, certainly stronger than my sheseru or my sylvan or my beset. That Yuri and Mikhail and Crane had been able to keep from shifting into panthers was hard for him to accept. The others—Logan, Domin—they were semels, so it made sense. But not him. It was good that we had talked and would be parting ways on good terms.

As I stood beside Logan, silently waiting along with everyone else, including the semel of Khertet and his household, I watched Domin and held my breath. He looked good this morning: shaved, hair still pulled back in a queue, every bit the new leader of the werepanther world. When he turned, giving Logan the playboy smile, my heart stopped.

"Anyone, semel-netjer?"

"Anyone," Logan said, nodding. "I want the semel-aten to be safe."

Domin nodded, smiling bigger, and looked over all of us, all of Logan's household.

"And you don't have to choose from those here," Logan told him. "If you want Ivan or—"

"No," Domin called over to Logan. "I would never ask Ivan or Markel again. They both have their lives there with you, especially Markel."

"Yes," Logan agreed, smiling back at him. "It's amazing how many good things came out of something that was hard for all of us."

Domin nodded, and I saw his jaw clench with emotion before his eyes found what he wanted.

I caught my breath.

"Mikhail," Domin said softly, "come with me to Sobek."

And I watched Mikhail Gorgerin smile slowly before he bowed. "It would be my privilege, semel-aten."

Domin's eyes then flicked to Yuri, who was barely standing still.

And every part of me screamed, *No, not like that, not to be sheseru.*

"Taj," Domin said, looking away, "come and be the sheseru of the tribe of Rahotep. I need someone I trust completely to carry out my orders until I become fluent in the language and customs of my new tribe."

Taj was touched by the depth of Domin's faith, and it was there on display for everyone to see. He nodded and bowed low. "Yes, my semel, it would be my honor."

I didn't want either of them to go, but I didn't want Domin to leave either; I wanted my family and my tribe together forever.

"This is *maat*," Domin said as Mikhail took his duffel bag and walked over to Domin to stand at his side. Taj did the same, and so he was flanked on either side by his sylvan and sheseru.

When Mikhail's eyes met Logan's, there was the slightest nod of understanding. They each knew what they meant to one another, and it was up to Logan to take care of Mikhail's family, parents, siblings, as well as his business there in Nevada. He would make the transition seamless for Mikhail, making sure that everything he needed would be shipped to Egypt, and if any member of Logan's tribe wanted to follow him, they too would be allowed to go. Only semels released tribe members, and Logan always did what was best.

He would do the same for Taj, although for him, returning to Sobek was more homecoming than leaving.

"As for the maahes of the tribe of Rahotep...." Domin took a breath and looked at me. "It's time, isn't it?"

Logan put an arm around me and tucked me against his side.

"I need my circle to be impenetrable against corruption. I cannot ever, for a moment, not trust my sylvan, my sheseru, or my maahes."

And then I knew what he wanted, but I also knew that unless I nodded, gave him my blessing, that he would not take what was mine. Only I could release Crane Adams; only I could release my beset and my promise at the same time.

I nodded because it was the right and best thing to do for my friend.

"As Crane Adams remains forever the beset of a reah, he is able, under that aegis, to defend my honor in the pit should there ever come a time. So I choose for the maahes of the tribe of Rahotep the beset of the reah of the tribe of Mafdet."

"Thank you, semel-aten." Crane bowed low.

I sucked in my breath as my best friend threw away all propriety and bolted toward me. He filled my arms and hugged me tight.

"I love you," I told him, whispering urgently.

"Me too." He nodded, squeezed me tighter, and kissed my cheek and then the side of my neck.

He let go first, and when I let my arms fall away, Mikhail was suddenly there, and Taj. There was a time to honor tradition and a time to let it fall to the wayside. I hugged the other two men and then watched Logan embrace them all as well.

"You all will always have a place in my tribe," he told them. "And you, Crane, will remain beset of my reah from this day forward. You will never be replaced."

He couldn't speak. No one could, and as Domin joined us, the two semels shook hands.

"I'm not done taking from you." Domin smiled at my mate.

"I know, but I approve."

"Which means more than you know," Domin said, gripping Logan's bicep tight before he released him and turned around to face Yuri, standing still and alone.

He moved quickly, stopping in front of my sheseru, staring into his eyes. "Come with me. Artem will care for your company; I talked to him last night."

Yuri just stared at him.

"Your reah has his mate to protect and care for him, don't worry about your duty."

Yuri's eyes flicked to mine, and I smiled and nodded. *Go, don't hesitate.*

"If you come," Domin said, sucking in his breath, "you will be the mate of the semel-aten."

Mate.

"I want you at my side forever."

I held my breath and watched Yuri's jaw clench even as he looked at Logan. He had to honor his semel even as what he wanted more than life itself was offered to him.

Logan nodded, just as I had.

Go.

"I love you," Domin said, in front of everyone, loud and clear. "You know I do."

With that, Yuri lunged at Domin, the emotion too much to contain.

And if the priest was surprised at Domin's choice of mate, he had the presence of mind to say nothing. Because, really, with Domin having made Ebere mastaba, he already had his children, as he had laid claim to hers. Hamid could make no claim that Domin needed a yareah, as procreation had already been dealt with.

Domin Thorne was always thinking, and sometimes I missed how critically fast his mind worked.

When Yuri released Domin, I was surprised that the smaller man grabbed his face and bent him forward into a kiss. "You're mine," he said, looking up into Yuri's eyes. "So says the mark I put on you, so says everyone here to bear witness. You belong to me, Yuri Kosa. Never forget it."

He let him go then, and Yuri turned and came for me.

Not for Logan, for me.

He grabbed me and crushed me in his arms. I lifted my head and kissed under his chin, and he shuddered hard.

"I'll miss your face."

"And I'll miss yours," I murmured. "But I'm so happy for you. Take good care of him and make sure he takes care of you."

"I'll look after Crane."

"Look after all of them. You're his mate, Yuri, your position is highest."

"It will take time to sink in."

"I suspect so." I sighed deeply.

He hugged Logan after me, and the two men stood for long minutes before Domin told him they had to go.

We promised to visit before the next Feast of the Valley. Domin said there would always be a place for all of us with him, and Logan told him that it was the same for all of them. Wherever Logan was, all of them were welcome. We all bowed low and then watched them all start walking away. But when Domin stopped suddenly, everyone had to; he was the semel-aten, after all. He turned and looked at Logan.

"Semel-netjer," he called formally over to Logan while putting on his sunglasses. "I will give your mate's father your regards when we reach Sobek."

"Please do." Logan smiled in return.

"And I will give your regards, my reah," Yuri told me, as Domin took his hand, "to the father of your beset."

The look in his eyes, deadly and dark, let me know exactly what would transpire. When I found Crane in the crowd, I saw the bittersweet smile. He would be able to stand before them, his father and mine, and let them see that they had not broken him, before they were put to death. It was fitting and final.

I had no more tears to shed for my father or Crane's. "Show them who you are," I called over to my best friend.

He nodded, turned away to follow after Domin, and lifted his hand one final time in farewell.

Logan's fingers threaded into my hair, and when he tugged gently, I lifted my brimming eyes to his. "I haven't cried this much in years."

"It's okay," he told me as he lifted his other hand to my cheek and brushed the tears away with his fingertips. "We all cry when we lose something, and you just lost half of your family."

Yes.

"But we're about to build a new one," he said, tipping his head up, and I saw that he was looking at Danny and Yusuke. "He will make a good sylvan, and she will make a wonderful maahen, don't you think?"

I was surprised. "You'll have a princess of your tribe instead of a prince?"

"You disagree?"

"No, I think it's wonderful."

"Her loyalty to her mate was boundless until he broke the bond between them. Now her oath will be to me, and I can return her status and power. She'll be strong and devout and terrifying to anyone that would ever think of attacking me or my tribe."

He was right, and as Yusuke became aware of his regard, I watched her smile before giving him a slight bow. The eye patch she wore was white and blended well with her porcelain complexion. She was still a stunning woman, but harder than she had been, with steely strength now on display, hidden no more. I liked the way she looked at Logan, the reverence there for anyone to see. He was the instrument of her resurrection, and she would never forget that he, and he alone, had provided shelter in the storm.

And Danny's smile as he looked at me was bright and full of hope. With my father's training and our acceptance, yes, he would make a very capable sylvan.

"What if, when we visit, Yusuke asks to stay with Crane? It might be love between the two of them someday."

"I'll cross that bridge when I come to it. As for now, they can see if corresponding strengthens their new bond or destroys it."

"You could just let her go with him now."

"She's not ready," my mate informed me. "And neither is he, not really."

I believed him. "So are you going to ask Artem to be sheseru?" I asked as Logan began leading me toward the semel of Khertet and his yareah to say our good-byes.

"No. Artem shifted too easily with your power, and besides, I have someone else in mind."

"Who?"

"Avery Cadim."

I was surprised. "But he's Christophe's sheseru. You can't just take the enforcer of another tribe, and I doubt that Christophe would ever release him."

"He will. If word got out that he was keeping Avery against his will, he'd lose honor in front of his tribe."

"But Avery hates me."

"No, he doesn't," Logan assured me, "and he wants to be my right hand very badly, and if you gave him a chance to be your champion... I think he would make an excellent one."

"He was just married, you know. His mate might not take too kindly to him becoming the sheseru of a gay man."

He scoffed, brushing his lips over my forehead. "The lady in question is one of Delphine's good friends, Jin, and a member of our tribe that I had to give permission to join Christophe's."

I didn't recall that.

"You've been dealing with your power for some time." He smiled, easing me forward so I could shake Khongordzol's hand and thank her.

"Saikhan zochluullaa," I said, using the words Danny had taught me.

"Zugeer." She smiled at me, telling me it was nothing, patting my hand. "Sain yavaarai," she finished, wishing me a safe journey.

"Sain suuj baigaarai," I sighed, hoping that she would, of course, stay well.

After Logan thanked Orso for his gracious hospitality and extended an invitation for him and his family to come and hunt with him on his land whenever they wanted, we headed toward the waiting Jeeps.

"So." Logan picked the conversation back up. "I know Avery's mate well; she will be thrilled to see Avery change tribes so she can return to her own."

"What if Avery doesn't want to be your sheseru?"

Logan chuckled as he held open the door of the first Jeep for me.

He was right; I knew how badly Avery wanted to be Logan Church's sheseru. He would come running when Logan called. To be the hand of the semel-netjer, his enforcer, the protector of his greatest treasure, me. Oh yeah, Avery had been *praying* for the chance to take Yuri's place, and finally, the opportunity was there. If Logan called for a challenge in the pit, which he never would, Avery would kill anyone who stood in his way.

"There will be new faces in our home, Jin," he said, leaning me against him once we were on our way, making the long drive back to Ulaanbaatar from the semel of Khertet's home in the mountains. "But it will always be our home, and the people in it will always be a family."

I nuzzled against him and felt his hands in my hair, stroking.

"And now I get to have my mate share my name and see the birth of my child," he said as he inhaled my scent. "But for me, wherever you are, that's my home. I see you, and I'm home."

I pressed into him, my face burrowed in the side of his neck as he held me tight.

"I love you, Jin Church. You're all there is."

He was the same for me, and I didn't need to tell him.

Read this excerpt of

Crucible of Fate

By Mary Calmes

A Change of Heart Novel

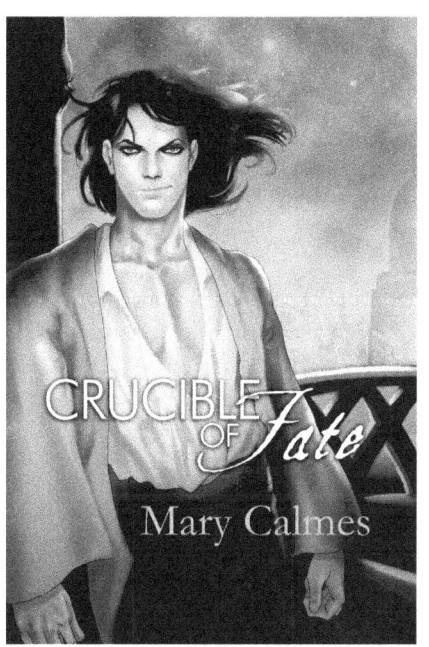

In the secret city of Sobek, Domin Thorne is making his way as the newly chosen semel-aten, the leader of the werepanther world. He aspires to make sweeping changes—he's set goals for himself and the people he chose to bring with him, modeling his reign after that of his friend, Logan Church. But Domin may have set too lofty a goal: his normal leadership style isn't working.

While juggling a homesick Crane, a moody Mikhail, a bullwhip-wielding Taj, servants with murderous intentions, a visiting ex, and a mate on a dangerous goodwill mission, Domin has to figure out his new role alone. He also must determine how to deal with a conspiracy, all the while falling hard for a man who, for the first time in Domin's life, reciprocates that love. Whether Domin is ready or not, Fate has stepped in to teach him a lesson: internal threats are just as dangerous as external ones.

Available at
http://www.dreamspinnerpress.com

Chapter One

IT MADE no sense, and they were all tired of hearing me ask the same questions. But until I had an answer I understood, how was I supposed to simply accept it?

"What did your father tell you when you became a semel?" I inquired of every single tribe leader who visited Sobek.

They all regarded me oddly, the last one being Maroz Amadu of the tribe of Serabit from Giza. He was confused.

Yuri translated. "Specifically, he wants to know what would happen to you if you failed as a semel. Where would the people in your territory go for help, if, let's say, you decided that two panthers of different races couldn't be married in your territory."

"But that's absurd," Maroz said to Yuri. "It doesn't matter who you—"

"The sekhem of the semel-aten is hypothesizing," his yareah, Hesi Amadu, remarked.

Apparently we needed our mates to do the talking for us.

"Oh, I see." He plastered on a smile. "Well, I was told that if I was not a good ruler, that the panthers in my tribe could contact the semel-aten, and he would hear the case against me and pass judgment."

"Exactly." I pointed at him, then whirled around to face Yuri. "You see?"

He crossed his thickly muscled arms across his wide, bulky chest and fixed me with a stare that made me question my sanity. "What do I see?"

"I was a bad semel."

"'Was.' Past tense. What does—"

"So does that mean no one ever reported me to Ammon El Masry when he was semel-aten? That seems odd, doesn't it?"

"I don't know. How would I know?"

"And therein lies my question."

There was a soft clearing of a throat behind me.

Pivoting, I found Maroz and his mate still there. "May we go to the grand salon now, my lord? We're both famished."

"Oh yeah, go ahead," I said, waving them away. "Sorry."

Maroz grabbed his mate by the hand and tugged her away from me quickly. They all ended up doing that, concerned about my state of mind, I was certain.

"Okay, so what now?" Yuri asked, stepping in front of me.

"It's what I was told as a new semel, what Logan was, what we all were."

"That the semel-aten would come get you if you were bad," Yuri paraphrased. "Right? Like the bogeyman?"

"Yeah. And if that's true, if millions of panthers are supposed to be calling me or e-mailing me and complaining—where is it?"

"What? You're asking if there's, like, a command center or something for all this correspondence?"

"That's exactly what I'm asking. I mean, who checks to make sure no panther is ever seen? Who spins an attack? Who basically has kept werepanthers off human radar for centuries?"

His eyes narrowed as he regarded me.

"So maybe whoever it is started small and now covers the entire world."

"You're nuts. You know that, right?"

"Yuri, there has to be a bigger body, a level up from semel-aten, like a werepanther CIA or something. There has to be. Someone is handling situations, and we know it's not me. I'm a figurehead with no power."

"You make law for everyone."

I dismissed that with a wave.

"And it just so happens that the tribe of Rahotep is the largest single tribe in the world."

"Yes, but if you put it into perspective and say every panther in the world…." The number was just staggering. "Who does that? Who is responsible for everyone?"

"I think, in all seriousness, everyone is responsible for their own and maybe the tribe closest to them. I mean, it was on Logan to make you stop when you were out of control; maybe that's how it is everywhere."

I shook my head. "That's too simple. Think about it. What if Logan and Christophe were just as fucked up as me? If that was true, then the entire corner of Nevada would have crazed werepanthers running around."

"Yes, but Logan ended your tribe," he reminded me. "He ended your reign as semel. Who's to say something similar doesn't occur every day?"

"But if single semels are just policing themselves, why doesn't the whole thing just collapse and we're on the six o'clock news everywhere?"

He shook his head. "You're overthinking this."

I wasn't, though; he was just missing it. There had to be a big brother—there simply had to be—but who or what that was, that was the question. I didn't want to be a figurehead. I wanted to make a difference, and on a larger stage than my own tribe. But I had no idea how to do it.

I did have the power to change the law, though, and that was where I was planning to focus all my energy, if I could just figure out what to start with and how. Everything had to be revamped, but I was buried under the weight of what I *should* have been doing versus what I *was* doing. I was on my second rant of the night. If the first was the conspiracy of silence, my next familiar tangent was change.

Yuri said the time for me to simply *be* had passed. I had to embody the revolution I wanted to see, not simply hope for it. I alone could become a catalyst for action.

"There's no way," I railed, pacing in our room, back and forth at the foot of the bed as he lay stretched out on the mattress watching me. It was how it always went, from firebrand to quitter; I swung back and forth daily. "How do I, the infidel, expect to simply upend thousands of years of *this-is-how-we-do-things*?"

He was waggling his eyebrows.

"What?" I yelled.

"You simply say 'this is the way we're going to do it from now on.' You do what we've discussed—proclaim yourself akhen-aten and begin a new reign with *your* players on the board."

I found myself staring at him. "It's not that easy."

"I think it is."

"That's because you're not the semel-aten!"

"And you're not either." He tipped his head to one side. "Well, at least you don't want to be."

"Yuri—"

"You hate it here," he said, cutting me off. "Not because you're here in Egypt, but because you don't like how the upper class treats the lower, how the priest keeps his temple, or how you are supposed to treat the servants in your own villa. You hate the classes of people instead of one tribe that stands together, and you hate that a hundred semel-atens before you and a hundred priests have kept this city in the Dark Ages instead of letting it join the modern world."

"Yes!"

"Then fucking fix it, my lord," he placated me.

"It's not that easy."

"Change is never easy." He shrugged. "Who lied and said it would be?"

I flopped down on the end of the bed.

After a moment, I felt the mattress lift and dip and realized he was moving behind me. When his strong arms wrapped around my neck, I grunted and leaned back against him.

"You'll do the right thing." He sounded so sure.

"How do you know?"

"Because you always do."

"That's not true." I closed my eyes, savoring the feel of his skin, the heat of his chest against my back, and the stubble-covered jaw grazing mine.

Did he know what a simple comfort his touch was? How did everyone in the world not want a mate? Having someone to listen when you unburden your soul and to sleep wrapped around in the night? How was that not a prerequisite for life?

"You are inherently good," he said, his voice a vibrating purr against the side of my throat. "And once you set your sight on a course of action, you will not be able to push it from your mind."

He was so right.

I was assaulted by everything that needed to be changed on a daily basis and crushed under the weight of the status quo. The landslide of obligations from the vital to the mundane never stopped. There were expectations and demands and endless responsibilities.

I hated it.

The Change of Heart series

http://www.dreamspinnerpress.com

MARY CALMES lives in Lexington, Kentucky, with her husband and two children and loves all the seasons except summer. She graduated from the University of the Pacific in Stockton, California, with a bachelor's degree in English literature. Due to the fact that it is English lit and not English grammar, do not ask her to point out a clause for you, as it will *so* not happen. She loves writing, becoming immersed in the process, and falling into the work. She can even tell you what her characters smell like. She loves buying books and going to conventions to meet her fans.

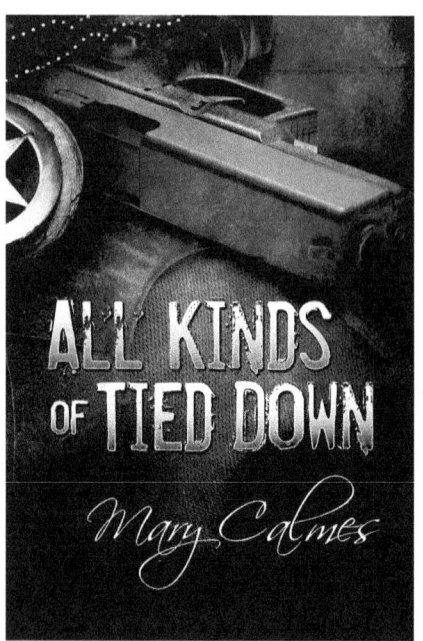

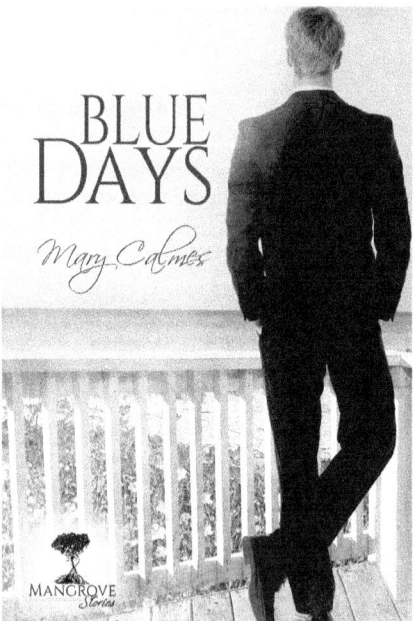

http://www.dreamspinnerpress.com

By Mary Calmes

Acrobat
Again
All Kinds of Tied Down
Any Closer
With Cardeno C.: Control
With Poppy Dennison: Creature Feature
Floodgates
Frog
Grand Adventures (Dreamspinner Anthology)
The Guardian
Heart of the Race
Ice Around the Edges
Judgment
Mine
Romanus
The Servant
Steamroller
Still
Three Fates (Multiple Author Anthology)
Timing • After the Sunset
What Can Be
Where You Lead
Wishing on a Blue Star (Dreamspinner Anthology)

Change of Heart
Change of Heart • Trusted Bond • Honored Vow
Crucible of Fate • Forging the Future

L'Ange
Old Loyalty, New Love • Fighting Instinct

Mangrove Stories
Blue Days • Quiet Nights • Sultry Sunset

A Matter of Time
A Matter of Time: Vol. 1 • A Matter of Time: Vol. 2
Bulletproof • But For You • Parting Shot

The Warder Series
His Hearth • Tooth & Nail • Heart in Hand
Sinnerman • Nexus • Cherish Your Name
Warders Vol. 1 & 2

Published by Dreamspinner Press
http://www.dreamspinnerpress.com

FOR **MORE** OF THE **BEST GAY** ROMANCE

DREAMSPINNER
PRESS
dreamspinnerpress.com